Children of Bacchus

Andrew Grey

Dreamspinner Press

Published by
Dreamspinner Press
4760 Preston Road
Suite 244-149
Frisco, TX 75034
http://www.dreamspinnerpress.com/

Children of Bacchus
Copyright © 2008 by Andrew Grey

Cover Art by Dan Skinner/Cerberus Inc. cerberusinc@hotmail.com
Cover Design by Mara McKennen

ISBN: 978-1-935192-13-8

Printed in the United States of America
First Edition
September, 2008

eBook edition available
eBook ISBN: 978-1-935192-14-5

To my partner Dominic for all your love and support and to an unknown 19th century French sculptor who created the spectacular bronze that inspired this story.

Prologue

Long ago…

Cembran was happy, truly happy for the first time in a very long time. He sat in his small shelter tending his family's flock of sheep on the mountain slopes of a small valley in what are now known as the Jura Mountains of Switzerland. The sheep grazed contentedly as Cembran sat with the last of the day's sun shining on his back, warming him on the outside as the memory of Gathod warmed him on the inside. Even more exciting was that he knew Gathod was coming to him. Cembran knew that tonight they would join together for the first time and his body tingled with anticipation, mixed with a touch of fear. His father would be angry if he found out about them, but his love for Gathod vastly outweighed his fear of his father.

Cembran's father was very strong and powerful, particularly in their little village deep in the mountains. Even though he was almost thirty years old, his father still controlled much of his life. His brother Fartham, on the other hand, was always his father's favorite, so he always got whatever he wanted. Lucky for Cembran, Fartham was basically a good brother who looked out for him and even stood up for him with their father.

As the sun set behind the mountains, he saw Gathod walking along the path to his shelter. Cembran stood and smiled broadly as his lover approached. Gathod dropped his pack in the shelter and without wasting time, wrapped Cembran in a tight embrace, kissing him deeply. They'd been apart for less than twelve hours, but it seemed like much longer.

As darkness approached, Cembran built a small fire near the shelter entrance. Even during the summer months, the temperature dropped dramatically at night. Gathod sat near the fire and Cembran sat at his side. Strong arms wrapped around his back, pulling him into a deep, penetrating kiss.

"Have I told you I love you?" Gathod's deep, rich voice swelled with passion.

"Not since you arrived, no," Cembran whispered playfully.

"Well, I do love you."

A gentle but determined set of lips pressed to his. Cembran opened into the kiss, giving himself over to the sensations and his own desire and need.

Gathod broke the kiss reluctantly, "We should eat. I think we'll need our strength."

Cembran brought out the food he'd planned for dinner and the two of them ate. He watched each bite Gathod took, the way his lips moved, the way his tongue savored the cheese, the way the wine lingered on his lips. Finally, Cembran could wait no longer.

"Gathod, I need you." He turned and headed into the shelter. "Love me."

After a few minutes, Gathod joined him. Cembran was lying on his back on a bed of soft, thick blankets, his clothes folded and stacked at his feet. Gathod followed his lead, slowly removing his clothes as Cembran watched every movement. After what seemed like an eternity, Gathod was nude as well. His body was wide, strong, and it felt good as his weight pressed Cembran into the blankets. Their lips kissed, hands explored, legs entwined, cocks rubbed. Each movement, each sensation felt new, heightened, special.

"I love you, Gathod." The words were whispered as lips found and sucked Cembran's sensitive nipples. Those lips continued down his body, opening for him, taking him in. The hot wetness of Gathod's mouth nearly sent him over the edge. Gathod added suction and worked his tongue across the base of the head, again and again, making Cembran moan and plead for more. It wasn't long before he felt his climax building. His lover must have felt it too, because he sucked harder, sending Cembran over the edge. His climax seemed to come from deep in his soul as he spilled himself into Gathod's mouth.

Gathod smiled as he swallowed everything Cembran could give him. Bringing their mouths together, he kissed Cembran deeply as he parted and lifted Cembran's legs to expose his most private opening. Gathod looked at Cembran, questioning.

Cembran responded by pulling his legs up farther, completely exposing himself, giving himself to this man, the man he loved. Gathod reached for the small bottle of oil he'd brought with him and slicked his fingers, slowly and carefully making Cembran ready for him: first one finger, and then two, checking for any sign of discomfort or doubt. There was none. A third finger had Cembran opened and ready. After oiling his cock, Gathod pressed the head to Cembran's entrance. Slowly, deliberately, he pressed into Cembran's strong, hot body.

Cembran had waited for this for a very long time. He had longed to be with Gathod since that first awakening of desire years before, but he never dreamed it could be like this. Gathod pushed into his body, entering him, filling him, completing him. Looking into Gathod's eyes, he saw only love and affection.

"Love me." The words came breathlessly as Gathod filled him to completion. The rest of the world faded away as they started to move, slowly at first, then increasing speed and intensity.

Gathod leaned forward, kissing Cembran deeply, pulling on his lips. He returned the kiss, thrusting his tongue into Gathod's mouth, kissing passionately. "I love you, Cembran. I want to be with you forever."

Uttering those words made Cembran's heart swell and his soul fly. He never thought he'd be loved like this and it filled him with absolute joy. He could deeply feel every movement Gathod made inside his body, every inch, as he filled and retreated only to fill him again. Cembran reached to Gathod, stroking his face letting his hands run down his chest, wanting as much contact as possible.

Pressure again built deep inside and he tried to signal Gathod, who kissed him again whispering, "Come with me, Cembran." The words were barely out of his lover's mouth when Cembran came on his stomach as Gathod spent deep inside his lover. Gathod slowly separated himself, then lay down next to him on the blankets.

"Stay with me, please."

Gathod nodded, "Of course I'll stay with you." The small fire cast shadows into the shelter, the darkness beyond wrapped them in quiet and peace. Gathod banked the fire before pulling the blanket over both of them. Wrapping his strong arms around Cembran, he pulled him to his body, pressing his chest to Cembran's back. "Sleep, my love."

He slept, contented and happy, in the arms of the man he loved.

Cembran woke to Gathod shifting next to him, rolling over to see him getting out of their warm blankets, saying "I have to get back before I'm missed." It was still dark, but the first rays of the sun had started to turn the eastern sky from black to gray. Gathod leaned forward, kissing Cembran fully and lovingly. After breaking the kiss, he dressed hastily and, turning to kiss Cembran again, disappeared into the early morning darkness.

He got up, dressed, gathered his things into his pack, and headed home with a spring in his step, a smile on his face, and a soreness that reminded him of last night's joy with each step he took.

Entering the house through the back door, Cembran was surprised to see his father sitting at the table, and he appeared to be waiting for him. His face showed little emotion.

"Cembran, sit down. I will speak with you." The voice was rough, the tone clipped. Cembran put down his pack and sat across the table. "I know where you were last night. I know what you did and I know who you were with."

"How could…?"

His father cut him off. "I know, and I won't tolerate it. I will not have a son of mine acting like a woman." Cembran tried to say something, but his father cut him off again. "I have decided that you have two choices." His father's voice was getting louder. "I have decided that you are to marry and stop this foolishness, or you must leave."

Cembran's breath caught. "Leave?"

"Yes. Either you stop this foolishness with Gathod or you will be banished from my house and this village." His father's eyes were as cold as stone. "What is your answer?"

Cembran was stunned and shocked into non-movement. He couldn't breathe and he couldn't think. "I—" No further sounds would come out. What a choice: marry someone to satisfy his father or leave the only place, the only life, he'd ever known.

His father continued, ignoring Cembran's reaction completely. "I will be out for most of the day. If you are here when I return, I expect you to marry; otherwise I expect you to be gone! Never show your face here again!" With those last words, Cembran's father stormed out of the room and a few seconds later he heard the front door slam hard enough the shake the small house.

He sat at the table, head in his hands, completely despondent. He jerked as a pair of hands rested on his shoulders. Turning his head he saw Fartham standing behind him.

"I'm sorry, Cembran."

"What am I to do?" Tears were starting to well in his eyes.

"There are worse things than getting married." Fartham sat in the chair that their father had occupied a few minutes before. "I'll help you find a suitable woman."

Something either broke inside Cembran or crystallized into clarity; he was never sure which, but at that moment, he knew what he had to do. "Fartham, I cannot get married. It wouldn't be fair to her. I could never love a woman, not in that way."

"But Cembran?"

He held up his hand. He knew he'd have only one chance to make his brother understand. Cembran's voice was slow and measured. "Fartham, you love Lita. With everything you have?"

Fartham nodded. "Yes, with all my soul. She's perfect for me."

Cembran smiled weakly; he knew Lita would make his brother very happy. He could see it each time he saw them together. "The way you feel about Lita is the way I feel about Gathod. I love him with everything I am."

"But Cembran, Gathod is...." Confusion was written all over his face.

"The way you feel about women, I feel about men. I can't change it and," taking a deep breath he continued, "I love Gathod."

Fartham sat still and quiet for a long time. "Then you have no choice; you must leave." He looked at Cembran with sadness. "I will miss you, but you deserve to be happy and you can't be happy here." He paused. "Does Gathod love you?"

"He said he did and I believe him." He had too. His happiness and sanity depended on that belief.

"Maybe Gathod will go with you."

It was almost a thought spoken out loud, but it made Cembran's heart jump. Yes, maybe it was possible.

"Come with me, I'll help you get ready, we have much to do."

Fartham turned into a whirl of activity. He pulled the small chest out of his room. It was sturdy, with a single drawer on the bottom. "You can use this, it's not too heavy and it should travel easily with you." Clothes, boots, blankets, and other items were neatly and carefully stowed in the chest. Once it was packed, Fartham put the chest back in its usual spot in case their father came home.

He turned to Cembran, opened his shirt, and pulled the pendant from around his neck and placed it around Cembran's neck. "Take this with you, to remember me and protect yourself." Cembran hugged him tightly. "Go find Gathod."

Cembran thanked his brother and headed out of the house. He knew he'd find Gathod tending his family's flocks and he raced to find him. He had gone only a few steps when he saw Gathod coming toward him.

"I was just looking for you." Gathod was smiling.

"I was looking for you as well. I need to talk to you." Cembran led Gathod back to the house. Fartham left the room as soon as they entered.

"What's wrong? You look so serious."

"My father knows about us." His lover's face fell, smile replaced with fear. "He told me this morning that I must leave you and get married, or leave the village." Gathod started shaking. "I cannot get married, so I have decided to leave." Gathod looked at the floor. "Come with me." Cembran's voice was urgent. "We'll find a place where we can be together," he said, his eyes full of hope, his heart full of love.

Gathod still looked at the floor. "I don't know. This is all so sudden. I…." His feet shifted nervously as he ran his fingers through his hair.

Cembran knew his heart was breaking, right then. But he also knew he couldn't force Gathod to come with him and he wouldn't make his lover feel guilty. Placing a hand on his shoulder, he said, "I understand. It's a lot to ask."

"Cembran, I do love you. I just don't know." The indecision was plain on Gathod's face and Cembran knew.

"I know you do and I love you." He gently kissed Gathod's lips. "I have to leave today. Will you meet me at the shelter on the high ridge at sundown?" This shelter was near the top of one of the mountains surrounding the village.

Gathod nodded, "Okay. I'll meet you there." He walked to the door and with a glance back, stepped out of the house.

Cembran collapsed into a chair as the door closed, tears streaming down his face, sobs wracking his body. It took some effort, but he finally regained control of himself as his brother came back into the room.

"Gathod's not going?"

Cembran shook his head in response.

"What do you want me to do for you?" Fartham had always looked out for Cembran and he was still doing it.

"Would you take the chest to the high shelter on the ridge? I have an errand that I need to run before I leave." Fartham nodded his assent. "Thank you."

Cembran stepped out of the house and walked through the village to the home of his most trusted friend. He had known Old Hans since he was a child and trusted him completely. He approached the house and knocked softly on the door.

"Come in, Cembran."

He opened the door and stepped inside.

"I was expecting you." From the tone of his voice, Cembran figured Old Hans already knew. "My boy, are you all right?"

He nodded. "As well as I can be. I'm leaving the village today. I will not marry to satisfy my father."

Old Hans nodded and disappeared into another room. After a few minutes, he returned carrying a small bag. "I figure you'll need this."

Cembran nodded; it was his life's savings. Actually it was almost every cent he'd ever earned in his life. He'd never trusted his father with his money, so Old Hans had held on to it for him. He took the bag and threw his arms around Hans's shoulders. "I will miss you." Tears welled in his eyes again.

"I will miss you too. Have you eaten?"

Cembran shook his head.

"Then come and we will eat a last meal together before you leave." Hans set out a fine meal and they ate together quietly, Cembran lost in his thoughts. "Where are you going?"

"I don't know. I'll decide in a few days when I've had a chance to think." Hans just nodded. After eating, he hugged his friend again and said goodbye. Placing the bag under his clothes, next to his skin, he stepped out of the house.

Late in the day, after he had made all his arrangements, he headed up the mountain to the shelter. This one was near the summit and, unlike the shelter he and Gathod had used the previous night, this one wasn't known to his father; Fartham, Gathod, and Cembran had only built it last spring.

Cembran found his brother waiting for him in the shelter; the small chest was sitting near the back.

"I wanted to say goodbye." Fartham hugged Cembran tightly. "Please be careful and take care of yourself."

"I will."

Fartham hugged his younger brother again and handed him a small bag of coins before turning quickly and heading back towards the village. He turned and waved just before he stepped out of sight.

The sun was setting when Cembran heard Gathod approaching the shelter. He saw him a minute later. Gathod started to speak, but Cembran silenced him. "No apologies, no regrets." Gathod opened his small pack and took out the food he'd brought while Cembran started a small fire. They ate quietly together, watching the sun set and the darkness descend around them.

After they'd eaten, Cembran took Gathod's hand in his. "Love me, Gathod. Give me something to remember forever."

Gathod quietly led him into the shelter. Their lovemaking was intense and passionate, lasting well into the night. Knowing they would part in the morning, they both made the most of the time they had together. Satiated and exhausted, they fell asleep in each other's arms, clinging together tightly for those last few hours.

The sun was rising as Cembran woke, Gathod's warm, strong body entwined with his. Gathod's hands stroked his back. Cembran reluctantly got out of the blankets and dressed quickly in the cold morning air. Gathod dressed as well and handed him the last of the food they had shared. They held each other as Cembran ate. Finally, he packed the blankets away and was ready to go.

"Cembran, I made this for you. I was saving it for your birthday, but—" Gathod's voice broke and tears ran down his face. He tugged Cembran into his embrace and kissed him deeply. "Goodbye."

With that Gathod turned and walked slowly down the path back toward the village. Cembran wrapped the gift in a blanket and stowed it in his chest. He'd open it later when he wasn't feeling so distraught. Slinging the chest onto his back, he headed down the mountain toward something he'd never known − the outside world.

Part One

Journey
to
Childhood

Chapter One

"This is ours, Dad? All of it? It's so beautiful." He whirled around with his arms outstretched, trying to take it all in.

"Yes, Travis, this is ours now." What he was going to do with it was another question.

"But how?" The look on his son's face was wide-eyed with wonder as he stood by the edge of the small lake.

"Uncle John, my brother from California, passed away and left me the land in his will. It's been in the family for a long time."

"Oh." Travis was barely paying attention. His thoughts were on the landscape around him. The trees around the lake were resplendent with their bright fall colors shining off the surface of the lake. "Can we come up here in the summer and go swimming?" His mind was flooded with all kinds of possibilities.

"Maybe," he answered, mind wandering to other worries, and there were plenty of those. Hell, he could barely afford the gas to make the trip to see what it was that his brother had left him. In his will, John had specified that the land couldn't be sold and there was a cryptic note about a tenant whose annual rent was to pay the property taxes. He looked around, but there was no sign of a tenant or anyone else. He was pulled out of his thoughts by another of Travis's questions; he seemed to have a million of them today.

"Dad, how much land is there?"

"Over 400 acres."

Travis whistled. "That's a lot of land. We're rich."

"Not exactly, Trav."

The lawyer had told him that it was mostly wooded land that contained a lake as well as a small stream. He'd also told him that one corner of the property had been cleared to make a small farm, where the tenant lived, tending goats and sheep."

"Can I take a walk around the lake? I won't be long, I promise."

"Sure. I'll wait for you in the car."

Travis was off in a flash. The lake wasn't particularly large and it would probably only take about twenty minutes to walk around it, but to Travis, it felt like another world. His family lived in the city; their house was small and there wasn't much of a yard, so this much open space was fascinating for him.

When he was almost back at the car, he turned around to look at the lake one last time. On the far side, near where the stream entered the lake, he saw a man emerge from the woods, looking at him. The man raised his hand and waved. Travis waved back and smiled; he couldn't seem to pull his gaze away from the stranger. Both of them just watched each other across the lake for a few minutes. Eventually, the man turned and walked back into the woods. Travis turned and headed back to the car before his dad got mad because he was taking too much time.

Travis climbed into the car. His mind was on the man he'd seen across the lake. He figured he must be the tenant who lived on the small farm. On the trip home, he was very quiet, which was unusual for him. Even he knew that he had a tendency to talk and ask a lot of questions, but right now, his mind was occupied by the man by the lake.

After about an hour he heard his dad speaking to him, "Sorry Dad, what did you say?"

Shaking his head, he repeated, "I asked you what you wanted for your sixteenth birthday."

Travis knew what he really wanted - a video game set like most of his friends had - but he also knew his folks couldn't afford it, so he said he just wanted to get his driver's license. His dad seemed to accept the answer and returned his attention to the road.

The following summer, Travis had gotten his driver's license and he begged his dad to take him back to the family property so he could see it again and go swimming in the lake.

"Trav, I just don't have time to take you with my new job and everything."

He'd been extremely disappointed, but he also knew that his dad's new job was making things much easier for the entire family.

His dad surprised him by continuing: "I'll loan you the car this Saturday and you can go on your own, provided you promise to be careful."

Travis was overjoyed and started to plan all the things he wanted to take.

On Saturday morning, he got up early and packed his swimming gear, lunch, and a few snacks and drinks into the car. He said goodbye to his mom and started the drive to the property and what he saw as a day of freedom. He loved his parents, but they were strict disciplinarians in every sense of the word. If Travis wanted something, he'd ask once and only once. Asking for something twice would get you slapped. Begging for anything would get you hit with the belt. Talking back got your mouth washed out with soap. The worst punishment of all would come if anyone ever found out about his feelings for other boys. He just knew that he had to control those thoughts or he was going to Hell and only God knew what sort of punishment he'd get from his dad.

Heading out of the city, he enjoyed the ride, and the farther he got from home, the freer and more relaxed he felt. It took him about an hour and a half to drive to the property. When he arrived, he parked the car in the same spot his dad had parked when they'd come in the Fall, and walked down to the lake.

The lake was even more beautiful than he remembered. The sun shone off the crystal clear water, and the trees around it were thick and lush. Setting his things by the shore, he changed his clothes and waded into the water. It was cool but not cold, the perfect temperature for swimming, and he spent the next few hours splashing and swimming in the shallow water.

At about noon, while Travis was eating his lunch, he saw some movement on the other side of the lake. Three sheep emerged from what looked like a path, followed by the man he'd seen last Fall. He was sitting in the tall grass and didn't think the man could see him. The man led the sheep to the stream for a drink before sitting on a rock. The sheep wandered through the little clearing near the lake, munching on the grass.

Eventually, the man took off his clothes and walked into the lake. Travis wasn't close enough to see much, but he could tell that the man was really handsome and strong. The man looked like he was washing his hair and Travis realized he wasn't swimming, but taking a bath. When he was finished, he seemed to lie in the grass to dry himself in the sun. After about half an hour, he got up, dressed, and led the sheep back into the woods.

When the man was gone, Travis finished his lunch and walked back to the edge of the lake. His mind was a torrent of feelings he didn't understand. Seeing the man naked, even from a distance, had turned Travis's mind into a whirl of confusion and feelings that he knew he shouldn't be having.

As the afternoon wore on, he packed up his things, loaded them in the car, and headed home. He knew he'd better not be late or he'd be in trouble, and his dad wouldn't let him use the car again. On the way home, he thought about what he'd seen and how he felt about it. While his feelings confused him, one thing was for sure - he hoped he saw the man again when he came back to the lake.

When he got home, his mom asked him about his trip. He told her he spent the day swimming and lying in the sun. "The lake is really peaceful and beautiful. I'd like to take you there sometime," he added.

His mom just nodded and went back to her housework. He was relieved she didn't ask any more questions. When his dad came home, he only asked if he'd put gas in the car. He smiled and assured him that he had, and they sat down for supper.

The July heat was oppressive and Travis was almost shaking with excitement. His dad had let him use the car for the day and he was already on his way to the lake again. He could almost feel the relief from the cool water. Throughout the past year, Travis drove to the lake as often as he could get permission. The property was quickly becoming his escape from his parents and their rigorous sense of discipline. He'd built himself a small rock-lined fire pit near the lake and even erected a small shelter. In all his visits, he'd never again seen the man or any of the sheep.

Arriving at the lake, Travis parked in his usual spot and walked down to the shore. The first thing he did was look across the lake to the stream, hoping to see the man again. The area around the lake was deserted, though, and he went back to the car to unload his things. Once everything was unloaded and stowed in his little shelter, he changed his clothes and ran into the lake. The cool water felt wonderful on his skin. After swimming, he spread a blanket on the ground before lying in the sun to dry.

He must have dozed off for a while, because he was suddenly very hungry. Getting out his lunch, he savored each bite as he listened to the sounds of the birds and squirrels. After lunch, he decided to swim across the lake to see what the stream looked like. Wading into the water, he started swimming toward the opposite shore. Travis was a strong swimmer and he was soon gliding quickly through the water.

As he approached the other shore and the water became shallow enough to stand, he saw that a small lamb was stuck in the mud near the stream. Stepping onto the shore, he slowly approached the lamb, trying his best not to scare it. As he got closer he could see that the lamb was buried in the mud to its knees. Thinking fast, Travis gathered small sticks and spread them on top of the mud around the lamb. The sticks allowed the animal to get some traction and it was able to free itself.

Travis sat on a rock near the lake shore watching the lamb munch on the nearby grass. When it got close, he slowly reached out and stroked the soft wool on its head and neck; the lamb moved closer, and seemed to enjoy his touch.

A soft noise alerted Travis to another presence. Shifting his gaze, he found himself staring into the deep blue eyes of a god. Travis knew this was the man he'd seen the year before, bathing in the lake. Startled, he stood up, unsure of how the man would react. The man was wearing a pair of rough wool shorts, plain rustic-looking shoes, a pendant around his neck, and nothing else.

The man just looked at him and his gaze somehow made Travis's stomach flutter and his mind whirl. He tried to find his voice and finally stammered, "The lamb was caught in the mud." The man looked over at the sticks. "I helped it get free."

The animal was now rubbing gently against the man's legs, and he bent down, lifting it in his arms.

"I'm Travis, my dad owns the land." He wasn't sure what to say and the silence was a little oppressive.

The man smiled, "Thank you for helping her out of the mud." His voice was deep, rich, and smooth.

Travis gently extended his hand, stroking the lamb's neck and back. The man watched attentively as the lamb nuzzled his hand with its nose.

"I have to be getting back, thank you again." The man smiled and slowly turned, disappearing into the woods.

Travis sat on the rock for a moment longer, then waded back into the water, and swam back across the lake. When he reached the other side, he couldn't help looking at the spot where the path entered the woods. Gathering up his stuff, he changed clothes, loaded the car, and headed home. The entire drive home, he couldn't seem to get the image of the man out of his mind.

About a week later, Travis woke in the middle of the night from a very intense, very erotic dream. In his dream, he had been lying in the sunlight by the lake when a shadow passed over the sun. Opening his eyes, he could see the body of a beautiful man. The man knelt next to him, and he felt their lips touch, very tentatively at first. Travis felt his body react and he returned the kiss, wrapping his arms around the man's neck, the kiss building in heat and intensity. He couldn't see who the man was, but he could feel his lips and the man's touch on his body, making him soar with delight and passion. The sensations of touch roamed over his body, across his chest, and arms, down his back, cupping his butt. The man's hands felt hot, almost burning, spreading heat through his entire body. Travis held the man close, allowing himself to float on the waves of sensation. He felt the man's hands pushing his shorts past his hips, down his legs, and over his feet.

The man whispered, "You're beautiful, Love."

Travis woke from the dream with a start, sitting straight up in bed, unsure where he was. When he realized he was home in his own bedroom, he relaxed back onto the sheets, somehow disappointed that the dream wasn't real.

A soft rap and his bedroom door opened, knocking him out of his reverie as he saw his mom's head peer around the door. "Are you okay, Trav?"

"Yes, Mom, I just had a dream." He was a little embarrassed and hoped his mother couldn't see his excitement through the sheets. Thankfully the door closed and he was again alone in the dark room. It took him just a few minutes to get back to sleep. In the morning, he could barely remember having dreamed at all.

Chapter Two

"Sorry Trav, but it just isn't working for me."

The fateful words ended yet another relationship. This time at least, the guy had had the decency to tell him face to face. Travis and his now ex-boyfriend Brock were sitting in a coffee shop across the street from the gym they both used. Travis couldn't say he was surprised; it really hadn't been working for him either. They'd been too much alike to really make it in the long run. He'd been dating Brock for about two months, and while he was a great guy and terrific to look at, it just wasn't going to last.

"It's okay. I understand."

This seemed to be the story of Travis's love life. Most of his relationships lasted two, maybe three months, and then either he'd become bored and break it off or they would. It was almost inevitable. Sometimes, he'd find out it was over when they just stopped returning his phone calls.

"You're a great guy; you deserve to be happy." Standing up, Travis gently squeezed Brock's shoulder and left the coffee shop.

It had simply happened too many times for him to get upset. He always seemed to fall for the same type of guys: young, tall, muscular, and gym-built. Brock had been different and Travis thought that maybe this time….

Walking down the sidewalk to his car, he told himself, "I've got to break this pattern and find someone I really like. I'm getting too old to do this over and over." Thinking back on it, he realized he'd been in this pattern for years now. Arriving at his car, he opened the door, threw his gym bag in the back seat, started the engine, and drove home.

For Travis, home was a small one-bedroom apartment on the third floor in a turn-of-the-century building on the Eastern section of the city. Finding a parking space near his building, he unloaded the car and headed up the stairs. The phone was ringing as he unlocked the door. Quickly dropping his gym bag on the floor, he answered it just before the machine picked up.

"Travis, this is Aunt Kathy," said his father's sister.

He couldn't help smiling. She called every couple of weeks and she was the one family member he'd remained close to over the years. "Hey, Auntie, how are you?" He always enjoyed talking to her; it made him feel less alone.

"Trav, you're dad is in the hospital. He had a heart attack."

Travis didn't feel anything. He and his father hadn't really spoken in years, for a number of reasons - his job, where he lived, and liking men. "He's been asking for you."

That was a surprise. "You're sure?" It was just hard to believe.

"Yes, he's been asking for you and he keeps asking. Please come to the hospital, this may be your last chance." There was a real sadness in her voice, beyond the usual sadness involved with visiting a sick relative.

"Is it that bad?"

"Travis, they don't know how much longer he has." He could tell she was holding back tears. "He's at Butterworth Hospital."

"Okay, I'll be right there." He figured he'd go, if only to be with his aunt. Grabbing his keys, he closed and locked the door, rushed down the stairs, and headed to his car.

It was a short drive to the hospital and after parking the car he went into the hospital and inquired about his father at the visitor's desk. He was directed to the cardiac unit on the fourth floor. When he arrived, he saw his aunt waiting for him. She looked harried. She stood when she saw Travis and hugged him tightly.

"You need to see him now." She wiped away a few tears.

"Is he really that bad?"

She nodded, "I don't know how much time we have." She led Travis into a small room. His dad was lying in a bed connected to a bunch of clicking monitors, breathing machines, and flashing screens.

"Dad, I'm here; it's Travis." The words were spoken tentatively.

"He's very weak Trav, but he can see and hear you."

His father raised his hand slightly and he seemed to be motioning him to come closer.

He approached the side of his father's bed. "I'm here, Dad."

Slowly his dad lifted his hand, placing it on the back of his neck, squeezing very softly. The touch was so gentle. "I'm sorry, Son." The words were soft and barely audible. Tears formed in Travis's eyes and he brushed them away. The hand slipped from his neck, back onto the bed.

"It's okay, Dad." Travis took his father's hand in his, stroking it gently.

His dad's face had a very peaceful look as he closed his eyes. The pinging of the monitors slowed and quieted until only a single tone sounded. A nurse came into the room and slowly shut off the machines one by one until the room was silent. Travis held his dad's hand for a few more minutes before placing it back on the bed. He felt his aunt touch his shoulder and placed his hand over hers. Slowly, he got up from the chair, hugged her, and walked out of the room into the hall. His aunt followed him.

"Why didn't they try to revive him?" He wasn't angry, just curious.

"Your dad's had a heart condition for a few years. He knew this could happen and he'd already signed a 'do not resuscitate' order." She dabbed a tear from her eye with a tissue. "I'll call the church and the funeral home and make all the arrangements." She reached into her purse and took out an envelope. "When he called me early this morning with chest pains, he made me promise to give this to you."

"Thank you." Travis opened the envelope and removed the contents. Inside was a list of information he would need, including the name of a lawyer, bank accounts, deposit boxes, etc. Travis almost laughed; this was the dad he knew, practical to the end. His mind abruptly wandered back to his dad's last moments of life and he couldn't help but smile; at least they'd made some form of peace before he died.

The next few days were a whirl, busy with arrangements, the funeral, cleaning out the house, and just taking care of all the details. He'd met with the lawyer this morning and his father's will had been very simple - everything went to Travis. He and the lawyer reviewed all of his dad's assets and made plans for their liquidation.

At the bottom of the list was the acreage that Travis had escaped to when he was a teenager. He hadn't been there in about eight years, but he had fond memories of his time at the lake. "Your dad spoke with me about two months ago and he'd planned to put that property up for sale. There are a number of people who would be interested; it's worth a lot of money."

Travis thought about the fun he'd had there, and a vision of the handsome man he'd seen by the lake flashed into his mind. "No, I think I'll hang on to the land for now. We'll sell the house and liquidate the other investments. I've already taken what I want."

The lawyer nodded, "I'll call an auction house, and they'll remove and sell the contents of the house and garage. Then we'll put the house on the market."

Travis held out his hand, "Thank you." The lawyer had been very helpful.

Leaving the law office, Travis decided that since it was still early on Friday, he'd take a drive. He didn't have to work again until Monday and he'd like to see the lake property. Travis was actually smiling for the first time in days. Driving back to his apartment, he packed the car with what he thought he'd need and headed North out of the city.

In some ways the drive seemed very familiar and in some ways, he noticed that a lot had changed in the last eight years. There was a lot more development. Areas that used to be fields were now full of new homes, a few shopping centers had been built, and the roads had been improved.

Arriving at the property, he parked where he always did and walked down to the lake. The path to the lake hadn't changed at all. The woods and trees were still thick and lush, just as he remembered. On the way, he found the small fire ring he'd made years before. The stones were still there, but overgrown with weeds. The small shelter had collapsed long ago and had mostly disappeared. The lake itself hadn't changed; the water was still clear as crystal, the early July sun shining brightly on the water, and he could see where the small stream emptied into the lake. The large trees still stood around the lake, framing the water in a backdrop of thick greenery.

Travis decided to walk to the other side of the lake to see if the path through the woods was still there. As a kid he had never explored the path. For some reason, he'd never been that curious. When he was here, he was just grateful for the few hours of freedom.

Stepping carefully, he walked around the lake, stopping at the stream to watch the water cascade over the small stones. The bank was muddy in the same place that the small lamb had gotten stuck. Just beyond the stream was the path into the woods. As he followed it, Travis noticed how dense and thick the woods were on both sides. The trees were huge and they looked like they'd been there forever. Light dappled the ground through the canopy of leaves overhead.

After walking for about ten minutes, he saw what looked like a clearing up ahead. As he approached the edge of the woods, he stopped dead in his tracks. He was standing on a slight rise and below him was a small farm consisting of two barns, a small house, and a number of animal pens and cleared fields. The entire area was probably about twelve to fifteen acres. The house looked to be about two or three rooms, rustic, but well built with a stone foundation and log construction. It looked somehow graceful and absolutely perfect in this almost surreal setting. The barns were located a small distance from the house, one on each side. Around each of the barns were small fenced animal pens and pastures. One of the barns appeared to house goats, while the other held sheep. The entire scene was incredibly pastoral and looked like something from the past, almost like something from a fairy tale.

Slowly, Travis continued down the path, which seemed to lead to the barns and house. He didn't see anyone around, so he walked up to the house and knocked on the door. He waited a few minutes and was about to leave, when the door was suddenly opened with a jerk.

"I told you before—" The words stopped in mid sentence.

Travis was looking into the face of the same man he'd seen all those years ago. In fact, he looked like he hadn't changed much. "I'm Travis Freeman, my father passed away recently and I inherited the land..." The look on the man's face stopped his words.

His expression was a mixture of surprise and confusion. "I know who you are. We met some years ago when you rescued one of my lambs."

The voice was just as he remembered; only hearing it as an adult, it made him feel warm from the inside out. Travis smiled, somehow thankful that the man had remembered him after all these years. "As I said, my father just died, and I inherited the land."

The man nodded and a dark look briefly passed across his face. "What are your plans for it?"

Travis recognized the look as fear. "I haven't decided. The lawyer told me that my dad was considering selling the land. But I have fond memories here...."

As he was speaking, the wind came up and clouds passed in front of the sun. The man looked up at the sky and sprang into action. "I have to get the animals inside before this storm breaks." The man was racing down the path toward one of the barns before Travis could move. Without thinking, Travis ran after him, asking if there was anything he could do to help. "Run down to the other barn and open the doors that lead to the pens. The sheep should come inside by themselves."

Travis followed the path to the other barn, opened the small door and stepped inside. Stepping into the pens, he opened the doors to allow the sheep inside. Like the man said, they walked inside obediently and waited for Travis to close the doors behind them. Once the animals were inside, he left the barn, closing the door behind him.

Outside, the sky looked dark and menacing, where half an hour before there had been blue sky. Travis saw lightning and heard thunder as he was hurrying up the path toward the house. As he passed the last pen, he saw a small lamb still wandering in the field. Reacting almost out of instinct, he jumped the fence, scooped the lamb into his arms, and stepped over the fence again. Raindrops had started falling as he raced for the house. Travis was surprised to find himself speaking softly to the lamb, telling it that everything would be okay.

He slowed as he approached the house, and the door opened as he came closer. The man stood in the doorway, looking unsure of what he should do. A burst of lightning and a crack of thunder seemed to erase his confusion and he stepped back to let Travis inside. The man closed the door as the sky opened up.

Travis was standing on a homespun wool rug just inside the door, still stroking the lamb's soft head and neck. The man stepped forward and gently took the lamb out of his arms. "After I let the sheep into the barn, I noticed this little one still in the field. I picked him up as I was coming back to the house."

"How did you catch him?"

Travis looked confused. "I didn't. I just picked him up and carried him with me."

The man looked puzzled. "They usually run away." He shook his head. "I'm Cembran, Cembran Bacch, by the way. Thank you for helping with the sheep and for bringing in this little one." He was smiling for the first time, his face lit up, and the heat Travis had been feeling through his body increased to a dull ache. The man was average height and he looked lean, trim, and strong. His face was the same face Travis remembered from years before, with warm piercing eyes, aquiline nose, and full luscious lips. His light sun-bleached hair framed his face with tight curls and ringlets.

"I'm glad I could help." Travis didn't know what to do, so he just stood on the rug by the door. Cembran took the lamb to a rug in the corner of the living room, gently setting it down, and it curled up like it belonged there.

Travis used the opportunity to look around the room. The inside of the small house was dominated by a fieldstone fireplace. The décor was rustic in the extreme; the walls were paneled with what looked like hand-sawn planks. The floors had woven wool rugs covering honey-colored plank floors. The furniture looked all handmade and the small kitchen looked primitive. The only modern conveniences apparent were a small stove, a refrigerator, and a few electric lights.

"Please sit down; the storm shouldn't last long. Then I'll lead you back to your car." Cembran indicated for Travis to sit in one of the chairs by the fireplace.

"Thank you." Almost gingerly, Travis sat down. The wood was smooth and conformed to his body. Travis heard movement in the kitchen and after a few minutes, Cembran brought two glass mugs filled with what looked like a medium-dark beer. He thanked his host and took the offered mug. After taking a sip, he couldn't help smiling. It was obviously beer, but it was unlike any beer he'd drank before. The color was medium-brown; the taste was rich and slightly sweet, and incredibly smooth. "This is incredible, probably the best beer I've ever had. Did you make this?"

Cembran just nodded and returned the smile. "It's an old family recipe. I had to modify it for the ingredients I have here."

As they sat, Travis kept looking around the room. In one corner near the kitchen was a small homemade dining table and two chairs. There were no pictures on the walls, but the mantle was filled with carvings of sheep, goats, and other animals. They were quite detailed and lifelike. "The carvings on the mantle − is that your work? They're so detailed and beautifully done."

"Yes, during the winter the farm largely goes to sleep. I take care of the animals and wait until spring." For the first time, Cembran had spoken enough that Travis realized he had a slight accent. He guessed it was European. "I fill some of the time carving." Getting up from his chair, Cembran went to the mantle and brought down two of the carvings. One was a lamb and another was a full-grown sheep. "Both of those are the lamb you rescued from the mud years ago. I carved them over the next couple of winters. The one you carried in today is one of her children."

Travis turned the carving in his hand, marveling at the intricacy. Closing his eyes, he tried to remember that day he'd helped the lamb get out of the mud. He tried to remember the animal, but his strongest memory of that day was the vision of Cembran wearing only a pair of wool shorts.

He didn't know what to say. Each carving seemed imbued with great care and love; it was as if they were portraits of family members or close friends. Travis looked over at Cembran and a sense of understanding overcame him. This was a man who spent almost all of his time alone. On some level, these were portraits of friends. The animals were his companions.

Cembran sat back and nodded, whispering almost to himself, "You do understand, don't you?"

"Yeah, I think I do." Nothing further was said, but Travis felt as though he was being given a look into this man that very few had ever gotten before. The thought made him smile. "Can I ask you where you come from? Have you lived here long?"

Cembran looked at him quizzically.

"You have a slight accent when you speak."

"My family comes from the Jura mountains, in Switzerland. I came to this country years ago. How about you?"

"I grew up in Grand Rapids. I've lived there all my life."

"You said your father died recently?"

Travis nodded. He wasn't sure how he felt; it was hard for him to grieve for a man he barely knew. Mostly he grieved for what might have been.

"We weren't close. He and I had different ideas of things." He took a breath, unsure if he should continue. "He didn't agree with many things, the job I chose, or what he saw as my lifestyle."

Cembran crumpled his brow. "Lifestyle?" He seemed confused by the word.

Travis decided to plow on. If Cembran kicked him out, he'd walk back to the car. "I'm attracted to men, not women." Cembran just nodded as a soft, sad look crossed his face. Travis knew that look well; he'd seen it in the mirror many times. "You too?"

Cembran nodded. "Yes." Finishing his beer, he got up and went into the kitchen area. It was still raining heavily and had started to get quite dark. "It looks like the rain isn't letting up and it's too dark to walk through the woods. You can stay here tonight and head back to your car in the morning."

The thought intrigued Travis and he was fascinated with Cembran.

"Thank you."

"I'll make some dinner and then set up a bed for you." Over the next half hour, Cembran made a basic meal of pancakes, berries, and what appeared to be venison. As he cooked, he hummed softly to himself, and the lamb in the corner perked up its head, watching Cembran's every move.

Dinner was incredible. Travis had never felt so full and satisfied. Cembran had brought out more beer and Travis was feeling a little tipsy. After dinner, Cembran made a bed for him on the floor in front of the fireplace. With the rain, the night had turned chilly. After finishing the bed, Cembran said goodnight and disappeared into the other room.

After cleaning up a little, he climbed into the blankets. All of the bedding appeared to be homemade and was incredibly comfortable, like he was wrapped in a cocoon of warmth and softness, and he fell into a deep sleep almost immediately.

Travis couldn't tell where he was, but he could feel someone kneeling next to him, a pair of lips gently touching his. His body reacted to the first touch as he returned the kiss. He pulled the man down onto his body, wrapping his arms around him, feeling the hot, smooth skin and taut muscles. Hands freely explored his body, his chest, stomach, and back. Lips pulled on his and a tongue explored his mouth. Lips and tongue soon joined hands caressing and tweaking his nipples. Travis pressed his chest toward the moist source of pleasure.

The lips continued exploring down his stomach to the elastic of his briefs, hands teasing the contents through the fabric. Slowly, the man pulled the waistband over his throbbing manhood, past his hips, and finally off his body. His dream-lover pulled away and Travis could tell he was looking at him. "You're beautiful, Love." The words seemed to be impressed into his mind rather than heard.

Without hesitation, Travis pulled him close, the man's skin hot against his own, his own hands exploring, chest, back, butt, and legs - all muscular, strong, and powerful. Lips pulling on his own, hard cock against hard cock sending waves of electric passion through his spine, directly to his mind. Fingers explored his buttocks, pulling the cheeks apart, teasing his crack, making him throb and ache, hips and legs pressing against his. Slow, fluid movement, almost too slow, knowing what he wanted, how to build, and make it last. The hands continued their searing explorations, lips pulling and tugging, while they kissed, throbbing and tasting, desire increasing, mounting, then retreating only to build again and again. Pressure built without retreat, building until finally, a hot explosion. The words "You're beautiful, Love," again etched themselves into his brain.

Waking with a start, Travis was disoriented, not knowing where he was. Slowly, he remembered the day before; he was in Cembran's house. The room was pitch-black and he fumbled for his pants, hoping he had tissues in his pocket. He had had these dreams off and on for years, but never before had they been so intense or this real, and never before had his body reacted so forcefully. Travis was embarrassed. Finding his pants, he fished in his pocket, finding what he was looking for. After cleaning himself up, he settled back into the bed and quickly fell into a deep sleep.

Chapter Three

Waking in the morning, Travis felt an incredible sense of contentment. He'd slept more soundly than he could remember. As he continued waking up, he realized there was a weight on the covers near his legs, and he couldn't help smiling as he looked down and saw the white body of the lamb curled up near his legs. The animal appeared to still be asleep and he didn't want to disturb it.

A few minutes later, the door to Cembran's bedroom opened and he stepped into the room. Travis had to keep from laughing at the shocked look on Cembran's face when he looked down and saw the lamb curled up next to Travis. His shocked expression was quickly replaced with an ear-to-ear grin. "Looks like you found a friend."

"Yeah, he helped me keep warm."

Cembran bent down and gently lifted the lamb off the blankets. "Come, little one; let's let Travis get out of bed." The lamb stirred as he shifted it from the blanket to the rug in the corner. "I need to see to the animals; I'll be back soon." Cembran left the house, giving Travis some privacy so he could get dressed.

He cleaned up quickly and left the house. Travis was able to find Cembran by following the sound of his humming and soft singing. The storm was long gone and the sun was shining brightly as he followed the path to the sheep barn. Stepping inside, he made a soft noise so he didn't startle his host, then asked "Can I help?"

Cembran smiled brightly, "Sure, would you open the doors on the other side? The sheep will head out on their own".

Sure enough, as he opened the door, all the sheep lined up and one by one exited the barn into the pasture. The barn now empty, Cembran began to clean the pens. Travis watched for a few minutes, then picked up a shovel, and mimicking his movements, pitched in to help. Travis wasn't as adept as Cembran, but he was in good shape from years of gym workouts. After working a while, they had cleaned all the pens and spread clean bedding.

"Thank you for the help. Let's head in for breakfast."

"What about the other barn, doesn't that need to be cleaned?" Travis was curious, and he had to admit that he'd enjoyed looking at Cembran as he worked; his taut muscles flexing under his clothes was a sight to behold.

"I already let them out and I'll clean the pens after breakfast." Cembran was already starting to exit the barn.

"*We'll* clean the pens after breakfast."

Cembran stopped in his tracks.

"You've been very hospitable and I want to repay you for your kindness." Travis stopped; he wasn't quite sure how to continue. "Besides, I like the animals." He wanted to add "and their owner" but restrained himself.

"The animals sure seem to like you." Cembran nodded as he headed out of the barn. Travis followed him up the path. "Did you have animals when you were growing up?"

"No, my parents would never let me have a pet. I had to make the most of my friends' pets. I always loved animals, though, and used to go to the zoo a lot as a kid."

They were quiet for the rest of the walk back to the house.

Once inside, Cembran washed up and started breakfast. Travis cleaned up as well. Stepping back into the main room, Cembran had set out cheese, fresh milk, bread, homemade jam, and an assortment of wild berries.

"Cembran, there's something that puzzles me. You seem surprised at the animals' reaction to me. Is there something wrong?"

Cembran shook his head and smiled. "No, nothing is wrong. The animals just seem to have taken to you, or at least the sheep have. It's quite unusual and really special."

"Oh." Travis looked at him quizzically.

"You don't have to stay and help. After breakfast, you can head along the path through the woods and back to your car."

Travis shook his head, "No, I'm going to help you clean the goat pens. I said I would and I meant it." He smiled, a glint in his eye, and added, "Besides, I want to see the goats." Cembran smiled back.

After breakfast, Cembran was cleaning up when a pounding on the door made Travis jump in his chair.

Cembran huffed out his breath in exasperation and opened the door. "What do you want?" His tone was confrontational, the same tone he'd used when he first opened the door to Travis the previous day. He'd obviously met the person before. Travis turned his chair to get a better look at the man at the door.

"I'm here to give you notice that I intend to buy this property and as soon as I do, I'm kicking you off."

"I didn't know it was for sale." Cembran looked over to where Travis was sitting, questioning. Travis shook his head slightly in answer.

"I was able to convince the man who owns the property to put it up for sale and I intend to buy it. I expect he'll do so in the next few weeks."

Travis wanted to slap the self-satisfied look off the man's face, but he kept quiet.

"What do you intend to do, if you buy it?" Travis couldn't see Cembran's face, but he could see that every muscle in his body was tensed.

"Create a small exclusive resort community around the lake. Hell, I might even turn this into a petting zoo." He swept his arms indicating the small farm, a sneer firmly plastered on his face.

Travis had heard enough and he could see Cembran was starting to tremble a little. Slowly, he got up from the chair he was sitting on and walked to the door. Cembran turned towards him, his face showing fear and sadness.

Travis stood next to Cembran, looking into his face, "Who is this guy?"

Without letting him answer, the man stepped forward. "I'm Joe Palumbo; I'm a developer of recreational properties. Who are you?"

A small smile twisted Travis's face. "I'm Travis Freeman; my father was the man you convinced to sell the property." The smirk on Joe's face began to fade. "My father passed away a week ago, so now I'm the new owner of the property and it's not for sale, and it won't *be* for sale." Travis could see the anger build on Joe's face. "Now, you have five minutes to get off my property or I'll call the state police and have you arrested for trespassing. You're not welcome on this property, now or ever."

Joe didn't move, so Travis pulled out his cell phone and dialed the number – which he happened to have because he'd dated a state policeman a few years ago. Just before the call connected, Joe finally turned and headed back down the path. Travis turned off the phone, watching to make sure Joe left, then closed the door.

"Did you mean what you just said?" Cembran's voice was soft and Travis looked into his eyes.

"Yes, I did. I have no intention of selling the property, to him or anyone else." A twinkle shone in Travis's eyes. "Come on; we have pens to clean." Travis opened the door and waited for Cembran to lead the way down the path to the barn.

As they walked, Travis took out his cell phone and made a call to the lawyer. He knew it was Saturday, but he hoped he might be in the office anyway. He was in luck.

"Earl, this is Travis."

"How are you doing? Where are you?"

"I'm at the lake property. Look, I met a Joe Palumbo today." Earl was silent. "I need you to check to make sure there are no outstanding debts, liens, taxes, or anything else on the property. I need to know that I own it free and clear."

"You do. I already checked when your dad asked about selling. There's nothing outstanding."

"Good."

"Travis, be careful, Joe's brother is the local Sheriff. So you won't get help from that quarter if you need it."

"Thanks for the warning, but I have a friend with the state police in this area. I'll call him if there's any trouble."

"Good, let me know if you need anything."

Travis ended the call as they arrived at the barn. The two of them spent the next few hours cleaning it out and arranging fresh bedding for the goats. When they were done, the barn smelled of straw and the breeze that was blowing through open doors. Cembran let a few of the goats inside. They nuzzled him before walking up to Travis and nuzzling his hands, too. Travis petted each of the goats as they pressed their noses against his legs.

"If I hadn't seen it with my own eyes, I wouldn't have believed it." Cembran was shaking his head in disbelief. "The last person who visited the farm, the animals wouldn't even come in from the field for me, and here they nuzzle you like an old friend."

All Travis could do was shrug his shoulders; he had no explanation.

They had both been working hard for the past few hours and they were covered in sweat. The day was turning out to be a hot one. After making sure all the animals had plenty of water, they headed back to the house.

"I think we should cool off. Let's go down to the lake," Cembran suggested, his face unreadable.

Travis smiled, "Sounds like a good idea."

Cembran grabbed a large blanket and led the way down the path and through the woods to the lake. The sunlight danced off the surface of the water as they reached the grassy bank. Cembran spread out a blanket. He toed off his shoes, pulled off his shirt, and unfastened his pants. They slipped silently around his ankles. Cembran stepped out of them and walked into the cool water.

Travis was mesmerized. Cembran's body was lean and powerful. Hard muscle covered his lithe frame with no hint of fat. Except for the area from his hips to mid-thigh, his smooth skin was tanned to a deep golden brown. Pulling himself out of his reverie, Travis slipped out of his clothes as well. He was slightly taller than Cembran, with dark hair and a sculpted gym-built body. Unfortunately, he hadn't had any time in the sun, so his smooth skin was pale, but he'd tan quickly.

Stepping into the water, he walked out until he was waist deep, then dove under, swimming gracefully and swiftly through the cool, sun lit water. Looking back at the bank, he realized he'd left Cembran behind. Turning around, he swam back. Cembran was looking at him, fascinated.

"No wonder you're good with the animals, you're part fish."

Travis looked at Cembran, confused, "Do you know how to swim?"

Cembran returned his look, shaking his head, "No."

"I learned as a kid and actually competed on swim teams while I was in high school. I could teach you."

Cembran was enthralled, "I think I'd like that."

Travis showed him some of the beginning swimming movements before they started getting chilled in the cool water. Stepping out on the bank, Cembran stretched out on his stomach on one side of the blanket to dry off in the sun. Travis joined him.

"Thank you. I never knew you could propel yourself through the water like that."

Travis turned his head to face Cembran. "You never saw people swim when you grew up?"

"No, growing up in the mountains, we didn't swim. We might walk into the water, but it was often too cold."

Cembran was quiet and still for a long moment. Then, he slowly lifted his upper body off the blanket, bringing his face close to Travis. His lips gently brushed Travis's in a very tentative kiss.

The image of the man from his dreams came unbidden to Travis's mind, and he realized that all these years he'd been dreaming of Cembran. Smiling slightly, Travis moved his head closer, encouraging him to continue. The kiss intensified and his body reacted with gusto. Tingles rushed up and down his spine, heat spread though his body, and he was instantly hard as stone. Gently, he cupped Cembran's head in his hand, parting his lips, letting Cembran's tongue explore his mouth, a soft moan escaping.

Cembran broke the kiss, looking a little embarrassed. "Travis, I'm—"

"Shhhh." Travis cut off further words by pulling Cembran into another kiss. Their bodies were still lying on the blanket and neither man moved or shifted. Their lips were hotter than the sun on their skin. Cembran parted his mouth and Travis used his tongue to explore, his lips gently tugging and squeezing, hands and fingers stroking Cembran's soft curls. He heard a quiet moan as Cembran increased the intensity of the kiss, using his own lips to suck and tug on Travis's. Reluctantly, Travis pulled back, breaking the kiss. His head was throbbing, his back taught, his skin burning from the inside, his body tingling. Without saying a word, Travis looked into Cembran's dazzling blue eyes and kissed him again. This time, the kiss was soft and tender, almost as if their lips were barely touching, yet the sparks and tingles began in earnest.

Travis knew he wanted Cembran, wanted him badly. He also knew that he'd always rushed into sex with every man he'd ever been involved with and he decided that this time, he was going to take it slower, so he resisted the urge to pull their bodies together. Instead, he lost himself in the kiss, letting his mind whirl in the wonder, and fly from the joy received from a single tender kiss.

Slowly, Cembran sat up without taking his eyes off Travis and his gaze seemed to pull Travis along. Cembran slowly traced the features of Travis's face with the tips of his fingers, touching his cheek, caressing his chin. Travis closed his eyes as the fingertips brushed his forehead, nose, and back to his cheeks.

Cembran took his hands, caressing his fingers and along the back of his arms. Turning them over, Cembran stopped his ministrations. Both of Travis's hands were blistered from helping clean out the barns.

A scowl crossed Cembran's face. "You should have told me."

Travis lifted his eyes to Cembran's. "They don't hurt." And at that moment, looking in his eyes, the memory of his kiss still fresh in his mind, they didn't hurt at all.

"Come, I need to see to those blisters." Cembran stood up and slipped on his pants. Travis slowly got up as well, putting on his pants and shoes. He was about to put on his shirt when he noticed that Cembran had just flung his over his shoulder. Travis couldn't help smiling, knowing he'd be treated to the sight of his hard muscles as they walked back to the house.

Cembran picked up the blanket and headed down the path. Travis walked just behind him, enjoying the view. After a few steps, Cembran stopped, took Travis's hand gently in his, and they continued their walk to the house. It had been a long time since Travis had just held hands with someone and it felt glorious.

Once in the house, Cembran brought out a jar of what looked like ointment and gently rubbed it into Travis's hands. It felt cool and soothing. "This will help your hands heal."

"Thank you."

Cembran got up, went to the kitchen, and started making lunch. During lunch, he was quiet. While they ate, he spent most of the time looking at the floor, not meeting Travis's gaze.

"Cembran, is something wrong?"

Cembran lifted his head, finally looking at Travis. "I just need to think for while." Travis didn't know what to say. So he waited for Cembran to continue. "It's been a long time."

Travis smiled, "Are you trying to tell me you need to take things slowly?"

He nodded, "I just need to think."

Travis nodded too. "I should probably get home. I'd like to see you again, soon. Can I come back next weekend?"

Cembran nodded and smiled as they stood up. Travis stepped in front of him, wrapped his arms around his back and pulled him into a deep, penetrating kiss. After breaking the kiss Travis whispered, "Remember that when you're thinking." Cembran nodded.

Travis put on his shirt, said good-bye, and slowly opened the door, stepping out into the bright sunshine. Cembran was standing in the doorway, and Travis watched as he smiled and gently touched his lips with his fingers before silently closing the door.

His feet hardly touched the ground as Travis walked down the path past the barns, through the woods, and to the shore of the lake. Sitting on the rock near the stream, he paused quietly in the sun, letting his mind wander. The thought that he'd been dreaming of Cembran since he was a teenager brought a smile to his face. Standing up again, he walked back to his car, grinning the entire time.

Chapter Four

The week had gone by agonizingly slowly. Travis kept looking forward to the weekend. On Wednesday, he'd visited the lawyer to see check on the estate liquidation.

"Everything is going well. The proceeds from the sale of your father's investments have been deposited in the estate account we set up. The estate sale is in two weeks and the house goes on the market tomorrow. Have you made a decision on the lake property?" he asked, leaning back in his desk chair.

"Yes. I'm going to keep it."

"Oh." He wrinkled his brow in surprise.

"Is there an issue?"

"No, I'm just surprised, I guess. I mean the property is worth a lot of money and I've received inquiries from a number of developers about purchasing it."

"Joe Palumbo, no doubt."

"No, actually he hasn't called me. But now I know how to address any inquiries."

Travis was relieved there were no issues. He thanked Earl for all his help, and left the office.

Right after work on Friday, Travis left his office and headed north toward the lake. He couldn't help smiling as he drove. Arriving at the property, he discovered a small road that allowed him to park closer to the little farm. He left his bag in the car and walked down the path. A few minutes later he was at Cembran's door, knocking. Cembran opened the door and Travis smiled brightly, leaned forward, and kissed him. Cembran stepped back and motioned him inside.

Cembran closed the door and Travis wrapped his arms around him, pulling him to his body, but Cembran put his hands on his chest to stop him. "I need to talk to you," he said. Travis didn't like the sound of that at all. "Please sit down." He sat in the offered chair, near the fireplace, and Cembran took the one opposite. "Travis, I can't do this."

"Cembran."

He held up his hand to stop Travis. "I can't do this to you. There are things you don't know, that could hurt you deeply." Travis opened his mouth to say something, but closed it again. "I just can't allow that to happen. I'm sorry. You'll be much better off if you go home and just forget about me, forget you ever met me."

Travis shook his head.

"It's better this way." Cembran got up from his chair. Travis followed him to the door without a word.

Cembran opened the door and Travis stepped out and started down the path, heart heavy. After taking a few steps he turned back, a lump firmly lodged in his throat.

"It's for the best, Travis." The door closed silently.

Shocked and dejected, Travis walked back toward his car. There was barely enough light to see the path. By the time he got to the woods, dejection had turned to anger and he was about to turn back when he heard whispers and footsteps off to his side.

"Why are we doing this?" a voice asked, so quiet Travis could barely hear the words.

Another voice whispered back, but he couldn't hear the response. Travis heard sticks breaking. "Shhh, be careful where you step."

His heart started racing; he wasn't sure what they were up to, but it didn't seem like it would be good for Cembran. Travis headed back toward the house. As he reached the clearing, he heard the strangers banging on Cembran's door. He picked up his pace and reached the clearing to see Cembran's door open and him step outside. Travis watched as one of the men hit Cembran on the side of the head and he saw him fall to the ground.

From the woods, he called out as load as he could, yelling, "What are you doing?" The two men looked at each other and ran into the woods. Travis could hear them running as fast as they could.

He rushed to Cembran. He'd been knocked out and was bleeding from the gash on his head. Travis went inside and found a clean cloth to stop the bleeding. As he was tying the cloth around Cembran's head, he heard a car start in the distance and drive away. Carefully, Travis lifted him and carried him into the bedroom, placing him gingerly on his back on the bed. The bleeding was slowing and Travis went to get a clean cloth. Once he found one, Travis stepped back into the bedroom, looked at Cembran, and gasped involuntarily.

Travis tried to move, but he couldn't. He blinked his eyes a few time and tried to make sure he wasn't imaging things. Slowly, he regained control of himself and edged closer. It was undeniable. Two small horns, like those on the goats, were sticking out of Cembran's forehead near the hairline.

Moving forward, he sat on the edge of the bed and started to clean the blood off Cembran's face. The bleeding had stopped so he removed the cloth from around Cembran's head and finished cleaning up the blood. He was nearly finished when Cembran started to wake up. The cloth was red and Travis went to rinse it out. When he returned, Cembran's eyes were open and he was trying to get out of bed. "Just lay there for a while." Travis noticed that the small horns had disappeared.

"What happened?" Cembran asked, relaxing back onto the bed. "I remember hearing someone banging and then opening the door?"

"Two men came through the woods. I heard them as I was heading back to my car. One of them hit you on the head." Travis stopped for a minute and decided not to say anything about the horns just yet. "I stopped the bleeding and carried you in here." He continued cleaning the last of the blood from Cembran's face. He was about to suggest that they call the police, but the words died on his lips.

Cembran was getting edgy and fidgety. Travis was confused and a little scared about what he'd seen and his mind was a whirl of possibilities. Once all the blood had been cleaned up, Cembran gingerly sat up on the edge of the bed. Slowly, he raised himself to his feet and carefully tested his legs before sitting back on the edge of the bed. "Thank you for taking care of me. You better go before...."

The fear that Travis had been feeling was replaced with anger. "Okay. I'll go, but would you answer some questions for me?"

Cembran nodded tentatively. "If I can."

"Did you get a look at the men? Did you see who hit you?"

Cembran shook his head slowly and looked relieved, "I didn't get a good look at them before they hit me."

Looking Cembran square in the eyes, he asked, "What are you Cembran? I saw the horns." Cembran's hands immediately went to his forehead, a defeated and fearful look crossing his face as he lowered his head.

Taking a deep breath, he said, "It's a long story. We may as well sit down." Cembran got up and moved into the living room, sitting in one of the chairs by the fireplace; he waited for Travis to join him.

Cembran took a deep breath. "I'm a satyr, or more precisely, part satyr." Travis furled his brow in confusion. "It's complicated, but basically, my father is a satyr and my mother is part satyr. I don't have all the satyr characteristics, but I do have the small horns that you saw, as well as a small tail. Physically, a satyr is part human and part goat." Cembran had never explained this to anyone before and was finding it difficult. "Travis, I know you have a number of questions and I don't know where to start, so I'll try to start at the beginning." Cembran got up from the chair - he was much steadier on his feet already - and got two mugs of beer. After handing one to Travis, he sat back down.

"I was born in 1697 in the Jura mountains of Switzerland." Travis's eyes widened but he said nothing. "My father is a powerful satyr. He has most of the characteristics - horns, tail, cloven feet, goat legs, and the ability to enter the dreams of others. My mother is part satyr, but mostly human. So I didn't inherit many satyr characteristics, just the horns you saw, a small tail, and I did inherit the satyr immunity; I can't contract or spread any human diseases. Anyway, my family raised sheep and goats deep in an isolated mountain valley, they still do as far as I know, and I spent most of my childhood and adolescent years working with the family animals. Satyrs mature more slowly than humans; we generally don't reach full adulthood until we're about 22." Cembran stopped and looked over at Travis before continuing. "When I was about 30, I met Gathod. He was part satyr, part human like me, and we found that we were attracted to one another. We were inseparable for two months and I was growing to love him." Cembran had a faraway look on his face. "After that time, my father found out about us and he was furious and told me that I had to stop seeing Gathod and find a full satyr woman to have children with or leave." The memory was obviously painful for Cembran. "To add insult to injury, Gathod decided he didn't love me enough to leave with me."

"Who told your father about you and Gathod?" Travis was curious.

Cembran visibly tensed. "No one told him, he stole the knowledge."

"I don't understand."

"My father forced his way into my dreams and stole the knowledge from my mind while I slept." Travis just looked at Cembran, clearly not understanding. "Think of it as a type of mental rape." Travis's eyes went wide and he couldn't help a small shiver. "We all have little secrets and parts of ourselves that are private. Imagine those things being stolen from you against your will. That's what my father did to me." Cembran was breathing heavily as he continued: "Anyway, I left my home and wandered through Europe working as a shepherd for years. Luckily, I have the ability to hide my satyr characteristics, so I could exist in the human world. Almost 200 years ago, I traveled to this country. I met an ancestor of yours and he let me farm this land in exchange for part of the wool. Through the years, the land has passed from family member to family member. Most of them were just happy to own the land. I have lived here for over 100 years now."

"You said your father can enter dreams; can you as well?" Travis was thinking about the dreams he'd been having of Cembran since he was a boy - were they his? Was Cembran somehow responsible?

"No, I've never been able to enter the dreams of others." Opening his shirt, he showed Travis a small medallion. "This pendant is a charm that keeps other satyrs from entering my dreams. I've worn it since shortly after my father attacked me. My brother gave it to me before I left."

"Oh." Travis felt relieved, and his mind was buzzing. Cembran looked at him, waiting for him to speak. "I don't know what to say. I'm so confused." His mind was spinning: Cembran was a satyr, something that shouldn't exist; people were trying to hurt him; and the police probably wouldn't help. "I need to think." The things Cembran had told him, his own feelings, his memories, as well as thoughts of his dreams all rapidly played in his head.

Cembran took Travis's hand, his eyes pleading, "Travis, I sent you away because I was scared of how you'd react if I told you what I was and I didn't want to get hurt, or hurt you." Looking totally defeated he said, "If you want to go, I'll walk you back to your car."

"I just need some time to think." Travis looked at his watch and realized it was almost midnight. Slowly, he got up, handed Cembran the empty mug and walked to the door. "I'll be fine getting to my car." He left the small house and carefully followed the path through the woods. As he walked, his mind was flooded with images, the first time he'd seen Cembran up close, helping Cembran with the animals, swimming in the lake. Travis thought of those sweet, tender kisses lying in the sun. The memory made his skin warm and his cock take notice. Reaching his car, he crawled into the back, stretching out on the seat, and thinking. He thought of driving home, but he was so tired and distracted that he didn't want to risk it until morning.

He must have fallen asleep because Travis woke with a start. His back hurt and he remembered that he was in his car. He'd had another dream. This time, he was at the farm, but it was empty, no goats, no sheep, and no Cembran. The buildings and barns were empty, lifeless, and starting to decay. The small, once-neat fields were overgrown. The door to the small house stood open. Peering inside, the house was empty except for two carved sheep on the mantle. Taking the sheep down, he held them in his hands. Leaving the house, he'd walked up the path to his car. Unhappily, he'd driven home to his empty apartment. Then he'd awoken.

"Damn it!" he thought. "I have to know." Getting out of the car, he shut the door, grabbed his small case from the seat and headed up the path through the woods. The night was clear and the moon provided enough light for him to see where he was going. With each step he took, his determination built. The house was dark and silent as he reached the door. Taking a deep breath, he knocked on the door and waited. Hearing no movement, he pounded again. Still there was no movement. He was about to see if Cembran was in one of the barns when he saw a light come on in the house. The door opened and Cembran stood in the light, wearing only a shirt and a pair of rough wool shorts.

Travis set the case he was carrying at his feet, "I have to know." He seemed to be repeating it almost to himself. Before Cembran could say a word, Travis stepped forward, placed his hands on either side of Cembran's face and pulled him into a scalding kiss. Travis's body instantly flooded with heat, his cock went rigid, and his spine tingled. Cembran opened his mouth and Travis grabbed the invitation, thrusting his tongue deep. His lips pulled gently on Cembran's as he kissed him like his life depended on it. He knew he wasn't letting go.

Cembran's arms wrapped around Travis' shoulders as he gave himself over to the kiss, sighing deeply into Travis' mouth. Travis ran his hands down Cembran's powerful back, stroking the strong, taut muscles, before coming to rest at the small of his back, pulling them closer, pressing their bodies together. Almost as if they had a mind of their own, Travis's hands slipped into Cembran's shorts to cup the tight, hard globes of his ass. Cembran's last remaining resistance seemed to crumble with a whimper and a gasp as Travis slowly opened his pants and ran his hands down, sliding the shorts off until they slipped to the floor.

Without breaking the kiss, Travis placed his left arm under Cembran's back, his right arm under his knees, picked him up off the floor, and kicked the door closed before carrying him to the bedroom. Travis carried Cembran to the bed, placing him in the soft mattress. Their lips hadn't separated the entire time. Travis toed off his shoes as he leaned over the bed, lips pulling and sucking on Cembran's, his tongue exploring his mouth, running over his teeth. Cembran's hands clutched at the bedding.

Travis nibbled Cembran's ear and cheek as he unbuttoned his shirt, kissing his neck. Cembran gave up trying to get Travis's shirt off as his shoulders was nibbled and licked. With a cry, he threw his head back as Travis gently sucked on his neck. As Travis moved to the other shoulder, sucking and nibbling, he managed to get his shirt off and unfasten his pants. They slipped off his hips and puddled on the floor. Stepping out of them he climbed onto the bed, straddling Cembran's tanned, toned, and now wonderfully naked body.

His lips moved down Cembran's chest, licking their way to one of the large protruding nipples. Cembran moaned as Travis licked the nipple gently while he rubbed the other between his fingers. Cembran thrust his chest toward Travis's eager lips, moaning and writhing beneath him. Clenching his teeth, he hissed, "Travis, oohhh!" Travis just smiled and increased the pressure on the fleshy disks.

Cembran's breath was coming in short gasps and he was trying to form words, but they just wouldn't come. Eventually, he gave up and completely gave himself over to Travis as he felt hot lips move to the other nipple, giving it the same erotically delicious treatment.

Deliberately, Travis kissed his way down Cembran's hips and stomach, tracing his abs with his tongue, before kissing his mouth again. He pressed his body down on top of Cembran, skin-to-skin, lips to lips. Cembran's hands caressed his back. Travis stroked Cembran's face and hair for a moment, then he pulled back. Getting up slowly, Travis slipped off his briefs and looked down at Cembran.

"Lamb, you look so perfect, so handsome." Leaning forward he pressed his lips to his lover's, before climbing onto the bed and pressed his body onto his. They rocked gently against each other, Cembran's hands cupping Travis's butt and stroking his back. Cembran's moans were coming faster and louder and his hips started bucking urgently as Travis nibbled and sucked again on his shoulder, his fingers teasing and tweaking the beefy nipples. Travis was thrusting wildly as well, and he cried out as he gushed onto Cembran's stomach. Cembran moaned deeply and came hard, bucking against Travis.

They both lay still for a few minutes, catching their breath and enjoying the post-orgasmic high. Travis kissed Cembran gently before rolling next to him on the bed. Cembran got up and brought a cloth. He cleaned up Travis, then himself, before climbing back into bed curling up next to Travis.

"Travis, we need to—"

"Shhhh, Lamb, we'll talk in the morning." He pulled Cembran to him, spooning into his back with his arms wrapped around his chest.

Chapter Five

Travis woke with a smile on his face, "Cembran, good—"
The words died on his lips; he was in Cembran's bed, but he was alone. The small room was furnished like the rest of the house, with very rustic handmade furniture. The bedposts and frame were made of tree limbs and trunks that had been stripped of their bark and joined together. The most refined piece of furniture in the room was a small clothing chest that looked quite old. Travis figured Cembran must have brought it from Switzerland with him.

Slowly, he got out of bed. His small case had been put in one corner of the room. As he was getting dressed, details of the night before flashed through his mind. What was he going to do? Last night had been intense and he *did* like Cembran. As he thought, he realized that in the cold light of day, he should just go and leave Cembran alone. Travis knew he had feelings for Cembran, but he'd had feelings for most of the other men he'd dated, too. No, this was different. He knew he could really get hurt, and it scared him.

Once he finished dressing, he packed his clothes into the small case, resolving to head back to the car and go home. Stepping outside the house, he turned toward the path leading to his car and he stopped. The breeze carried a melody, a happy, soaring melody. Without thinking, he put his case back inside and followed the music down the path to the goat barn. Stepping inside, Travis saw Cembran milking one of the goats, singing. The words were foreign, but the joy expressed in the song reached into the depths of Travis's soul. Leaning against the doorframe, he listened to the soaring notes and brilliant cadences and he realized that if he was in any way responsible for Cembran feeling this way, he couldn't leave.

Travis watched and listened until suddenly the singing stopped. Cembran was smiling at him brightly, and he returned the smile, "I'll be done in a while." His hands didn't stop moving as he spoke. Travis watched as he finished milking the goat and patted her rump. She moved into the pen and Cembran moved on to milk the next one. As he worked, he started singing again. When he finished his song, he asked, "Would you like to try?" Travis moved forward agreeably and Cembran showed him the proper hand movements. "She's very sweet tempered."

Travis sat on the small stool and after a few mishaps and some laughter on Cembran's part, he actually managed to milk the goat. Cembran brought in the next one and started milking her. After about an hour, Travis had managed to milk three goats, while Cembran finished about twelve. He had a million questions and they talked while they worked.

"Is an affinity for animals part of being a satyr?"

"In some ways, since we are technically part goat. But not all satyrs are good with animals, just like not all humans are good with people. Most satyrs make their living raising goats and sheep, but not all. I always had a special bond with the animals in my care. My mother always said it was a gift." When he spoke of his mother, a faraway look spread across his face.

"Do you miss her?" He looked at Cembran over the back of the goat, his voice quiet and soft.

"Sometimes. She died many years ago, just before I left home. I probably wouldn't have left after my father's attack if she'd been alive. She was a sweet, kind person." He shook his head, "I don't know how she ever put up with my father." They were quiet for a while. Travis concentrating on milking his goat and Cembran appeared to be lost in thoughts and memories. The goat felt warm and he leaned his head against its body as she nuzzled his arm with her head. He finished milking her and gave her a pat like Cembran had done as she moved out into the pen.

"Cembran, will you grow old?" He'd been wondering if he'd age like normal and Cembran would always stay young. After all, he'd been alive for over three hundred years.

"In a way. For a satyr, our appearance changes based upon different life events. If I were to get married and have children, then my appearance would age as they grew older; the same is true if I were to have grandchildren. Since I haven't had either, my appearance remains as you see it, and has for almost 300 years."

"Can you die?" It sounded as though Cembran was immortal.

"Yes, I can die. I heal faster than humans, but I can be killed and I can die. It's hard to explain. Eventually, our life force is used up and we die, but our appearance doesn't age like that of a human. In satyr terms, I'm middle aged."

Travis was trying to take all of this in. "So, you still have hundreds of years yet to live?" This was confusing and very disheartening.

"I could, yes. But let's not talk about that right now." Cembran had just finished milking the last goat and after making sure they had food and water, he put the milk away and led them up the path into the house for breakfast.

"What do you do with the milk?" He was following just behind as they walked up the path.

"I use it to make cheese, among other things." Travis remembered the wonderful cheese he'd had on his last visit.

After breakfast, they spent the afternoon working in the vegetable garden. Travis loved this kind of work. He had always enjoyed making things grow. He spent most of the morning on his hands and knees pulling weeds and tending the young plants. He enjoyed himself immensely.

They talked while they worked, their conversation becoming more companionable. "I'm worried about something." Travis had been thinking about the attack on Cembran the night before. "I think you were attacked in order to scare you into leaving. Someone wants this land very badly and they are willing to hurt you to get it."

Cembran looked up, a concerned look on his face. "I know. I'm going to keep one of the sheepdogs up closer to the house. If anyone approaches, they'll bark and let me know." Travis was mildly reassured, and he let the matter go for now.

Travis smeared his face with dirt, as he tried to wipe off the sweat, "When we're done here, do you think we have time for a swim?"

A big smile lit Cembran's face. "I think we've earned a cool swim in the lake," He winked and Travis's pants suddenly started to get tight.

Once the vegetable garden was weed-free, they went inside. Cembran packed a lunch into a basket and grabbed the beach blanket before leading them down the path to the lake. The sun shone on the surface of the water as Cembran spread out the blanket. "Are you hungry?"

Travis nodded before sitting on the blanket and gently tugging Cembran onto his lap. Their kiss was soft and long, Cembran's body warm in the sun. "I've wanted to do that all morning." Before Cembran could answer, Travis kissed him again as he cradled his body in his arms. Cembran leaned back, giving himself over to the kiss and the pleasure. Slowly, Travis broke the kiss, "Lamb, if we go much farther, I won't be able to control myself."

Cembran stole one more kiss before opening the basket and setting out their lunch. He couldn't help smiling as he watched Cembran set out a wonderful lunch of cheese, bread, fruit, dried meat, and beer. Once they'd eaten, Cembran gently reclined, his head resting in Travis's lap, looking up at him.

Bending forward to kiss him, he murmured, "Lamb, you take my breath away."

Their lips brushed together in a soft, tender kiss. Travis could feel Cembran relax. After a short while, Cembran dozed off with his head on his lap.

Travis was utterly content. Cembran had dozed off about fifteen minutes ago, and Travis was stroking his hair and petting his cheek. Whenever the breeze became still, Cembran's sweet musky scent would waft up to him. Each time it happened, he could feel his body react with arousal. Looking down, he couldn't help smiling as he saw Cembran's eyes flutter and open.

"I'm sorry I dozed off." He looked slightly embarrassed.

"Don't be," Travis bent forward touching his lips to Cembran's. "I watched you sleep. We had a late night and you got up early." Travis kissed him again, adding a touch of passion.   He moaned into Cembran's mouth as his lover stroked his ears and neck, the simple, gentle touch sending shivers through him.   Slowly, Travis lifted Cembran's shoulders and carefully shifted his body from beneath him before laying him onto the blanket. Travis stopped moving and looked down at Cembran taking him all in.

Slowly Cembran cocked his head as if to say, "What?"

Travis smiled, "Just looking."   Cembran returned the smile and pulled Travis's body more firmly onto his as their lips met in a scalding kiss. Travis's tongue pressed for entrance and Cembran parted his lips, allowing the tongue to explore, and explore it did. He ran his tongue across the front of Cembran's teeth as his lips gently pulled on Cembran's. With each gentle tug, his lover moaned and whimpered, his hips bucking against Travis.

Placing his hands gently on Cembran's hips, Travis stilled his movements. "Relax, Lamb. I want to take my time and explore every inch of you." His voice was husky and rough, his eyes looking deeply. Cembran threw his head back and moaned loudly as Travis found a sensitive spot on the base of his neck. "Okay?" Cembran just nodded as he gave himself completely over to Travis's ministrations.

The sun bathed them in warmth as Travis sucked a small mark on Cembran's neck, licking and nibbling the hot, sweaty, sweet skin. With each touch of Travis's tongue, Cembran would moan; when Travis ran his fingertips through Cembran's curls, he whimpered. He kissed Cembran hard before returning his attention to the feast that was his lover's body. Licking Cembran's throat, he slowly opened the rough wool shirt, kissing and nibbling on the tan exposed skin. With each button, he licked lower and lower, down his sternum and his stomach, before swirling his tongue in his navel. Unfastening the last button, Travis opened the shirt completely, exposing the hard, muscular chest.

Cembran's large fleshy nipples were standing at attention as Travis circled them with his fingertips. Taking the left one between his lips, he licked small circles around the nipple, sucking gently, as he used his fingers to tease and play with the right one.

Cembran's breathing came in short gasps, "Travis, oh, my, that's so good!"

Travis smiled and sucked a little harder and he got a loud moan in return. He kept teasing the left nipple until Cembran begged him to stop, then he switched to the other side, licking the right nipple while his fingers teased and circled the left. Over and over his lips sucked and licked the left, then the right, then back to the left. Cembran had stopped moaning, had transcended words or even sounds. His head was thrown back, his mouth was open, his hands gripped the blanket in tight fists, and his feet rocking gently against the blanket.

Giving the nipples a reprieve, Travis ran his hands down Cembran's sides as his tongue explored and traced the lines on Cembran's hard stomach. Travis slipped his hands beneath Cembran, cradling the curve of his butt. His tongue swirled in Cembran's navel as he softly ran his fingers along Cembran's cleft fingering him gently through his clothing. Slowly, Travis withdrew his hands and kissed Cembran's stomach before opening his pants and slowly wriggling them over his lover's hips, down his legs, and off his body.

Travis stood on the blanket, looking down at Cembran's now naked body. No words were spoken because none were necessary, and the sight of Cembran's strong naked body had left Travis speechless anyway. Slowly, Travis peeled off his shirt before opening his pants and letting them fall to the ground. The only sounds besides their breathing were the songs of birds and the babble of the stream as it entered the lake. After peeling off his briefs, Travis laid his body on Cembran, their lips pressed together, hands running through soft curls, hard cocks pressed together, legs entwining, and hard, strong, smooth chests radiating heat. Without breaking their kiss, Travis worked his hands beneath Cembran, cradling his butt in his hands. Fingertips zeroed in on the hot, puckered skin of Cembran's most private self. A soft hiss escaped Cembran's lips, as fingertips brushed and caressed the tight opening.

"Do you like that?" Travis whispered.

Cembran nodded, "Oh yes, it's just been a long time."

Travis would have smiled at the understatement if he wasn't so turned on by the way Cembran gave himself to him. Shifting positions, he straddled Cembran's legs, taking the long sleek cock in his hand. He heard Cembran gasp at the first direct touch. Travis stroked gently with one hand as the other cradled his balls. Slowly, almost teasingly, he took the head in his mouth, his tongue swirling around the base. Deliberately, Travis worked his lips down the shaft to a chorus of moans and whimpers, as he ran his tongue along the ridge on the underside. Travis took more and more of Cembran into his mouth until his nose was buried in the curls at the base. Cembran was moaning loudly as Travis sucked and bobbed.

"Travis, I'm going to—"

Travis deep-throated Cembran, sucking him with everything he had and Cembran cried out as he exploded down Travis's throat. Without releasing his hold, he swallowed everything Cembran could give him.

Once Cembran's breathing returned to normal, Travis let his cock slip from between his lips. Cembran pulled his lover's face to his, kissing him deeply. When Travis opened his eyes, he saw that Cembran's were filled with tears. "What's wrong?"

Shaking his head, he answered, "Nothing; it's just that no one has done that in a very—" Cembran couldn't finish his thought because Travis's lips were kissing him again, tongue pressing for entrance. Cembran wrapped his arms around Travis's neck, pulling their bodies together. The sun warmed them and the breeze caressed them as they kissed and petted.

Slowly, Travis lifted himself off Cembran, gently clasped his ankles, and spread them apart, lifting them toward his chest. Cembran's pink puckered opening pulsed and throbbed as Travis circled it with his fingers. Cembran whimpered and wriggled with each touch.

His voice was quiet, but deep with lust and want, "Are you going to...?"

Regaining some control, Travis shook his head. "Not right now. There are things we need and I don't want to hurt you." Slowly, Travis lowered Cembran's legs back to the blanket.

Cembran quickly shifted to where Travis was kneeling and took Travis's cock into his mouth. The feel of Cembran's hot lips and mouth around him was an unexpected surprise. Gradually, Cembran took more and more of him. Travis was over the moon with lust and want and he had to keep from bucking wildly into Cembran's throat.

What Cembran lacked in experience, he made up for in desire and effort. Soon Travis was moaning loudly and thrusting carefully into Cembran's movements. "Lamb, not going to last." Travis thought Cembran would pull back, but instead he took as much as he could and Travis came with a yell, shooting down Cembran's throat. He collapsed back onto the blanket, pulling his love with him. The weight on his body felt solid as he wrapped his arms around Cembran, kissing him deeply. "You were incredible."

Cembran rested his head on Travis's shoulder, his lips near his ear. "It's been a long time and I—" Cembran's voice broke and Travis felt tears on his skin.

Travis turned and raised his head to see tears welling in Cembran's eyes. "Lamb, why the tears?"

"It's been a long time since anyone made me feel...." He was going to say loved, but he suddenly became cautious, ending, "...special."

Travis settled back onto the blanket, hugging the other man tight to him. A lonely thought occurred to Travis, "Was Gathod the last person?" Cembran shook his head. "Do you want to tell me?" Cembran didn't move or say anything for the longest time. The breeze blew through the trees and birds flew and chirped overhead. "It's all right if you're not ready."

Cembran shook his head and turned towards Travis, "Can we cool off first?"

Travis kissed him gently, "Good idea." Getting up from the blanket, they both waded into the lake. After splashing and dunking each other, Travis swam for a while, gliding effortlessly through the water. After his swim, he worked with Cembran to help him learn to float and to use his arms to pull himself through the water. Travis could tell Cembran was preoccupied by his thoughts. He was curious as well, but he didn't want to push.

Once they'd cooled off, Cembran walked out of the lake, lying on the blanket in the warm sun. Travis followed, lying next to him. He took Cembran in his arms, kissing him deeply. Cembran returned the kiss before resting on the blanket.

"I think I told you I came to this country 200 years ago." Travis nodded. "I arrived in Maryland and immediately headed north. I settled in Pennsylvania near a small town called Carlisle. I worked as a farm hand for many years, often moving from farm to farm so no one would get suspicious about my age and keeping myself as isolated from other people as I could. In early 1863, I met a man named Joseph; he was the son of the farmer I tended sheep for at the time. I fell for him as soon as I saw him and I guess he really liked me too, because he kept seeking me out. He had just turned eighteen and he was going to join the Union army." Cembran looked down at the blanket. Travis lifted his head, kissing him gently. "One winter night, just after dark, he came to my small cabin. That night we made love." Travis couldn't help notice the words he used. Not *had sex*, but *made love*. "He told me he was leaving to join the army and asked me if I'd go with him."

"Did he know about you?" Travis's words were soft, without judgment.

"No, but I was so enamored with him, I agreed to go. We signed up together and ended up in the same unit. We looked after each other and helped each other." He swallowed hard. "I really did love him, but something held me back from giving him my Triuwe." The term wasn't familiar to Travis, but he didn't want to interrupt. "About three months after we joined up, we were sent to a small town called Gettysburg with a large portion of the Union army." Travis's eyes got wide, but he said nothing. "We arrived at the end of the second day of the battle and were dispatched to help hold the Union lines. The night before the battle, we knew we might not survive, so I snuck Joseph into the woods, away from the rest of the camp. We made love quietly under a large tree. Afterwards, I told Joseph about me and I showed him who I really was." Cembran's voice broke and tears rolled down his face. "He started screaming that I was the devil and that I was going to kill him and take his soul. One of the other men heard him and came to see what was going on. Luckily for me, they thought he was shell-shocked and didn't pay much attention to his ravings, and after while, he seemed to calm down."

"The next morning, we were told to line up and repel any Rebel advances. We were lined up shoulder to shoulder, three or four men deep. Luckily for us, we were near the rear of the formation. Late in the day, we saw a large group of Rebel soldiers charging across the field in front of us. I believe you call it Pickett's Charge today... Anyway, we got in formation and started firing. The smoke from the muskets and rifles was almost blinding. The noise, the shouting, the smell of blood, and the cries of men when they were hit are hard to describe. Our line held and we were able to repel the charge, but Joseph was hit late in the battle. I found him on the ground toward the rear. He was bleeding badly from his belly and I knew there was no hope for him. I held him close and whispered that I loved him." Tears were running unhindered down his cheeks. "He just looked up at me, but he couldn't speak." Cembran stopped talking and wiped the tears from his face. "I like to think that he understood that I loved him. A few minutes later he died in my arms." The tears came again and he made no effort to wipe them away. "Once the battle was over, I buried him where he fell, and a part of me died with him. I stayed in the army for another year and I eventually returned to the farm to tell his family what happened and where he was buried."

Travis wrapped his arms around Cembran, kissing him, their lips barely touching. "When you saw who I was yesterday, the first words that sprang to my mind were Joseph's words of rejection." Cembran was looking intently at Travis, waiting.

Travis's answer was to pull Cembran to his body, kissing him deeply, "Lamb, I will never reject you for who you are and you don't have to be afraid to show your true self to me." Cembran returned the kiss, relief flowing through his body. "Was Joseph the last person you loved?"

Cembran shook his head, "He was the last person I made love to, but he wasn't the last person I loved." Travis was confused and it showed on his face. "Travis, I loved your grandfather. He was a wise, kind, and caring person. I knew him for over forty years. After the war, I traveled to this area and again worked as a farm hand.

Eventually I met your ancestors and settled on this farm about 120 years ago. I first met your grandfather when he was a young man. He became suspicious when I didn't age and started asking questions. I told him the truth and he accepted me for who I was. He was a good friend and protector for many years."

Cembran looked around and realized it was starting to get late. "We need to get back, I need to check on the animals and I still have a few chores to finish." Travis was really enjoying having Cembran in his arms and he really didn't want to move, but he knew Cembran was right. Slowly, they got up from the blanket and started getting dressed. "After dinner, will you tell me your story?"

Travis smiled, "Sure, but it isn't as interesting as yours." When they were dressed, they gathered the picnic supplies and headed down the path through the woods and to the house. When they reached the door, Travis took Cembran's hand, saying, "Let's put this away and I'll help you with the chores."

It took them a few hours to complete the tasks. To say that Travis was tired was an understatement, but he also had an incredible sense of accomplishment. The goat milking was becoming easier and he enjoyed the time he spent with the animals and Cembran. Once the chores were complete, they headed back toward the house. The sun was casting warm light and long shadows across the farm. After cleaning up, they worked together to make dinner.

"Cembran, earlier you used the word Triuwe, but I don't know what that means."

"It's a satyr word that means 'special heart.' It's hard to explain, but by giving someone else my Triuwe, it means that I'm binding my life to theirs." He stopped, unsure how to explain further.

"Sort of like blood brothers?" Travis was trying to understand.

"No, more like a life bond or a life mating. It's hard to describe, but basically, my life becomes permanently linked to that person." He went back to preparing dinner.

Travis furrowed his brow, "Does that mean you'd die when they die?"

"No, but my lifetime becomes linked to theirs. To give someone my Triuwe means that I love them enough to not want to go on forever. It's hard to explain, but for a satyr it is the ultimate act of love." Cembran kissed Travis gently as he continued making dinner.

When the food was ready, they sat down at the small table to eat. "Travis, you promised me you'd tell me your story."

Travis finished chewing and answered, "I did, didn't I?"

Cembran smiled, "Yes, you did." The glint in his eye told Travis he was going to be held to that promise.

After dinner, they sat together and Travis told Cembran about his family, the men he'd dated, his job, and the fact that he'd never been in love. He told him how he always seemed to date the same type of men, but something was always missing. He didn't add that he thought he now knew what it was; it was too soon. "Basically, my life until now has been uninteresting and boring."

The sun had set by the time Travis had finished regaling Cembran with his life story. Cembran yawned. "We should go to bed. The farm work starts early and I'm still tired from last night."

Travis just nodded and went to get cleaned up. Once he'd finished, he went into the bedroom, got undressed, and climbed into Cembran's bed as though it was the most natural thing in the world. Once he'd cleaned up, Cembran joined him. It was a warm night and Travis was lying on top of the covers. Cembran just stared at the man in his bed, taking him all in, admiring. "You're beautiful, Lemmle." The words were barely whispered.

Travis looked intently at Cembran. "Lemmle?"

His lover nodded, "It means 'precious one.'" Slowly he climbed into bed next to Travis. "Good night, Lemmle."

"Good night, Lamb."

Cembran kissed Travis warmly before turned out the light.

Chapter Six

Travis was lost in what appeared to be woods. He kept wandering and getting nowhere, becoming more afraid and disoriented. Everything was dark and close, increasing his fear. "Where am I?" An unseen voice kept asking questions. Questions that rolled through his mind like they had an echo. Questions he couldn't answer or didn't want to answer. "Who are you?" The unseen voice kept bombarding him with the same demands again and again. "Where is he?" Images flooded through him, horrible images of death, blood, gore. Every time he thought he saw light, he'd find himself lost again, the questions repeating over and over. Sometimes the questions were gibberish, as though they were being asked in a language he didn't understand.

"Go away!" Travis found himself sitting straight up in bed, sweating and shaking. The questions finally stopped; his head was quiet.

A soft voice next to him whispered, "Where should I go?"

Travis looked over at the man next to him. "Lamb, I'm sorry - I was having a nightmare." The room was very dark, but Travis could feel a pair of gentle hands stroke his back and shoulders, soothing his tight muscles.

"Lie back down. I'm here, Lemmle." The words were whispered, almost sung like a lullaby. Slowly, Travis relaxed back onto the soft mattress. Cembran's arms wrapped around his chest, drawing him close. "Have you had nightmares before?"

Travis relaxed into the comfort of the embrace. "No, I've had dreams, but I don't remember having nightmares like that before." Fingers gently massaged his scalp.

"Go back to sleep." Cembran's voice was soft and soothing, with a touch of worry. Gently, Cembran massaged his back, easing all the tension from his body, soothing him back to sleep.

The sun was beating through the small windows when Travis woke in the morning. The bed was empty and Travis felt lonely for some unexplained reason. He got up and dressed in work clothes, figuring Cembran was already hard at work completing his morning chores. He had left some food in the kitchen for Travis, and he smiled at the thoughtfulness as he ate.

After eating, he left the house and headed down the path to the goat barn. As he approached, he heard Cembran working. He was surprised because he didn't hear singing; Cembran always sang to himself while he worked. Slowly, Travis stepped into the barn. He bent behind Cembran, softly nuzzling his cheek, whispering good morning before picking up a stool and helping with the milking. Cembran had been at it for a while and there weren't many goats left, but Travis figured the practice would do him good. Once the goats were milked, they finished the rest of the morning chores before heading back to the house for lunch.

Cembran had been quiet through the morning, and he remained quiet while he made lunch. It looked like he was going to remain quiet while they ate as well.

"Lamb, is there something bothering you? You seem so withdrawn," Travis asked between bites.

Cembran looked up from the table, "I've just been thinking. Would you tell me about your nightmare last night?"

Travis crinkled his nose, "I'll try. I really don't remember all of it." He paused. "I remember feeling like I was lost in the woods and an unseen voice kept asking questions over and over again."

"What sort of questions?" Cembran was starting to get concerned.

"'Where is he?' 'Who are you?' And sometimes the words were gibberish, like in a language I didn't understand?"

"Those gibberish words, could they have been, *Washe int hash*?" Cembran pronounced them carefully, almost whispered as if he was afraid of the answer.

"Yeah, I think that may be it, but I can't be sure... How did you know?"

All color drained from Cembran's face. He was a white as a ghost and he started swearing and cursing. Travis was surprised at the reaction. "What is it?"

Cembran looked him straight in the eye, "You must leave right now and never come back." Cembran pushed the chair away from the table and went into the bedroom. He returned a few minutes later with Travis's suitcase, dropping it by the door. Coming back to the table, he grabbed Travis's hand and forcibly pulled him to his feet. "Go now, forget you ever met me, hell, forget you ever saw me." Travis saw fear tinged with terror in his eyes, "Please... Just go." Cembran pushed him toward the door.

Travis was at the door almost before he could think. "Why? What are you afraid of?" He took Cembran's wrists in his hands. "Look at me." Slowly, Cembran lifted his eyes to Travis, and they were filled with tears. "What are you afraid of? It was only a nightmare."

Cembran was shaking his head. "No it wasn't. I think it was an attack." Travis almost laughed. "The reason I was able to guess the words from your dream is because those words mean, 'Who are you' in satyr. I think my father or someone is trying to get to me through you." He looked at Travis, "Remember, my father attacked me using my dreams."

Travis was stunned and shocked, but he was also angry that Cembran would send him away. Then he realized Cembran was probably sending him away for his own safety and his anger faded as quickly as it had risen. "Lamb, you're making a lot of assumptions on something I can barely remember, and I want to tell you something else." Travis took his hand and led him back to the table. "I started

having the most incredible, sensual, erotic dreams about ten years ago."
Cembran was giving him a confused look at this change of topic.

"I was lying in the sun by a lake when a shadow passed over the
sun. Opening my eyes, I could see the body of a stunningly beautiful
man. The man knelt gently next to me and I felt his lips touch mine,
very tentatively at first. I felt my body react and I returned the kiss,
wrapping my arms around the man's neck, the kiss building in heat and
intensity to white-hot levels. I couldn't clearly see who the man was,
but I could feel his lips and his touch on my body, making me soar with
delight and passion in a way I had never felt with anyone. The touch
roamed over my body, across my chest, and arms, down my back,
cupping my butt in strong hands. The man's hands felt hot, almost
burning, spreading heat through my entire body. I held him, allowing
myself to float on the waves of sensation flowing through my body. I
felt the man's hands gently pushing my shorts past my hips, down my
legs, and over my feet. I lay naked, exposed under his hot, penetrating
gaze. I was so hard, my entire body throbbing for release. Gently, his
hands take stroked me, again and again." Travis swallowed before
continuing, "At this point I usually woke up, disappointed and alone."

Cembran looked confused, "Why are you telling me this? I don't
understand." He actually appeared to be a little jealous.

"At first I didn't understand the dreams either, but once I met you I
realized that the man in the dreams is you." Cembran opened his
mouth to say something, but no words came. "Over the last few weeks,
I've realized that all the men I dated till I met you were a vain attempt
to find the person from my dreams." Travis's face became set and his
eyes drilled into Cembran's, "I looked for my dream man for years and
now that I've found him, I'm not letting him go easily!"

Slowly Travis got up from the table, extending his hands to
Cembran. Cembran took them. "Come with me." Cembran got up
from the table and let Travis lead him into the bedroom.

Travis stood next to the bed, face to face with Cembran. Gently, he
leaned in and captured his soft full lips. Travis's arms wrapped
themselves around his back, pulling him closer, hands resting near the
base of his spine. Lips pressed together firmly, mouths opened,
tongues explored, Cembran moaned and gave himself over to the

feelings. Nothing he had ever experienced compared to Cembran's willingness to give himself to Travis the way he did. It made Travis always want to make sure that each time was better then the last. Whispering softly, he asked, "Lamb, do you really want me to leave?" Cembran shook his head negative as Travis captured his mouth again in a scalding kiss. "Do you want me to stay?" Cembran managed to nod slightly as his lips were captured yet again. Travis nibbled Cembran's ear, "Do you want me to stop?"

"Noooo," Cembran moaned, the word trailing off in a deep-throated groan as Travis lips sucked and nuzzled his neck.

Slowly, Travis pulled his head back, looking Cembran in the eyes, his hands now still. He was not going to use sex to get what he wanted. He knew he was being pushy and aggressive, and he needed to know for sure that this was what Cembran wanted. If he truly wanted Travis to go, it would be easier now than later. "Cembran, I need to know. If you want me to leave, I will."

Cembran looked disappointed and confused, like what happened to the lips and hands? "I don't want you to go. I reacted out of fear, for you and myself."

Travis raised his eyebrows, "You're sure?" His voice was soft, but the feeling behind the words was strong.

Cembran was nodding his head affirmatively, "You may be right. After all, it was only one dream, but you have to promise me that you'll tell me if you have any more of them, okay?" Cembran wasn't fully convinced that the dreams weren't an attack, but he was willing to wait and see.

"Okay and you have to promise me that you won't tell me to leave unless you truly mean it." Cembran nodded his agreement as Travis guided him down onto the bed. Travis captured his lover's mouth with his own and he could feel him melt into the kisses, giving Travis control, letting him take what he wanted, knowing that what Travis wanted was to please him.

Travis knelt over Cembran, kissing his lips, nuzzling his neck, and using his hands to massage and stroke his scalp. His pace was almost languid, meant to tease, build Cembran's need and want to a frenzy of longing, and from the way Cembran returned his kisses, Travis could tell it was working. Cembran was wriggling in delight on the bed. Hell, he was practically vibrating with anticipation and Travis had yet to remove a single piece of clothing.

Travis stepped back, toed off his shoes and removed his socks. Cembran sat up and started removing his shirt, but Travis stilled him, gently settling his back on the bed. "Lay down with your arms spread out, Lamb." His voice was husky, filled with passion. Cembran rested himself back on the bed with a moan, his eyes never wavering from Travis. Slowly, button by button, Travis opened his shirt and removed the garment, letting it fall to the floor. Next he unfastened his jeans, pulling them open, almost in slow motion. Once they were unfastened, he wriggled his hips and the jeans fell to the floor. Cembran whimpered at the sight of Travis wearing nothing but a tight pair of briefs, with a very prominent bulge.

Travis knelt back onto the bed, holding his body just above Cembran's. "Don't move," he ordered, his voice deep and sort of growly, his desire plain. Travis's kisses started gentle, but quickly built in intensity, driven by heat, passion, and downright need. He nibbled on the base of Cembran's neck, getting a whispered "So good" in response. As he nibbled, Travis slipped his hands beneath Cembran's shirt, caressing deliberately up his stomach to Cembran's hard, fleshy nipples, worrying them gently between his fingers.

Cembran writhed on the bed as Travis continued sucking on his neck and worked each nipple between his fingers in turn, back and forth, again and again. Cembran's moans and whimpers continued almost non-stop, filling the small room with the sounds of pleasure. Travis smiled into Cembran's shoulder; those moans and whimpers were music to his ears.

He gripped Cembran's shirt, lifting it over his head and pulled it from his body. Travis gasped involuntarily at the sight of Cembran's hard, tanned chest. He knew he could look at this man forever. His lips were drawn to the large nipples. Travis licked and sucked gently on each one. The moans and whimpers started again as he alternated between licking and caressing the sensitive nubs. Travis had never had a lover as responsive and downright hedonistic as Cembran, and it thrilled him to think he could make Cembran writhe and moan with such pleasure.

The sensations were driving Cembran out of his mind, fists gripped the sheets. "Please. Need more." He was reduced to short phrases, gasped between breaths.

Fingers slipped beneath the waist of Cembran's pants, teasing the smooth skin. Cembran raised his hips and sucked in his breath, encouraging Travis to go further. He wanted, no he *needed* the feel of Travis's hands on his skin. With nimble fingers, Travis unfastened his pants, teasing the hot skin beneath. Cembran's breath turned into in short gasps as Travis opened his pants and slowly slipped them off his hips and legs. His cock was rigid and leaking steadily as Travis gently ran his fingertips down the length of the shaft.

Cembran hissed his breath through his teeth, "That feels so good." He was practically whining as Travis cupped his balls in his palm.

"So hot. So sexy." Travis whispered into Cembran's ear as he carefully rolled his balls in his fingers.

Cembran hissed as the hand released his balls and traveled the short distance to lightly finger his opening. "You like that, Lamb?" Travis teased the opening again, watching Cembran's face.

His head thrown back, his mouth wide, and Cembran could only nod as Travis continued to tease and stroke his opening with those magic fingers. Travis gently lifted Cembran's legs to his chest, exposing the tight, puckered entrance. "If you liked that, you'll love this," he whispered slyly before circling the opening with his fingertip one last time.

Travis bent down and gingerly swirled his tongue around the opening. Cembran gasped and cried out, "Oh god," as Travis licked again, getting another moan before he darted his tongue over the opening. After a little more teasing, the muscles relaxed and Travis was able to dart his tongue in and out, skewering Cembran with the muscle. Cembran's moans were increasing in intensity, as he rocked his hips into each thrust.

A loud cry burst from Cembran as he suddenly erupted onto his chest and stomach. Travis smiled as he lowered his legs and licked the salty cum off Cembran's chest on his way to his lips.

Cembran tasted both Travis and himself in the kiss as he wrapped his arms around Travis's back, pulling him to his body. Cembran's hands slipped into the waistband of Travis's briefs, shoving them over his tight butt and past his hips.

Travis hissed as his cock came in contact with Cembran's skin. He bucked against his lover's hip, erection gliding easily, sending jolts through his body. Cembran pulled their mouths together, teasing Travis's tongue with his own. He felt the pressure build in his balls as Cembran cupped his butt with his hands and devoured his mouth. With a whimper, Travis came on Cembran's scalding hot skin.

After catching his breath, Travis lifted himself up, settling next to Cembran on the bed. Cembran got a cloth and cleaned them both before relaxing. They held each other, enjoying the closeness.

"Trav," Cembran said, in a tone that seemed almost shy, "I've never felt anything like that before."

"Like what?"

"I've never had anyone use their mouth like that before."

Travis was surprised and pleased at the same time. "I'm glad I could be the first." He looked mischievously at Cembran, "Maybe we can find other fun things you haven't done before..." He arched his eyebrows at Cembran.

Cembran's answer was to pull Travis into a deep, contented kiss. Their lips savored each other, tongues explored lazily, hands caressing and petting. After a while, Travis raised himself on his elbows, looking at Cembran still lying beneath. "Lamb, I have to go back to work. If you want, I'll return next weekend, but if you don't—" His words were cut off by Cembran's lips on his.

"I'm looking forward to it, Lemmle."

Travis smiled brightly, kissing Cembran again before getting up from the bed and putting on his clothes. As Travis was getting ready to leave, he again became concerned for Cembran's safety. "Promise me you'll be careful; the men who tried to hurt you will probably be back."

Cembran nodded, "I will. I'll move one of the dogs near the house as soon as you leave."

Travis was mildly reassured. He was feeling really protective and possessive of Cembran, something he'd never felt for any of the other men he'd dated. When he was ready to leave, he kissed Cembran goodbye at the door before heading down the path to his car.

Chapter Seven

Travis had just left his office and was heading towards the farm and Cembran. He'd had to work late and was disappointed that he wouldn't arrive until close to sunset. Over the last month, he'd spent all of his weekends with Cembran at the farm. Their visits had quickly become the highlight of Travis's week.

In the past few weeks, his father's estate had largely been settled. The house had been sold and the contents that Travis hadn't wanted had been liquidated in an estate sale. It looked as though he was going to end up with a nice nest egg once the estate was finally resolved. He had thanked the lawyer for all his help, sincerely relieved that was behind him. The memories of his father had already started to mellow.

Travis continued to have occasional nightmares and from what he could remember in the mornings, they seemed to be along the same line - a constant barrage of questions as he appeared to be lost and confused. Thankfully, they'd gotten less frequent and he hadn't had one in the last week or so.

The sun was setting as Travis pulled into the small parking area he'd made near the farm. He grabbed his suitcase and a bag of supplies and headed down the path to Cembran's small house. As Travis approached, he noticed that the door was open and he heard voices coming from inside. As he got closer he realized the voices were speaking a language he didn't understand. They sounded happy and he heard laughter, Cembran's laughter, coming from inside. Travis released the breath he hadn't realized he was holding and stepped into the doorway.

"Cembran?" Travis called out tentatively, before stepping into the house.

"Travis." Cembran turned toward the door, his smile bright. Travis noticed that there was another man in the house, seated in the living room. He stood up as Travis entered. After placing the bag he was carrying in the kitchen, Travis went into the living room, standing next to Cembran. "Travis, this is Gathod." Travis extended his hand, hoping he was able to keep the surprise off his face. "Gathod, this is Travis." The two men shook hands and exchanged greetings.

Gathod and Cembran couldn't have been more different. Where Cembran was rather slight, lean, and almost beautifully handsome, Gathod, was short, stocky, built for strength, with very rugged chiseled features.

"Gathod arrived a few hours ago." Travis could tell that Cembran was happy to see Gathod, but he appeared apprehensive as well. "We were just catching up on things when you arrived." Cembran pulled up another chair and Travis sat down; he was very curious to know what Gathod wanted and he figured Cembran was as well.

"I was just telling Cembran when you arrived, that I have been looking for him for a very long time."

"Have you been in the country long?" Gathod had a pronounced accent when he spoke and Travis figured he must have just come recently.

"I arrived in the U.S. about two weeks ago." Gathod's words were measured and tentative. Travis figured he didn't speak English much and he had to think about each phrase. "I've spent most of that time looking for him," Gathod said, indicating Cembran.

"Travis, do you need something to eat?" Cembran knew Travis was usually hungry and Travis suspected that Cembran needed something to do.

"Yes, I left right from the office and only stopped for a quick bite on the road."

Cembran got up and made a quick snack that he placed on the table. The three of them spent the next hour or so snacking and talking about general topics. Travis could feel the tension in the room, particularly between himself and Gathod. Travis wasn't jealous of Gathod; his relationship with Cembran was in the distant past. He just couldn't figure out why Gathod was here and what he wanted.

Gathod filled in Cembran about some of his family; he didn't mention Cembran's father, which Travis thought peculiar. He even told Cembran that he had a cousin, Brock, who was a lawyer in Grand Rapids.

Travis had been quietly listening to the conversation, letting it swirl around him, but he perked up when he heard that. "What's his name?"

Gathod looked puzzled, "Brock Kraus." Travis was stunned and a little surprised. Cembran looked at Travis with a puzzled look on his face. Travis mouthed, "I'll tell you later." Cembran nodded and returned his attention to the conversation.

Travis was getting tired and he could tell Cembran was as well. Travis yawned involuntarily and tried to stifle it, but didn't have much luck. He kept expecting Gathod to get ready to leave.

Travis was surprised when eventually Cembran got up and brought the blankets and bedding to make up a bed in the living room. They moved the furniture back and Travis helped Cembran get everything set up. He knew it was getting late and he knew Cembran would be up early in the morning with farm chores. Over the last few weeks, Travis had gotten used to getting up with Cembran, and they did the chores together. With the two of them working together, they were able to get things done quickly and they usually had time for some fun in the afternoon.

When the bed was made up, Cembran said goodnight and headed into the bedroom. Travis went into the kitchen to put away the supplies he'd brought with him before going to bed. As he was standing in the kitchen, Gathod said good-night and went into Cembran's bedroom, shutting the door. Travis was floored, his mouth hung open, a knot forming in his stomach, and he couldn't move.

Almost immediately, the door to the bedroom burst open. "Gathod, what do you think you're doing?"

"I thought…." Gathod looked crestfallen.

Both Gathod and Cembran came back in the living room. "Gathod, that bed is for you." Cembran pointed at the bed on the living room floor. "I don't love you like that anymore. It's been too long, way too long."

Travis almost snickered, but managed to stifle it, thinking to himself, "Yeah, 280 years too long."

"I figured. I've looked for you for so long." Gathod's voice was filled with disappointment and confusion. As Travis watched his expression, he could see that Gathod truly didn't understand.

"Gathod, you need to know that I share my bed with only one person and that person is Travis. I love him." That declaration stopped Travis's breath. His head snapped up and he looked Cembran in the face, his mouth open. "Good night, Gathod, we'll see you in the morning. We'll talk more then." Travis left the supplies on the small counter and followed Cembran into the bedroom.

As soon as the bedroom door closed, Travis had his arms around Cembran, their lips pressing together in a passionate kiss. "You really love me?" he whispered between kisses. It was as though he didn't trust his ears. No one other than his mother had ever told him that they loved him.

"Yes, Lemmle, I do." Cembran's bright eyes looked directly into Travis's and he felt a warmth and comfort that he'd never felt before in his life. "I love you, Travis."

Travis eyes were dancing and his heart was pounding in his chest. "Good, because I love you, Lamb." The lump in his throat was so large, his words were barely a whisper. Neither of them moved; their eyes were locked on each other, bodies pulled together. Heads tilted and finally their lips touched again, sending fire and passion through both of them. Travis's hand cupped Cembran's head, pushing their lips together. Tongues explored, lips pulled, Travis's fingers combed through Cembran's soft curls. Travis could feel Cembran give himself over to the kiss and their passion. The way Cembran, his little hedonist, gave himself over to Travis, trusting him, always increased Travis's passion. Without breaking their hold on each other, he led Cembran to the bed.

"Lamb, what do you want?" His voice was deep, uncontrollable passion just below the surface ready to burst through at any time.

"I want you, all of you." Cembran's voice was very soft, very urgent, full of want, communicating in a few words the love and trust he felt for Travis.

"My suitcase is still in the other room. I need to get something." Travis reluctantly broke their kiss, opened the bedroom door and quietly stepped into the living room.

Gathod was still awake and Travis smiled at him before quickly retrieving his suitcase and stepping back into the bedroom. As he closed the door, he looked toward the bed. Cembran had removed all his clothes, pulled down the covers, and was lying on his back with his hands beneath his pillow. His entire body was vibrating with excitement; his eyes were wide and expectant. Travis opened his case and retrieved the small bottle of lubricant, placing it next to the bed.

Standing at the foot of the bed, Travis pulled off his shirt and slowly started to remove his pants, making sure he gave Cembran an enjoyable show. With the removal of each article of clothing, Cembran's excitement increased visibly. His hips were moving gently against the bed; his cock was rock hard, straining towards his navel, his stomach glistening with the wetness already flowing from his cock. "Lemmle, please," he begged, "Hurry."

Travis removed the last of his clothes before lying next to Cembran and pulling his lover onto his body. Cembran's lips locked on to his, Cembran's tongue sliding into his mouth. His hands stroked Cembran's back, caressing the soft skin. His lover's lips pulled on Travis's as he cupped Cembran's butt, kneading the firm globes.

Cembran whimpered into Travis's mouth as fingers slowly slid along his cleft, teasing his opening as they moved. "Trav, I need you." The words, moaned into Travis's mouth, were barely coherent.

Stroking his soft curls, Travis whispered, "Are you sure?" A quick nod was the response and they found each other's lips again. As they kissed, Travis used his weight to shift them until his weight pressed Cembran into the soft bedding.

Travis reached for the lube and liberally applied it to his fingers. Cembran's eyes never left him. "How do you want me, Trav?"

"Roll over on your stomach, Lamb."

"But I really want to see you."

Travis nodded, "Okay." He grabbed a pillow from the bed and placed it beneath Cembran's hips before lifting his knees to his chest. "Are you comfortable?"

Cembran nodded as Travis gently probed his opening with a finger. The entrance was tight, really tight. Slowly and gingerly, he worked a finger inside Cembran. "Relax, Lamb." Travis felt the muscles soften as he worked his finger in and out. Cembran was moaning steadily as Travis added a second finger, and he threw his head back as Travis found his pleasure spot again and again. Travis removed his hands, placed Cembran's calves on his shoulder, and pressed the head of his lubed cock at Cembran's entrance.

Cembran gasped as Travis breached him for the first time. Slowly he pressed forward, giving Cembran time to adjust to the new sensations. Travis continued to be amazed at his lover's responsiveness as he pressed himself inside, wanting more, needing everything. When Travis had buried himself to the root, he stopped moving, waiting for Cembran to indicate he was ready.

He didn't have to wait long. Cembran rocked his hips as he pulled Travis into a deep penetrating kiss. "You feel so good inside me."

Travis started to thrust, using short, slow strokes, extending the length with each movement. Soon he was pressing into Cembran with long, fluid strokes, making sure he could feel every inch of every stroke. Cembran moaned with each thrust and whimpered slightly with each withdrawal.

"Lamb, you feel amazing! So hot!" Travis thrust deeply into Cembran as he mouthed breathlessly.

"Feel so full, so close to you. Like you're part of me," Cembran gasped, "Don't stop, don't ever stop."

"Don't intend to. Want to love you forever." The sentiments just poured unhindered from Travis. It was like they filled him so completely, he couldn't hold them inside any more. "My Lamb, my love." Each declaration was punctuated with a deep penetrating thrust as Cembran met each one with his hips.

Cembran reached to stroke his cock, but Travis gently batted his hand away. "Let me." He wrapped his lubed fingers around Cembran's cock, stroking in rhythm with his thrusts. Cembran was moaning steadily as Travis whispered, "Come for me, Lamb." Cembran's cock throbbed and he threw his head back as he came on Travis's hand and onto his stomach and chest.

Cembran's climax sent Travis soaring and he filled Cembran with his release. Bringing his lips to Cembran's he kissed him with all of the feelings swelling inside him. Slowly he withdrew, lying on the bed next to Cembran, caressing his face and nuzzling his neck.

A while later, Travis got out of bed and got a cloth. After cleaning up Cembran, he climbed back into bed, pulling Cembran close. "You're incredible Lamb." Their kiss was slow and languid, full of love, their embrace comforting and warm. Travis put out the light, plunging the room into near total darkness.

"Travis, can I ask you a question?" Cembran sounded tentative.

"You can ask me anything, Lamb. What is it?"

"Earlier, you asked about my cousin and you told me you'd tell me later."

Travis smiled to himself. "A few months ago, I dated your cousin Brock."

"Oh." Cembran was quiet.

Travis wrapped Cembran in his arms. "Lamb, no one can hold a candle to you." Travis could almost feel Cembran smile. "If you like, I'll take you to meet him."

"You would?"

"Of course, he's part of your family and I think you'll like him. He's a really good person, especially for a lawyer."

"I think I'd like that." Cembran kissed Travis gently and slipped out of bed, "I have something to show you." He moved to the small clothing chest, opening its lid. Cembran looked at Travis, "Most of the things in here, I brought with me when I left my village." Cembran reached inside the chest and brought out what looked like a very old blanket. He unrolled the blanket and inside was a carved wooden box. The box was decorated with geometric designs that were very colorfully painted. "The night before I left the village, Gathod gave me this box as a gift." Cembran opened the box. Inside was a delicate carving of two people standing side by side; the wood had darkened with age. Cembran removed the carving from the box and handed it to Travis. There was enough detail for Travis to see that it was a carving of Cembran and Gathod.

Both men had small horns on their foreheads and both had small tails on their lower backs. Travis gently handed the carving back to Cembran. "For the longest time, the only love in my life was memories." Cembran looked at Travis as he added, "But now…."

Travis didn't know what to say to this beautiful man standing in front of him, naked and exposed, holding a memory in his hand, looking so vulnerable. This man had the chance to recapture that memory and instead, he'd chosen Travis. The realization of what Cembran's declaration of love meant filled Travis with warmth. "Lamb, sweet Lamb." Travis moved closer, pressing his chest to Cembran's back as he slipped his arms around his waist. "I love you too." Travis let his hands wander over Cembran's chest and stomach as he whispered words of love in his ears.

Cembran gently wrapped the carving and put it back in its box. He then rewrapped the box before carefully placing it back in the chest.

"Come to bed, Lamb." Travis took Cembran's hand and led him back to bed. Cembran snuggled right next to Travis, burrowing in close. Travis had never liked to sleep close to anyone before, but with Cembran, it just felt right, it felt damn near perfect. "Goodnight, Lemmle."

Travis smiled at the use of Cembran's pet name for him. "Goodnight Lamb." Travis lay awake in bed unable to turn off his mind or to stop smiling. Cembran quickly fell asleep curled right up next to him.

Travis eventually fell asleep only to be awakened a few hours later by the sound of the dog near the house barking furiously. He woke Cembran as he got out of bed.

Dressing quickly, they were outside in a matter of seconds, Travis nearly tripping over Gathod, who was still sleeping on the floor. Cembran immediately let the dog loose and it raced down the path to the sheep barn. Cembran followed the dog down the path with Travis close behind, calling to him to be careful.

They slowed their pace and listened as they approached the barn. They couldn't hear anything from inside. Travis whispered, "Stand back," then threw open the barn door and yelled. Nothing happened. Cembran turned on the lights. Nothing seemed out of place, but the dog started nosing around one of the feeders Cembran used for the sheep. "Is anything out of place or different from what you'd expect?"

Cembran was shaking his head negative, when he abruptly stopped. "Why is that door ajar?"

Travis walked over to the door and looked out. The sheep from the pasture were lined up outside. Travis closed and re-latched the door firmly. "Cembran, look at the dog."

"Sham, get down, bad dog." The dog was on her hind legs sniffing around the feed.

"I think she's trying to tell you something. There's feed in there."

Cembran's eyes got wide. "Oh my god. The feeders were almost empty when I let the sheep out for the night." Cembran started looking closely at the food. "This doesn't seem right. Check the others." Travis and Cembran raced around to the other feeders. They all looked fine. "Okay, cover this one and don't touch anything."

They covered the feeder so none of the animals could get to it and checked the rest of the barn. Then they walked to the goat barn to make sure everything was okay and it didn't look as though anything had been disturbed.

"Lamb, let's go back to the house. I need to make a phone call." Travis could tell Cembran was upset and nervous.

"Who are you going to call at this time of night?"

"I'm going to call a friend with the state police. I think they better investigate what's going on."

Cembran and Travis went along the path to the house with Sham following behind them. When they got to the house, she curled up near the door. Both Cembran and Travis petted and praised her as they went back inside.

Gathod was awake when they entered. "What's going on? Are you all right?" He seemed genuinely concerned and Cembran filled him in while Travis made a call on his cell phone.

"Doug, it's Travis, I'm sorry to bother you so late, but we need your help."

"What's going on Trav?" He didn't sound angry which was good.

Travis explained where he was, and explained, "We think someone tried to poison some of the animals. We covered the feed and didn't touch it."

"What about the local police?"

"The person we suspect may be behind this happens to be the Sheriff's brother."

"Say no more. You've got to be talking about the Palumbos. Do you need me now, or can I come first thing in the morning?"

"The morning should be fine. We'll have breakfast for you."

"Deal."

Travis gave Doug directions to the farm and hung up the phone. Both Gathod and Cembran were standing in the living area watching Travis expectantly.

"We should all go back to bed. Doug is with the State Police and he'll be here in the morning. We should all get some rest." Travis walked toward the bedroom, taking Cembran's hand in his as he passed. "Come on, we need to try to sleep." Travis led him to the bedroom, shutting the door quietly and they undressed and got into bed.

"I know you're upset Lamb, but please try to sleep." Travis wrapped Cembran in his arms, kissing him sweetly. It was then that he realized Cembran's cheeks were wet with tears. Travis tightened his embrace, holding Cembran tight, trying to comfort him. Eventually Cembran did fall asleep, but Travis stayed awake all night, holding him close and listening. The sun had started to rise when he finally drifted off.

Chapter Eight

Travis woke in the morning to Cembran sneaking out of bed. He shifted and looked questioningly at Cembran, who answered "Go back to sleep. I'll start chores. I know you were up most of the night."

Travis yawned, pulling him back into the bed. "Lamb, you didn't get much sleep either." Travis pulled Cembran back to the bed, spooning their bodies, kissing his shoulders and neck.

Cembran protested mildly. "I need to start chores. The animals won't wait because I'm tired," but he made no effort to get out of Travis's embrace.

"I know and I'll help you; I just want a few minutes alone with you, Lamb."

Shifting in the bed to face Travis, Cembran pressed their bodies together. Travis rolled his lover on top of him, weight pressing him into the mattress. They kissed warmly and Travis luxuriated in the feel and taste of his gorgeous, generous lover. Their quiet morning was suddenly interrupted by Gathod, tromping around the other room like a herd of cows.

Travis sighed, "I guess we better get up. I'll help you with chores in the goat barn until Doug gets here. We shouldn't touch anything in the sheep barn until Doug can look around. Will the sheep be all right for a few hours?"

Cembran nodded and kissed him again before reluctantly getting out of bed. Travis watched the tanned, lithe body move around the room. The sight got him hard, but he knew he had to ignore it, for now.

As he got out of bed, he couldn't help wonder what he'd ever done to deserve having this kind, beautiful soul in his life. Cembran was washing up and Travis slipped his arms around his waist, grinding his hardness into his butt. "I have something for you and only you..."

"Mmmm." Cembran tilted his head back to get a kiss as Travis ran his hands up and down his chest and stomach. After another kiss, Travis pulled back and started getting dressed.

Gathod was already waiting for them in the other room. Cembran wished Gathod a good morning as he left the house to get started on the morning chores.

Travis came into the room, saying, "Gathod, would you mind waiting here? Someone from the police will be stopping by this morning."

"Sure, I'll stay here. Do you want me to send him to the barn or have him wait for you?"

"Ask him to wait. We shouldn't be long." Gathod smiled and nodded. Travis thanked him and headed out to help with the chores.

Working together, they finished in the goat barn in record time. Cembran was visibly tense from the night before and a few times between milking the goats, Travis slipped behind Cembran, nuzzling his neck or gently massaging his shoulders. Once the chores were finished, they were heading back to the house when Travis saw Doug approaching.

Travis waved as they caught up with him. "Doug, thank you for coming." The two men shook hands. "Doug, this is Cembran." Travis slipped his arm around Cembran's waist. "Cembran, this is Officer Doug Green, with the State Police."

Cembran extended his hand, "Thank you for coming." They shook hands and Cembran ushered them into the house. The three of them stepped inside and Travis introduced Gathod.

After a few pleasantries, Doug took out a notebook. "Please tell me what happened."

Travis looked at Cembran and then spoke, "The dogs around the house woke us at about two in the morning. After getting dressed,

Cembran let the dog loose and she raced to the sheep barn. There was no one inside, but the dog kept pacing and sniffing at one of the feed bins."

Cembran interrupted, "When I looked at the feed, it didn't look or smell right and I knew there wasn't that much feed in the bin when I let the sheep out at night. I thought it had been tampered with."

"What leads you to that conclusion?"

"I can just tell. It comes with experience. You learn to recognize bad feed, it can cost you everything."

Travis picked up the story. "We covered the bin and kept the sheep outside."

"Has there been anything else unusual?"

Travis looked at Cembran and he could tell he was concerned, but Travis figured Doug needed to know everything in order to help them. "Cembran was attacked on the property about a month ago. I scared them off."

"Did you report this?"

Cembran shook his head as Travis spoke for him, "We didn't know who to call because earlier in the day, Joe Palumbo had been here making threats. We figured he was behind the attack, but his brother's the Sheriff."

Doug made a few more notes, "Trav, can you show me the barn?" Travis figured Doug wanted to talk to him alone.

"We won't be long, Cembran."

"I'll start breakfast. Gathod, will you give me a hand?" Travis kissed him gently, then led Doug out to the sheep barn. They passed fields of animals happily munching the grass.

"Travis, what brings you here?" Doug seemed curious.

"I inherited the land and Cembran is my tenant."

Doug stopped walking, "There's a lot more than that going on, isn't there?"

Travis smiled. "Oh yes, I'm in love with him."

Doug's smile was big and genuine. "I'm happy for you."

Travis relaxed a little and actually chuckled, "I thought you might be angry."

"No, when we dated, we had a good time, but you always seemed to be looking for something you yourself couldn't put your finger on. I'm happy you found it."

"So am I." Travis opened the door to the barn and led Doug to the covered bin. After lifting the cover, Travis could see for himself that the feed didn't look right. Doug took out a plastic bag and took a sample.

"Was there anything else unusual?"

Travis nodded, "We think whoever did this, opened this door," Travis indicated the door they'd found unlatched. "The sheep would have eaten the bad feed before we got up."

"Tell me about this trouble with Palumbo."

"He wants to buy the land and turn it into a recreational area. I could make a lot of money if I sold, but...." He had too many memories, and he couldn't ever do that to Cembran. "This land is unspoiled and should stay that way."

Doug smiled at him knowingly. "I know there's more to it than that, but I'm glad you're not selling. This is a beautiful piece of property and I'd hate to see it spoiled. Look, I'll have a talk with the local Sheriff. I can probably put enough heat on him that he'll tell his brother to lay off."

Travis covered the bin back up and they headed out of the barn and back to the house.

"Travis, can I ask you a question?"

"Sure."

"Who is this Gathod? He's hot!" Doug tried to look lecherous, but Travis knew better.

Laughing, he answered, "He's an old friend of Cembran's. I don't know how long he's staying though."

"Oh." Doug seemed disappointed but Travis didn't know Gathod very well and he wasn't playing matchmaker… yet.

When they entered the house, Cembran and Gathod were putting breakfast on the table. Travis slipped his arms around Cembran and nuzzled his neck. "Thank you, Lamb," he whispered.

The four of them sat at the small table and ate Cembran's hearty farm breakfast. "Doug took some samples of the feed," Travis said, filling them in on what was happening.

"Yeah, I'll get it analyzed. If it is contaminated, we may be able to establish a link." He took a bite of the fluffy pancakes. "I really want to nail Palumbo. From your description, it sounds like his method of operation."

Travis noticed that Doug kept looking at Gathod. Furtive glances that lasted just a few seconds, but enough for Travis to notice. He didn't think Cembran noticed; he seemed lost in his own thoughts.

After breakfast, Doug said goodbye and told them he'd call as soon as he received the test results. Travis turned to Gathod and asked him to help clean up. After giving Travis a kiss, Cembran headed out to finish his chores, leaving Gathod and Travis alone.

Gathod looked uncomfortable as he helped Travis with the dishes. "You know about Cembran and me?" Gathod's voice was tentative, nervousness clear in his tone.

Travis put down the dish he was washing and looked at Gathod. "Yes. Cembran told me you were his first."

"I know. I think I broke his heart." The regret was plain on his face.

"Gathod, Cembran hasn't shared all of the details with me, but I know from experience that not every relationship works out. I don't think you meant to hurt him, and if you had left with him, you might have resented him eventually. Besides, it was a long time ago and I bet Cembran's forgiven you. Talk to him about it."

Gathod was quiet and Travis went back to washing the dishes and Gathod continued drying. "Travis, I'm sorry about last night. I was a fool." Travis kept washing the dishes without looking up. "I mean, I was looking for him for a long time and when I found him, I thought—"

"It's okay." He was going to say he understood, but he really didn't.

"No, it's not." The two of them were quiet again; the only sounds were the clinking of the dishes and the birds singing in the trees outside the house.

Travis got the feeling there was more Gathod wanted to say, but he offered no more and Travis didn't know him well enough to press. Once the dishes were done, he said, "I'm going to help Cembran finish the chores. It shouldn't take long."

"Okay. Can I help?" His offer seemed sincere.

Travis smiled, "Sure."

A few minutes later they were heading down the path to the sheep barn. Travis noticed that it was quiet, too quiet. Entering the barn, the scene that greeted them nearly broke his heart.

Cembran was sitting on the floor of the barn cradling a lamb on his lap. Tears were flowing down his cheeks. Travis knelt next to Cembran, his hands on his shoulders. "What happened?"

Cembran lifted his head, the tears flowing freely. "I was cleaning out the bad feed." He sniffled loudly. "When some fell on the floor, I didn't notice, and he ate it before I could—" The words stopped as Cembran cradled the lamb in his arms, his face nuzzling its neck. Travis stroked the soft wool. The lamb was still alive, but its body was limp in Cembran's arms.

Tears were streaming down Travis's cheeks as well when he realized the lamb was the same one he'd rescued during the storm a month or so earlier. His hands slipped around Cembran, head resting against his lover's shoulder as they watched the lamb breathe, fearing each breath would be its last. "Is there anything we can do?"

Cembran just shook his head, unable to form words.

Travis couldn't believe the feelings racing through him. He'd never thought he had a particular affinity for animals. He'd not had pets growing up and rarely came in contact with animals. But over the past month or so, he'd grown to love Cembran and those feelings encompassed the animals he cared for.

Travis had completely forgotten Gathod until he bent down in front of them. His hands were deeply stroking the lamb's wool. Gathod closed his eyes and seemed to be concentrating. There was no sound except Cembran's choked up breathing and an occasional sniffle. Travis held Cembran close, not knowing how he'd react when the lamb died.

"Baahh..." The bleating of the lamb knocked Travis back to the present. Looking at Cembran's lap, the lamb had lifted its head and licked Cembran's shoulder and Travis's hand. It struggled a little, so Cembran set him on the floor and the lamb walked, almost ran, out the barn door into the pasture to find its mother.

Travis was bewildered, "Cembran, what did you do?"

"It wasn't me." Cembran was looking at Gathod. Travis followed his gaze, his eyes questioning.

Gathod was looking at the floor, "I saw its pain and took it away."

"But how?"

"I found out shortly after you left that I have the ability to heal. Well, animals at least."

Travis was overwhelmed. "Thank you." Travis stood and clasped Gathod on the shoulder, "Thank you," he said again from his heart.

Cembran got up from the floor, "Yes, thank you. I heard as a child that there were satyrs with the ability to heal, but it's very rare." Cembran hugged Gathod. "Thank you."

Gathod smiled, but he looked pale, "I need to lie down, it takes a lot out of me." Travis and Cembran helped Gathod to his feet and half-walked, half-carried him to the house, laying him on his bed. "Do you need anything?" they said together.

Gathod shook his head, "Just rest."

"Cembran and I will finish the chores." Travis knelt next to Gathod, "You rest, and thank you again."

Travis and Cembran left the house, closing the door quietly before heading down the path to the sheep barn. When they got to the barn, Cembran grabbed Travis and pulled him into a deep kiss. Travis wrapped his arms around Cembran, combing his fingers through tight curls.

"What was that for, Lamb?" Travis smiled looking into Cembran's eyes.

"I just needed—"

Travis silenced him with another kiss whispering, "I needed it too."

Cembran looked up towards the hay loft, "Do you want to...?" Cembran's eyes indicated the loft above them.

"What I want, I want in a nice soft bed." He punctuated each word with a kiss. Travis whispered conspiratorially, "Let's get the chores done. We need to check on Gathod, and then...." The rest was left unsaid as he let his kiss speak for him.

They finished their chores in record time and as they were heading back to the house, Travis stopped Cembran. "I know he saved the lamb, but there is still something he's not telling us."

Cembran touched Travis on the shoulder. "I know, but he'll tell us when he's ready." He thought a minute, "Later, if I have to, I'll see if I can pave the way for him, but for now, we won't worry about it." Cembran smiled and took Travis's hand and they walked the rest of the way to the house.

Gathod was asleep when they returned. Travis whispered, "Let's go down to the lake." He grabbed a bag he'd left by the door the night before and they headed down the path to the lake. The sun sparkled on the water as Travis spread out two large, thick beach towels. Cembran felt the soft towels and smiled. "I brought this one especially for you."

Travis sat down on his towel, gently pulling Cembran onto his lap. "I love you, Lamb," whispered very softly as he took Cembran's mouth, his tongue pressing for entrance. Cembran opened for him, letting him in, giving himself to Travis. The kisses spread heat through both their bodies as Travis slipped his hand beneath Cembran's shirt, working a nipple between his fingers. Cembran moaned into his mouth as he worked each nipple in turn, back and forth. Eventually his lover broke the kiss and, standing in front of Travis, pulled off his shirt, toed off his shoes and slipped his pants around his ankles.

"You're spectacular."

Cembran tilted his head, "And you're wearing too many clothes."

Travis smiled as he quickly shucked his clothes, standing naked in front of Cembran.

"You're beautiful, Love."

Travis's smile shone like the sun, "That's what you always said in my dreams." Travis pulled Cembran to him, standing together in the sun, lips to lips, chest to chest, cock-to-cock, hands stroking and cupping each other's butts.

"Lamb, I want...." Cembran kissed him. "I want to see you."

Cembran looked at Travis with a puzzled look. Then he backed away, fear showing in his eyes as he shook his head.

Travis stepped forward closing the gap between them that Cembran had created. "I love you for who you are. You don't need to hide yourself from me." His arms were around Cembran, his lips kissing him. He wasn't going to push further.

Gently, he maneuvered Cembran onto his back on his towel. Travis laid his body onto Cembran's, whose legs parted automatically. Lips kissed, tongues explored, cocks rubbed against hot skin, chests heaved. Travis loved Cembran's soft curls and he took every opportunity to comb his fingers through those silky ringlets. As he combed through his hair, his fingers encountered two small nubs near the hairline. Without looking up, Travis knew what they were and what it meant. Travis attached Cembran's lips communicating his desire and love as he circled his fingers around the small horns. They were about an inch high now and as he circled the base with his finger, Cembran squirmed and moaned.

"You like that?"

Cembran nodded.

Shifting their weight, Travis rolled them so Cembran was on top. Travis liked being in control, but he also liked the feel of his lover's weight on his body. His hands framed Cembran's face as he pulled him down for a kiss.

"What do you want, Lamb?" The whispered words were meant to entice.

Cembran's reply was breathy, "I want you to show me that you still love me, like this."

The tentativeness in Cembran's voice tugged at his heart; of course Travis still loved him. He grabbed the bottle of lube from the bag and slicked his fingers. Pressing two of them to Cembran's entrance, he asked "Like this?" Cembran moaned as the fingers slipped inside. It was so hot, so tight.

"Yes!" Cembran leaned against the fingers, pressing them deeper. "Need more."

Travis slicked one of Cembran's own fingers and brought it to his entrance, "See how good you feel, Lamb."

Cembran pressed one of his own fingers alongside Travis's, moaning as it slipped inside. He withdrew his finger and slicked Travis's cock with the lubricant. Travis withdrew his hand and Cembran positioned himself onto Travis's cock and thrust down on it in one rapid movement that stole Travis's breath away. Cembran drew himself up and impaled himself again and again, moaning with each movement.

Cembran couldn't get enough and Travis let him take what he wanted, giving him everything he had. He wrapped his hand around Cembran's cock, pulling in time with their movement. With almost no warning, Cembran shouted, "Travis, Love!" as he shot hot streams onto Travis's stomach and chest. Cembran hadn't finished coming as Travis peaked and came deep inside Cembran's body. "Love you, Lamb," he whispered.

Cembran collapsed onto Travis's body, arms around his neck, lips pressing together.

Travis's hands ran down Cembran's back, encountering the small tail near the base of his spine. The silky hairs were about a foot long, curling away and then back toward Cembran's body. Travis didn't know what to think about the tail, it didn't bother him, but it didn't excite him either. It was just a part of the person he loved. The small horns, on the other hand, gave Cembran an air of mischief that Travis really liked.

Cembran curled up next to Travis on the towel, kissing and petting.

"I love you." The words were heartfelt and meant to reassure.

"I love you too." Cembran's eyes were full of tears and Travis gently wiped them away.

"Lamb, let's cool off before we head back to the house."

Cembran smiled, "Yes, let's. I've been practicing."

Travis raised his eyebrows as Cembran got up from the towel. The horns and tail were again invisible as Cembran walked naked into the water. "What are you waiting for he asked?"

Travis smiled as he ran into the lake, hugging Cembran tight as they both fell into the water with a splash. Cembran had indeed been practicing, and they swam together, enjoying the feel of the cool water on their hot, satiated bodies.

Chapter Nine

Travis was lost in the woods, which were very dark and foreboding; he couldn't find his way out. Confusion reigned supreme and the questions came over and over again, "Where is he? Who are you?" He didn't answer, ignoring the questions, just searching for a way out. Then a light appeared in the distance. Travis headed toward the light, but instead of the way out, he found himself in Cembran's small house. It was empty and quiet. He moved from the main room to the bedroom. There was a shape in the bed with a head of curls on the pillow.

Sitting on the edge of the bed, he said "Lamb, it's me." There was no movement. Pulling back the covers, the bed was a sea of blood, Cembran's lifeless body pale and stiff.

"No!" he screamed at the top of his lungs.

The room disappeared, replaced by the blackness of Cembran's bedroom as he awoke. Arms cradled his shaking, sweaty body. Hands caressed his cheeks and face. "Lemmle, what happened?" Cembran's tone was soft and full of concern.

Travis looked around trying to get his bearings; the room looked the same and Cembran was next to him in bed. It was just a nightmare. Cembran was alive and cradling him against that body he knew. Slowly, his breathing returned to normal.

The bedroom door opened and Gathod raced into the room, wearing only a pair of boxers on his stocky frame. "What happened? I heard a scream." His voice had a definite sense of urgency and concern.

"I just had a nightmare." Travis rested his head against Cembran. The dream had been so real.

Gathod looked at Cembran, concern plain on his face. Gathod suddenly became aware of his dress, or the lack there of, and quickly stepped out of the room, only to return a minute later in a pair of jeans and a shirt.

"Travis, I need you to describe the nightmare. Have you had them before?"

Travis looked at Cembran, fear and concern plain on his face.

"Lemmle, please tell him your dream," Cembran said, voice shaky and wavering.

"Yes, I have had them before, off and on for the last month or so. But not like this." Travis went on to describe the dream to them. When he was done, both Cembran and Gathod looked concerned.

"Travis, go back to sleep." Gathod looked conflicted, but then he seemed to make up his mind. "We'll talk in the morning. There are things I need to tell you both. I was hoping it wouldn't come to this but." He paused. "We'll talk in the morning. Good night." Gathod closed the door, leaving Travis and Cembran alone.

Cembran turned off the light and soothed Travis back into bed. Arms folding around him, comforting, his words soothing, he whispered, "I'm here. Not going anywhere."

"I know. I'll be okay. It was just a dream." Travis curled against Cembran, kissing him and holding him tight before falling asleep again.

In the morning, Travis woke as Cembran got out of bed. This time Travis pulled him back, demanding.

"Travis, I have to—" A passionate kiss melted him into Travis's arms and cut off his protest. The kisses continued as Travis's body pressed Cembran into the mattress, his legs spreading. Lips kissed and licked as his fingers teased Cembran's cleft, searching and exploring his most private places.

"Want you, Trav, need you now!" His voice was soft, but the tone was urgent, needy almost wanton. Travis slicked his fingers, pressing two of them inside, kissing Cembran deeply, earning a deep throaty moan. "More, need you, need more." Cembran sounded raw, almost pleading. After slicking his cock, Travis removed his fingers and pressed the head to his lover's small, tight opening. "Yes, want all of you."

Slowly and steadily, Travis pressed into Cembran, their joining magical and fulfilling, Cembran's channel taking him, surrounding him.

He moved slowly at first. With each entry, a moan; with each retreat, a gasp, as if there wouldn't be another. Hands caressed Cembran's body, lips pulled and sucked, kisses scalding hot, taking their breath. With each thrust, Cembran's moans increased in volume and intensity, sending Travis high on waves of passionate pleasure. Knowing he was bringing his lover to such heights made him soar. Travis was close, but determined that Cembran would climax first. Taking Cembran into his hand, he caressed and pulled with a twisting motion as his thumb rubbed over the head.

Shouting, Cembran shot his climax as Travis hit his own deep inside Cembran. Carefully, Travis pulled out a few moments later and rested his body on the bed next to Cembran, cradling him in his arms. The kisses were languid, passion replaced with love and tenderness. Cembran stroked Travis's cheek as he finally got out of bed, then dressed, and headed out to see to the animals, humming quietly to himself.

After the chores were done and breakfast completed and cleaned up, Gathod reminded Cembran and Travis that he needed to speak with them, saying, "This may take a while." The three of them sat together in the living room. "I'm not sure where to begin, but I'll try."

Gathod turned to Cembran, "The morning after our last night together, you headed out of the valley and I walked back to the village. When I arrived, the entire village was in an uproar. Your father was furious that you'd left rather than submit to what he wanted. He was organizing groups to look for you and bring you back." Gathod was looking at and talking to Cembran; Travis just listened quietly. "Most people in the village knew why you'd left, so while they did look for you, they only looked where they knew you wouldn't be. They had no intention of finding you." Cembran looked disappointed that the others has not cared to find him. Gathod continued, "It's not that they wanted you gone. We all knew your father would make your life hell, so everyone thought it best to leave you alone." Cembran relaxed, nodding. "Over time, when there was no word of you, he finally gave up looking, but he never allowed anyone to speak of you."

"Eventually, life returned to normal, except that your father clung to your brother Fartham more than he had in the past. He could do no wrong. He also seemed to tighten his grip on everyone. Periodically, when I could get away, I left the village and looked for you, but I never found any trace of you. Eventually I met Linal and we married." Cembran raised his eyebrows in mild surprise. Gathod continued with a sad look in his eyes, "We had a good life together for a number of years. She couldn't have children. She was part satyr like me, but unfortunately, she was susceptible to human diseases and died after a long illness." Gathod paused and wiped his eyes. "I never thought I could love a woman, but she was vibrant, smart, independent, and forgiving of my proclivities." He turned back to Cembran, and said, "Even during my marriage, I continued looking for you."

"Eventually, your father trained Fartham to take over for him and he even transitioned some of his duties to your brother."

Travis was getting antsy, and interrupted: "What happened."

"A year ago, Fartham was hunting wolves with friends and he got separated from the group. The pack found him before we could." Tears came to Cembran's eyes and he covered his face with his hands. "When we did find him he was barely alive." Gathod touched Cembran's shoulder gently. "He was my friend and I held his hand as he died." He paused, giving Cembran a chance to digest the bad news.

"Did Fartham marry?" Travis asked, as he tried to comfort Cembran.

"He wanted to and your father pressed him to marry, but your father hated the girls he dated and made them miserable. Fartham actually had a widow woman in the village that he visited often and cared for a great deal. They were together until she died, but your father never knew, and the village kept their secret. He was never in want for female company and he was happy; they were happy."

Cembran had composed himself and indicated to Gathod to go on. "Once Fartham died, your father decided that you had to be found, but he couldn't locate you anywhere. It wasn't until Travis started having feelings for you, that he was able to get a link to you."

"Hence my nightmares?"

"Exactly, Travis. He's trying to find Cembran and you are the only link he has. Luckily for you he can't disguise his satyr appearance like Cembran and I can, so he can't leave the village. But he can keep attacking your dreams, and I suspect that as your feelings for Cembran grow and deepen, he will have more ammunition to use against you."

Travis was puzzled. "After all this time, why look now? There has to be more to it than him just having an heir."

Gathod nodded, "There is." He looked at Cembran.

Cembran took a deep breath, "Travis, I told you my father was a very powerful satyr and he is. What I didn't tell you, and I should have, is that he's sort of the King of Satyrs."

Travis was wide eyed, "You mean you're a prince?"

"Well, sort of; I gave that up a long time ago. What's important is that as King, my father presides over the Bacchanal, which is a huge honor, the highest for any satyr. In order to preside over the Bacchanal, you must be a descendant of the first satyr leader, Bacchus. My father is a direct descendant of Bacchus." Cembran shook his head and it looked to Travis as though a weight had descended on him. "With my brother dead, it means that in my father's mind he must find me to continue his legacy and that of Bacchus."

"What is the Bacchanal?"

Gathod looked at Cembran and then explained, "I need to give you some background. Satyrs at one time were strictly hedonistic creatures living on wine, women and song. We had the power to bestow dreams, often erotic dreams, on others. However, with the power to bestow dreams came the power to also give nightmares. This power was abused. As time passed and humans evolved, it was determined that we shouldn't meddle in others' dreams; it was too open to abuse. Now interfering with another's dreams is highly frowned upon."

"My father never paid attention to that."

Gathod turned to Travis, "No, he didn't and still doesn't, from the description of your nightmares. Anyway, the Bacchanal is a throwback to the hedonistic satyrs of old. It's a monthly gathering of satyrs that performs two functions. First it gives satyrs a regular outlet for our hedonistic tendencies, and second, the Bacchanal is timed for the full moon, which is the only time our children can be conceived. At the Bacchanal there's plenty of food, wine, and everyone has sex until they can't move. We're sort of driven to it."

Cembran looked at Travis. "I'm one of the few who doesn't feel the pull of the Bacchanal."

Travis turned to Gathod, "Do you?"

Gathod nodded. "The full moon was two days ago." Travis nodded; that explained Gathod's odd behavior the night he arrived. "Cembran's father is going to keep trying to find him. He wants him to return and take his place as his successor."

"Why now?"

"His time is running out and he knows it. Satyrs can live a long time and in some cases a very long time, but we are not immortal and Cembran's father's time is coming to an end."

"Is there no one else beside Cembran who can step up?"

"By tradition, whoever leads the Bacchanal must be a descendant of Bacchus and Cembran is the one with the strongest connection. There are cousins, but they don't have as strong a tie as Cembran does."

Travis was drained and Cembran looked lost, like his whole world had just collapsed around him.

Cembran's voice seemed small, timid as he asked, "What do we do now?"

Travis spoke up. "Nothing at all." Gathod and Cembran looked at him. "He doesn't know where you are and he can't come here. His time is running out, so all I have to do is put up with a few nightmares until he either gives up or dies. Big deal."

"Travis, you need to know that he could make your dreams so bad that you don't sleep at all. He could—"

Travis stopped Gathod, "I'm not giving up Cembran to a father who attacked him and discarded him. No way!"

Cembran looked at Travis, "What do we do?"

"For now, nothing... We'll wait and see. Time is on our side for now." Travis gently stroked Cembran's neck and shoulders. "The most important thing to me is that you're safe."

Travis turned to Gathod, still stroking Cembran's skin. "Can he get to you?"

Gathod shook his head, "I have a pendant, just like Cembran, that protects my dreams."

"Can we get another one for me?" Cembran asked hopefully.

"Unfortunately, they only work for satyrs; otherwise I could make you one." The room got quiet and the conversation seemed to wind down.

Cembran slowly rose from his chair and without a word, or a glance at Travis, left the room, the door to the house closing quietly behind him.

Travis got up to follow him, but Gathod placed his hand on his arms. "Let him go. He needs to think." Travis glared at Gathod as he continued, "He needs to digest all that's happening with his family."

Travis's face relaxed, "I know. I can see the fear in his eyes; he thought he'd left all that behind long ago and suddenly it looks like it's being dumped on him again. Tearing his world apart. I do know." Travis was seething, "God damn it! I'm not going to let anyone hurt him!"

Gathod remained quiet through the outburst. When Travis sat back down, he nodded knowingly. "You really love him, don't you?"

"Yes, I do. I first saw him over ten years ago. I dreamed about him for most of that time. I dated other men, looking for the man of my dreams. I finally found him and I'm not letting go!" The determination was clear in Travis's voice, "If he wants to go, I won't fight him, but—" Travis was about to say something selfish, but stopped himself. He knew he'd do what was best for Cembran, even if he got hurt in the process.

Slowly, Travis lifted himself out of the chair and headed out of the house, down the path to the barns to find Cembran. He checked the goat barn, but it was empty. The sheep barn was quiet as well. Then Travis headed to the lake.

Cembran was sitting on the rock near where the creek emptied into the lake. It reminded Travis of the first time he saw Cembran, all those years ago. In his arms was the lamb Gathod had saved the night before.

"Lamb, are you going to be all right?" Travis stepped behind Cembran, curling his arms around his waist, lips and nose nuzzling his neck.

"Aren't you mad at me?" Cembran's voice was soft and very tentative.

Travis's voice was surprised, "What for?"

"For not telling you about my father."

He shook his head. "I don't think so. Maybe a little confused, but not mad."

They were quiet and Travis could feel Cembran leaning against him, relaxing into his body. "I guess it just never occurred to me. I mean, I thought I'd left all that behind me. It wasn't relevant to anything."

Travis could understand that. "So what do I call you now that I know you're a prince? Your Highness? Prince Cembran?" Travis was teasing, but Cembran didn't smile.

"Actually, I have a title that's better than any of those." Travis raised an eyebrow, unsure what to expect. "Lamb." Cembran turned his head, angling for a kiss. Travis leaned forward and met his lips in a sweet, tender kiss.

They kept kissing until the lamb Cembran was holding decided he wanted in on the action and started licking Travis's face and they both laughed.

The laugh felt good, but the lightness didn't last.

"Travis, I feel so guilty."

"What do you have to feel guilty about?"

"My father is attacking you because of me." Cembran was looking at the ground, unable to meet his eyes.

Travis almost laughed. "Cembran, your father is attacking my dreams because of his own selfishness and pride. Not because of you."

"But—"

Travis kissed away his argument. "No buts about it. This is all his fault and his doing. He, and he alone, is responsible."

"I'm afraid that you'll hate and resent me for what he's doing to you." Cembran was again looking down at the ground.

Travis gently placed his hand beneath Cembran's chin, lifting his head to meet his eyes. "I resent your father for doing this to me." His voice got louder, "I resent your father for making you feel guilty. I resent your father for interfering in our lives!" Travis let the anger melt away. "But I love you for caring." He kissed Cembran's forehead. "I love you for wanted to protect me." Travis kissed his cheek. "And I love you for being you." He kissed his lips, wrapping his arms around Cembran's neck, pulling their bodies into a tight, encompassing embrace.

After releasing Cembran, Travis picked up the lamb. "Come on, Lamb, we need to get back. We have more important things that worrying about your father." Holding the lamb against his body with one arm, he extended his other hand to Cembran, who smiled. Taking Travis's hand, they walked together back to the house.

Late in the afternoon, Travis was working in the vegetable garden as Gathod approached.

"Travis, could I talk to you?"

Travis nodded and stopped working as Gathod sat on the ground near where he'd been weeding. "

I have asked Cembran if I could stay here. I don't want to go back to the village, but he told me that he couldn't give me an answer." Travis looked at Gathod, confused. "He said that the land was yours and that I needed to ask you." Gathod looked at the ground. "I know we don't know each other very well. Hell, Cembran and I don't know each other very well either, but I do know that I would never hurt either of you."

Travis thought for a minute. "You do understand that I love Cembran very much?"

Gathod nodded and smiled, "And I can tell he loves you as well. I would do nothing to harm either of you."

Travis looked Gathod in the eye, studying his face. Gathod met his gaze without flinching. "I know Cembran meant a lot to you and you meant a lot to him, and I know that was a long time ago." Travis paused making sure his words conveyed the correct sentiment. "I also know that I would feel better if Cembran weren't alone right now." Images of the attack on his lover flashed through his mind. "If you wish to stay and if Cembran approves, it's fine with me. However, you will need to build your own place to live."

Gathod looked at Travis with relief. "I built my own house before, I could build another here."

Travis nodded, "Next weekend, when I'm back, you can show me where you'd like to build and we'll work out the details." Gathod was speechless, but the smile on his face spoke volumes. Gathod thanked him profusely and got up to leave. Travis held up his hand. "I'll talk to Cembran before I leave to make sure we're agreed."

Gathod was practically walking on air as he stepped out of the garden and Travis smiled to himself as he returned to work.

After dinner that evening, Travis was in Cembran's bedroom, packing his things when Cembran joined him with a longing look on his face. "I wish you didn't have to go."

"I know, Lamb. So do I, but I need to work tomorrow." Cembran sat on the edge of the bed and Travis stopped packing to sit next to him. "Gathod told me he wants to stay."

Cembran nodded, "I told him he had to speak with you."

"He did. I told him it was okay, but he needs to build his own place to live. Are you all right with him staying?"

Cembran looked at Travis with a surprised look. "Yes, I'm just surprised that you'd let him stay. I mean how can you trust him so soon?"

Travis wrapped his arms around Cembran, bringing their lips together in a gentle kiss, "I trust *you*, Lamb." He pulled Cembran into a long hot kiss. Cembran melted into the kiss, whimpering weakly into his mouth. He pushed Cembran back onto the bed as he started removing his clothes. Their love making was slow and hot, Cembran making small whimpery noises. Afterwards, Travis held him close, not wanting to leave.

Eventually, he knew he had to go, but as he was getting dressed he remembered, "Cembran, I brought you something." Reaching into his suitcase he pulled out a small cellular phone and handed it to Cembran, who looked confused. Travis smiled, "It's a cellular telephone. I got it for you so we can talk during the week, and in case you need anything."

Cembran smiled and Travis spent the next few minutes showing Cembran how it worked. "I programmed in my work number and my cellular number. I also added Doug's number in case you need the police." He really hoped he wouldn't. "Please carry it with you in case something happens."

"I will."

Travis went into the other room and dialed Cembran's phone so he could hear what the ring sounded like. He answered the phone right away and immediately started talking to Travis like he was in the room. Travis then had Cembran call him. He was pleased that Cembran seemed comfortable with his new phone.

After dinner, Travis was saying goodbye. He, Cembran, and Gathod were sitting in the living area talking. Travis kissed Cembran and told him he'd see him next weekend.

"Travis, I was wondering, could I stay with you next weekend?" Travis was surprised because Cembran had never shown any particular interest in coming to the city. "Gathod has said he'd care for the animals. So I was wondering…."

He gave Cembran a long, sweet kiss. "That would be great. I'll pick you up on Friday. I'll call you during the week, Lamb." Travis kissed Cembran again and nuzzled his neck before heading to his car, smiling the entire way.

Chapter Ten

Travis was ecstatic. Work was over and the highlight of his week was about to begin. Over the past few months, Cembran, the animals, and the small farm had become as essential to Travis as oxygen. The city was fading in the distance as he headed North. He was whistling and singing along with the radio as he drove. The days were getting shorter and the sun was already getting low in the sky, but it was still light enough to see that the trees had started to turn and the hills were a mixture of green, orange, red, and yellow.

Travis smiled to himself as he recalled the last month or so. It had truly been a happy time in his life. His father's estate was almost settled. The house had been sold and the contents liquidated. He had found it surprisingly hard when he'd walked through the home he'd grown up in for the last time. He'd allowed himself to accept his father's deathbed apology and he'd even gone to the cemetery to visit his parents' graves and say his final goodbye. Standing in front of their graves, he'd actually talked to them, thanking them for everything they'd done for him and letting them know that he understood that they'd done the best they could.

Cembran had indeed spent a weekend with him in Grand Rapids. They'd had a good time together, even though Cembran had been very intimidated by the noise and all the people. Travis had taken Cembran to a movie and Cembran had been fascinated throughout the entire film. After they left the theater, Cembran confessed that he had really enjoyed the experience, but he actually had no idea what the movie was about. They'd laughed as they walked back to the apartment. Travis took him out to eat several times and Cembran found out he liked hamburgers, pizza, and ice cream. Travis had showed him television, but he had no interest at all. He did love Travis's king-sized bed, and asked Travis if he'd help him get a new mattress to replace his homemade one at the farm. Travis had also called Brock so Cembran could meet him, but he hadn't been in town that weekend.

On Saturday night, Travis had made Cembran dinner and then took him dancing. When Travis asked him if he'd like to go dancing, Cembran had been taken aback: "Won't people be shocked?" He just couldn't understand the concept.

Travis had responded, "Lamb, trust me, there are places that we can go where there will be many other couples like us." He took Cembran to a small bar that had a dance floor and played soft, slow music. Travis would never forget the look on his lover's face when they walked into the bar and the head of every man in the place turned to look at them. Cembran had turned around as well to see what they were looking at, and Travis had whispered, "Lamb, they're looking at you."

Cembran had turned to Travis, confused and scared; he actually touched his forehead, feeling for his horns. "Why? I don't understand." His voice showed a touch of fear.

Travis took Cembran's hand and whispered, "It's because you're so handsome," as he led them to a table. Travis got Cembran and himself a good rich dark beer and they spent time together drinking and enjoying the music.

Cembran watched the couples dance and Travis was pleased to see him tap his feet and move his body naturally to the beat of the music. "Would you like to dance?" he asked. Cembran nodded and Travis led him to the dance floor, wrapping him in his arms and pulling him to his body. The man was a natural and he molded his body to Travis, rested his head on his shoulder, and moved to the beat. "You're a wonderful dancer."

Cembran smiled and whispered so only Travis could hear, "One thing we satyrs can do is dance." Travis smiled as he slipped his hands beneath Cembran's shirt, stroking his back as they moved to the music. They danced for hours wrapped in each other's arms, the music providing an almost protective cloak around them. They barely saw or heard anyone else as they moved to the rhythm of each other's bodies.

Now it was the weekend again and Travis couldn't help smiling as he drove. He'd packed a portable CD player and some music, and he was hoping that he and Cembran would be able to dance this weekend, right there in the living room.

Earlier that week, Doug had called to tell Travis that the tests had come back and the feed had indeed been poisoned. He'd had a conversation with the Sheriff, too. Doug had laughed, "The Sheriff didn't seem very happy, particularly when I told him about his brother making threats. I think I put the fear of God in him when I told him that the state police were starting to take an interest in what was happening in his jurisdiction. So I don't think you'll be having any more issues." Travis had thanked Doug for his help.

Travis arrived at the farm just before dark. After parking the car, he headed down the now familiar path to Cembran's house. As he approached the house, Sham perked up. Travis called her gently and scratched her ears before going inside. Gathod was in the kitchen making dinner and Travis looked around for Cembran. Gathod smiled knowingly; "He's finishing up the chores in the sheep barn. He should be up soon."

"Thanks. How's the house coming?"

Gathod and Travis had become friends over the past month, particularly since Gathod had started building a home of his own. Travis had given him a spot in the woods for a small house and Gathod had set to work right away. Travis brought in a couple of friends to help with the plumbing and wiring. The house was quite small, just two rooms and a bathroom, but Gathod was thrilled and looked forward to moving in. This weekend, they hoped to finish the interior walls, and if everything went according to plan, he would move into his new house in early October. For now, he was still staying with Cembran. They seemed to get along well, but Travis could tell Cembran was ready for Gathod to move into his own home.

Gathod's face brightened, "Great. I can't wait to show you the progress." The two of them had worked together to build the house and this shared activity had helped build their friendship.

Travis put the groceries he'd brought on the counter before putting his suitcase in the bedroom. As he was unpacking, he felt a pair of hands circle around his waist and a pair of warm lips kiss his neck. Travis smiled and slowly turned into his lover's embrace. "Hello, Lamb." Travis leaned to Cembran, kissing him deeply as his hands ran through Cembran's soft ringlets. Travis had to be careful not to get carried away. Last weekend, he'd immediately dragged Cembran onto the bed when he'd arrived. Within minutes he'd had Cembran naked and down his throat, with Cembran whimpering and moaning loudly. Their lovemaking had been passionate, hot, and unfortunately for Gathod, loud. When they were done, Gathod was nowhere to be found and dinner was burning on the stove.

Reluctantly, Travis pulled away, saying, "If we keep this up, Gathod will burn dinner again." They both laughed and after one last kiss, Travis finished unpacking, then joined the other two in the kitchen. Gathod and Cembran were finishing making dinner and Cembran motioned Travis to sit until it was ready. He sat in one of the comfortable handmade chairs, relaxing. His eyes wandered as they usually did to the mantle and the delicately carved animals. Those small, life-like carvings always drew his attention. Next to the chair, Travis noticed a small basket with a block of wood and carving tools. "Cembran, are you carving?"

Cembran continued working on the food, "Yes. I just started."

"What is it going to be?" Travis picked up the piece of wood, rolling it in his hands.

"I haven't decided yet. I'm just getting the feel of the wood." Travis glanced at Cembran through the corner of his eye and realized that Cembran was being evasive on purpose. Travis nodded and put the piece of wood back in the basket. As he relaxed in the chair, his eyes closed and the sounds in the room drifted around him. Hands kneaded his shoulders and lips brushed his cheek, waking him from his doze as a voice whispered that dinner was ready.

After dinner, Travis and Cembran went to bed early. Gathod had smiled saying he was going to make sure the animals were all right before going to bed. Travis and Cembran shared a look as Travis took his lover by the hand and led him to the bedroom, shutting the door quietly behind them.

He undressed quickly before getting into the bed, watching Cembran with attention as he slowly removed his clothing. "Lamb, you are so beautiful." The shirt came off and Travis hissed softly at the sight of Cembran's lithe chest and grooved stomach. The pants went next, unfastened, opened, and then allowed to drop to the floor. Cembran was already hard. The low light in the room played off Cembran's hair and eyes as he moved around the bed. Standing next to Travis, he saw the small horns appear near Cembran's hairline. For the last few weeks, Cembran had let Travis see him as a satyr whenever they made love. Travis knew it was a sign of deep love and trust. Just the thought of seeing Cembran this way could make him hard in an instant, but the actual sight of those small horns caused his body to ache and pulse with unbridled desire.

Cembran threw back the covers as he got into bed, "I need to see you." Travis smiled as he pulled Cembran into the bed, their bodies instantly wrapping and tangling together. Usually when they made love Cembran was happy to let Travis take control, but tonight was different. He took Travis's mouth in a ravenous kiss, demanding, taking, wanting him. Travis wrapped his arms around him, returning his kiss, giving as well as he was getting.

Travis felt his toes curl as Cembran's kisses became more heated, more demanding, and he gave himself over, letting him take whatever he wanted. Cembran's tongue thrust deeply into Travis's mouth, his lips pulling and tugging fiercely. He pulled back, looking deeply into Travis's eyes. They were both breathing deeply, panting into each other's mouths. "Is this okay?" The words were rough with lust between Cembran's breaths.

"Oh yes, Love. It's more than okay. It's hot as hell." Travis was trying to catch the breath that Cembran had stolen away. Before he could, though, the lips were back, kissing, filling his mouth, consuming him in a frenzy of love and passion. "I missed you so much, Lamb."

"I missed you too. Need you." Lips and mouth latched onto Travis's nipple, pulling nibbling, sucking hard. Fingers circled the other one as Travis writhed on the bed, hissing breath between his teeth. Using his lips and tongue, Cembran laved and nibbled at the now sensitive buds. He'd never done this before, but he loved it when Travis did it to him, so he was determined to return the favor.

Cembran straddled Travis body, his buttocks against Travis's hips while his busy hands and tongue explored and teased Travis's neck, shoulders, and chest. Slowly Cembran reached for the lube from the bedside table. Travis was willing to give Cembran whatever he wanted, and he watched as Cembran lubed his fingers, lifting his legs to give Cembran access. He moaned loudly as his lover reached around to prepare himself. "Lamb, let me watch." Travis's voice was husky, deep with need and outright lust. Cembran smiled and turned around so Travis could see the fingers working their way into Cembran's small, tight entrance. Travis's cock was rock hard and the view made him throb, oozing onto his stomach. "Please, Lamb I need you now. Don't make me wait any more."

Cembran turned to Travis, straddling his hips with his back to Travis. After positioning Travis's cock at his entrance, Cembran thrust his body down onto Travis's cock in one quick movement, taking him to the hilt.

Travis could barely breathe as the sensations overwhelmed his brain. Cembran, however, was a man possessed. He lifted his body and thrust himself onto Travis again and again, almost pulling off completely and them thrusting again, over and over. Travis was breathless, his body on absolute sensory overload. With each thrust, he could feel the pressure building. Then Cembran added a new twist, literally. After thrusting downward, he twisted his body so he was facing Travis. The pressure inside Travis was becoming uncontrollable. He took Cembran in his hands and worked his cock as his lover thrust himself down again and again.

Cembran was moaning, Travis was whimpering; he cried out and shot like a bullet deep into Cembran's body. Travis had barely finished coming when Cembran climaxed, releasing onto Travis's chest and stomach.

They both needed a long time to catch their breath. Eventually Cembran lifted himself off Travis before collapsing onto the bed.

Travis grabbed a towel from the bedside table and cleaned them both before pulling Cembran into a deep kiss. "Lamb, you were amazing."

"That was okay then?" Cembran sounded tentative.

"That was the hottest, most incredibly mind-blowing sex I have ever had in my life. You were absolutely unbelievable." Travis pulled Cembran next to him, snuggling their bodies together.

They held each other, petting and kissing. Cembran kept looking up at Travis like he wanted to ask something. "Trav, have you had any more nightmares?" This was becoming a question that Cembran asked each weekend, ever since Travis had woken up screaming.

"A few, but not very often and none that have had me too upset. Mostly, I don't wake up during the dream and I can't really remember them in the morning. I promise I will tell you about them if I do. Okay?"

Cembran nodded and Travis turned off the light, smiling. He made the same promise each week, but it was Cembran's care and concern that had Travis he loved; it had been a long time since he'd had someone that felt strongly enough about him to be protective, and he liked it.

Travis heard the front door to the house open and close. Smiling to himself, thinking that Cembran hadn't woken him up to help with chores again, he started to get out of bed. Rolling over, though, he felt a warm, sleeping Cembran curled up next to him. Who was in the house? Carefully, Travis got up, trying not to disturb Cembran, and walked into the other room to see what was going on. Standing in the middle of the room was a person he didn't know.

"Where is Cembran? I know you have him. I'm here to take him with me, now!" The man's voice was familiar.

Travis became angry and stood his ground, "You can't have him!" He stepped closer, but the shadows didn't allow him to see the person clearly.

"I will have him! I must have him! He belongs with me, with his own kind!" The words were short, clipped and carried a heavy accent. The person stepped forward, grabbing Travis by the arm. The grip was like a vice and he immediately started to struggle and fight. He heard laughter, "You can't fight me, Human." Travis continued to struggle, kicking the person in the leg. The stranger yelled in pain and his grip loosened on Travis's arm enough that he could get free. Travis then felt fingers gripping his throat and he tried to pry them away. "You can't fight me." Travis used both hands to grab an arm and pull the hand away from his throat. His grip intensified; he gave it everything he had.

Travis felt his body being shaken, his name screamed into his ears. "Travis, please wake up!" Shaking his head, Travis opened his eyes. Gathod was standing in front of him, holding his wrists tightly. Travis shook his head and let his arms go limp, and Gathod released his grip. Travis was standing in the living room near Gathod's temporary bed.

"What happened?" His voice was weak, fearful. "Did I hurt someone? What have I done?" A hand covered his mouth in horror.

Travis looked at Cembran, now standing beside him, hoping he'd have the answer. "You got out of bed and I thought you were going to the bathroom. I heard struggling out here and when I came into the room, you were attacking Gathod."

Travis collapsed into a nearby chair. "What did I do?" His face anguished.

Gathod took a deep breath, "You came into the room, said, 'You can't have him,' and then you grabbed my arm. I thought you were going for my throat, but you grabbed my arm instead."

"Gathod and I were trying to wake you for several minutes before you finally woke up." Cembran's voice echoed Travis's fears. Gathod was rubbing his arm.

Travis just shook his head, "What have I done? I'm sorry Gathod." He buried his face in his hands. "It was so real."

Gathod and Cembran looked at each other. Finally Gathod spoke, "Travis, you didn't do anything. I think Cembran's father entered your dreams again and this time, he had enough information to make the dream very real." Travis looked up at Gathod, his face a study in misery. Gathod gripped him by the shoulder, "I know you'd never hurt me or Cembran. This isn't your fault and you can't feel guilty. That will only play into his hand." Travis looked up at Gathod apologetically. "I'm serious. He will use your guilt against you." Gathod thought a minute, the suggested, "Travis, you need to describe your dream to us before it starts to fade."

Travis described the dream in as much detail as he could remember. When he was done, Gathod nodded. "It's as I feared. This wasn't you, it was Cembran's father. He really gave himself away." He gripped Travis's shoulder, "Go back to bed and please don't worry. It's not your fault."

Travis looked at Gathod's face, "Thank you."

Gathod's face was stern, "Tomorrow, we need to figure out what we're going to do. We can't let this continue." Travis nodded his agreement.

Cembran hugged him close and walked him back into the bedroom, helping him back into bed. He still felt bad, though Gathod's forgiveness was starting to sink in. Cembran held him close and stroked his hair. "Are you feeling better?"

Travis nodded, "Yes, I just don't want to hurt either you or Gathod. I mean…."

Cembran continued stroking his hair, "I know. I feel really bad too. Maybe I should just go."

Travis jerked his body to face Cembran, "No. He can't have you." Travis took a deep breath to calm down. "I don't know what I'd do without you." The words were out of his mouth before he could stop them. He knew he loved Cembran, but at that moment he realized just how important he had become to him. The thought of losing him made Travis's insides churn and twist. He kissed Cembran, letting all his feelings for him flow into that kiss. "Whatever happens, we face it together. Agreed?"

Cembran nodded and slipped his arms around Travis, gently maneuvering him so his head was on the pillow. "God, you're stubborn. Okay, we'll face this together."

Travis smiled and settled next to Cembran, holding him tightly. He finally fell asleep, safe in Cembran's embrace.

Chapter Eleven

His morning chores were finished and Travis was sitting in Cembran's living room. He was still tired from last night's ordeal, but he knew that they needed to discuss what they could do to try to stop these nightmares. Up until last night, they had been an annoyance. However, Travis now knew that they could be intense enough and real enough for him to hurt Cembran, Gathod, or even himself, and he couldn't have that. As he was sitting, staring at the carved animals on the mantle, he heard Cembran and Gathod come in and join him.

Travis didn't know where to start, so he kept quiet, hoping either Gathod or Cembran would take the lead. This was unusual behavior for him, and it worried Cembran to see him looking so defeated.

Gathod cleared his throat. "I've given this some thought, but I need more information. Travis, can you think back to when you had the first nightmare?" Travis nodded. "I need to know when that was." Travis thought for a while, trying to place other events so he could derive a date. Finally he figured it out and told Gathod, who smiled and seemed relieved. "This confirms my suspicions and may actually help us. Two months ago you had the first dream, where you appeared lost and confused. Last month you had the first gruesome nightmare, and last night you actually had a very realistic dream that had you sleepwalking." Travis nodded. "All of those dreams happened near the full moon, near the Bacchanal."

Travis furrowed his brow, asking, "But what does that have to do with anything?"

"Cembran's father, the Baccharist, is strongest during the time of the Bacchanal. I think he's using that strength to attack your dreams. During other times of the month, he can enter your dreams, but he isn't strong enough for the really nightmarish or intense dream experiences like he is around the Bacchanal. This is a just theory, I don't know for sure, but his behavior and the pattern of dreams leads me to believe it."

"Baccharist, what's that?"

Cembran answered, "The leader of the Bacchanal is called the Baccharist. That's my father's official title. That's what everyone in the village calls him."

"Oh." Travis thought for a minute. "So what do we do? I mean, I know I can't get a dream protection amulet like you and Cembran wear, but I don't want to chance hurting anyone." He was scared and angry at the same time. The more he thought about it, the angrier he got.

Cembran seemed to know Travis was getting upset and he took his lover's hand in his. "Gathod, what options do we have? I mean, I see only two. One is to do nothing and wait my father out. I hate that option, because it puts Travis in jeopardy. The other is to confront my father and somehow get him to back off." Cembran looked at Travis and Gathod, searching their faces. "Do you see any other choices?"

Both Gathod and Travis shook their heads. "If we do confront him, and I'm only saying if at this point, how do we do that?" Travis asked.

Gathod spoke up, "You must do it at the Bacchanal in front of everyone. You have to stand together."

Cembran looked at Gathod, "Won't me bringing my human, male lover to the Bacchanal incense my father?"

Gathod smiled a wicked smile, "I'm hoping it will and I'm hoping the others in attendance will see that he's not being reasonable." Gathod paused. "The other thing is that you need to surprise him if you can; that will put him on edge."

Travis looked to Cembran, "Okay, Lamb - it looks like we're going to Switzerland." Both Gathod and Cembran nodded. Once that was settled, Travis felt much better and he was able to relax some. "Gathod, tonight is the full moon, correct?"

Gathod looked warily at Travis, "Yes. I was thinking that I'll sleep outside tonight."

Travis jumped up from his chair, suddenly a bundle of energy, "Nonsense, tonight is the Bacchanal and we have our very own descendant of Bacchus, right?"

Gathod looked skeptical, "So?"

"So, we're going to have our own Bacchanal right here. I mean, it's basically a party. We've got Cembran's wonderful beer, wine, food, music; we could build a fire down by the lake and have our own party. It should be a beautiful September night." Travis looked at the other two alternately.

Gathod was grinning from ear to ear, "You'd do that for me?"

"Sure, it'll be fun." Travis felt arms wind around his waist, lips brushing the back of his neck. Cembran indicated his pleasure by nibbling on Travis's ear. "Okay, then... let's have a party."

Travis spent part of the day with party preparations, and the rest of the time working with Gathod on his house. Working together, they were able to get a lot of things accomplished. They finished the last big interior projects. The rest of the work Gathod would be able to get done on his own during the next week or two.

After completing work on Gathod's house, Travis cleaned up and started carrying some things down to the lake. Once they were set up to his satisfaction, he headed back to the house. Gathod had told him that the Bacchanal officially began at sundown, so they had decided to eat dinner before starting the party. Dinner was ready when Travis went inside. The whole house smelled wonderful. Once they were done eating, Travis cleaned up while the other two got ready to go down to the lake.

Just before sundown, Travis made his way down the path. He lit a large fire and made sure everything was ready for the satyrs. At sundown, Cembran and Gathod made their appearance. The light from the fire reflected on the smooth water and danced on the tall trees surrounding the lake. Cembran started pouring beer and the three of them sat around the fire, drinking and talking. They took turns telling stories. Gathod told about fighting during the Napoleonic wars: he'd actually met Wellington during the battle of Waterloo. Cembran told stories about his travels after he left the village. Travis was fascinated as Cembran described living on the American frontier.

Cembran smiled broadly, "Say, I remember a story my mother used to tell me." Travis scooted closer, leaning against his lover's shoulder. "My favorite bedtime story was William Tell." Cembran thought a minute as Travis and Gathod waited for him to continue. "Long ago now, the hated Austrian Hapsburgs sent Gessler to be the governor of the town of Altdorf. Gessler was a mean, cruel, self-obsessed man." Travis smiled at the faces Cembran made as he described the villain. "Now, Gessler had a large pole built in the center of town and had his hat placed on top of it." Cembran looked at Travis with a smile, "He decreed that everyone had to bow before his hat."

"William Tell was a proud man and he refused to bow before a stupid hat on a pole." Travis was enraptured as Cembran's rich voice continued with the story. "When William passed in front of the hat, he was arrested because he didn't bow. In addition to being cruel, Gessler had a sinister sense of humor. As punishment for not bowing, he decreed that William Tell had to shoot an apple off the head of his son Walter, or Gessler would execute them both." Travis was enthralled with the story and Gathod was hanging on every word, even though he'd heard it many times before. "If William Tell was successful, both he and Walter could go free."

"Gessler stood Walter in front of the pole in the town square and placed an apple on the boy's head. With a single shot," Cembran mimicked aiming a crossbow, "William Tell split the apple in two." Travis thought the story was over and started to get up. "But...." Travis sat back down. "Gessler noticed a second bolt in the crossbow. When asked, William Tell told Gessler that if he'd failed the challenge, the second bolt was to kill him." Cembran looked at both Gathod and Travis, building tension before continuing.

"Gessler was furious and had William bound and gave orders to have him taken to his castle on an island in Lake Lucerne." Cembran stood up, making wave-like motions with his arms. "When they were on the lake, a storm came up, bouncing the small boat on the water." Cembran pantomimed the action of the rocking and twisting boat.

"William Tell managed to escape during the storm and he hid on the island. When Gessler arrived a few days later, William was waiting for him and shot him with an arrow."

Travis looked at Cembran and waited, figuring there had to be more. "Gessler's cruelty and William Tell's bravery emboldened the people to rebel against the Hapsburgs." He looked to Travis, his eyes softened and his voice returning to a normal tone, "That rebellion resulted in the first Swiss Federation and the birth of what we know today as Switzerland."

"That was a great story, and you tell it so well." Travis kissed him gently. After a brief lull it was his turn, so he told some stories about the crazy things he did in college, particularly the time some of his friends decided that Travis needed to get himself a woman. Luckily for him, the "woman" they chose happened to be a very good drag queen, so everything turned out just fine. The three young men laughed and carried on for hours.

As the stories started to wind down, Travis put some techno-club music on the portable CD player he'd brought down earlier, and the three of them danced around the fire, gyrating madly as they whooped and hollered. As they danced, Travis noticed that Gathod disappeared into the woods for a while and then returned to dance again. Cembran just kept dancing, paying no attention to Gathod, so Travis followed his lead. As the night wore on, Travis realized he was starting to get drunk, so he stopped drinking the beer. Cembran did the same, but Gathod kept drinking and disappearing into the woods every so often.

When Travis could barely move any more, he sat down on a blanket next to the fire. Cembran joined him as Gathod kept dancing and partying on his own. Cembran started kissing him and pushed Travis back onto the blanket. He returned the kiss, thrusting his tongue into Cembran's willing, hot mouth. Cembran moaned wantonly as Travis slipped his hand down the back of Cembran's pants, caressing the smooth skin of his butt. Cembran started to remove Travis's clothes, but Travis stopped him. "We can't do this here."

As if on cue, Gathod stopped dancing, staggered a few steps away from the fire and collapsed onto the sand. Travis was concerned, "Is he all right?" Loud snoring confirmed that Gathod was fine. Travis got up and covered Gathod with a blanket and then rejoined Cembran.

Travis pressed their lips together and Cembran responded immediately with wanton moans and whimpers. He slipped his hand beneath Cembran's shirt, working first one nipple and then the other between his fingers. His lover pressed his chest forward, moaning loudly and melting into his kisses.

He used Cembran's pliancy to position him on his back on the blanket without separating their mouths. The kisses continued as Travis opened Cembran's pants and slipped his hand inside. Cembran whimpered into his mouth as he gently and teasingly stroked his cock.

"More, please Travis, I need more." Cembran threw his head back as Travis teased him.

Taking pity on Cembran, Travis slipped his pants past his hips, then pulled off his shirt, admiring his skin in the firelight. Cembran was now nude, lying on the blanket, vibrating with excitement. "You are so incredible, Lamb." Travis pulled his shirt over his head. "My beautiful satyr." Travis toed off his shoes as the small horns appeared. Cembran was whimpering as Travis started opening his pants. "I love that you get so excited for me." He pushed his pants off, stepping out of them as gracefully as possible, then knelt next to Cembran kissing him hard. Cembran pulled him onto his body, the need to be skin to skin overpowering. Lips pulled on lips, chests heaved, hard leaking cocks rubbed together sending ripples up their spines.

Travis straddled Cembran's body, resting his butt on his lover's legs as he leaned forward to capture one of Cembran's fleshy nipples between his lips. His tongue danced around the deep pink disk as Cembran writhed, squirmed, and gasped with pleasure. "Do you want more?" Cembran just nodded his head, quivering beneath Travis's ministrations. "What do you want?" Travis switched nipples, laving the other disk with his tongue.

Gasping, Cembran managed to gasp out, "Need you." Cembran then gave up trying to form words, throwing his head back as waves of pleasure coursed through his body. Travis repositioned his body between Cembran's legs, lifting his knees to his chest. Fingers caressed his crease, teasing and circling the tight opening. Cembran nodded, his head still thrown back, his eyes rolling in his head, his mouth open. Travis brought his tongue to the tiny opening, laving and circling; he smiled as the muscles pulsed and throbbed at his touch. Again and again, he teased and thrust his tongue into the opening, getting Cembran relaxed for him. "Are you ready for me?"

"Oh god! Yes!" The words were hoarse and rough. "Now, please!" Cembran was reduced to single-syllable words as Travis wet his cock and pressed the head to the tight ring of muscle. Cembran was so ready and so hot that his body almost seemed to pull Travis inside. Travis positioned Cembran's calves on his shoulders as he buried himself to the hilt and leaned forward to capture his lover's lips. Without breaking the kiss, he started thrusting. Cembran moved into each thrust, his rhythm perfectly matching Travis's.

"I love you, Travis. Love how I feel when we're together like this," he moaned.

"And I love you, Lamb. I love how you feel, how you look, who you are." Travis's breathing was coming in short bursts, his body covered in sweat as he continued driving deep into Cembran. "I love who I am when I'm with you. How happy you make me." Travis leaned forward and kissed Cembran again, encouraging, "Come for me, Lamb," and he did. Those words sent Cembran flying and he came hard, his cock pulsing again and again. The muscles flexed, traveling through Cembran's body and breaking the last of Travis's control, and he gushed his essence deep into Cembran, filling him with everything he had.

With kisses and soft words, Travis slowly pulled out of Cembran. Using a corner of the blanket, he cleaned them both up, then added more wood to the fire, and snuggled next to Cembran on the blanket before covering them both with a second blanket.

Before going to sleep, Travis glanced over at Gathod. His eyes were closed and he appeared to be asleep. It may have been a trick of the light, but he thought he saw tears falling from Gathod's eyes. Cembran rested his head on Travis's shoulder as they both fell into a deep, contented, passion-spent sleep.

The first rays of the sun were peeking over the trees by the lake when Travis woke. Cembran was still asleep next to him. Gently, Travis stroked his hair as he felt Cembran shift slightly and snuggle his body closer. Travis looked around. Gathod was still asleep where he'd fallen the night before. Cembran's body provided a cocoon of warmth and Travis quickly dozed off again.

He woke again to Cembran shifting next to him. "Morning, Lamb." He pulled Cembran's body to his, spooning them together. Travis nestled his head next to warm shoulders, kissing and nuzzling the hot, smooth skin.

Cembran slowly extricated himself from their cocoon and started getting dressed. Travis watched him put on his clothes, admiring every movement of his body. He finally got moving as well, got out of the blankets, and started pulling on his own clothes. He looked over to where Gathod had been sleeping, but saw only the empty blanket. Cembran kissed Travis and went to start the morning chores. Travis began cleaning up the mess from the previous night's revels, hauling things back to the house. Once everything had been put away, he went to find Gathod.

Travis figured Gathod was working on the house, so he tried there first. Gathod was sitting on the floor looking at the floor boards. "Gathod, are you all right?"

Gathod looked up at Travis and blushed. "I saw you and Cembran make love last night." Travis wasn't sure what to think. "I passed out and someone must have put a blanket over me. I woke up and you and Cembran were making love by the fire. I know I shouldn't have watched, but I couldn't help it." He looked down at the floor again. "I have never seen or felt the love that you two showed each other last night except with Cembran, and I let him go." Travis didn't know what to say, so he just listened. "I hope that I'll have someone to love me like that again."

Travis thought he understood. "Gathod, you know I love Cembran and I believe you love him, too. But the passionate love you shared was a long time ago. I know you think you made mistakes and maybe you did, but regret is a waste. It keeps us from being happy and it keeps us from moving on. Forgive yourself and allow yourself to be happy again." Gathod looked up and Travis gently squeezed his shoulder, "You're a good friend, and we're both glad you're here." Figuring that Gathod needed some time alone, he quietly left the house and headed down to the sheep barn to find Cembran.

Travis heard him before he saw him; the sound of Cembran humming and singing audible from outside the barn. He went inside and watched Cembran for a few minutes before getting his attention. Travis slipped his arms around his waist and nuzzled his neck, "Morning, handsome." Cembran leaned his head back for a kiss. "We had an audience last night," Travis told him. Cembran turned around to face him. "Gathod wasn't as passed out as we thought." He related to Cembran what Gathod had told him. After another hug and a kiss, they finished the chores and headed up to the house.

Cembran made a quick breakfast and Gathod joined them just as Cembran was setting the food on the table. Travis patted him on the back. "It's all right, Gathod." The other man's face brightened up, and once breakfast was done, Gathod went back to work on his house. Cembran led Travis to the bedroom.

Their kisses were hot and slow. Hands stroked and caressed smooth, scorching skin. Chests heaved, legs entwined, and the room filled with the moans and whimpers of love and pleasure. Hard flesh pressed against hard flesh. The passion built until they could no longer contain it, begging for release.

Travis held Cembran tight, whispering "I love you, Lamb." Cembran kissed him gently, snuggling against his body. "Are you all right?"

Cembran's voice seemed small, "I'm worried, I guess, about facing my father, about leaving the farm, and being in an airplane."

Travis cuddled him close, reassuring him. "I'll be with you and I won't let anything happen to you. I can promise that." Cembran rested his head on Travis's shoulder.

Chapter Twelve

Early the next week, Travis requested vacation time from work, and made the airline, hotel, and transportation arrangements for their trip to Switzerland. He knew he needed more information on what he could expect from Cembran's father, so on Wednesday he called his ex-boyfriend, Cembran's cousin, Brock.

"Hello, Brock Kraus speaking."

"Hey, Brock, it's Travis."

"Travis, how are you doing? I haven't talked to you in a while." Brock sounded wary.

"I'm doing well, but I need your help."

"What kind of help? Is this a legal matter?"

"No, it's personal. Could you come over this evening?" Brock hesitated. "It's important, I wouldn't have called you otherwise."

"All right, I'll be there in an hour."

"Thanks, Brock. I'll have a beer ready for you."

Brock arrived on time and Travis ushered him into the apartment, seating him on the sofa and getting him a drink. "Travis, are you trying to get back together? Because...."

Travis shook his head, "Brock, I'm going to come right to the point. I met a relative of yours about three months ago, your cousin Cembran." A shadow of fear passed across Brock's face. Travis saw it and tried to allay those fears. "I know that both you and Cembran are satyrs. Your secret is safe with me." The tension seemed to flow out of Brock.

"You know where Cembran is?" Brock asked, holding up his hands. "Please don't tell me."

"From your reaction, I take it you're not a fan of his father."

Brock shook his head vigorously. "The Baccharist is the reason my parents left the village and came to this country. So no, we are not fans of Cembran's father."

Brock seemed to relax as Travis continued. "The reason I called is because I need your help. I've been seeing Cembran for the last three months or so. A couple of months ago, I started having nightmares. However, they've been getting worse and more realistic, particularly around the time of the Bacchanal at the full moon."

"That would make sense. His power is greatest leading up to the Bacchanal."

Travis nodded; that confirmed what Gathod had thought. "We believe that Cembran's father is trying to get to him through me. During the last full moon, I was sleepwalking and attacked someone thinking that he was someone else, from a dream." Travis took a deep breath. "So, to try and make a long story short, we've decided that we need to go to Switzerland and confront his father. But I need some information. I need to know more about his father, and if he has any weaknesses."

Brock thought a minute, "I don't think I can help you. But I know who can. Have you had dinner?"

"No, not yet."

"Good, get your coat. I'm supposed to have dinner with my parents tonight. They may be able to help." Travis grabbed a jacket and followed Brock to his car. "You can ride with me; I'll bring you home."

On the way, Brock kept looking over at Travis. "What's Cembran like? I mean, my parents always spoke of him in almost reverential terms. He was the first person to have enough courage to leave the village. I think he inspired them."

A smile lit Travis's face as he thought of Cembran. "He's beautiful. He's slender, and strong, with smooth tanned skin. His face looks almost angelic, which makes his small satyr horns incredibly sexy." Brock smiled as he drove. "He has light hair that he wears in ringlets with sun-kissed highlights." Travis paused, sighing softly, "He's kind, thoughtful, with an innocence about him, like the world hasn't touched him. Brock, he is the most loving, sensual person I've ever met."

"He sounds perfect." Brock's voice sounded a little hurt.

Travis laughed, "He's not perfect any more than the rest of us are, but he has some wonderful qualities."

Brock was quiet for a while, "Do you love him?"

"Oh, yes. Very much." A warm happy feeling filled Travis as he talked about Cembran.

"Good. You deserve to be happy." They pulled up to Brock's parent's home just North of Grand Rapids. It was a small, well-kept home surrounded by flowers.

Brock led the way up the walk, opening the door and ushering him inside. Brock's parents were seated in the living room. They both rose when they saw they had a guest. "Travis, these are my parents, Sue and Jim. Mom and Dad, you remember Travis?"

"Of course." They all shook hands and offered Travis a seat. Brock's parents looked to be in their mid-fifties, but Travis knew they were probably much older.

Brock's mother looked uncomfortable and seemed a little flustered, "Brock, I didn't know you were bringing company. Are you two dating again?"

Brock and Travis both smiled, "No, Mom." Brock was trying to figure out where to start. "Travis called me earlier today asking for my help, but I think he really needs to talk to you." Brock looked at Travis. "I'll let him fill you in."

"About three months ago, I met a wonderful man. I believe he's your nephew, Cembran."

Their mouths flew open and they gasped together. It was almost cute. "Don't tell us where he is," they said in unison.

Travis told them about the dreams, and about their plans to confront Cembran's father. "What I am hoping for is some information."

"Do you love Cembran?" Sue asked, almost tentatively.

Travis smiled big, "With everything I have."

Jim nodded. "Good; you'll need that in dealing with his father. Has he given you his Triuwe?"

Travis shook his head. "No."

"That's good too, at least for dealing with The Baccharist."

"I don't understand."

Jim smiled, "You wouldn't. When you give someone your Triuwe, particularly a non-satyr, you give them part of yourself, your strength. If Cembran had given you or anyone his Triuwe, he might not have the strength he'll need to deal with his father. I know it's hard to understand."

"What is Cembran's father like?"

Jim looked at Sue and Brock and then at Travis. "The Baccharist, Cembran's father, is a classic tyrant. He rules that small village and the people in it with an iron hand. He was always controlling, but after Cembran left, he became even more so. His word was law and he broached no dissention. The only person who seemed to be able to have any influence was Fartham." Jim thought a minute as he looked at his wife. "We couldn't take him anymore, so we decided to leave." Sue picked up the story. "About fifty years ago, we decided we had to go, so we packed only what we could carry and left during the night. Eventually we made our way here."

"Does he have any weaknesses? Anything that can be used against him?"

Jim answered the question as best he could; "His main weakness is that he can't understand anything but influence and power. That's what he lives for and that's why you can't tell us where Cembran is. He could get that information from us if he tried, and he would use it against his son somehow."

Sue had been quiet, thinking. "My brother became the Baccharist after my father was killed in an accident. I always thought my brother had something to do with that, but I could never prove anything. It's just a feeling. Anyway, part of the ceremony involved him changing his name. That name is the one thing he guards most passionately. Very few people know what it is, and most, if not all, of them are dead now. I'm not sure why, but I think that the name is somehow the key to his power. If you could find out that name, you might have some leverage."

Jim spoke up, saying, "The one thing that bothers me the most is that he's attacking your dreams. While we do have that ability, dreamweaving is something that is now highly frowned upon, particularly when performed on humans. But in keeping with his character, he just ignores any rules that aren't convenient for him."

Sue got up and walked into the kitchen, calling back into the room, "Dinner will be ready in ten minutes."

"Jim, I wanted to let you know that Gathod is here with Cembran."

"That's good. The Baccharist can't get to either of them."

"Yes, I know. They have dream protection amulets." Jim nodded and Travis continued, "Gathod told us when he arrived that Fartham was killed in a hunting accident."

Jim's eyes got wide, tinged with sadness. "That explains why he's so desperate to find Cembran and why he's invading your dreams. He feels he must have an heir. He knows he can't get to Cembran directly and your love for him is the only connection to Cembran he can find. I don't envy what you're doing, but I think it's the only way. You have our good wishes."

Sue entered the room and announced that dinner was ready. The food was delicious and Travis enjoyed talking to Brock's parents. They seemed like happy, fun people. When dinner was over, they talked a little more before the two younger men had to leave.

Travis thanked them both for the information and the dinner. "When this is over, I'll arrange for you to see Cembran. I'm sure he'll be thrilled to see all of you."

Travis and Brock got into the car and drove back to Travis's apartment. "Thanks, Brock, for all your help." Travis gave him a hug and went inside to call Cembran and tell him what he'd found out.

The weekend before they were to leave for Switzerland, Travis arrived at the farm at his usual time on Friday night. When he arrived, Cembran was cooking dinner. He set down the things he was carrying and took his boyfriend in his arms, kissing him passionately before hugging him tight. "Lamb, I missed you."

Cembran smiled, "I missed you too. Dinner will be ready soon. Gathod is joining us; he says that we need to make final plans."

Travis nodded his head, "Yeah, we do, but I was hoping to have you all to myself tonight." He ground his hips into Cembran's body.

"You'll get yours after he leaves." Cembran giggled a little, "I'm starting to wonder who the satyr is in this relationship." Travis laughed as well and set his things in the bedroom before putting away the food he'd brought with him. He's had started bringing groceries on the weekends, to help out, and now Cembran was starting to request some of the things he particularly liked.

"Cembran, have you thought about what your father's Baccharist name might be?"

Cembran continued getting dinner ready while they talked. "I have given it some thought and I seem to remember an instance where it might have been used, but I just can't recall the details. I'm hoping it'll come to me, but I know I can't force it."

Travis knew that he had to be patient, but he was finding it difficult. "Okay. By the way, I talked Brock this week; he and his parents send their best and wanted me to tell you that they're looking forward to seeing you when this is over."

A smile lit up Cembran's face. "It'll be nice to know family members again. It's been a long time."

A sharp knock on the door was followed by "Hope you're decent!" Cembran and Travis laughed as the door opened and Gathod practically bounced into the room.

Travis snickered a little. "You're in a good mood. Did you get lucky?"

"No. But I did finish the last work on the house!"

"Great - we have something to celebrate." Travis hugged Gathod hello and they all helped Cembran set the table and lay out the food. While they were eating, the conversation turned to their upcoming trip. Travis reviewed the plans: "We leave Friday morning. I'll pick Cembran up Thursday night and we'll stay at my apartment. We'll arrive in Switzerland on Saturday."

Gathod added his information, "The Bacchanal will be held on Monday night. Don't show yourselves until midnight for the most impact. The Bacchanal will be going full-tilt by then and your appearance will garner a lot of attention."

"I still don't have anything to use against him and we really don't know how he'll react." Travis was starting to worry again.

"I've been giving this some thought. You don't need to beat him, just stand up to him. He's all about power. Just standing up to him is a win for you. Besides, he's not supposed to be using dream control anymore. That alone can be used against him. Remember, you're playing to the crowd, and they may fear him, but they don't like him. So use that."

"If we can figure out his secret name, how do we use that?"

"I don't know. If you find out that information and you decide to use it, don't use it as leverage, use it forcefully. I believe that's the only way."

Travis turned to Cembran, "Lamb, are you okay with this? I mean, he is your father."

"I'm fine with it. He stopped being my father a long time ago. A real father wouldn't have treated me that way he did."

"As long as you're sure." Travis looked Cembran directly in the eyes.

"I'm sure."

"Good. Let's talk about something more pleasant." The three of them spent the rest of the evening talking and laughing together. There was still a sense of nervous anticipation in the room, but it was tempered by the good company and a lot of laughter. As the evening wore on, Gathod said good-night and headed home. Cembran turned out the lights, took Travis's hand, and led him to the bedroom.

Chapter Thirteen

The night before they were to leave for Switzerland, Cembran and Travis slept at Travis's apartment in the city. Cembran was a nervous wreck. The prospect of riding in an airplane, as well as the thought of dealing with his father, had reduced him to a bundle of nerves. Travis stayed close, making sure Cembran knew he wasn't alone. That night, he held Cembran tightly, calming and reassuring them both.

Travis made sure they arrived at the airport early. Once they checked in for the flight and checked their bags to Zurich, he took Cembran to the observation lounge. He wanted him to see planes taking off and landing. Cembran was absolutely fascinated. "How do they get those big machines to fly?" He was full of questions, and Travis answered them to the best of his ability with patience and kindness.

Travis was careful to maintain physical contact with Cembran. They did get some looks when he slipped his arm around Cembran's waist, but Travis ignored them and he didn't think his lover noticed at all. Travis concentrated on making sure Cembran felt as comfortable as possible.

Their flight to Atlanta was announced and Travis directed Cembran to the boarding gate. As they took their place in line, Cembran was nervous and shaking. Travis slipped his arm around his waist, whispering, "I'm here, Lamb, and I'm not going to let anything happen to you." Cembran leaned close and his shaking subsided.

Boarding the plane, Cembran remarked that there was more space than he thought, which surprised Travis, because he always found airplanes cramped. After finding their seats, Travis stowed their carry-on luggage. Cembran was seated by the window and seemed content and calm, knowing he could look outside.

Travis reached in his pocket, "Here, Lamb, take a piece."

"What is it?" Cembran asked, accepting a piece.

"It's chewing gum." Travis opened the wrapper for Cembran. "Don't swallow it, just chew. It helps relieve the pressure on your ears as the plane takes off."

Cembran nodded and put the gum in his mouth. Smiling, he said, "It's sweet." Travis nodded and returned his smile.

The doors to the plane were closed and Cembran tensed as they pushed away from the gate and taxied for takeoff. The engines revved and he grabbed the armrest holding on for dear life. Travis placed his hand on Cembran's as the plane picked up speed and lifted into the air. He was wide-eyed as the ground fell away. Once aloft, Cembran started to relax, and after a while started to get comfortable. Cembran got nervous again as they started the landing process, but once on the ground in Atlanta, he said he was surprised how easy the trip had been. Travis was extremely relieved.

Their flight to Switzerland was long and relatively uneventful. Travis was relieved when Cembran fell asleep after dinner. Travis had never been able to sleep on airplanes, so he read. A few times Cembran woke, looking around. "I keep seeing my father and remembering things I haven't thought about in a long time."

Travis put his book down, turning to Cembran, concerned, "He's not...?"

"No. I'm just remembering. There are so many things I want to show you." Cembran's expression changed from excitement to sadness, "But most of them are probably gone."

Travis leaned close, "Lamb, after almost 300 years, things are bound to have changed." Travis held his hand and Cembran drifted back off to sleep.

Halfway through the flight, Cembran jerked himself awake. The flight attendant happened to be passing, and asked "Are you okay?"

"Yes, it's his first flight. He's a little nervous," Travis explained.

She smiled at Cembran as Travis patted his hand gently as she walked away.

"I remembered something - well actually two things. Before I left, I hid my money from my father." Travis looked at him confused. Cembran explained, "Fartham was my half-brother. My father married my mother for her money, but he never saw any of it. She was too smart for him and managed to keep it away from him. She told me where to find it just before she died. I couldn't take it with me, so I hid it."

"Will it still be there after all this time?"

Cembran smiled and leaned close. "Oh yes. I hid it in a place that was sure to be maintained and undisturbed." Travis waited. "I can't tell you where it is, in case my father...." Cembran let his voice trail off. He hated that his father was making him keep secrets from Travis.

Travis smiled and squeezed his hand, "A wise precaution. Will the money still be good? I mean, a lot has changed."

The twinkle in Cembran's eye should have been the tip-off. "Gold is always good."

Travis nodded. "What else did you remember?" He wanted to change the subject in case they were overheard.

"I remember where I heard his secret name." Travis was all ears. "Father was threatening my mother, trying to beat her. He needed the money she had and she wouldn't give it to him." The look on Cembran's face was pure pain, and Travis knew he'd walk through fire to keep that look off Cembran's face in the future. "She was yelling at him to stop, but he wouldn't. He just got angrier. Finally she looked him in the eye and said...." In frustration, Cembran hit the arm of his seat with his fist. "I was so close! I just can't remember."

Travis leaned over, nuzzling Cembran's neck, "It's okay, Lamb. How did you hear all this?" Travis kept his head close to Cembran's, enjoying the closeness and the smell of the man he loved.

"I was young and scared of my father. I hid in the cupboard when he came home because I was supposed to be in the field with the animals, but I was hungry. Neither of them knew I was there."

Travis shook his head as he comforted the loving, caring man in the seat next to him, thinking to himself, *"What kind of monster would hurt a person as wonderful as Cembran?"* Gently, he wrapped an arm around his lover, pulling his head against his shoulder. After a few minutes, Cembran's breathing became regular, and soon he was snoring gently, cradled in Travis's arms.

After landing in Zurich, passing through immigration and passport control, getting their luggage, and passing customs, Travis rented a car, and soon they were on their way to the hotel. He had arranged for them to spend Saturday and Sunday in Zurich. On Monday, they would move to a small farm hotel near the satyr village. Travis explained to Cembran, "We don't want to take the chance of being recognized." Arriving at the hotel, they took a quick nap before spending the rest of the day seeing the sights.

Travis and Cembran wandered through the Old Town district of the city with its narrow streets and interesting shops. Travis saw a small shop specializing in wood carvings, and Cembran was fascinated to see what other people were doing. Travis leaned close to his ear and whispered, "I like yours better; they're done with such love," as they wandered through the shop. At the back of the store, there was a case of antique carvings. They looked very different from the recent one. The wood had oxidized and aged, the color darkened. Cembran pointed to one of the carvings and got excited. The shopkeeper came over and Cembran asked to see the carving. When the shopkeeper handed it to Cembran, his demeanor changed. It was as though he was holding a holy object. Cembran caressed the carved figure with his hands. As Travis looked at the figure his eyes widened – the figure was a carving of Cembran. The shopkeeper noticed the resemblance as well. Cembran turned to Travis, and said with awe, "This is Fartham's work."

The shopkeeper was floored, "You know this?"

Cembran nodded, "This was carved by a relative of mine."

"You are from the area?"

"My family lives in Jura."

"I have more that I bought at the same time. Would you like to see them?" Cembran nodded and followed the man to the back room of the shop. On a small shelf were six similar carvings. Cembran reverently picked up one, turning them in his hand. From the expression on his face, it almost seemed as though he was communicating with it. As he set each one down, he placed them in groups.

"This one, I don't know who carved it. These two were carved by a man named Cembran Bacch. These three were carved by a man named Fartham Bacch. They were brothers. All of the carvings are between 250 and 300 years old," the shopkeeper said.

Cembran set the last of the carvings back on the shelf and slowly walked out of the shop. Travis followed, and once Cembran reached the street, he crumpled onto a bench.

"Lamb, what is it? Did you really carve those before you left?" Travis was speaking very quietly.

Cembran's hands were pressed to his face as tears ran down his cheeks. "Those were Fartham's. The one he carved of me. The two that I carved are Fartham and my mother. The others, while carved by Fartham, are unknown to me."

"Wait here." Travis went back into the shop. "What is your best price on these three carvings?" Travis indicated the carvings of Cembran, Fartham, and Cembran's mother.

The shopkeeper looked out the window at Cembran sitting miserably on the bench and then back at Travis. "Those really are ancestors of his?" Travis nodded. The shopkeeper named a price that Travis thought was very fair and Travis handed over his credit card. After the financial transaction was complete, the shopkeeper wrote a detailed receipt that Travis could use when going through customs on the return trip, and carefully packed each carving in tissue and a separate small box. Travis shook the shopkeeper's hand, thanked him, and exited the store.

Cembran was still sitting on the bench looking miserable. "Lamb, let's go." Cembran looked up and saw the bag that Travis was carrying.

"What did you do?" Cembran wiped the tears from his now puffy eyes.

"I bought the carvings of you, Fartham, and your mother." Slipping his hand around Cembran's waist, he added, "Come on, Love, let's get back to the hotel, it's getting late and we should have dinner and then get some sleep." Travis could tell that things were starting to wear on Cembran; he hoped Cembran would feel better after he'd slept.

Sunday morning was bright and beautiful. They'd both slept very well, which surprised Travis, since he'd been expecting a nocturnal visit from Cembran's father. They spent the day seeing a few more of the sights around Zurich, the Fraumünster Church with its incredible Chagall windows, and the Swiss National Museum. They also had a wonderful lunch and dinner before taking a quiet walk as the sun was setting.

Sunday night, Cembran was a bundle of nerves. The closer it got to the Bacchanal, the more nervous, skittish, and emotional he became. By three in the morning, he was tossing and turning, unable to sleep at all. Travis was awake as well. He had been having another nightmare, but Cembran's tossing had woken him up. On top of that, he was becoming more and more worried about his lover. "Come here, Lamb."

Cembran scooted next to Travis. Strong arms wrapped around him, pulling their bodies together. "It's okay, Lamb. I know you're nervous." Travis threaded his fingers through Cembran's soft ringlets. Getting out of bed, he got a bottle of lotion from his kit. Pulling back the covers he suggested, "Lie on your stomach, Lamb."

Cembran rolled over as Travis straddled his legs. Using the lotion, Travis stroked and rubbed Cembran's shoulders, soothing tension from the taut muscles. His shoulders started to relax under the ministrations, and Travis's hands moved to his back, working those muscles with deep, long strokes from shoulder blade to round, firm butt. Low moans and deep breaths accompanied the strokes as Cembran's muscles let go of the nervous energy they were storing. Legs were stretched, thighs were stroked, and buttocks kneaded repeatedly until they too relaxed. Travis found that he was getting excited, but pushed his desire aside in order to concentrate on Cembran's need.

"Roll over, Lamb," the words were whispered softly as Cembran slowly rolled onto his back. Travis's hands caressed the strong, broad chest muscles, stretching and stroking. Stomach muscles were rubbed, arms kneaded and stretched, legs and feet stroked.

"Feel better?" He straddled Cembran's legs, butt resting on Cembran's thighs.

Cembran smiled a wicked smile, "Yes, but you missed the best part."

Travis returned his grin, "I did, huh?" He used his fingertips to trace the length of Cembran's rigid cock. "That just won't do at all." Reaching for the lube on the bedside table, he lubed his fingers, then bringing those fingers to his ass, prepared himself for Cembran.

"Travis, what...?" Travis took Cembran in his lubed hand, slicking him. "Are you sure?"

"Shhh, Lamb." The words were barely audible. Travis positioned Cembran's cock at his entrance and slowly took him into his body. Cembran whimpered and hissed as his senses were overwhelmed.

"Trav, I never knew." Cembran threw his head back as Travis's butt sank down onto his hips.

"Never knew what, Love?" Travis lifted again and sank back down.

"I never... knew... it could... be like... this." Cembran was breathing in small, shallow breaths, barely able to form words.

Travis smiled wickedly as he lifted his body again and again. "Are you telling me you've never topped?" Travis plunged himself onto Cembran yet again. Cembran could only shake his head as the power of speech left him. Travis lifted up, "Well, I'm glad I'm the first." Cembran bounced on the bed as Travis pounded himself onto him again and again. Just knowing that he was the first to do this for Cembran thrilled him beyond belief.

Travis was determined to give Cembran everything he had, everything he could want. Sweat was pouring off his body as he ground down onto Cembran's cock. Cembran was meeting every downward thrust and soon they were moving together. Tears were running down Cembran's cheeks, their movements a wonderful dance of love.

"Trav, I can't hold...." Cembran lost his last bit of control and Travis could feel his lover's cock throb as he emptied deep inside his body. He clamped his muscles tightly onto Cembran and vigorously stroked his cock. The need to mark Cembran as his was overpowering. Cembran was still inside him as he came hard on Cembran's chest and stomach; the word "Mine" ripped from his lips.

Slowly, Travis let Cembran slip from his body. After cleaning up, Cembran snuggled close to him murmuring, "Thank you. I had no idea."

"I wanted to give you something special."

"Mmmm, you did." The room was dark, and after a final kiss, Travis held Cembran close and soon he was snoring softly. Travis relaxed and fell asleep as well.

Chapter Fourteen

Travis woke Monday morning to the sun streaming in the windows and a gentle morning breeze moving the curtains. Cembran was still asleep as Travis got out of bed, being extra careful not to wake him. After dressing quietly, he left to get some breakfast. He returned about fifteen minutes later to an adorable sight. Opening the door to the room, he saw Cembran still asleep, his arms patting the bed trying to find Travis.

Setting down the breakfast tray, he sat on the edge of the bed. Cembran found him and wrapped his body around him. "Lamb, I have breakfast for you." Cembran's deep blue eyes opened and he stared at Travis. Travis wanted to remain in the gaze of those eyes forever. "I have breakfast for us." Bringing the tray over, he waited for Cembran to sit up before setting the tray on his lap, then undressed and got back into bed.

After breakfast and some morning snuggling, they got cleaned up, dressed, packed, and checked out of the hotel. Travis had booked them into a small farm hotel just over the ridge from the satyr village. The hour-long drive was spectacular as they passed through beautifully mountainous terrain with its jagged, rocky peaks covered with snow.

Arriving at the hotel, Cembran was surprised that the small inn was, in addition to a hotel, an actual working farm. "I thought you'd be comfortable here," Travis said. The lady of the house showed them their small but comfortable room. Everyone at the farm was welcoming and made them feel at ease. Once they were settled, Cembran went out to visit with the animals, while Travis spoke to their hostess, inquiring about a path into the mountains, explaining that they wanted to do some hiking.

She was pleasant and gave him directions, but cautioned him, "Stay out of the mountains at night. We sometimes hear strange noises on the wind and see strange things." Travis assured her they would stay close, thinking to himself, *"If you only knew."*

Late in the evening, Travis and Cembran dressed in dark clothes and headed up the path toward the location of the Bacchanal. They had agreed that Cembran would confront his father alone. Travis wasn't happy about it, but he had reluctantly agreed to Cembran's wishes. Travis would join Cembran if things got out of hand or if Cembran signaled.

It took them about an hour to reach the edge of the clearing. The scene that greeted them was almost beyond Travis's belief. The clearing was a large oval with a huge bonfire in the middle, casting flickering shadows on the surrounding trees. Scattered around the edge of the clearing were tables overflowing with every food imaginable, barrels of wine, and casks of beer. Satyrs were milling around eating and drinking. Some of the men looked like Cembran, with horns and a tail, but most were full satyrs with larger horns, tails, legs that looked goat-like and hooves instead of feet. Most of the men also had dark, curly-haired beards. The women looked human, with no discernable satyr characteristics. Cembran whispered very softly, "Only the males display the characteristic satyr traits. Satyr women look human." Very few of the men in attendance were wearing clothes, and those who were had on loose tunics or open shirts. Most of the women were dressed in loose, simply cut dresses decorated in exuberant colors and embroidered in wild, flowing patterns. Travis could feel the temperature rise as they approached the clearing. The October night had been quite cool, but the closer they'd gotten to the clearing, the warmer it became. It was like a bubble of warmth enclosed the space and surrounding forest. Travis would have to ask Cembran about it later.

At the edge of the clearing was a dais with a large chair. Seated in the chair was a huge satyr. Travis assumed that this was Cembran's father. He had horns about eight inches long, a long, full beard, and very curly black hair. Travis knew where Cembran got the ringlets he loved so much. The Baccharist's chest was covered with dark, curly hair. His torso looked strong, and at his hips, his body changed to that of a goat with powerful legs and hooves. He looked extremely intimidating and menacing.

As they watched the scene, music started playing and the satyrs started dancing a wild, uninhibited dance. As the dance progressed, couples could be seen disappearing into the woods. Cembran again whispered very softly, "They're leaving to have sex. That will occur throughout the night. Some will have sex five, even six, or seven times before morning."

Travis could hear the nervousness in Cembran's voice as he spoke. Travis turned toward Cembran, stroked his cheek, and kissed him gently. "I love you."

"I love you too." Taking a deep breath, he squeezed Travis's shoulder, "Time to face my father." With those words, he stood up straight and tall. Travis could see Cembran's horns peeking through his hair. With a smile at Travis, he stepped from the cover of the trees and toward the clearing, strong and confident.

Cembran strode to the center of the clearing, standing in direct line of sight between the fire and his father, and waited. His father's attention was momentarily diverted to the side of the clearing, but when his head turned, he saw Cembran looking straight at him, unmoving. A broad smile formed on his father's face. "Cembran!" He stood up and signaled. The music stopped immediately and the clearing quickly became still. "Cembran, welcome home! I thought you might come back. It's good to see you."

"Is it?" Cembran's tone was ice.

"Of course it is. I'm your father; I'm thrilled that you have returned to us." He signaled again and a striking woman glided from the edge of the clearing to where Cembran was standing. "Cembran, this is Chrystianne." Cembran furrowed his brow, wondering what his father was up to. "You two will make beautiful, strong satyr babies." The crowd murmured slightly.

Cembran was absolutely furious. "No!" he spat vehemently. The woman stopped approaching. "I came back to tell you to leave us alone! You were a horrible father then and you are still a horrible father, and I have no intention of marrying any woman, satyr or otherwise!" The clearing became silent except for the sound of the fire.

"You will stay and you will." The Baccharist signaled and two large men stepped from the side of the clearing.

Cembran gave a signal of his own and Travis stepped into the clearing pointing at the two satyrs advancing on Cembran. "Stop! This is between them!" Travis reached Cembran's side, placing his arms around his waist. The two men halted. "Can't fight your own battles, Baccharist?" The two men stepped back to the edge of the clearing.

"Puny human." Cembran's father drew himself to his full height. "This does not concern you!"

"That's where you're wrong. If it concerns Cembran, the person I love, then it concerns me." Travis stared at Cembran's father. "I may be a puny human, but I was strong enough to keep you from getting what you wanted from me after you attacked my dreams for months." The crowd murmured and Travis knew he had to get them on his side. "You, Baccharist, are nothing but a bully and a thief who steals the dreams and thoughts of others. You stole Cembran's private thoughts and you tried to steal mine." Travis could see Cembran's father was seething. "You're a tyrant who terrorizes your own village for power and your own enjoyment, and worst of all you're a rotten father." The crowd was buzzing softly and Travis could tell he was hitting a chord with them. He turned to the others. "How many of you have felt the brunt of his controlling, tyrannical nature? Who among you has he attacked and stolen your thoughts and dreams? After all, he stole his own son's."

The Baccharist signaled again and a few men stepped into the clearing toward them. Travis knew he had to act fast. "What, not able to fight your own battles? Scared? Afraid of the truth? Need your minions to do your dirty work for you!" Travis made sure his voice carried all through the clearing.

Travis could see the rage building in Cembran's father, but he could also see his confusion. He signaled with his head and the men stopped advancing. Travis knew that his only hope was to attack Cembran's father's honor.

Cembran's father pointed at Travis, his voice seething with rage, "I challenge you to the Traumsinn!" The crowd gasped and the murmurs started again. Travis could tell they were shocked.

Travis whispered to Cembran, "What's the Traumsinn?"

Cembran whispered, "It's a challenge of minds, like a dream challenge."

Cembran's father continued, "My prize is Cembran. If I win, he stays in the village, marries the woman of my choice, and the human goes home alone."

Travis spoke up, cutting off Cembran's father, "If I win, the Baccharist steps down and is banished from all satyr contact for the rest of his life."

Cembran's father knew he was losing control of the situation and tried to take it back, "I'll set the terms."

Travis cut him off again, "The terms are set! Do you agree or are you afraid?" He knew he'd upped the stakes for Cembran's father. Now he had a lot to lose.

Cembran's father agreed, "The Traumsinn will take place here at midnight tomorrow! No one here is to help him."

"Except Cembran! But no one is to help you at all!" Travis was starting to get a kick out of flustering Cembran's father. "Midnight tomorrow!"

Travis and Cembran walked to the edge of the clearing, past the people gathered there, into the forest, and back to the hotel. As they walked, the only sound was the wind and their footsteps on the forest floor. Travis kept looking at Cembran, but his face was set and he said nothing as they walked. Once they reached the hotel, they very quietly headed up to their room.

In the room, Travis collapsed on the bed shaking and visibly upset. Cembran was vibrating, his anger overwhelming him. "What in hell were you thinking? If you lose, I'll have to stay here." Cembran wasn't shouting, but by his tone, Travis knew he was barely controlling his emotions. Travis had never seen Cembran angry before and his first instinct was to lash out, but he couldn't. The words died on his lips as

Cembran continued venting his anger using words Travis didn't understand. Cembran paced around the room like a cat hunting its prey before turning to Travis. His anger died instantly once he saw the anguish and pain on Travis's face. "I'm sorry, Lemmle."

Cembran sat on the bed next to Travis and they cradled each other. "I know." A tear rolled down Travis's cheek, "He issued the challenge and I didn't know what to do. If I lose, which is likely since I don't know anything about this Traumsinn, at least you'll be alive and well." The tears came unbidden now as they held each other. Travis sniffled, "If by some miracle I win, you're free and so is the village."

"What we need to do is find out what we can about the Traumsinn. I've never seen one, but no one can help us directly."

Travis smiled as he wiped his face. "He did say that no one *there* could help me."

"Then we should find out if Gathod knows anything about the Traumsinn."

Travis kissed Cembran, "Good idea." He got out his phone and called the number of the cell phone he'd gotten Cembran. They had left it for Gathod in case of emergencies. *"Please answer,"* Travis thought to himself.

Gathod answered the phone very tentatively, "Hello?"

"Gathod, it's Travis."

"How is it going? Did you confront Cembran's father?"

"Yes." Travis put the phone on speaker so Cembran could listen and explained what had happened and about the Traumsinn challenge.

"The Traumsinn is a dream or thought challenge. Between satyrs, both of them open their minds and assault each other with images and emotions, trying to get the other to close his mind. However, with a human the rules are different. Cembran's father will place images in your mind, probably painful, highly emotional images that generate a strong negative emotional response. He'll try to use any emotional insecurity you might have against you, cast doubt about the people you love, any fears you have, any jealousies you harbor."

"How do I fight him?"

"What you'll need to do is turn the images he uses against him. If he shows you death, you concentrate on birth. He wins if you ask him to stop, or if you collapse or lose consciousness. You win if you last until the sun comes up, or if the spectators declare you the winner."

"Spectators?"

"Yes, every satyr at the Traumsinn will be able to see the images he places in your mind and your response to them. If he tries to cheat everyone will know. So play to the spectators − if you win them over, he loses. Now, there is some good news: he doesn't know you very well. While he can still conjure up some very powerful images, he has less ammunition that he would have with someone he knew."

"Gathod, I…." Travis sounded frightened and unsure of himself. Cembran rubbed Travis's back, letting him know he was there.

"Listen to me. You have to trust in yourself and what you know, no matter what. While I can't help you, I will be thinking positively of you and Cembran."

"Thank you, Gathod."

Travis hung up the phone, and after cleaning up, they both climbed into bed. Cembran was scared; Travis was nervous and uptight. "He's going to try to use every painful memory you have against you."

Pulling Cembran close, he replied, "Then I need to think good thoughts." Travis turned out the light. Cembran curled next to him, holding him tight. Eventually they both fell asleep, clinging to each other as if they expected to be separated at any time.

In the middle of the night, Cembran bolted upright in the bed. Travis was still asleep next to him, "Travis, Travis!" Cembran shook him awake.

"What is it, Lamb?" he yawned.

"I remembered! It came to me in a dream."

Travis brain wasn't functioning. "What came to you?"

"The name! In my dream, I heard my mother say the name, Vindionum, to get my father to stop attacking her." Travis was awake now.

Travis kissed his lover appreciatively, "Thank you so much, Lamb. How did you remember?"

"I dreamed the answer. The scene replayed in my dream, but this time, I heard my mother say the name. When she did, my father immediately backed down."

Travis was quiet, thinking for a minute as he slipped his arm around Cembran, "How do we use it?"

Cembran shrugged his shoulders and shook his head. "Ask Gathod in the morning, or you might call Brock's parents. They may have an idea."

"I'm afraid to go to sleep. In case he...."

"This I know - he can't get to you now. The invocation of the Traumsinn closes your mind to him until the challenge." They snuggled back under the soft, warm bedding, kissing and holding each other. The thought kept going through Travis's mind that this could be the last time he got to do this.

Chapter Fifteen

Tuesday night just before midnight, Travis and Cembran were at the edge of the clearing. Unlike last night, the clearing was dark except for the lights carried by the satyrs who lined the edge of the circle. Cembran's father was standing toward one side, looking confident and ready for the contest. Earlier in the day, Travis had called Brock, as well as Jim and Sue, but they had no additional advice regarding the Traumsinn or how to use the name Cembran had remembered. They did all tell him that they wished him luck and that their thoughts were with him.

Travis and Cembran stepped into the clearing; the low talking and murmuring that could be heard died away quickly. Travis took his place, facing Cembran's father. He turned to Cembran, pulling him into a bone-crushing hug. "I love you. No matter what happens, I love you," he said, his fingers combing through Cembran's hair.

Tears ran down Cembran's cheeks, wetting the shoulder of Travis's shirt. "I love you. I'll always love you." Travis released Cembran from the hug. Placing his hands on both of his cheeks, Travis pulled him into a searing kiss.

Cembran's father sneered. "How touching," his voice dripping with sarcasm.

Cembran slowly pulled away from Travis and stepped to the edge of the clearing, making sure he was in Travis's line of sight. Travis turned to face Cembran's father. The clock in the village in the valley below started to strike the hour. When the last strike faded, Travis was standing in the house he'd grown up in. He had just finished telling his parents that he was gay. His father was yelling, "No child of mine is going to behave that way." Travis's mother was sitting in a chair weeping into her hands. "See, you've broken your mother's heart."

Travis was immediately assaulted by the pain those memories released. He knelt at his mother's side trying to explain, "I'm the same person. I haven't changed. I still love you, Mom." Slowly, Travis stood up and faced his father. After staring at each other, Travis went to pack his bags and left the house. The next time he'd see his father would be at his mother's funeral.

Travis realized he'd been floating on waves of grief and regret, remembering that it was part of the Traumsinn. It had been so real, like he was there. Concentrating hard, the scene changed to his father's hospital room. His father placed his hand on Travis's neck, saying, "I'm sorry, Travis." Those simple words of apology and Travis's simple words of forgiveness, "It's okay, Dad," and the regret and pain from the earlier images were gone. Travis opened his eyes and stared at Cembran's father.

Travis was sitting in Cembran's main room and Cembran was telling him that he couldn't be with him. "You have to go. There are things about me that could hurt you." Dejected, Travis left. He remembered that evening very well and he almost laughed as Cembran's father conjured up the images. He fast-forwarded the memory to later that evening, after Cembran had explained about being a satyr, when he'd pounded on Cembran's door demanding, "I have to know!" The kiss that followed caused murmurs through the crowd. Travis then focused his mind on some clear, simple words - "That was the first night we made love." He then cleared his mind; he wasn't going to show them those images.

Travis was becoming tired and he realized that the Traumsinn was draining his physical as well as emotional strength. He concentrated on taking deep, cleansing breaths.

He was subjected to some of the most disturbing images he'd ever seen. Image after image of gruesome death, people torn apart by dogs, shot, blown into pieces in explosions. Blood was everywhere. The last image tapped into one of Travis's greatest fears; Cembran was lying in a bed, bleeding. Travis could tell he was getting weaker and weaker. He could see him, but he couldn't reach him; an invisible force kept him away. Travis could hear his own voice shouting for Cembran. Then someone came by Cembran's bed and pulled the sheet over his face. Travis was nearly consumed by grief and rage.

Focusing his attention from the images in his mind, he looked across the clearing at Cembran's father, who had a self-satisfied smile on his face. Suddenly, Gathod's words came to Travis's mind and he gathered his powers of concentration. The image in his mind transformed to the sheep barn. Cembran was holding a dying lamb and Travis comforted him. Gathod reached to the lamb and concentrated. "Baahh." The lamb moved and licked Cembran's face before squirming from his arms and running into the field to its mother. When Travis looked up this time, the self-satisfied look was gone from the Baccharist's face.

Travis was feeling very tired; the challenge was definitely taking a toll on him. He looked at Cembran's loving face for support and felt a surge of energy radiate through him as though a reservoir containing inner peace and strength had been released, and he could almost feel Gathod, Jim, and Sue sending him their good thoughts, too.

Cembran and Gathod were together in a small shelter. Cembran reached to Gathod, slowly removing his clothes, before slipping off his own clothing. They kissed deeply and lovingly as their bodies moved together. Gathod entered Cembran slowly and gently, their union spirited, quiet, their passion evident. Travis was filled with feelings of jealousy. He'd known about Cembran and Gathod, but to see them together was almost too much. Cembran and Gathod's lovemaking reached a frenzy as they climaxed together.

It took all of Travis's self-control to keep from crying out. "*Trust in what you know*," – the words came unbidden to his mind. He took a deep breath and concentrated. The scene morphed to a dark night by the lake. Travis and Cembran were making love by the fire, the night of their Bacchanal. Travis was slipping off Cembran's clothes. As the memories of that night flooded through Travis, the jealousy evaporated; Cembran loved him and only him. Travis concentrated, blocking out all other thoughts. The memories were fresh, happy, passionate, and extremely strong. Their words of love echoed through Travis and across the clearing as everyone in attendance witnessed the love and passion that he and Cembran shared. The declarations of love and devotion brought some of the satyrs to tears. As the memory of their lovemaking ended, Travis concentrated hard, thinking, *"He is my passion, my love, and my life. He is mine and I am his, forever and always. Period."* Travis's eyes were closed, his concentration taking all his mental energy.

A hand gripped his shoulder and Travis jumped at the touch. Opening his eyes and looking around, he saw many of the satyrs wiping their eyes and smiling. One of the men had his hand on Travis's shoulder. The man said nothing, but stood nearby. Soon, other people in the crowd moved forward, standing behind and around Travis, filling his side of the clearing. Travis looked at Cembran and saw that he was smiling broadly.

Cembran took a step forward, then another, and finally ran into Travis's arms. The minute their lips touched the satyrs cheered and applauded. "You won, Travis. You used our love to defeat him." Travis kissed Cembran again and again, crushing his lips to his, as he lifted him off the ground.

After putting Cembran down, Travis's attention was drawn to Cembran's father, standing alone on the other end of the clearing. He knew he'd lost, but he stood erect and tall as he watched the celebration. Travis moved away from the crowd and walked toward Cembran's father. As he approached he held out his hand as an offering of peace. Cembran's father grimaced and turned away. Travis shrugged, turned, and started walking back toward Cembran.

"Travis, look out!"

Travis turned quickly to see Cembran's father charging at him. His head was down and his horns pointed at Travis. Travis pointed and yelled, "Vindionum, freeze!"

Cembran's father froze in mid-stride; not a muscle moved. His eyes didn't even blink. Cembran stepped over to his father, waving a hand in front of his face. "What happened?"

Travis shrugged as he watched the frozen figure. "I guess that the name *was* powerful."

Cembran's attention was drawn away from his father, "Travis, look." He pointed to the center of the clearing. As they watched, a mist formed, thickened, and started to glow. The mist vibrated and shifted as a figure coalesced. Everyone watched the figure as the mist evaporated. The figure was definitely a satyr, with all the satyr characteristics – horns, tail, goat legs, and cloven feet. He also had a wreath of grape leaves in his hair and a musical pipe around his neck. He stood about seven feet tall with broad shoulders and powerful muscles.

"Bacchus." Cembran whispered in Travis's ear.

Travis watched as the figure stepped in front of Cembran's father and touched him on the shoulder. He collapsed onto the ground and slowly got to his feet. "Darthan," the figure's voice boomed across the clearing, "Your time is over and you must now move on." The figure then turned to where Travis stood with his arm around Cembran's waist. "Travis, I am Bacchus. My time is short, but—" His words stopped as he looked Travis up and down, nodding his head. "Yes, you are truly worthy."

"Worthy of what? I don't understand."

"You will." Turning to Cembran, the god asked, "Does he make you happy?"

Cembran nodded, "Yes, very much."

"Then be happy with my blessing." Bacchus stepped back to Darthan and the mist formed again. When the mist cleared both Bacchus and Cembran's father were gone.

The clearing was silent as everyone digested what had happened. One by one, they drifted out of the clearing and back toward their homes. Travis looked at Cembran, unsure how he would react. Cembran wiped away all doubt as he threw his arms around Travis's shoulder, his needy lips pressing to his lover's. "Thank you."

"I was worried you'd… I mean he is your father."

Cembran kissed Travis again. "He stopped being a father to me long ago. Besides you didn't do anything, Bacchus did, and he said you were worthy!" Cembran's voice was full of excitement. "Besides, he gave us his blessing. That means a lot, particularly to satyrs."

"But, how will they know? I mean who's going to tell them."

"No one. They'll just know." Cembran took Travis's hand and led him into the woods and up onto one of the mountains that surrounded the clearing. It didn't take them long to reach the top, where there was a small stone shelter. Cembran led Travis inside. In the back of the shelter was a secured wooden box containing bedding and blankets. Cembran spread them out on the ground. "Come join me," Cembran asked, laying on the bedding, "Make love to me. Show me why you're worthy."

"I hope I'm always worthy of you, Lamb." Travis slipped off his clothes as Cembran scrambled out of his. Lying down next to Cembran, Travis pulled a heavy blanket over them against the cool mountain air. "I love you, Cembran, and I hope I always make you happy."

Cembran threaded his arms around Travis's neck, pulling him in for a kiss. "I love you, Travis, and I know you'll make me happy." Cembran's kiss curled Travis's toes with its intensity and passion. He returned those kisses, adding his own love. Their bodies melded together as though they were made for one another. Their kisses fueled their passion. Cembran moaned, "I need you, Travis," as he lifted his legs to his chest, "I want you."

Travis licked his fingers before working two of them into Cembran, watching for any signs of discomfort. All he saw was Cembran's desire and love shining on that angelic face. Travis withdrew his fingers and positioned himself at Cembran's entrance. Pressing in for entry, he whispered, "Show me, Love." As he slipped inside, Cembran's small horns appeared at his hair line. Travis bent forward kissing Cembran deeply as he buried himself deep inside. "I love you."

Travis's movements were measured and slow; he wanted this to last. Cembran writhed and moved with his steady, mind-blowing rhythm. Their bodies were hot, skin searing to the touch even in the cool mountain air. "I love you, Travis, my knight in shining armor." Pressure built inside and Travis came hard, Cembran's name echoing out over the mountains. Cembran's climax quickly followed and the

Travis's name was carried by the breeze to the valley and mountains beyond.

Darkness still covered the mountain when Travis woke, Cembran curled around him, sleeping contentedly. Gently, Travis shook his shoulder. "Lamb, we should get back to the hotel before they send out a search party for us."

Cembran's lips found his, arms pulling them back together. "Love you." Slowly in the dark, they dressed and stowed the bedding and blankets back in the box. The sun was just peeking over the horizon as they headed down the mountain toward the hotel. The family was waking as they arrived. Travis and Cembran went into the barn and started hauling water for the animals. When the family's children entered the barn, they thought Cembran and Travis had gotten up early and wanted to spend some time with the animals.

After working for an hour or so, they headed up to their room. Travis undressed and climbed back into bed, holding the covers open as an invitation. Cembran stripped and got into bed, snuggling close, both of them falling back asleep for another few hours.

Chapter Sixteen

A knock on their door woke Cembran and Travis and a soft voice
called, "Breakfast in half an hour." Travis rolled over and looked
at the clock. They'd been asleep for just a little while. He got
out of bed, padding into the bathroom to clean up and shower. Their
room was unusual in that it was the only guest room in the house with
its own bathroom; the other guest rooms shared a bathroom.

The water was steaming under the shower as Travis felt a pair of
hands wrap around his waist. "Mind if I join you?" Cembran stepped
in with him. Lips found lips and bodies pressed together as the water
cascaded over them. Cembran stepped back, soaping his hands,
washing Travis's body. Those hands that worked so hard on the farm
felt so good on Travis's body that he felt his knees going weak. Once
he was rinsed and clean, Travis washed Cembran in return, stroking all
that hot, smooth skin.

Travis felt himself reacting and Cembran stroked him with his
hand, bringing his cock to full strength. "I don't think we have time,
Lamb." Cembran's eyes danced as he continued his slow stroking.
"You're just mean, Love," Travis scolded playfully.

Both of them rinsed off and stepped out of the shower. "Travis, I
was wondering – at the house, I just have a bathtub. Can we get a
shower? I'm starting to see the beauty of them." Travis wrapped
Cembran in a large towel, quickly rubbing his body dry, before drying
himself.

"That would be wonderful. I think I can help with that." They
finished their morning routines, dressed, and headed to the dining room
for breakfast.

Travis had finished his breakfast, waiting for Cembran, when a small, shy-looking man was escorted into the dining room. He approached, "Are you Mr. Travis?"

Travis nodded, "Yes. Can I help you?"

The young man was shifting from foot to foot, obviously a little nervous. "I'm Dovino." He looked around the room; everyone was watching him. "Can I speak with you and Cembran?" His eyes darted around the room, "Alone."

Travis turned to his lover, "We'll go outside." He touched Cembran's shoulder as he followed Dovino out of the hotel. Cembran nodded silently.

Once they were outside, Dovino became less nervous and more animated, "I was sent to extend an invitation to you both from everyone in the village." Cembran joined them, having finished his breakfast. "We know that your visit here is short, but we would be honored to have you stay in our village." Travis had been wondering what the reaction of the satyrs would be and this looked like a good sign.

"Cembran, what do you think?" This decision was his. If he wanted to go, that was fine, but if he didn't, Travis would take him wherever he wanted.

Cembran looked at Travis and then back at Dovino, "We'll come to the village." So they went up to their room to get what they'd need for the day, met Dovino outside the hotel, and followed him back. At the top of the mountain pass, Dovino took a horn from his pack and blew a long note before leading them down into the village. Travis was amazed – there was no sign of the small houses until they were practically in the middle of them. The tall trees and rugged terrain completely blocked any view of the village. Once there, tall trees seemed to form almost a natural roof over it

"This is incredible." Travis was overwhelmed. It was as though time had stood still. The buildings were small, well-built, sturdy structures that looked like they hadn't changed in hundreds of years. There were no cars or any other modern influences for that matter. Everything was as it had always been. Travis took Cembran's hand as they walked down the narrow main street, with its small shops, village hall, and cobbled road. As they passed, each door opened and satyrs spilled into the street, smiling and waving. Soon a throng of people was waving and cheering as they walked to the far end of the village. "Dovino, where are you leading us?" Travis asked, as more and more people came forward to shake their hands.

"I'm taking you to my father." Dovino led them to a house a little larger that some of the others. A satyr came out of the house, walking confidently to Travis and Cembran. Dovino made introductions, "This is my father, Darifo."

The young satyr then stood next to his father, "Welcome to our village, we are very pleased you could come. I'm Cembran's cousin."

Cembran smiled, "We are pleased you invited us." He stepped forward and embraced his cousin tightly. After a brief hesitation, Darifo returned the hug. When the two of them separated, they both seemed very pleased.

"Would you like a tour of the village?"

Travis was still looking around him, trying to take it all in. "That would be incredible. This is the most beautiful place I've ever seen." Darifo led them back down the narrow main street, pointing out each building or house. To Travis, the village looked like something out of a history book or maybe a fairy tale.

Darifo led them to what appeared to be the largest house in the village. It was still small by modern standards, with what looked like four or five rooms. "This was where the Baccharist lived."

Travis immediately turned to Cembran and he noticed the sad look on his face. "Is this where you grew up?" Cembran nodded. "Do you want to go inside?" Cembran didn't answer or move; he just stood and stared at the house. Finally, he moved down the small walk. Opening the door, Cembran stepped inside. Travis followed right behind him. Darifo and Dovino stayed outside and waited.

The house was rustic, but very well built. Simple, graceful, furniture was placed in the living and dining areas. The walls were covered with plaster and painted bright cheerful colors. There was little decoration or ornamentation anywhere. Cembran looked around the rooms and then headed into what looked like one of the bedrooms.

Travis followed, placing his hand on Cembran's shoulder as he said, "This was Fartham's sleeping room." There was a bed and a chest in the corner. Cembran opened the chest, but it was empty. Disappointment was written on his face as he looked around the room again before pushing the bed away from the wall. "Travis would you help me?" Where the bed had been, Cembran indicated a floorboard with a knot in it. "Put your finger on the knot and press the lever you'll feel on the left."

Surprised, Travis put a finger into the hole and pressed a small lever. Cembran then lifted one edge of the board and it came out of the floor. "Fartham built this when we were kids. We used it to hide things from our father." Inside the small compartment were two cloth bags. Travis gently lifted out both bags and handed them to Cembran. One was heavy but the other was quite light.

Cembran placed the heavy bag on the bed and opened the light one. Inside were a few small trinkets, including a pendant like the one Cembran wore and a few pieces of jewelry. Cembran placed the jewelry on the bed and started to cry softly. "These were my mother's and I couldn't find them when I left. Fartham must have found them and hidden them, knowing my father would sell them." He put the items back in the bag and then opened the other one, dumping the contents on the bed. Travis's eyes bugged from his head as shiny gold coins fell from the bag. Dozens of them. Travis picked one up and looked at it. He had never seen a coin like it. There was a date, clearly readable - 1699. Cembran carefully gathered up the coins, placing them back in the pouch. He then placed both bags in his pack.

Heading down the hall, he went into the last room in the house. This was a larger bedroom, which had obviously been his father's. This room had a larger bed and a larger chest as well. The room was as neat as a pin. Cembran opened the chest and went through it. It was filled with clothes and a few personal objects. He carefully emptied the contents onto the bed. When the chest was empty, he tapped the bottom the chest, before lifting the false bottom out to reveal a small hiding space. Inside was a little bag. Cembran pulled out the bag and handed it to Travis, who opened it and found inside even more gold coins. Travis held the bag while Cembran put the bottom back and packed the clothes back in the chest. Travis handed the coins back to Cembran, but he shook his head, "Those are yours. You defeated him."

"Cembran, they belong to you along with everything else here."

His lover shook his head, "I can't take anything that belonged to him. Besides, I want you to have them; my knight in shining armor." Cembran moved to Travis and kissed him deeply. "It feels good to kiss you in this room, to be free of him in every way."

Travis put the bag of coins in the pack and they headed out of the house. Darifo and Dovino were waiting for them in front of the house. When Cembran and Travis joined them Darifo asked, "What are you going to do with the house, Cembran?"

Cembran looked at his lover, "I don't know. I don't want anything to do with what was his."

Travis hugged him, "Lamb, why don't you give it to the village. I'm sure they'll find a good use for it. Maybe there's a deserving family that needs a home." Cembran nodded and hugged him tight.

Darifo was smiling a huge smile, "Would you join our family for lunch? And after lunch Dovino will go back to the hotel, settle your bill, make arrangements for your car, and bring your things back here. You can stay with us until it's time for you to leave."

Travis returned his smile, "Thank you, that would be very nice, but we don't want to be any trouble."

"Trouble? You're family. It would be a pleasure. Come, let's have lunch before I fall over." Darifo laughed heartily as the walked back down the street to his home.

The next four days were a whirl. They stayed with Darifo and his wonderful wife Tona. She mothered them both incessantly; Travis grew to like her a great deal. Dovino was their constant companion. He seemed to worship them both and wanted to go everywhere they went. During that time, they ate each meal at a different house in the village; everyone wanted to meet them. The more time they spent there, the more Cembran and Travis felt the sense of community that permeated this place. Everyone helped each other without thinking or expecting something in return. One morning, Darifo's neighbor was working to repair his roof. An hour later there were six men working with him, including Cembran, and the roof was repaired before lunch.

The day before they were to leave, Cembran woke Travis early. "Would you come with me to my mother's grave?"

Travis kissed his love tenderly, "Of course, Lamb." Travis then realized the sun wasn't yet up and Cembran was already dressed and ready to leave. Travis dressed quickly and the two of them left the house with their packs quietly. "Why so early and why do we need two nearly empty packs?" he asked. Daylight was just beginning to appear.

Cembran whispered, "I don't want any watchful eyes. Trust me." Travis nodded as they walked down a narrow path to a small clearing away from the village. The clearing was filled with small, lovingly tended grave markers. Some were very faded and barely readable. Cembran walked through the cemetery and went directly to his mother's grave. The stone was still legible, but just barely: Isabella Bacch, gestorben 21 Juli 1726, 68 Jahre.

Cembran stood silently facing the stone for many minutes, his arm around Travis's waist. He then removed his pack and took out a small shovel and a piece of cloth. Behind his mother's grave marker, he bent down and started digging, being very careful to roll back the grass and place the dirt on the cloth. After about half an hour, he had cleared the dirt from the top of a wooden box. "Travis, the box is rotten. I need your pack." Cembran lifted the lid off the box in pieces, carefully placing them on the pile of dirt. Inside the box were several oilcloth bags. Cembran gently lifted them out and placed them one by one in Travis's pack. Then he filled his own pack. Once the box was empty, Cembran filled in the box with the pieces of lid, sticks, and leaves, filled in the hole with the dirt, and replaced the pieces of grass.

When Travis picked up his pack, he was surprised how heavy it was. "This weighs a ton."

Cembran laughed, "No, only about sixty pounds." Travis smiled. They walked back to the village hand in hand, looking for all the world, like they'd only been out for an early morning stroll. When they got back to the house, they quietly went to the room they'd been given and stowed their packs. Lucky for them, Darifo and his family weren't early risers. Sitting on the edge of the bed, Cembran asked, "Now that we have all this, what do we do with it?"

Travis leaned close to Cembran, "When we get back to Zurich tomorrow morning, we'll find a friendly Swiss banker. He'll be able to help us." Travis pulled Cembran onto the bed, kissing him and working off his shirt as he straddled his hips. Cembran hissed Travis's mouth as fingers circled and lightly pinched his nipple. Nimble fingers worked open Cembran's pants, freeing his throbbing erection. "Love you."

Cembran whispered, "Love you, too," into Travis's mouth as his lips were kissed hard. Fingers wrapped around Cembran's stiff, pulsing erection, the thumb rubbing the base of the head. Cembran moaned quietly into Travis's mouth. "Want to feel you." Travis lifted his body off Cembran's and pulled off his shirt before lowering himself again, pressing their chests together as their lips explored, and Travis's fingers stroked and teased Cembran's cock.

Cembran's fingers worked at Travis's pants, finally able to get them open. Travis moved away from the bed and pulled off Cembran's pants, before shoving his own to his ankles and stepping out of them. Travis returned to the bed and took Cembran into his mouth, working his tongue around the head of his erection. "Does that feel good?" Cembran nodded. "How about this?" Travis lifted Cembran's legs to his chest and thrust his tongue into Cembran's tight, puckered opening.

"Yes, that's so good." He licked, probed, and sucked on that tight muscle, opening Cembran, getting him ready. "Travis, please." Travis shifted on the bed, positioning the head of his cock at Cembran's entrance and slowly pressing forward. Cembran's body opened for him, joining them together. Travis slowly withdrew and pushed back inside. Leaning forward, they kissed ravenously, moving together.

Travis withdrew from Cembran and lay down on the bed next to him. "Ride me?" Cembran let out a little whoop as he straddled Travis and sank onto him with a sigh. Cembran was like a man possessed, bouncing on Travis with abandon, pulling himself up and then pounding himself down onto his lover again and again. Travis wrapped his fingers around Cembran's cock, pulling in time with his frenzied thrusts until the movements became ragged and he came with a soft cry on Travis's stomach and hand. Travis thrust deep and spilled himself into his lover.

Completely spent, Cembran collapsed onto Travis, kissing him deeply as their bodies entwined of their own accord. Cembran's breathing evened out and soon he was snoring lightly. Travis smiled as he allowed his eyes to close and he quickly dozed off as well.

That evening, the village held a celebration. Travis and Cembran were guests of honor as the town elected one of Cembran's cousins as the new Baccharist. Farbran seemed like a good, level-headed man. Cembran's name had been put forward, of course, but he'd declined. "You should choose the best person, not select a Baccharist based on family or tradition." The village also decided to separate the duties of running the village and running the monthly Bacchanal, so they elected Darifo the village's first mayor. The entire village sang, danced, and celebrated well into the night.

When it was time to go to bed, Travis could see the longing look on Cembran's face and he knew Cembran would miss the village. They'd both found a level of acceptance here that neither of them had felt before in their lives and it felt good.

Chapter Seventeen

"Travis, I'm going to miss this place." Cembran's voice was quiet. "I wish we could stay longer." They were cuddled together in the small bedroom of Darifo's house. Today they were leaving the village, going back to Zurich. Tomorrow they would catch their flight home. "I mean, I'm ready to go home, but I'll miss this place and the community."

Travis's arms snaked around Cembran's shoulders, pulling him close, their cheeks touching. "I know what you mean." Sounds could be heard coming from the kitchen and Travis knew Tona was already up, making breakfast for them. Reluctantly, Travis got out of bed, cleaned up, and dressed. While Cembran was getting ready, Travis completed their packing. By the time they were ready for breakfast, everything was ready for their hike through the mountain pass back to their car, which was still parked at the farm hotel.

During breakfast, a steady stream of villagers stopped by to wish Cembran and Travis a happy and safe journey and to congratulate the new mayor on his election. After breakfast, Darifo took them aside saying, "Dovino will help you get back to your car."

Travis smiled, "That isn't necessary, I'm sure he has things to do."

Darifo looked concerned, "He requested that I let him accompany you this morning. I think he wants to talk to you." Darifo hugged Cembran, lightly kissing him on both cheeks, "Good journey, Cembran." He then hugged Travis, kissing him on both cheeks as well, "Good journey, Travis. You are both welcome here in the village any time and we hope you'll visit us again soon."

Cembran clasped Darifo's hand, "Thank you, we will be back to visit." Tona entered the room, hugged and kissed them both, and gave them a packed lunch for their trip. Dovino followed his mother, looking a little nervous. After some final goodbyes, they donned their now-heavy packs and between the three of them carried the remaining luggage. Slowly they walked down the main street of the village returning waves and well-wishes.

A half hour later they reached the top of the pass through the mountains, taking a few minutes to rest. Travis sat next to Cembran, pulling him close as they looked back toward the village. They could see no trace of the small homes and other buildings.

Travis smiled and watched as Dovino nervously paced, "Dovino, is everything all right?"

The young satyr sat down on a rock near Travis and Cembran. "I wanted to say…." Travis waited for him to go on. "I think I'm like you and Cembran." Once the words were out of his mouth, the floodgates opened. "I don't know what to do. I haven't told my parents and I don't know how they'll feel about it."

Travis stood and put his hand on Dovino's shoulder, "Talk to your mother and father. They deserve to know who you are, and it may be easier than you think." Dovino looked up at Travis. "Your father told me he thought you wanted to talk to us. I think he may already suspect."

"But, how could he? I mean, I've never been with anyone yet." His face showed confusion.

"Your parents love and care for you and they know you better than you think."

Dovino seemed relieved and actually smiled. "When I get back, I'll talk to them." He was quiet for a few minutes, "I was wondering if I could come to America to visit you sometime."

Cembran smiled brightly, "Of course, Dovino. We would love to have you visit. You're always welcome." Dovino seemed overjoyed. Picking up the luggage, they walked the rest of the way down the path toward the car.

An hour later, Cembran and Travis had said goodbye to Dovino, packed the car, made sure their hotel bill was settled, and were on the road heading toward Zurich. They reached the city a little before noon, checked into their hotel, and found a small café for lunch before heading to one of the large banks in the financial district.

Walking into the bank was an experience. The lobby was immense, almost palatial. Travis and Cembran were still in their traveling clothes and looked a little rumpled, particularly with the packs they were carrying. A banker in an expensive-looking suit asked if he could help them. Travis told him that they would like to open an account and make a deposit. The banker directed them to a desk, but Travis shook his head, "We need to go to a private area."

The banker's eyebrows rose slightly, but directed them to a small room off the lobby. "How can I help you gentlemen?"

Cembran spoke a little nervously, "We'd like to make a large deposit in gold." He took off his pack, set it on the table, and started taking out the bags of gold coins. The banker's eyes briefly went wide as bag after bag of gold was removed and opened.

The banker, who introduced himself as Heinrich Mueller, indicated the coins, "May I?" Cembran nodded, and Heinrich picked up a few of them before making a quick telephone call. "I would like to ask a few of my colleagues to join us. We will need to inventory all the coins and then set up an account for you. What would you like to do with the coins?"

Cembran was confused, "Do?"

Travis knew what the banker was asking, "Cembran, he's asking if we want to keep the coins on deposit in their vault, or if we'd like to sell them and put the funds on deposit."

"Oh." Cembran turned to Heinrich, "I think we'd like to sell the coins over time to get the best prices and put the funds on deposit here in both of our names."

Travis was floored; the thought had never occurred to him. In his mind these coins were Cembran's and he was just helping him. He looked at his lover and asked Heinrich if he'd give them a minute. The banker stepped outside. "Cembran, are you sure? These are yours, your family's."

Cembran smiled and stroked Travis's cheek, "I've been thinking about this for the last three days. Yes, I'm sure." He leaned forward, letting their lips touch gently. "I'm very sure."

Over the next several hours, each coin was placed in a sleeve, numbered and inventoried. It took a while to inventory and catalog the hundreds of ducats, thalers, gold marks and other coins. An account was opened for them and the coins were deposited. A basic plan was developed for liquidating the coins, and Heinrich would construct a detailed plan over the next few weeks. Toward the end of the afternoon, Cembran and Travis thanked Heinrich for all his help and finally headed out of the bank.

"Lamb, we have one more stop to make." Travis took Cembran back to the wood-carving store and purchased the remaining three carvings that his brother Fartham had done. "These belong with you." After all that activity, they headed back to their hotel to rest and have dinner before collapsing into bed.

The next morning, they drove to the airport. After turning in their rental car, they checked in for their flight. The trip home was long and uneventful. Cembran dozed during the flight, but Travis's mind was awhirl. Thoughts of Cembran and his generosity, what Bacchus had said about him being worthy, and the wonderful sense of community and inclusion they'd felt while they were in the village. As Travis finally started to relax in his seat, a thought came to mind and he had a moment of crystal-clear realization. All these things were related and he knew what he needed to do.

Travis smiled as Cembran's blue eyes fluttered open, saying, "Lamb, I love you." He leaned down, kissing him softly but insistently. Cembran rested his head on his shoulder, their hands finding each other's. A few people on the plane looked at them curled together, but they were happy and neither of them noticed.

The end of a very long travel day found Travis and Cembran arriving back at the farm. They were both tired and happy to be home. Travis was thrilled because he had taken two weeks off work and still had some time to rest and spend with Cembran.

Gathod met them as they drove up and helped them unload their luggage. "Everything went fine while you were gone." He talked a blue streak as they unloaded the car. "The policeman stopped by while you were gone; he said he just wanted to make sure there wasn't any more trouble. He seems really nice. We talked for a while and I showed him all around the farm."

Travis looked at Cembran and smiled. He had a feeling that Doug would be visiting often.

"Your last call said that some strange things happened after you defeated Cembran's father, but you didn't say what," Gathod prompted.

"We'll tell you all about it. Right now, though, we need some food and a lot of sleep. Tomorrow we'll have lunch together and tell you everything that happened, okay?"

Gathod nodded, "I'll take care of the morning chores so you two can sleep in." He pulled each of them into a big hug. "I missed you both. See you in the morning," he called out over his shoulder.

The other two went into the house, "Cembran, will you see if we have something for dinner? I'll put the bags away and unpack." Travis took the baggage into the bedroom and put things away. The six carved figures he placed on the mantle in the living room. By the time he was done, Cembran had managed to put together a light dinner.

Early in the evening, just before going to bed, Travis and Cembran were quietly sitting in front of the fireplace admiring the carved figures. "I think two of them are your aunt and uncle, Brock's parents," Travis suggested. Cembran smiled and seemed content. Travis got out of his seat and quietly walked into the bedroom, sitting on the edge of the bed. A few minutes later he heard Cembran's chair move on the floor as he got up. Seconds later, his lover poked his head in the bedroom and Travis patted the bed next to him.

They both started to talk at the same time, both saying "I need—" They laughed.

"Lamb, you go first."

Cembran took a deep breath, "Travis, I wanted to ask you." He was suddenly very shy. Travis thought it was cute and incredibly arousing. "I know you haven't been happy at work and I wanted to ask you if you'd...." Cembran was looking at his lap and Travis gently lifted his chin to meet his eyes. "Would you be willing...? Oh, hell. Travis, would you live here with me?"

The smile that lit Travis's face could have put the sun to shame. "I'd love to, Lamb. You're right. I haven't been happy at work and I can't think of anything I'd like more than to wake up every morning next to you." Cembran returned the smile as Travis pushed him back onto the bed, scooting their bodies until Cembran's head rested on the pillow. The kiss that followed was almost bruising in its intensity. "Lamb, I have something to ask you." His body pressed Cembran to the bed, looking deeply into his eyes. "I think I know what Bacchus meant when he said I was worthy."

Cembran grin was mischievous, "Took you long enough. I figured it out days ago."

"Why didn't you tell me?" Travis was confused, but still smiling.

"You needed to find out for yourself. It has to be your decision." Cembran leaned forward and captured Travis's lips. "Make love to me in our bed."

Travis got up and slowly removed his clothing, while Cembran wriggled out of his. "I love you." Skin met skin, lips kissed, as tongues probed and tasted. Hands caressed hard firm muscles, rubbed against soft flesh. Mouths searched, finding nipples, lips, and smooth, firm hardness. Moans and gasps filled the small room as their pleasure in each other's bodies and spirits built and soared. Words of love poured from them. Travis entered Cembran, slowly and lovingly, their bodies moving together in a symphony of joy. Their lovemaking took them to heights most could only fantasize about. Love poured from them as they came together in waves of passion.

The November evening was cold. The large fire cast shadows on the lake and trees, creating a bubble of warmth against the cold. The full moon shown down on the lake, its light rippling on the surface of the water. Everything was ready for the Bacchanal. Food had been set up, wine and beer were ready. Gathod, Cembran, Brock, Jim, and Sue were all there, laughing and having a good time. Cembran had already explained that Travis would be joining them in few minutes. Travis had brought Cembran to visit his aunt and uncle and to meet his cousin Brock a few weeks earlier. Cembran had been so thrilled to see his aunt and uncle again, and to meet Brock, that he'd invited them to the farm for the Bacchanal.

Travis was standing in the woods, watching the festivities, waiting for the appointed hour. At midnight, he stepped into the clearing by the lake and into the light of the fire. He was wearing a flowing white robe and simple sandals on his feet. He knew he should feel cold, but he wasn't. "Thank you all for coming. Tonight is a very special Bacchanal for me and I'm pleased you could all be here." Travis opened his robe and the cloth slipped from his shoulders to reveal his naked body. Closing his eyes, he concentrated. "Vindionum," he said aloud, "Please join us. You are welcome."

On the edge of the lake, a mist formed and moved until it coalesced into the figure of Bacchus. Bacchus looked around at those in attendance, smiling at each person and greeting them by name, before turning his attention to Travis. "Have you decided?"

"Yes, with Cembran's blessing, I have decided to accept your generous offer." Travis stood in front of Bacchus, his arms at his side.

Bacchus smiled, "You have proven yourself worthy and I am pleased to welcome you as one of my children." The god touched Travis's shoulders with his hands. "I know you will use your gifts wisely; that is why they are given. Love and care for my other children." Bacchus stepped back, gestured to everyone present, and then faded back into the mist and was gone.

Cembran moved to Travis, slipped the robe back onto his body, and threw his arms around his neck, kissing him deeply. "Now I have my own satyr to play with." Travis raised his hand and felt his forehead.

Sure enough, he could feel two small horns at his hair line. "Do you feel different?"

Travis grinned, "The tail tickles a little." Turning to Cembran, his expression turning serious, he answered, "Yes, I do feel different; I love you now more than ever."

Part Two

Community
of
Children

Chapter Eighteen

Steven loved his job at the law firm of Goode, Goode, and Kraus. He'd worked there for years, starting as a clerk, but Mr. Goode, Sr. had recognized that he had a talent for finding and correcting the mistakes in legal documents. When the firm decided to open a side publishing business in conjunction with the Bar Association, Steven was made an editor/proofreader. A few years ago he'd been promoted to Editor of Legal Publications.

Steven was always notoriously early for work. He often came in an hour early, particularly when he had work that required a lot of concentration. This morning, Steven was surprised when Mr. Goode, Sr. knocked on his office door. "I figured you'd be here early." Jack Goode was one of those people who noticed everything. He'd been the Senior Partner in the firm for over twenty years. He'd run the business efficiently for years and Steven could never remember him raising his voice.

He entered Steven's office and sat in one of the chairs. "Steven, you know that we have a website for the firm."

Steven nodded. "What we want to do is add the ability to purchase our publications through the website."

Steven smiled; he'd suggested that a number of years ago.

"We'd like you to work with Brock to get us up and running as soon as is safely possible."

Brock? Oh god.

He tried to keep the fear off his face as Mr. Goode continued. "I know we can count on you, Steven." With those final words, he raised himself from the chair, squeezed his shoulder, and headed down the hall to his own office.

Steven was floored. Brock – how was he going to survive it? He thought Brock Kraus was the most attractive man he'd ever seen, but he knew that any sort of office romance was out of the question. He had always been cordial to the other man, but did his best to keep his distance. He'd always thought of himself as plain, and Brock in Steven's opinion, was a walking, talking wet dream. Tall, tan skin, muscled, with dark, thick hair that Steven always imagined extended to his broad chest and flat stomach, and those eyes, deep brown with gold flecks. Steven shook his head to knock himself back to reality. How was he going to deal with it? Well, he was going to have to be professional and just try to get the project completed as soon as possible. With that resolved, he tried to bring his mind back to the work he'd come in early to complete.

A few hours later, Steven was engrossed in a book he was editing when he heard a soft knock on his door. He raised his head, finding himself looking into Brock's incredibly deep eyes. Brock came into Steven's office and immediately sat down, saying, "I understand Jack spoke with you this morning?" Steven nodded. "I just stopped by to see how your schedule looks this afternoon; I have a few hours and I thought we could get started."

"Great. I'm free this afternoon. I'm just finishing this up," Steven tried to keep his voice level, but it was hard, and so was his cock, for that matter.

"Good, why don't you come to my office at two and we'll get started?" Brock stood and quickly left the office.

Steven breathed a sigh of relief when Brock left. *Get hold of yourself,* he thought. *He's a co-worker, he's probably straight, and he's way out of my league. Even if he is gay, he'd never be interested in me, so just stop it.* Steven kept repeating those thoughts, trying to get himself under control.

He knew he wasn't ugly, but he'd never considered himself handsome either. He was about six feet tall, but thin. Heck, he considered himself to be almost scrawny, with pale skin and light hair.

That afternoon, he approached Helen's desk promptly at two, who greeted him with, "Hey, handsome; Brock told me to send you right in."

Steven smiled. "Thanks, gorgeous." Helen was in her fifties and she and Steven always flirted playfully with each other. She giggled a little as Steven headed to Brock's door.

He entered Brock's expansive office and was motioned to the conference table. He took a seat and was surprised when Brock took the chair directly diagonal to his. Brock was so close that Steven could smell his deep, musky scent. Thank god he was seated, because his cock reacted immediately. Steven listened as Brock outlined his plans for the website. He added his own ideas occasionally, and soon they were deep in work. Before Steven noticed, it was already five o'clock; they'd been working for hours and it had seemed like just a few minutes.

Brock looked at his watch, "I have an appointment in an hour, why don't we pick this up tomorrow?"

Steven stood up and headed for the door, "Have a good evening, Brock." He closed the door behind him and headed quickly to his office. That hadn't been so bad. They'd worked well together, maybe this could work.

Over the next three weeks, Brock and Steven worked together a lot, often working late together three or four nights a week. They'd set an aggressive deadline for delivery and they were both determined to meet it. This particular Thursday evening was unusually warm for March. Steven and Brock had been working for hours – the project was nearing completion and they were trying to make sure all the last minute details were addressed. The office was warm, so Brock removed his tie and loosened the collar of his shirt.

Steven almost groaned out loud as another button popped loose, giving Steven a peek at the thick, dark hair on Brock's chest. "Oh God," he actually said to himself. He was standing across the table and his dick reacted in a big way. Steven was trying not to let it show.

"Well, I think we've done all we can for tonight." Brock squeezed Steven's shoulder, "You've done really good work."

"Thank you." Steven gathered his papers and left the office quickly, almost hastily, hoping Brock didn't notice the bulge in his pants.

The next morning, Steven had been in the office about an hour when Brock phoned him asking him to come to his office. Helen wasn't in yet, so Steven knocked and entered. Brock was sitting behind his desk, looking very serious. Over the past few weeks when they were working together, they'd worked together as equals, but when Steven looked at Brock, he could tell Brock was now the high-powered attorney. "Steven, please sit down," he said.

Steven took one of the chairs in front of the desk, wondering what he'd done wrong. He felt like a kid who'd been called to the principal's office.

"Steven, why don't you like me? What did I ever do to you?"

"I don't understand." Steven was definitely confused. "I like you fine."

Brock leaned forward in his chair, "Over the past few weeks whenever we're finished, you'd gather your things, say good-night and almost run back to your office." Steven didn't know what Brock was getting at, so he waited. "Last night when we finished, you rushed out of here like I had the plague."

Steven was finding it difficult to look at Brock. He couldn't tell him, "*I rushed out because I had got a raging hard-on the minute you opened your shirt.*" He tried to sound convincing as he answered, "I had to be somewhere and I realized I was late."

Brock, however, wasn't buying it, but Steven was reprieved when Helen knocked and told the other man that his first appointment was here. "I'm not finished. We'll talk about this later." Steven stood up and headed for the door. He passed the client as he entered Brock's office.

"Steven, honey, don't pay any attention to him. He probably just came in grumpy this morning," Helen smiled as Steven walked back to his office.

Steven managed to avoid Brock for the rest of the day. At five o'clock the next day, Friday, the office was quiet. Steven gathered his things in his briefcase, threw his coat over his arm, and headed for the exit. He had to walk past Brock's office on his way out, and he'd been hoping to avoid him, but no such luck.

"Steven, could you step in here please?" While the words sounded polite, the tone was definitely assertive-lawyer. Steven let out the breath he'd been holding, put his case and coat on Helen's chair, and stepped into Brock's office. "Close the door." Steven complied. Brock was standing behind his desk. "You never gave me an answer to my question." Brock was staring at Steven waiting for an answer. Steven looked at the floor. "What is wrong? You can't even look at me." Steven remained silent. "I think I deserve an answer." Brock's tone was becoming confrontational.

Steven was getting tired of Brock questioning; in fact he was starting to get angry. "You want to know? Do you really want to know?" Steven burst, building a head of steam, "Fine, I'll tell you." His voice got louder with each word: "I'm attracted to you, okay? You're strong, intelligent, hell you're the most handsome man I have ever met in my life." Steven took a breath, "Fuck, you're way out of my league, probably straight, and even if you're gay, why would you want me anyway?" He was practically yelling at this point. He took a second to get his voice under control, "So now that I've made a fool of myself, I'm going home."

Steven turned and walked toward the door. As he grabbed the knob, he felt his body being turned around and before he knew what was happening, a pair of hot, full lips was pressed to his, stealing his breath. The kiss was hard, insistent, and Steven parted his lips as a tongue entered his mouth. This was definitely a man who knew what he wanted and how to take it. Hands cupped the back of Steven's head as the lips increased pressure, pulling on his.

"Brock, we can't do this. You're a partner." Steven could barely think; it felt as though Brock had sucked his brains out with his kisses.

"You're right. We can't do this here." Steven looked into his eyes to make sure he was serious. "Get your coat; I'll follow you to your place." Steven nodded and somehow made it out of the building and

into his car. Steven had never been aggressive in his life, but the
thought of strong, confident Brock, made his dick throb. *"Fuck it, if I
only get him once, I'll take it,"* he thought. Almost in a daze, he drove
home with Brock following him.

Steven led the other man into his condo. Once they were inside,
Brock took charge. Steven had barely turned on the light before Brock
had pressed his body against the wall, kissing him hard. He put his
arms around Brock's neck, and in one quick movement, Brock lifted
him off the floor, slipped his legs around his waist, and carried him to
the bedroom.

Brock laid him on the bed, "Put your hands over your head."
Brock's voice was firm and strong. Steven complied. Brock quickly
opened the buttons of Steven's shirt, slipping it off his shoulders before
throwing it on the floor. Steven was embarrassed and turned his head
away. Both his nipples had little silver bars through them that had been
a gift from a previous relationship. The only reason Steven kept them
was because they made his nipples really sensitive, but he still felt
embarrassed.

Brock kissed Steven as his fingers went right for the nipples, gently
tugging and twisting on the silver bars. Steven went wild, moaning and
whimpering into Brock's mouth. "You like having your nipples played
with?"

"Uh huh," he moaned, running his hands through Brock's thick
hair.

"Keep your hands over your head, Steven," Brock scolded,
twisting a nipple gently. Steven was now whimpering and moaning,
his hips bucking against the bed, cock throbbing in his pants. Brock
stilled his hips, "Just relax. We've got plenty of time, and I'm going to
make sure you enjoy every second." Brock continued working
Steven's nipples until they ached. His dick throbbed; he needed,
wanted Brock so bad. His mouth was dry and he could barely breathe.

Slowly, Brock got off the bed. When Steven started to sit up, he
repeated, "Keep your arms where they are." Steven relaxed back on
the bed and watched with rapt attention as he slowly removed his shirt.
He could barely breathe at the sight of Brock's sculpted chest and flat

stomach. Brock's chest looked like a plate of armor and his stomach was cut in deep grooves. Black hair covered his chest, narrowing as it proceeded down his stomach before disappearing into his pants. Steven whimpered like a puppy.

Over the years, Brock had had many lovers, but he had never gotten a reaction like that from any of them. "Like what you see?"

Steven nodded, "You're more spectacular that I ever imagined." His mouth was so dry, the words sounded raspy and rough. Brock leaned forward and took off Steven's shoes and socks. He then unfastened his pants, and in one swift movement pulled them and Steven's underwear off before dropping the clothing on the floor. Steven turned his head to the side again. He'd always been ashamed of his thin, scrawny body and he felt sure Brock would be disappointed.

"Steven, look at me." Steven turned his head and looked at Brock. He was surprised not to see disappointment and instead saw nothing but desire. Brock splayed his hand onto Steven's chest, feeling the smooth skin. He whimpered as Brock wrapped his fingers around his cock and cupped his balls. Brock knelt on the bed and pressed his lips to Steven's, "I don't know why you're embarrassed; you're beautiful, Steven." The words were punctuated by a kiss that melted him into the mattress.

Brock moved away from the bed again, releasing Steven's cock. He opened his pants, slipping them off his powerful legs, covered in the same black hair as his chest. He was wearing sexy black briefs and the bulge in the front made Steven's eyes pop. "I'm going to fuck you."

Steven started to squirm in anticipation, "Oh fuck, yes!" He turned his head toward the night stand and Brock opened the drawer, taking out the lube and condoms he found inside. Brock lifted his legs, exposing his tight, perfect opening before inserting a lubed finger, and Steven moaned and shifted forward, wanting more. Adding a second finger, Brock curled them, searching.

"Oh, god, Brock, do that again."

His lover smiled, "Right there, huh? You like that?" Steven nodded. "How about this?" Brock added a finger from his other hand while he curled his first two over the spot again and again. Steven's breath came in short gasps as waves of pleasure crashed through him. His first instinct was to reach for his cock, but as he lifted his hands, Brock opened his mouth and swallowed his cock to the hilt.

Steven was whimpering loudly as Brock worked both his ass and his cock at the same time. "Gonna come."

Brock lifted his head, "Not yet." The fingers and mouth disappeared and he stood between Steven's legs and slowly pulled down the black briefs.

Steven hissed as Brock's weighty cock bounced free of the fabric, "Oh god. Fuck me, Brock!"

Brock slipped on a condom, lubed his cock, and pressed the head to Steven's opening. Steven felt his body stretch and open as Brock pressed into him. Brock's cock filled him like he'd never been filled before. Fat, long, and hard, he could feel each inch as it slipped inside his body. Brock entered Steven slowly and steadily, stopping briefly before pressing his cock to the hilt. Brock leaned forward and brought his lips to Steven's in a crushing, hard, intense kiss.

He started thrusting slowly and deeply, steadily picking up the pace as Steven came unglued. Brock held his ankles as his powerfully muscled body thrust deeply into him.

"Oh god, Brock. Fuck me hard!"

"You like that?" Steven nodded. "How about this?" Brock changed the angle slightly and Steven was over the moon, each stroke making his head throb and his spine tingle.

"Oh yeah, right there!" His arms over his head, his head thrown back, Steven just rode the waves of ecstasy.

Brock took Steven's cock in his hand and started stroking, urging him, "Come for me Steven, come for me hard." Steven cried out as he shot like a rocket onto his chest and Brock's hand, tiny spots of light dancing before his eyes.

Two strokes later, Brock came with a shout, filling the condom. Brock stayed where he was, then slowly withdrew from Steven's body. After removing the condom, he went into the bathroom, grabbed a towel, and cleaned up Steven before joining him on the bed. Brock lay on his back.

"Can I put my arms down now?" There was a hint of humor in Steven's voice.

"Yeah, " Brock laughed, pulling him on top as he ran his hands down his back, cupping his smooth butt in his hands while he kissed Steven deeply.

Steven was all over Brock, kissing him with everything he had, while he carded his fingers through the thick hair on Brock's chest.

"You were amazing. Never think anyone is out of your league. Least of all me." Brock's lips found Steven's again, silencing any protests he might have.

Breaking the kiss, Steven rested his head on Brock's shoulder.

"What is it?"

Steven shrugged and started to get off the bed.

"Where are you going?" Brock asked.

Steven looked embarrassed, "I was getting up so you can go. I figured you'd...."

Powerful arms pulled Steven back onto the bed and back onto Brock's body. "I'm not going anywhere unless you make me."

"But...."

"No buts," Brock's arms wrapped around Steven pulling him into another kiss. The two men rested together for a long while, each content in the other's presence. "Steven?"

"Yeah," Steven's voice was soft, with just a touch of fear.

Brock took a deep breath that raised and lowered Steven, where he rested on Brock's chest. "I have something I need to tell you. After that you might want me to leave."

Steven shifted slightly so he could see Brock's eyes. Brock suddenly seemed unsure of himself, which was surprising, since he always seemed so confident. Steven sat up on the bed and watched as

Brock sat up as well. "I'm not sure how to say this. I've never told anyone before."

"Then why are you telling me?" Steven was a little confused, but he was also flattered that Brock would trust him with whatever secret he wanted to share.

"I like you and I want to continue seeing you, outside of work." Steven blinked – had he heard him right? Brock smiled, "You heard me right. I like you and I want to get to know you better, romantically, but I won't do that unless…."

"Brock, just tell me what you want to say."

"I'm not fully human." Steven opened his mouth, but Brock silenced him with a finger, "Let me say this; I'm part human, part satyr. See." Brock concentrated and a set of small horns appeared on his forehead and he twisted on the bed, so Steven could see the tail just above his buttocks. He stopped talking when he saw the look on Steven's face, unclear of what it meant.

Brock waited for Steven's reaction, but it wasn't what he expected, "Oh my god," were the only words Steven said before tears started to run down his cheeks. "Oh, my god."

"Steven, do you want me to leave?" Brock got off the bed and started picking up his clothes.

Suddenly Steven smiled, a bright warm smile, "Brock, oh my god." Before Brock knew what happened, Steven had thrown himself into his arms, hugging him tightly. Tears were still running down his cheeks, falling onto Brock's shoulder. "Oh my god."

"You keep saying that, but it is good or bad?"

Steven grinned and whispered in Brock's ear, "I think I have something to tell you." Now it was Brock's turn to be confused. Steven released his grip and settled back on the bed. "I don't know where to start, because I don't know the whole story, but I'll try." Brock sat back on the bed. "I was a late bloomer, or that was what my mother called it. Anyway, when I finally went through puberty, I started to get bumps on my forehead and lower back. My mother took me to the doctor and he said that there was abnormal bone growth and recommended surgery. Mom resisted until it became clear that I was growing what looked like horns and a tail. So she marched me down to the surgeon and had them removed."

"What are you saying?"

"Well, I think I'm saying that you finally provided me with the answer I've been looking for all my life. I always knew I was different, and as a teenager, I thought I was a freak."

"Oh my god, Steven, you're not a freak − you're one of us." Brock gathered Steven into his arms pulling him to his body as he relaxed back onto the bed. Brock brought their lips together again. Steven's hands were all over Brock; he thought he was in bed with an octopus with the way Steven's hands never seemed to settle anywhere. "I think I know some people you should meet."

Steven slid down Brock's body, relishing the rough, scratchy feel of his chest hair on this smooth skin, "You do?"

"Yeah I—" Brock's words were cut off as Steven took his cock in his mouth, swallowing it to the hilt. "Yeah, they live, oh fuck, Steven, that's good." Whatever else he wanted to say would keep until later.

Chapter Nineteen

Winter on the farm was a slow time, spent taking care of the animals and making plans for the coming year. When the weather was nice, Travis and Cembran had tried to make some progress on some of their projects, but most of the winter was quiet and uneventful. Travis spent much of the winter working with Cembran making plans for the farm and their lives. They decided that two additional rooms would be added to the house; a new master bedroom complete with master bath, as well as a room that Travis could use as a media room and office.

With Travis living with him, Cembran wanted to enlarge the sheep and goat herds. "I want to add some new breeding stock for both the sheep as well as the goats." They were sitting together in front of a roaring fire on a cold January afternoon.

"Okay. Why don't we plan to go to the Fair this year and we can buy the animals you want. Heck, Love, we can buy the Grand Champions if you want." Cembran was always surprised at the support he got from Travis. He sometimes found it hard to believe, but he was trying.

"If we're going to enlarge the herds, we'll need more pasture."

"I was thinking about that. We could clear the land next to the existing pastures. There's plenty of room, and we've already removed the brush. We could use the trees we need to fell to build the additional rooms. There are a number of huge trees that could be cut into lumber for the house."

They continued making their plans, including enlarging the vegetable garden, maybe planting a small orchard, and building a storage building.

"Storage building?" The look on Cembran's face was precious.

"Now Cembran, don't get mad." Cembran looked at Travis through squinty eyes. "I think we need to get some equipment. A tractor, garden tools, a brush cutter. We could build a storage building for them, with a loft above for additional hay storage."

"I've managed the farm the way it is for a very long time. Suddenly, you want to change things?"

Cembran had a point and Travis had been afraid Cembran would feel this way. "Lamb, I don't want to change what's important." Cembran's face was set and Travis thought he was going to become angry. "I'm proposing that we get some equipment to make some jobs easier, jobs like building fences, clearing brush, felling trees, helping in the vegetable garden, and cutting hay. Not the way we care for the sheep and goats."

Cembran didn't say anything. Travis knew Cembran wasn't keen on most modern equipment, so his answer surprised him: "Okay. But don't expect me to operate the stuff."

"That's a deal." Travis smiled as he raised himself from his seat and bent to kiss Cembran's soft, sweet lips. Cembran put down the block of wood he was carving, his fingers carding through Travis's hair. Travis's kisses became harder, turning needy. Cembran lifted himself out of the chair and followed his lover to the bedroom, thinking this was definitely the way to spend a cold January afternoon.

Over the past few months, Travis and Cembran had managed to make progress on their goals. The winter had been kind to them and they'd been able to start clearing the new pastures, and in the next few weeks, the storage shed would arrive. Travis had found a firm that built prefabricated farm buildings and they'd worked with Travis to design a storage shed that would fit in with the other farm buildings. In early

February, they'd gotten an unexpected thaw, so Travis had contacted a local mill and contracted with them to remove the large trees that were in what would be the new pasture, so they could be processed into the building materials they'd need for the addition to the house. The representative from the mill told Travis there was more than enough lumber there. The two men worked out how the lumber would be cut and prepared and the mill agreed to buy any excess from Travis. The first delivery was expected in the next week.

This particular evening, Travis and Cembran were preparing to have guests for the weekend. Brock had called a few days earlier and told them that he had someone he'd like them to meet.

"Is it serious?" Travis had asked.

He could almost hear Brock grinning as he replied, "Yeah, I think so." He paused a minute to add, "Travis, if this is uncomfortable for you, I'll understand."

Travis smiled to himself. "If me being in love with your cousin didn't bother you, then why would you finding someone who makes you happy bother me?"

"Good point."

"Why don't you plan to stay the weekend? It would be nice to see you."

Brock had accepted happily.

Just before dinner, Travis heard a knock on their door. When Travis opened the door, he saw Brock and Steven standing on their doorstep, shivering in the cold. Travis ushered them into the warm house and, after introductions, settled the newcomers in front of the fire to get warm.

After a hearty dinner, the four of them gathered in the living room. Travis broke the ice by making small talk: "Steven, how did you and Brock meet?"

Steven looked at Brock, his eyes sort of dreamy; Travis smiled as he saw the reaction. "I've worked at the same law firm for years, but I always avoided him." Brock put his hand in Steven's, and he continued, "I've been attracted to him for a long time, but...."

Brock took over as Steven started to feel embarrassed, "I thought Steven was incredible and watched him for a long time. I just thought he wasn't interested. It wasn't until we worked together on a project that we were finally able to get past our misconceptions."

"Brock," the one word carried a lot of meaning.

Brock smiled, "Steven, Travis knows about us. In fact, that's why we're here this weekend. When I told Steven I was a satyr, he was shocked, but not for the reason I expected."

"You didn't know he was a satyr as well?" Travis was very matter of fact.

Brock was completely shocked. "How did you know?"

Steven was absolutely floored too: "Yeah, how did you know?"

Travis looked at Cembran and then back at Brock and Steven, "I don't know, I just knew the minute he walked in the door. Must be one of the abilities I received from Bacchus."

Steven's eyes went wide, "Who?"

Travis looked at Brock and Steven, "I think we better start from the beginning."

Steven told his story while Cembran and Travis listened with shocked attention. "So I never knew until a few weeks ago that there was a reason why I always felt different, and that I wasn't some sort of freak. But I have a million questions, and Brock told me that you might be able to help answer some of them." Travis nodded and indicated for Steven to ask what he needed. "Well, each month, I get sort of...." Steven turned bright red.

Travis smiled, "Horny as hell, sort of a 'fuck or you'll explode' sensation?"

"Yeah, how did—" Steven stopped as Travis smiled.

Travis explained about the full moon, its role in procreation, and the Bacchanal. He also invited Steven and Brock to the April festivities. At that point, Cembran spoke up and explained about aging and how satyrs age based upon life events rather than merely because of chronological age. Cembran then explained about his family, and showed Steven the carvings on the mantle of his brother, mother, and Brock's parents. Brock and Steven were both enthralled when Travis told them how they had found the carvings in Switzerland.

Travis and Cembran spent the rest of the evening telling them stories about their histories, relating old legends, and Cembran even recounted some stories that his mother had told him as a child. Travis told Steven how he'd become a satyr a few months earlier.

"So you weren't born a satyr?"

Travis shook his head, "No, I was made a satyr by Bacchus himself." Travis told Steven the story of his contest with Cembran's father, about their meeting the god, about Bacchus's offer, and Travis's eventual understanding and acceptance. "The one thing I've never told anyone, except Cembran, is that I dreamed of Cembran for years. Those dreams started just after I met him for the first time."

As the evening wore on, Cembran made up a bed for Brock and Steven in front of the fireplace. While Steven was cleaning up, Travis gathered some blankets, and both he and Cembran headed for the door. "We're not kicking you out, are we?" Brock looked a little confused.

Travis whispered to Brock conspiratorially, "No, we're going to the lake shelter." Travis took Cembran's hand, "Enjoy yourselves in front of the fire. We'll see you in the morning."

Travis and Cembran shut the door quietly behind them and headed toward the lake. The fresh snow reflected the light of the stars as they walked down the path. Travis had built a sturdy, stone, three-sided shelter with a fireplace near where the creek entered the lake. This was one of their favorite places.

Once inside, Cembran opened the sealed box they'd built into the shelter and pulled out the soft mattress and bedding. Travis hung and fastened the heavy curtain he'd made across the opening before lighting the fire he'd laid earlier in the day. Soon the shelter was warm and filled with dancing light.

Travis slipped off his clothes and climbed under the heavy, thick blankets, wrapped in a cocoon of warmth. "Come here, Lamb." Travis watched as Cembran undressed, slowly, exposing his skin to Travis's eyes, the light dancing and playing as his muscles flexed and moved.

Once he was naked as well, Cembran knelt on the bed. Travis's arms wrapped around his waist as his tongue and lips latched onto a nipple, sucking and swirling. Cembran threw his head back in a silent cry as tongue and lips teased first one nipple and then the other. Travis knew what Cembran liked and he loved administering this particular delicious torture. Cembran's nipples were puffy and red as Travis helped him slip beneath the covers. Their kisses were deep and wonderful, each knowing what the other wanted and needed and each freely giving everything he had.

Travis's weight pressed Cembran into the bedding as lips kissed and hands explored territory already known and yet somehow seeming new each time they made love. "Roll over," Travis urged breathlessly. Cembran shifted beneath him and he slithered down his lover's back, his head disappearing beneath the blankets as his lips and tongue kissed their way down Cembran's spine to the cleft between his perfect butt cheeks. Hands spread those cheeks as lips and tongue explored and teased before finding the opening that provided such pleasure and warmth. Travis rimmed Cembran breathless, darting his tongue in and out of the puckered opening. At first, Cembran moaned and whimpered, but soon words failed him completely and he arched his back as Travis thrust his tongue deep, driving him insane with lustful, aching need.

Slowly, Travis kissed his way back up Cembran's spine until his weight again rested on Cembran's back. "Did you like that?"

"Mmmmmm, yeah, want more though." Cembran tilted his head so he could kiss Travis, "Want so much more, want you, all of you."

"Like this?" Travis positioned his cock against the now wet and slippery opening and slowly sank into Cembran's body.

"Mmmmmm. Aaaaahhhhhh." The sound was of Cembran slowly releasing his breath as Travis sank deeper and deeper into his body.

"Do you like it this way?"

"Uh huh, like it. Can give myself to you completely. I'm yours, Lemmle, all yours." Cembran's body was pressed flat against the bedding as Travis slowly lifted his hips and sank again into Cembran's hot, welcoming body.

"Show me, Lamb." Travis smiled as he felt Cembran's tail tickle his stomach as his cock again disappeared into Cembran's body. Travis let his own body go as well.

"Oh my god!" Cembran practically screamed.

"You like that? I've been practicing." Travis had found a way to use his tail to tickle Cembran's balls and he'd timed it to coincide with a deep penetrating thrust.

"Oh god, do that again."

Travis complied over and over, then slowly pulled out and rolled Cembran over before lifting his legs and re-entering him with a deep thrust. Leaning forward, Travis pressed his lips to Cembran's, kissing the man he loved deeply and with passion, letting him know that he was his whole world. "Love you, Lamb," Travis sucked on Cembran's lips as he buried himself deep in Cembran's body, filling him over and over.

Cembran exploded between their bodies as he felt the first of Travis's release fill his body, moaning "Lemmle," as he came.

After cleaning them both up a little, Travis banked the fire and settled back under the covers next to Cembran, who was already falling asleep. Travis kissed him gently before he too fell asleep.

In the morning, Cembran woke as Travis pulled him close, snuggling their bodies together. Cembran could tell that Travis wasn't awake yet, even though part of him was up, quite insistent, and pressing hard against his butt. "Morning, Travis," Cembran reached a hand around his back and stroked his lover's morning wood.

"Morning, Mr. Magic Hands," Travis smiled as Cembran continued stroking him languidly. Just as things were getting interesting, they could hear the sound of bleating goats drift softly across the snow. Cembran kissed Travis before releasing his cock from his hand, reluctantly got out from under the covers, and started to get dressed. Travis followed his lead, although he did manage to cop a feel of Cembran's butt before it disappeared into his pants. Once dressed, Cembran trudged through the snow to start their morning chores. Travis gathered up the blankets, packed the bedding back into the box, and dumped snow on the fire before picking up the extra blankets and heading back to the house.

Travis opened the door quietly; the fire had died down, but had not gone out. Brock and Steven were curled together under the blankets and Brock had pulled Steven into his body with his arms wrapped around him protectively. Brock must really care for Steven, he thought; he and Travis had dated for months and he'd never held Travis like that. The thought wasn't mean or even jealous – it was just a realization that Brock was as captivated with Steven as Steven obviously was with him.

Steven's eyes opened slowly and he started to squirm, feeling a little embarrassed. Travis smiled. "Shhh. Go back to sleep, it's early." Travis quietly put another log on the fire, put the blankets in the bedroom, and left the house before heading down to the barns to help Gathod and Cembran complete the morning chores.

That afternoon, once the chores and lunch were finished, Cembran took Steven on a tour of the farm, leaving Brock and Travis sitting in front of the fire. "Steven seems really great," he said.

"He is, Trav." Brock wasn't completely comfortable.

Travis had learned during their short relationship to read Brock pretty well, "Look, we didn't work out, but I'm happy and you're happy." Brock looked at Travis a little skeptically. "I can tell he makes you happy, so don't feel uncomfortable, there's no need."

Brock didn't seem to understand Travis's attitude. "Didn't you care for me?"

Travis smiled, "Yes, I did, and I still do, as a good friend." He changed tacks, "Brock, you instinctively need to protect and care for people. It's part of what makes you special. I didn't need that, but Steven does. I think you two are great together and I think you will grow together in ways you can't imagine yet." *We were too much alike*. Travis didn't say that, but he thought it.

"Brock, can I ask you…?" Brock's eyes had a soft look so Travis continued, "Do you love him?"

Brock hesitated, "I'm…."

"Let go of the defenses you've built up – let yourself feel and admit to yourself what you feel."

Brock looked deep into Travis's eyes, smiling, "How'd you get so smart?"

Travis beamed, "Having Cembran in my life showed me what it's like to truly love someone and to be loved just as much in return."

"I just don't know. I mean, Steven keeps expecting me to leave. He thinks I'm out of his league, or some such nonsense. I mean, if he loved me, he'd...."

Travis squeezed Brock's shoulder as he shook his head, "He's probably more scared than you are of getting hurt. Tell him how you feel. Take the chance and speak from your heart."

Cembran and Steven returned from their tour of the farm. Travis smiled as Steven went on and on about the lambs and kid goats. "Spoken like a true satyr. Steven, many of us have a connection with animals."

Cembran nodded, "It was what first drew me to Travis." The look on Steven's face was asked them to tell him more. "Travis rescued one of my lambs from the mud, and instead of fighting him, it let him and actually bonded with him." Travis nodded as Cembran continued, "Travis and Gathod even have the ability to heal them."

"I've never actually done it, but we both saw Gathod heal one of the lambs after it had been poisoned," Travis clarified. He and Cembran got up from their chairs, "We need to finish the chores for the day. You two stay here and relax. We shouldn't be too long." They put on their work coats and headed down the path toward the barns.

Once the chores were complete for the day, they walked up the path back to the house. "Gathod, would you like to join us for dinner?"

Gathod grinned, "No, thank you. I have plans for tonight. I'll see you both in the morning." He waved as he headed down the path to his house.

Travis was almost at the door when he heard Steven's voice saying, "Oh god, Brock. I love you too," followed by the unmistakable sound of flesh gently slapping against flesh. "Don't stop, please."

Cembran caught up to Travis. "You're—" Travis put his fingers to his lips to quiet Cembran.

Brock's voice echoed through the door, clear as day, "You are so special, Baby. I love you so much!"

"Oh god, Brock." It sounded like Steven was crying, "You make me feel special."

Travis smiled broadly as he whispered, "Come on, let's take a walk around the lake." Cembran smiled as he took Travis's hand, and they quietly headed down the path.

Chapter Twenty

"**B**rock, what should I take to the Bacchanal tomorrow?" Steven was a little flustered and a whole lot excited. "I mean, what should I make to bring?" They were in the kitchen of Steven's condo on a beautiful Friday afternoon in April.

Brock smiled, "Baby, you don't need to make anything."

"I don't understand; Travis and Cembran shouldn't have to make everything."

Brock wrapped his arms around Steven's waist, "That's why Travis invited you to come early. He wanted you to see the preparations." He bent forward, nibbling on Steven's ear.

Turning to face Brock Steven said, "I don't understand."

"You will, Baby, you will. Just trust me," as he captured those luscious lips.

"Okay. Umm. Do we have time for this before we leave?"

Brock leaned close, "We probably do, but if we hurry Travis said we could use the shelter by the lake tonight." To punctuate his meaning he placed his hands on Steven's butt.

Steven's eyes got wide, "You mean we can make love by...." His words trailed off as Brock again kissed him.

"Uh-huh, as long as we hurry."

"Oh boy!" Steven kissed Brock and squirmed out of his grasp before rushing to finish the packing. Suitcases appeared a few minutes later. "Brock, would you load these in the car?"

"Okay, but remember we have to stop at my house so I can pack."

Steven grinned. "No we don't," he said as he raised the larger suitcase, "I packed this one for you yesterday."

Brock was floored and he just laughed. Thank god he'd brought the special bag with him. Brock took the suitcases and loaded them in the car while Steven finished in the condo and locked the doors.

In the car, Steven settled in the passenger seat of Brock's BMW sedan, his hand resting on his lover's leg. "Uh, Brock?"

Brock looked over at Steven. He was so cute when he wasn't sure how to ask something. He'd gently bite his lower lip, and his eyes would get this shy, puppy dog look. Brock smiled. "What is it, Baby?" he asked softly.

"What's in the paper bag you stuffed under the seat?"

Damn, he'd hoped Steven hadn't noticed. "It's a surprise for later."

"Oh." Steven got quiet as he rested his head against the seat.

Brock had already noticed that when Steven was nervous or afraid, he got quiet and started to pull inward, and he could tell that was what Steven was doing now. He'd even removed his hand from Brock's leg. "Steven, what's wrong?"

The voice that answered was tentative and small, "I guess it's hard to explain. Growing up, my mother used to surprise me with things a lot."

"That must have been fun."

Steven shook his head. "No, she surprised me with things like, 'Pack your stuff, we're moving tomorrow' or 'We can't afford to keep the cat, so I took him to the pound.' The biggest surprise I got was the year I turned nine and my mother surprised me for my birthday with a new stepfather − no presents, just a strange man now living in our house. I mean, she meant well and she did her best for me, but she never discussed anything unpleasant, she just surprised me with it."

Brock was horrified; what a way to grow up! No wonder his boyfriend was so tentative: he never knew what was coming next. "Steven, Love, I promise that when I tell you I have a surprise, it's a good one that I think you'll like." Jesus, he and Steven had talked about growing up, but he had no idea. He reached to Steven and squeezed his leg, determined to re-establish a physical connection with the adorable man in the passenger seat.

"Okay." Brock could tell he wasn't fully convinced, but he was reassured when his hand again rested on his leg.

About an hour later, they arrived at the farm. Brock knocked on the door. Cembran answered, greeting them warmly and ushering them inside. Travis and Cembran already had company: Doug and Gathod had stopped by for a drink. Travis made introductions and re-introductions before finding everyone a seat. The conversation was light and pleasant.

Steven turned to Cembran, "Would it be all right if I went to see the lambs?"

Cembran smiled, "Sure. I'll get you a flashlight."

As Steven put on his coat, Doug asked if he'd mind if he tagged along. "That'd be great."

When Steven and Doug left, Gathod started to talk, "Travis, I need your help. I've been seeing Doug for a while and I need to tell him, but I don't know how."

"You should tell him soon. He's a good guy, Gathod. I think you can trust him. When did you want to tell him?"

Gathod demurred, "I was hoping you'd help me tell him tonight."

Cembran spoke up, "If you're determined to tell him tonight, then you don't need an audience. Brock, if you don't mind, when they get back, would you and Steven be willing to help me with the goats for a while?"

"Yeah, that's probably a good idea."

"I know I should tell him, but I just don't know how, and he's known you for a long time..." It was plain to everyone that Gathod was scared of how Doug might react.

Brock and Cembran put on their coats and were about to go outside when Steven and Doug returned. Brock nuzzled tenderly into Steven's cold cheeks, "We're going to help Cembran with the goats." Steven took the hint and headed down to the goat barn with the other two.

Travis, Gathod, and Doug sat in front of the fire. Gathod looked at Travis, asking for his help with his eyes. Travis took a deep breath, "Doug, Gathod has something that he wanted me to help him tell you." Doug looked alternately at Gathod and Travis, clearly wondering what was going on. "Before he does, I want you to know that Gathod cares for you enough and trusts you enough to tell you something very personal."

Doug smirked, "It sounds like he's coming out of the closet."

"Well, he is sort of."

"This sounds bad." Doug was starting to get really tense.

"No, it's just something that he hopes won't change the way you feel about him."

Gathod started to fidget, "Doug, I don't know how to tell you this, so I'm just going to say it. I'm not fully human. My father was a satyr."

Doug looked blankly at Gathod and Travis and started to laugh. "Okay, what's the joke?"

Travis stood up, "Doug, there's no joke. Gathod, Cembran, Brock, Steven, and I are all satyrs." Travis concentrated, allowing his horns to appear.

Doug stood rapidly, knocking over his chair and shouting, "Get away from me!" Those words shot like an arrow through Gathod's heart and the look on his face was of absolute heartbreak.

"Doug!" Travis knew he needed to regain control. "Please, sit down."

Warily, Doug picked up his chair and took a seat. He looked ready to bolt at any second. "What are you going to do to me?"

Travis shook his head as Gathod stepped forward, taking Doug's hands. "We're not going to do anything to you. I wanted to tell you this because I love you and I wanted you to know who I really am." Gathod's voice had an almost pleading quality.

"Doug, you know what that's like coming out. We all do."

Doug thought for a long time before nodding, "But what does this mean?"

"It means that Gathod has certain abilities. One of them is a gift that allows him to heal animals; it also means that he has horns and a tail when he wishes to show them. It means that he loves you and trusts you enough to tell you."

Doug looked at Gathod, "This is a shock."

"I know, and if you want to leave, I'll understand. That's the chance I took when I decide to tell you." Gathod looked down at the floor, clearly afraid of Doug's reaction.

One could have heard a pin drop as Gathod stared at the floor and Doug stared at Gathod. Finally, Gathod raised his head and Doug looked into his eyes, "Come on; let's go."

"Go where?"

"To your house, we've got some talking to do." Doug got up and headed toward the door with Gathod following dejectedly. After putting on their coats, they went outside. Just before they closed the door, Travis saw Doug reassuringly take Gathod's hand in his.

Cembran, Brock, and Steven returned a while later, their cheeks red from the cold night. Steven was very excited; "I got to milk a goat," he grinned. "Brock's goat didn't like him. Apparently he had cold hands and the poor thing kicked when he touched it."

Brock, always a good sport, grinned along with Steven, "Hey, it's getting late." Turning to Travis he asked, "How'd it go?"

"As well as could be expected," Travis knew Doug was a good man and he figured they'd be fine once the initial shock wore off.

Cembran had gone into the bedroom and returned with the extra blankets, handing them to Brock. "The shelter's all ready for you, all you have to do is light the fire and enjoy." There was a twinkle in Cembran's eyes.

"Thank you." Brock picked up the paper bag sitting next to his suitcase and after saying good-night, they headed outside and down the path toward the lake. Steven stared at the bag Brock was carrying, trying to figure out what was inside. When they arrived at the shelter, he pulled back the curtain, allowing Steven to enter first, following right behind. He lit the fire and its warmth soon filled the small shelter, while Steven spread out the blankets and got their bed ready.

The fire soon had the shelter toasty warm. "Steven, you can have your surprise now." Brock handed Steven the small paper bag.

Steven opened it and pulled out two long straps of leather with loops in the end. Confused, he looked at Brock. "What are these?"

"They're padded wrist restraints."

Steven went white, dropped the restraints onto the bed and started to curl into himself. "You want to tie me up?" He was actually shaking.

"Well actually…." Brock trusted Steven and he knew he'd never do anything to hurt him, but he also thought that if he gave Steven a little control, it might give him some confidence. "I was going to have you tie me up."

Steven relaxed and thought for a minute until a big grin crossed his face, "You'd trust me to do that? Have you done this before?"

Brock immediately knew he'd made the right decision. "Yes I trust you, and you are the first person that I've ever allowed—" Brock's words were cut off as Steven climbed into Brock's lap. Brock's arms cradled him as their lips came together in a hot, passionate kiss. When they broke their kiss, Brock unbuttoned his shirt and slipped it off his shoulders. He then slipped his wrists into the restraints and Steven hooked them to the curtain tie-down and the steel frame of the firewood holder. Steven stood at the base of the bed, the ceiling of the shelter just above his head, and looked down at Brock laying on his back, his powerful chest rising and falling with each breath.

Steven stood for a moment, silently looking at Brock all laid out before him. He wanted everything, but he wasn't sure where to start. Finally he smiled and started undressing, taking off his shirt, shoes, socks, and pants before slipping off his underwear. His cock was already rock hard and dripping a little. Slowly Steven straddled Brock's prone body, leaning forward to kiss those full lips.

"I like these, Brock," Steven whispered as his lips traveled to one of Brock's large, full nipples. Steven's lips clamped on the bud while his tongue licked swirls around the edge. Brock hissed and threw his head back as Steven worked the nipple with his lips and tongue. He smiled and transferred his attentions to the other nipple before licking and kissing his way down Brock's stomach. He traced every line and groove on Brock's hard stomach, loving the salty-sweet taste of Brock's skin.

Steven licked downward till he reached Brock's belt buckle. His tongue swirled around his lover's navel as he opened the belt buckle and slowly unzipped Brock's fly. "What's in here, I wonder?" Steve whispered with a grin as he spread the flaps of Brock's pants. He stood and pulled off Brock's pants with a whoop, leaving Brock wearing only his tight, black briefs. Steven grinned as he licked Brock's ankle, swirling his tongue up the leg until he reached Brock's ample bulge. After nuzzling his package, making Brock moan with anticipation, Steven slowly and deliberately licked his way up the other leg, paying special attention to those areas that made Brock flinch and writhe. Steven was really enjoying this; Brock always put him first when they made love, and Steven wanted to do that for Brock this time.

Slowly, Steven reached into Brock's waistband and tugged the briefs down as his tongue kissed the newly exposed skin. The base of Brock's cock appeared and Steven licked and nuzzled it as he continued to lower the briefs. As they slipped past Brock's hips, his cock sprang free of the fabric and Steven smiled and slipped the briefs down Brock's legs and off his body. Teasingly, Steven ran his tongue along the ridge of Brock's cock, earning a groan and a slight hiss. Steven looked at Brock's face, pleasure clearly written in his eyes. "I know you like that, but how about this?"

He opened his mouth and took just the head of Brock's cock into his mouth. Brock bucked trying to get Steven to take more. Using one of Brock's own movements, he placed his hand on Brock's hips to still him. "You're going to come, and you're going to come when you're deep down my throat, but not yet." Steven licked and swirled Brock's weighty balls in his mouth as he lifted Brock's legs to his chest. "There it is," Steve whispered to himself as he blew on Brock's tiny puckered opening. Brock whimpered deeply as Steven's tongue licked around the muscle.

Brock usually didn't allow this. It was too submissive an act for him. He liked rimming Steven, but he'd never allowed himself to be rimmed. He moaned deeply as Steven thrust his tongue against that tight muscle, sucking and probing that incredible ass. "Can I?" Steven looked up and Brock.

Brock's eyes danced, wondering what Steven had in mind, "You're in charge, Love." Steven read the trust in Brock's eyes.

Steven smiled as he pressed his lips to Brock's cheek and sucked hard while biting gently. He'd never felt the need before, but for some reason he wanted to mark the other man as his. "Mine." Slowly, he lowered Brock's legs back to the bedding and straddled Brock's body. Opening his mouth, he took Brock down his talented throat in one swift, sure movement. Brock writhed and moaned as Steven worked his cock like a pro. "God, Baby, that's so good." Steven stilled Brock's hips again as he worked that big cock with everything he had.

Brock moaned and writhed on the bedding as Steven picked up the pace, fucking his own mouth onto Brock's cock. "Steven, goddamn," was the only warning he got before Brock exploded down his throat. Steven swallowed every drop as he milked him dry.

Steven smiled as he raised his head, and, laying on top of Brock's strong body, Steven kissed him like the world was ending. Reaching to Brock's hands, he released them from the restraints and groaned as they wrapped around him, caressing his skin before latching hard onto his butt. "Did you like that, Love?"

"Uh huh."

Steven lifted his head and looked into Brock's eyes, "Did you?"

Brock nodded, "You were wonderful." His hands were already spreading Steven's cheeks, fingers working, locating his opening.

"Yesss, I want you," Steven hissed as a finger breached him.

Brock smiled as he kissed Steven again, "I know, Love." He flipped them on the bed, his weight pressing Steven into the blankets. "I want you too." He lifted Steven's legs, exposing his opening. Steven moaned as Brock blew onto the skin, the muscles pulsing. Brock ran his tongue around the muscle, teasing the tight opening.

"Oh god, I love that," Steven whimpered as a finger pressed against the muscle.

Brock smiled, "I know you do." He thrust his tongue deep into Steven, feeling that slim, lithe body vibrate from his ministrations.

"God, Brock, fuck me, please!" Brock was hard again, and it took only a second to lube himself and press the head of his cock against Steven's opening. "Give me all of you, now!"

Brock thrust forward in one swift movement, burying himself to the hilt. Steven gasped as he was filled. Brock pulled out and Steven whimpered, thrust again, and Steven repeated the gasp. Steven put his hand on Brock's leg, pulling him to his body, "More, Brock, faster, harder." Brock let loose and thrust into Steven like a man possessed. Steven rode the waves of pleasure as his lover pounded into his body. "I love you!"

They had both already expressed their love for each other, but hearing the sentiment again drove Brock to new heights of passion. He leaned forward, kissing Steven, while his hips pounded his cock deep into that incredibly welcoming body. "Oh god, Brock." Steven was stroking his cock as Brock rode his ass. With a yell, Steven came onto his stomach.

Brock leaned forward, his lips sucking the base of Steven's neck, sucking hard. Brock came deep in Steven's body as he hissed the word, "Mine!"

Brock collapsed onto Steven, who wrapped his arms around Brock's neck, pulling him into a kiss, "Yeah, yours. All yours. And you're mine and I love you!"

Brock lightly tickled Steven's stomach and he giggled and laughed as Brock settled on the blankets next to him. After a quick cleanup, they climbed under the blankets, Brock pulling Steven's body to his as

Steven snuggled close to Brock, sheltering himself against Brock's warm, hard body.

Steven smiled and squirmed a little. "Your chest hair tickles." Brock pulled away slightly. Steven turned his head to look at Brock's face, "I like it." He felt Brock's body get closer again. "It's part of what makes you the sexiest man I've ever met." Brock smiled as his hands stroked Steven's smooth chest and his nose and lips nuzzled Steven's neck.

"You're pretty sexy yourself, you know." Steven smiled as his eyes started getting heavy. "I love you, Steven."

"I love you too, Brock." Steven drifted off to sleep as those words happily bounced through his head.

The following afternoon, Steven and Travis headed down to the lake to the location they'd use for the Bacchanal that night. "This is something I usually do alone," Travis said, "but I thought you might benefit by seeing the preparations for the Bacchanal." As they arrived at the lake, Travis had Steven stand next to him. Travis concentrated and Steven thought he saw Travis glow with a transcendent, inner light. Travis spread out his hands, "Wine." A cask of wine and a stack of glasses appeared at the edge of the clearing. "Beer." A barrel of beer and chilled glassed appeared next to the wine. "Favorite food," he said, and tables of luscious looking food appeared next to the beer and wine. "Chocolate." A table of what looked like wonderful chocolates appeared next to the food tables. Travis waved his arms over his head and said, "Blessing." At first Steven didn't see anything, until the sun came out from behind a cloud. As he looked up, he saw a shimmer high above their heads. Travis then said, "Thank you," and opened his eyes.

Steven blinked his eyes and looked at Travis, "Where did all this come from and what is that?" Steven was pointing to the shimmer above their heads.

"This comes from Bacchus. He provides us with his gifts for each Bacchanal, and that is his blessing."

"I don't understand."

"I know. I call it his blessing because it's a sort of protection. Under that protection, it will be comfortably warm and pleasant even though the night will be cold. It allows our revelries to be conducted in comfort."

"Oh. How long does it last?"

Travis motioned around him, "At sunup tomorrow, it all disappears."

Steven was nodding. "So that's why Brock said I didn't need to bring anything."

Travis nodded. "Let's head back to the house, I need to rest before tonight. The preparations always make me tired." They headed back to the house for a quiet afternoon.

That evening was Steven's very first Bacchanal and he was so excited. Brock, Steven, Travis, and Cembran all headed down to the lake together. Steven noticed that it was indeed warmer near the lake. Jim and Sue arrived a few minutes later and the Bacchanal began. Steven turned to Travis, asking, "Isn't Gathod coming?"

"I think so, but I don't know." Travis hoped so.

Travis announced the Bacchanal and everyone gathered around the fire. "As usual, I'd like to begin our Bacchanal with some stories. Jim, would you start?"

Everyone took turns telling stories about their childhood, various adventures, or exciting experiences. As the stories were wrapping up, Gathod joined the gathering, with Doug a few steps behind him. Travis introduced Doug to everyone. Once the storytelling was finished, Travis turned on some music and everyone began to dance around the fire. Steven wasn't sure he wanted to join in, but Brock convinced him and soon he was whirling and twirling around the fire with everyone else.

"Brock, this is incredible," Steven shouted as they danced together. Suddenly he stopped and pulled his boyfriend aside, "I'm really horny. I feel like I'm going to explode."

Brock laughed, "That's part of the Bacchanal – it makes us really horny." He grabbed Steven's hand, whispering, "Come on," as he pulled Steven toward one of the shelters. Once inside, Brock opened Steven's pants, pushing them to his ankles, "What do you want, Love?"

"Fuck me hard, now!" Steven turned around and braced his hands against the wall of the shelter. Brock smiled as he opened his own pants, lubed his cock, and slowly pressed into Steven. Steven wasn't having any of it. Brock had just entered him when Steven pushed back hard against Brock, burying his cock deep inside. "Oh god, Brock! Fuck me!" And that's exactly what Brock did. Steven was moaning loudly as Brock fucked the living daylights out of him. Brock was afraid of hurting Steven, but every time he picked up the pace, Steven begged for more. He wrapped one hand around Steven's cock, stroking furiously, while the other hand lightly twisted the silver bar in Steven's nipple. Steven came with a moan of pleasure as Brock poured himself deep into Steven. After regaining his breath, Steven took Brock's hand, brought it to his mouth, and licked it clean before pulling up his pants and throwing his arms around Brock's neck. "I love you."

Brock thrust his tongue into Steven's mouth as he pulled the smaller man to his body. He'd never had a lover as responsive and tender as Steven and his heart melted every time Steven told him how he felt. "I love you too." After kissing for a few minutes, they stepped out of the shelter and rejoined the dance.

Hour after hour, they danced, ate, and drank. At one point, Steven got so aroused, he pulled Brock into the woods, opened his pants and swallowed his cock to the root. Brock fucked his mouth as Steven opened his own pants. Brock gushed down Steven's throat while Steven came on Brock's shoe. They both laughed as they cleaned themselves up, and headed back to the fire.

As the evening wore on, Doug, Travis, and Steven were talking together. Steven was finally satiated, much to Brock's relief and enjoyment.

"Travis, I've made a decision, I'm going to run for Sheriff. It's time we got rid of Palumbo," Doug said.

Travis was thrilled, "That's great! We'll do whatever we can." He hugged Doug as Gathod joined their group. "Are you enjoying yourself?"

Doug grinned, "Are you kidding? This is incredible." He grinned like a cat as Gathod dragged him toward one of the shelters.

Cembran joined the group around the fire a few minutes later, nuzzling Travis's neck gently.

"I know, Lamb, I'm impatient too. I need to speak with Brock and then we'll go to our shelter." Cembran nodded as Travis walked toward Brock, who was gorging himself at one of the food tables.

Travis patted him on the back, "I see you've got a live one in Steven."

Brock smiled, "You aren't kidding; I'm exhausted."

Travis laughed, "I wanted to ask you something. I'd like to incorporate the farm to help protect it in case something should happen to me. Could you help me?"

Brock spoke between mouthfuls, "Absolutely; come see me in the next few weeks and we'll get started." Steven joined Brock a few minutes later, both of them eating ravenously. Travis laughed to himself as he found Cembran and they headed toward their shelter together. A little while later the music faded and everyone bedded down for the night, exhausted from their revels.

Chapter Twenty-one

Travis woke to the first beams of the warm May sun streaming through their window. Cembran was awake next to him, his arm draped over Travis's chest. "What are you doing today, Lamb?" They'd already mapped out their strategies for the spring and there were a number of projects in progress.

"I want to get those fences for the new sheep pasture completed. How about you?"

Cembran nuzzled Travis's neck gently and the answer he wanted to give was to stay in bed and have sex all day. "I thought I'd help you so we can work on the house later." Thank goodness Gathod had agreed to take on most of the regular farm chores, freeing Travis and Cembran for the farm expansion work.

Over the last month, the addition to the house had progressed nicely. The foundations had been dug and laid, the exterior framing was complete, and they had started enclosing the roof and walls. They weren't expecting it to be done until late summer. Gathod had been helping them with the final phases of clearing the new pastures for the sheep and goats. The pastures wouldn't be ready for a while, but the new land allowed them to put the reserve pastures into use. It was these reserve pastures that Cembran and Travis were fencing. Cembran had cleared the ground a few years ago, but kept them fallow as a contingency. With the new pasture being cleared, he felt comfortable putting the land to use for the expanded sheep and goat herds.

The new storage building had been delivered about two weeks ago in large pieces. A week before delivery, a crew arrived to pour and complete the foundations. The crew then assembled the new building in about three days. The building was larger than what Travis knew they needed, but he wanted room for expansion, and the additional hay storage would come in handy. The company had done a spectacular job of designing the building to fit with the other farm buildings.

Travis and Cembran spent most of the morning stringing fences. They had already sunk the posts over the last few days. Cembran was amazed how quickly the job had gone once Travis hooked up the post hole digger to the tractor.

The sun was warm and the field smelled fresh and clean on the May breeze. "Cembran, I want to ask you something." Travis was attaching the fencing to the posts while Cembran held the fencing in place. "Am I pulling my weight here on the farm?"

Cembran smiled, "Yes, of course you are."

"It just seems as though you do a lot more of the work than I do." Travis was concerned that he was a burden here.

Cembran stopped working, leaning on one of the posts. "Yes, Travis, I do more of the physical work than you do. I'm good at it; I've done it for a long time. But you plan a lot more than I do. You planned the addition to the house and found some tools that would make the job go faster. You also planned, acquired, and had the new storage building built. You also take care of the vegetable garden, which was a chore I always disliked."

"Oh."

"And there are some things that you don't do well. Put a pair of shearing clippers in your hands and the sheep should run for their lives." Cembran chuckled to himself, remembering how bad Travis's sheep looked once he was done. He hadn't hurt the animal, but her coat looked like a moth-eaten patchwork quilt. "So, to answer your question, yes you pull your weight."

As the morning progressed, the air got warmer and Cembran pulled off his shirt, stuffing it through his belt, and they continued attaching the fencing to the posts. Travis was getting more and more distracted; he couldn't help watching Cembran as he worked - his muscles stretching, the light coating of sweat on his glistening skin, the outline of his cock occasionally visible through his pants.

By noon, they'd attached the fencing for three sides of the pasture and Travis had had enough. Cembran was leaning against one of the posts looking over their new fence. Travis came up behind him and slipped his arms around his waist as he pressed his body to Cembran's back.

Cembran smiled as he turned around. He opened his mouth to say something, but never got the chance. His lips were quickly occupied as Travis took his mouth in a searing, hot kiss. Travis lowered Cembran onto the soft grass. Cembran's hand cradled Travis's head as he returned the kiss, adding his own passion. Travis slipped his hand down Cembran's stomach to his cock, rubbing Cembran's hardness through his pants. Cembran whimpered softly as Travis fingers opened his clothes. Slowly, Travis stood up and slipped off his shirt, laying it on the grass. He then opened his pants and slipped them and his underwear off. Travis kissed Cembran softly as he slipped his clothes off. Lying on his back, with their clothes as a blanket, Travis pulled Cembran on top, wrapping his legs around Cembran's body. Their lips explored as they slowly rocked against each other.

"I want you, Lamb."

Cembran pulled back, looking at Travis's face. Travis heard a low growl as Cembran attacked his mouth, while fingers caressed and worked the skin around his opening. Those fingers carefully worked their way into Travis's body. "Yes..." Cembran's lips continued their assault on Travis's mouth, as his fingers performed magic in his body.

The breeze flowed gently over their bodies as Cembran removed his fingers and slowly pushed his cock into Travis. Inch after incredible inch of cock slipped into Travis's body, slowly filling him.

"Lamb," Travis moaned as Cembran entered him. Slowly and deliberately, Cembran pulled out before entering Travis again. Each movement was exquisite and both men felt as though they were part of each other. Cembran fucked him as though each thrust were rationed and he needed to wring maximum pleasure from each stroke – which is exactly what he did. Stroke after stroke, Cembran built a flame inside Travis that built into an inferno of love and desire.

When Cembran had Travis babbling incoherently, he wrapped his fingers around Travis's cock and stroked it, using his fingers to massage the head and tease his balls. Travis climaxed on waves of ecstasy, spots flashing before his eyes, as Cembran poured himself deep into his lover. "Lamb, love you."

Travis rolled Cembran onto his body as he felt Cembran pull out of him. The May sunshine warmed their bodies as they quietly held each other, while the breeze cooled their sweaty bodies. "Love you too, Lemmle." The words were soft, but full of emotion. Reluctantly, they helped each other get dressed before walking hand in hand back to the house for a quick lunch.

After lunch, Cembran and Travis were just finishing with the fencing as Doug walked across the field. "Hey, Doug, what brings you by?"

"Actually, a couple of things. I need to stop by the County Home for Children tomorrow and I was wondering if you'd go with me. I'd really like the director's support in my bid for Sheriff."

"Sure. But why me?"

Doug leaned against one of the fence posts. "I don't know how to explain it, but you exude a sense of joy to everyone around you. These kids need that."

Travis nodded slightly, "Okay, when did you want to go?"

"Is tomorrow afternoon all right?"

Travis looked at Cembran, who nodded. "That's good. Why don't you join us for lunch and we'll leave from here." Doug agreed. "You said a *couple* of things?"

"Well, I also stopped by to see if you needed help with the house, to make up for taking you away tomorrow."

"That's a deal. We just finished here and were heading that way." After gathering up their tools, they headed back to the house. They spent the rest of the afternoon working together and they were able to make a lot of progress getting the exterior of the addition enclosed. As the light started fading, Doug said he had to get home, but he'd see them tomorrow for lunch. Travis went inside to start dinner, while

Cembran spent some time in his small dairy making some of his incredible cheese. After dinner, they both collapsed into bed after a hard, but productive day.

The following afternoon, Doug stopped by at the appointed time and drove them to the County Home for Children after they ate. "How's the campaign going?" Travis hadn't heard much and he was more than a little curious.

"Jack is playing the gay card."

"You knew he would." The current Sheriff, Jack Palumbo, would do anything to keep his job.

"Yeah, I did. It's just that I don't want Gathod to become a target." Travis understood. Doug's feelings for Gathod were evident whenever they were together. "But I gave an interview to the paper. They even agreed to support me."

Travis had been surprised; the local newspaper was usually so conservative. "Yeah, I saw the article. I was glad to see you took the high road."

"I think my honesty surprised them. I mean, I told them I was gay, but I also told them I'd worked for the state police for ten years. Jack can't argue with my qualifications or my record, so he tries to get personal."

"How's the community support?"

Doug almost laughed, "One lady berated me in the street, but then lots of people volunteered to help with the campaign."

"Cembran and I will help; just let us know what we can do."

"I know, and you've got your hands full right now, but I'll need you later."

Travis was quiet for a while as they drove through the sleepy countryside. "Can I ask how you're dealing with the whole satyr thing? I was going to ask you at the Bacchanal, but didn't get a chance."

Doug concentrated on the road while he talked, "It was a shock, but I guess it doesn't really matter. I mean, I love Gathod and…."

Doug's cheeks started to get red and Travis smiled as he saw the blush. "The sex is absolutely mind-blowing?"

"Yeah, how did you…?"

"Let's just say it's a satyr thing." Travis smiled to himself as he thought of how Cembran always seemed to know, almost instinctively, how to make him happiest.

"I sort of figured that, but how?"

Travis had thought a lot about that himself, "I think," he started to explain and decided to change tactics. "Satyrs just seem to know what will give their partners, and by extension themselves, the most pleasure. We're very hedonistic creatures by nature, it's just part of who we are."

"Travis," Doug turned his head to look over at his passenger, "Why didn't you tell me when we dated?"

"I wasn't a satyr when we dated." He explained what had happened on the trip to Switzerland and how he had become a satyr.

"So this is all actually real? I mean, I knew about Gathod and I saw your horns and stuff, but the rest of what Gathod told me is true?"

Travis nodded.

Doug fell silent and Travis could tell he was lost in his own thoughts, so he settled back in the seat as they rode in comfortable silence.

Arriving at the home for children, Doug parked the car and they entered the fenced facility, looking for the director's office. From the outside, the building looked dismal, a square red brick facility, with small windows and very little yard. There did appear to be a small play area for the kids, but by and large the building screamed 1970s government construction at its worst. The inside of the building was a completely different matter. The hallways were decorated in bright colors, with posters and drawings lining the walls. The lighting was institutional, but everything from the paint colors to the curtains on the windows indicated that the person in charge really liked her job and cared for the children.

Arriving at the director's office, Doug knocked on the door. It was opened by a large woman with a bright cheerful face. He introduced himself and explained why they were here. Her face immediately clouded over, "So are you one of those 'spare the rod and spoil the child' type of people? The current Sheriff keeps...."

Doug raised his hand and smiled, "These children need all the support we can give them." He looked down the hall and shook his head, "This is incredible. From the outside you'd never know how homey and friendly this place is on the inside."

The stern look melted from her face, "I'm Paulette Brown." She extended her hand.

"I'm Doug Green and this is a good friend of mine, Travis Freeman." Travis shook Paulette's hand. "I was wondering if you'd give us a tour of the facility."

"It'd be a pleasure." Paulette led them though the building, explaining how it was laid out and the use of each area. She also explained the programs they ran and the support they gave the children. "Most of our children we are trying to find foster homes for," she explained as they walked, "Our goal is either adoption or placing the children back in their homes, once their parents have gotten the help they need." Paulette led them into the play yard behind the building. She was pointing out the equipment and other features, but Travis had tuned her out.

He actually interrupted saying, "Paulette, that boy sitting alone."

Paulette looked sadly at Travis, "That's Arthur, he's been here for about two weeks. Unfortunately, he hasn't uttered a word since he arrived. He just stares at a picture of his mother. She died of complications from HIV."

"Where is his father?"

"We don't even know who he is."

Paulette lead Doug back inside, but Travis stayed behind. Slowly, he walked to where Arthur was sitting and sat next to him. "Hi, I'm Travis." The boy raised his head a little. Travis leaned a little closer to look at the picture. "Is that your mom?" Arthur nodded a little as a tear ran down his cheek. "She's pretty, and she looks like you. Arthur, it's okay to miss her. My mom died a long time ago and I still miss her, too." Travis hadn't thought of his mother in a long time. He did miss her, especially her patience and understanding. Before he could stop it, a tear formed in his eye as he thought of her.

Arthur handed him a wadded Kleenex from his pocket. "Don't cry," the words were barely whispered. Travis was surprised at his own reaction and he used the Kleenex to dab his eyes. Before he knew what happened, Arthur had his arms around him. Now Travis really started to get choked up, not for himself, but for the sad little boy who was comforting him. Travis hugged him in return and he felt the small body convulse as Arthur sobbed.

Travis looked over the boy's shoulder and saw Paulette come back into the yard. She stopped dead in her tracks as she saw Arthur hugging Travis with everything he had as his body heaved with grief. Travis thought he saw her eyes look toward the sky. She went quietly back into the building dabbing her own eyes.

A while later, Paulette and Doug come back. Travis was still talking to Arthur. He was telling him about the farm and the lambs and kid goats. Arthur even asked a few questions. "I have to go, but I'll be back next week to visit you." The boy raised his head. The look on his face was pitiful. "I promise I won't forget. I'll even try to bring one of the lambs with me if you like."

"Okay." That got him a small smile. Travis stood up and Arthur stood up as well and gave Travis a hug. He said good-bye again and then headed inside with the other two adults.

"How old is Arthur?" he asked as they were walking back to Paulette's office.

"He's fifteen. The doctor says that he has a condition that delays puberty. That's part of the problem; he's small for his age and he's a little immature as well."

They stopped outside Paulette's office. "I'd like to visit him next week, and I'd like to bring a friend with me. A four-legged friend."

"Do you mean a dog?"

"No, a lamb. Arthur seemed to open up when I told him about the farm, he even asked questions."

"If it helps that boy, I'd let you bring an elephant. I don't know what you did, but I'm grateful." They shook hands and went back to the car.

On the drive back to the farm, a million thoughts were racing through Travis's head. He was knocked out of his thoughts by Doug's voice: "You sure made a connection with Arthur. I told you, you have a gift."

"Doug, there's a reason for Arthur's small size and his reaction to me, I think. His development isn't delayed; in fact, he's perfectly normal." Travis shifted in his seat, "He's a satyr, Doug. They mature later than humans, often when they're sixteen or seventeen."

"How do you know?"

"That is one of my gifts. I can tell, where most other satyrs can't. I can also tell that Arthur is going to start maturing and when he does he's going to get horns and a tail."

Travis was surprised by Doug's reaction, but he shouldn't have been.

"What are we going to do?"

"I don't know yet, but we are going to help him somehow." Travis only wished he knew how.

Arriving at the farm, Doug thanked Travis for going with him and then headed home. Travis headed into the house. Cembran was making dinner as Travis took off his coat and slipped his arms around his lover's waist, kissing his neck and ear.

"How did the visit go?" Travis told Cembran about the facility and about Arthur. "What are you going to do?" Cembran looked at Travis, "I know you're going to do something to help." Cembran turned around, putting his arms around Travis's neck, "It's part of why I love you."

Travis smiled as he kissed Cembran hard. "I don't know yet, Lamb. I just don't know, but you're right, I'm going to try to help."

Chapter Twenty-two

S teven's phone was ringing and he smiled involuntarily as he saw the name of the caller. "Hi Brock."

"Hey Steven, I was wondering if you're free for lunch today? Travis and Cembran are coming in to meet with me and I thought you'd like to join us."

That smile returned as a warm happy, feeling spread through Steven's entire body. "Sure, I'm free." Their conversations at the office were usually very businesslike. They hadn't told anyone at work that they were dating, which was fine with both of them. People tended to gossip and neither of them wanted the distraction. "Great, come to my office about noon and we'll all go from there." Brock's voice got very soft, "Love you."

Steven smiled into the phone, "Love you too." That was the most affection that either of them ever displayed in the office and only when they were sure they couldn't be overheard.

A few minutes later, Steven saw Cembran and Travis enter the office for their meeting with Brock. At noon, Steven locked his computer and headed down the hall to Brock's office. The door was closed and Helen appeared to have left for lunch, so he quietly tapped on the door.

"Come in, Steven." He couldn't help smiling as he peeked inside. Travis, Cembran, and Brock were seated around the large conference table, "We'll be done in a minute."

"Do you want me to come back later?" So much of Brock's business was confidential, involving attorney/client privilege, that Steven was already heading for the door.

Travis spoke up, "No, please join us. We have something we'd like to ask you." Steven was intrigued. He shut the door and took an empty seat around the table. "Cembran and I are working with Brock to incorporate the farm and all the land, including the land used for the Bacchanal, under the name Two Worlds Farms." Steven nodded, "We want to protect it as best we can. One of the things we need to do is set up a Board of Directors."

Steven was listening intently, "Okay, what can I do?"

Travis smiled and looked at Brock, "We need one more outside director and Brock suggested we ask you, and I thought that was a great idea."

Steven was taken aback, "Me? Why me? Why not Brock?"

"Brock is going to sit on the Board, as am I, Cembran, and Brock's father. We need one additional director and we all thought you'd be a good choice."

Steven smiled broadly, the pleasure and surprise at being asked plain on his face, "It would be an honor."

"Excellent."

Brock was thrilled. Over the past few months, he'd seen Steven blossom in so many ways. He spoke up more both at work and when he was with Brock, and he seemed so much happier and content. Brock still felt very protective of him, though; a few weeks back, he'd had to restrain himself when he heard a colleague giving Steven a hard time. His first instinct was to protect his lover. A few months ago, Steven would have taken the comments to heart, but this time he stuck up for himself and proved he was all right.

Brock stood up, "I think I have all the information I need to start the paperwork. Are you all ready for lunch?" He took them to a small café near the office that was relatively quiet.

"Brock, I need your advice, and yours too, Steven." Both men looked at Travis. "I visited the County Home for Children with Doug a few weeks ago and I met a boy, Arthur. I've been visiting him for the last few weeks. He's really an incredible kid." The waitress approached and took their orders. Once she'd left, Travis continued, "His mother died recently and he's alone. The saddest part is that he's fifteen and hasn't developed yet." Both Steven and Brock looked at Travis with rapt attention. Travis nodded to confirm their thoughts, "He's a satyr but he doesn't know it. Unfortunately, his mother probably didn't know either. Luckily he hasn't started maturing yet, but he will soon."

Brock nodded, but Steven looked appalled and scared. "We've got to do something. I don't want anyone to go through what I went through." Cembran and Travis looked at Steven as he continued, "Travis, someone has got to tell him. He's going to feel different and start to look different. He's going to think he's a freak." Brock placed his hand on Steven's to calm him.

"Steven, I promise, I'll explain things to him if I have to, but I'm really trying to find a supportive home for him." Steven started to relax as their food arrived. "Both of you, please let me know if you think of anything."

Steven spoke up, obviously feeling strongly, "We will." Brock couldn't help smiling at his boyfriend's conviction and his need to help.

After lunch, back in his office, Steven was working intently when he received a telephone call from Jack Goode, Sr. personally. Steven was a little surprised that Jack was calling him – usually his secretary called to make arrangements. "Steven, this is Jack. Could you please come to my office at your convenience?" Steven knew that the 'at your convenience' was a courtesy.

"Yes, I'll be right down." Steven hung up the phone and hustled to Jack's large corner office.

Gregory, Jack Goode's assistant, was hard at work when Steven approached. The door was closed, but Gregory smiled and told Steven to go right in. Steven knocked softly and opened the door.

Jack stood up from his desk chair and walked to Steven extending his hand. "I wanted to thank you and Brock for your long hours and hard work getting the website set up. It's been a huge success." He patted Steven on the back and led him to one of the chairs in front of his desk. Jack indicated for Steven to take a seat. He then realized that Brock was occupying the other one. Jack continued talking as he sat behind his desk. "The website has already increased the sales of our publications by twenty percent in just a few months, way beyond our expectations." Steven's eyes darted to Brock.

Steven was a little confused, but he noticed Brock was smiling, so it couldn't be that bad. "Steven, Brock tells me that you two have something you need to talk to me about?" Steven looked at Brock, a knot of fear in his stomach. Jack continued, "I think I can guess what it is." The man's eyes were twinkling. "I think this is Brock's way of telling me that you two are a couple. Am I right?" Jack sounded like a kid in a candy store for some reason.

Steven looked at Brock and then back at Jack before nodding his head. Brock reached to Steven patting his hand gently. "Now look, I won't have any inappropriate behavior in the office." The words sounded stern, but Jack's eyes were still twinkling, "But over the past few months both of you have been visibly happier and by the way, I'm not the only person to notice." Steven's eyes kept shifting to Brock, not sure he could believe his ears. "As long as both of you are professional at work, and you have been over the past few months, then I'm happy for both of you."

"But," Steven stammered. He couldn't believe his ears.

Jack smiled broadly, "As long as you don't report to Brock, there is no conflict of interest, and as of today, you report directly to me." Steven looked at his lover.

Brock smiled broadly, "Jack told me earlier that he wanted to promote you to Director of Publications. You'll be in charge of the entire legal publishing department, and reporting directly to Jack." Steven was shocked and confused. Had he gotten the job because of his relationship with Brock? "When Jack told me, I told him we had something to tell him."

Steven looked at both of them, "I didn't get this because of Brock?"

Brock shook his head. Jack smiled and chuckled lightly, "Steven, you got this position because of your hard work and only because of your work. Brock just confirmed my decision."

"Oh." Steven was overwhelmed. They spent the next hour discussing Steven's new job responsibilities and how the transition of his current duties would be accomplished. At the end of the conversation, his head was swimming. Slowly he stood up and thanked Jack before leaving the office. Brock followed him a few minutes later.

"Come to my office in a minute." Brock's eyes were dancing as he strode by. Steven hung back so he could watch Brock's gorgeous ass as he slowly followed him to his office. Once inside, Brock closed the door, arms wrapped around Steven's waist as their lips pressed together, hard and insistent. "I have an appointment soon, but I just wanted to give you that."

Steven smiled and his knees went a little weak as he opened the door and floated back to his office. A few minutes later, Gregory appeared at his door. "Yes, Gregory, can I help you?"

Gregory smiled, "I need you to follow me if you would." Steven got up and followed him down the hall. He led Steven to the front of the office, near where the partners had their large spacious suites. Gregory opened the door to the office next to Brock's, and led Steven inside. The office was a near duplicate of Brock's with a large walnut desk, plush chairs, and a conference table. Gregory smiled, "I'll have your things moved in here tomorrow."

"Huh?"

"This is your new office." Steven thought he was kidding, but one look at his face told him he wasn't. Steven smiled and looked around as Gregory left, shutting the door behind him.

After work, Steven went home to his condo. Brock had told him late that afternoon that he had an appointment in the evening. Steven was a little disappointed because he was so excited about the promotion and he really wanted to share his excitement with Brock.

Steven was eating dinner on the couch when he heard a key in the lock of the front door. It opened and Brock came inside, wearing a pair of tight black leather pants, a black leather jacket, and a huge smile, carrying a bottle of champagne. "I wasn't expecting you." Steven's smile was huge as he got up from table and jumped into Brock's waiting arms. Their kiss was intense, hot, and hard as Brock set down the bottle, pressing Steven to his body. "Do you need something to eat?"

Brock grabbed Steven's ass as he wrapped his long legs around Brock's waist. "Just you, Love!" he grunted, as he carried Steven to the bedroom, pressing their lips together. Setting Steven on the bed, Brock removed the leather jacket.

Steven growled at the sight of all that dark skin, taut muscle, black chest hair, and the large fleshy nipples. "Oh god, Brock." His mouth hung open as he was gripped by desire. "Wh... what about your meeting?"

"I cancelled it." Brock was leaning over the bed. "Get naked, Steven!" Steven shed his clothes so fast, his arms and legs looked like blurs. Soon Steven was standing in front of his lover, naked and panting, his cock leaking copiously in anticipation. "God, Baby, you are spectacular." Brock's gaze raked over Steven, "All that smooth alabaster skin and all for me." Brock gently pushed Steven back onto the bed.

Brock wrapped his hand around Steven's cock, "Yeah, all yours, Brock." Steven's head was already thrown back as Brock ran his tongue lightly across the head of his cock. The bars through Steven's nipples drew Brock's attention. His tongue teased one of the nipples, while his fingers lightly twisted the other. Steven moaned loudly as Brock teased and sucked his super-sensitive buds.

Brock whispered as he blew on Steven's nipples, sending visible shivers through his sweet body. "Want you, Love." Steven said nothing. He simply placed his hands above his head, holding on to the headboard. "Steven." The word was whispered softly as Brock realized the significance of Steven's actions. He was giving himself to Brock, telling him he trusted him.

Quietly, Brock opened Steven's closet, looking through his clothes. Brock smiled as he found a silk tie. "Raise your head, Love." Steven did as he was told and Brock wrapped the tie around his head, covering his eyes. "Tonight, you just feel."

Steven could see nothing as the tie covered his eyes. He heard the zipper of Brock's pants and he heard them drop to the floor. He felt Brock's weight on the bed, then lips touched his very gently, a hot tongue probed his mouth, lips pulled and sucked on his. Hands caressed his arms, tickling the sensitive skin of his underarms and side. Those same hands caressed his chest and stomach, while the lips slowly moved down his body, nibbling his neck, sucking on his shoulders, teasing his now ultra-sensitive nipples. "That's so good." Steven pushed his chest forward against the heat of Brock's tongue and lips, wanting more, needing more.

The tongue and lips kept exploring, his ribs and hips were laved and teased, his stomach was caressed, and Steven felt gentle kisses travel down his abdomen. God, he wanted to feel Brock's lips on his cock, but Brock wasn't quite ready yet. The tongue swirled into his navel before traveling along his hip to his leg. "Not fair; I need you."

The pleading made Brock throb with desire, but nothing would interfere with his plan. "Just relax, Love." His voice was rough.

Steven felt lips and tongue travel along his inner leg. His legs spread wide on their own, opening himself to Brock's ministrations. The tongue traveled up Steven's inner thigh and licked one of his balls. Steven hissed in surprise as they were sucked into that mouth.

"Brock." Steven's voice was really whiny as he begged Brock for more. "God, I need it."

"What do you need? This?" The tongue ran along the underside of Steven's cock, slowly and gently, as Steven's hips bucked toward the sensation, trying to get more. "How about this?" Steven's legs were lifted and he felt hot breath and then a scalding tongue press against his opening. The tongue teased around the edge before probing him.

"Yeah, Brock. Yes, more please!" Steven was pressing hard against Brock's mouth. Brock smiled as he slipped a finger into the tight opening, his mouth taking Steven's cock. Steven moaned loudly as his head thrashed back and forth on the pillow, his hands white-knuckled on the headboard. One finger became two as those fingers massaged his pleasure center. "I'm going to...."

His lover's mouth pulled off Steven's cock. "Not yet, Love." The weight on the bed shifted as fingers slid out of his body. Steven knew what was next, god, he hoped what was next. He felt a cock press at his entrance, pushing into him, his body opening, accepting Brock greedily. He felt it slide into his body steadily, deeper and deeper, until he was filled. Steven felt hot scalding lips press to his as Brock started to move inside him. He felt hands against the blindfold and then it was gone. He could see Brock's face and look into his eyes – eyes that were bursting with love. "I needed to see your face." The kisses kept coming as Brock thrust deep into him; sometimes it felt as though he were touching his very soul.

"I love you, Brock." Steven was so overwhelmed by the look on Brock's face that he couldn't control himself anymore and he came hard onto his stomach, his body shaking.

Brock cried, "Steven!" as he climaxed deep in his body. Steven finally let go of the headboard and wrapped his arms around Brock's neck, drawing him close. Brock collapsed, the weight of his body feeling good, solid, on top of him. Their kisses were hot and loving as they both relished the post-orgasmic high before their bodies started to recover.

Brock rolled onto his side, pulling Steven's body to his, arms wrapped protectively around the man he loved with all his heart. He gently nibbled on Steven's ear. "Would you come with me to my parents' house for dinner tomorrow?"

"Mmmm," those lips on his ear felt good, "Sure."

"I'd like you to get to know them." Steven tilted his head to look into Brock's face. "They're important to me; you're important to me." Steven snuggled close, extremely happy and content.

"I keep thinking about that boy Travis told us about at lunch."

Brock caressed Steven's cheek, "I know, me too. I want to discuss it with my parents tomorrow, they might have some ideas."

Steven nodded softly, "I just can't get him out of my mind." His voice got soft, "Although you were quite a distraction." Steven felt those arms squeeze him gently.

Brock smiled and kissed Steven, "Could we get a snack before we go to sleep? I seem to have missed dinner."

"As long as I get to be dessert," Steven wiggled his butt against Brock before getting out of bed.

Chapter Twenty-three

The June Bacchanal was in full swing. Brock's parents, Jim and Sue, had brought another couple with them. They seemed like a very nice, middle-aged couple. Greg was an artist and his wife Millie was a nurse. Their children had left home a few years ago and they were thrilled to be included in a Bacchanal. They said they hadn't attended one in over forty years. They even asked if they could bring their children. Millie had whispered, "Only the married ones, of course." She then started to giggle and Travis couldn't help laughing along with her.

At that point, Greg moved to his wife's side. "This is very different from the Bacchanals I remember." There was no criticism in his voice; he just seemed curious.

Travis and Millie were still laughing together. She really seemed to spread joy and happiness. "I'm sure it is. I mean, I know it's different from the Bacchanal I saw in Switzerland. But the purpose of this one is different."

"What do you mean?" they both said in unison. It was adorable.

"The primary purpose of the Bacchanal I witnessed was reproduction, since satyrs can only conceive beneath the full moon."

Greg nodded, "That's true, but what makes this any different?"

"Well most of us aren't going to conceive anything, full moon or not." Travis smiled. "The primary purpose here is community building. I mean, most of us didn't know each other a year ago and this is a chance to build a sense of community and identity with other satyrs. That is the main reason we start each Bacchanal telling stories – to help foster a sense of shared history and identity."

Greg appeared thoughtful, "I never thought of it that way, but you're right."

Travis whispered conspiratorially, "And it's a wonderful spot to be with the one you love." He looked around as the moon shone brightly on the lake.

Millie giggled again, "I couldn't agree more." Her smile didn't diminish as she took Greg by the hand, winking at Travis, "Please excuse us." Travis smiled as they headed into the woods toward one of the shelters built for the Bacchanal, giggling and laughing as they walked.

Cembran joined Travis a few minutes later, slipping his arms around Travis's waist, "Lemmle, I have our shelter ready for us." Cembran's voice was needy and his lips were already pulling on Travis's ear as he moaned softly. He pulled Travis by the hand toward the shelter. A small fire was burning in the fireplace, blankets and pillows had been set out. Cembran lowered himself to the blankets, pulling Travis down with him.

Generally, Cembran was not particularly aggressive in bed. He was usually content to let Travis take the lead, but tonight he was a tiger. He attacked Travis's lips with his own as he tore open Travis's shirt, sending buttons flying in every direction. Lips pulled on Travis's nipples while nimble fingers opened his pants before pulling them off. "Lie down, Lemmle. Tonight you're mine and I want you."

"Okay, Tiger, whatever you want." Travis was excited by this aggressive side of Cembran and he went with it. Whatever his lover had in mind, he was sure it was going to be memorable. Cembran lifted Travis's legs, pushing them toward his chest, before rimming him within an inch of his life. Travis's head rocked on the pillow as Cembran thrust his tongue deep. "Lamb, that's so good." Cembran smiled as he lifted his head, before swallowing Travis's cock to the root. Without lifting his head, Cembran shifted his body, his knees straddling Travis's head. Travis guided Cembran's hips lower and his cock to his lips.

He worked Cembran's cock down his throat as he slipped a finger into Cembran's hot, tight body. Cembran moaned gently around the cock in his mouth as Travis worked his finger over his gland again and again. Slowly, Cembran lifted his body. "You're mine and I'm going to have you now, just the way I want you." Cembran straddled Travis and thrust down onto Travis's spit- lubed cock. "Oh god, yes. That's just what I wanted!"

Travis moaned as Cembran's body gripped his cock like a vise. Cembran lifted and lowered himself while his fingers stroked and tweaked Travis's nipples. He worked Cembran's cock with his hand, the thumb massaging the head with each stroke, while Cembran pounded their bodies together. "Lamb, I'm coming." Travis's climax burst deep into Cembran. Travis withdrew and shifted their bodies, taking Cembran in his mouth where he sucked like a vacuum cleaner. Cembran cried out as he shot hard down Travis's throat.

Satiated and comfortable, they rested together before heading back to the Bacchanal. The clearing by the lake was quiet. Some people were in the shelters while some were sitting around the fire telling stories.

Brock and Steven were cuddled together around the bonfire, obviously satiated and just enjoying themselves. Travis and Cembran joined them. Cembran excused himself a few minutes later.

"Travis, have you had any luck finding a home for Arthur?" Steven seemed really concerned.

"No." The disappointment plain in Travis's voice, "I've visited him a couple times a week for the last month or so. He's a really smart, quiet kid."

Steven nodded, "I've spoken to a few people I know, but I haven't had any luck."

Travis exhaled deeply, "I'll keep trying." He was starting to give up hope.

Steven looked up, "So will we." His voice very determined. He got up and wandered away.

Brock whispered to Travis, "Steven would like to take Arthur, but he knows it isn't practical." They looked at Steven as he stood by the edge of the lake, the moon playing on the water. Travis nodded and Brock got up to join his boyfriend.

Travis watched as Cembran returned, then said, "I'll be right back, Lamb." Travis went to the shelter, doused the fire, grabbed some blankets and pillows, and rejoined Cembran at the main fire. Travis spread a blanket on the soft sand. "Come here, Lamb." Cembran curled onto the blanket next to Travis, their bodies pressing together, Travis's arms wrapping around him protectively as they watched the flames and whispered softly to one another.

The clearing near the lake was quiet when Travis woke in the morning. The sun danced on the surface of the calm water. Travis smiled to himself; even Cembran was still asleep. The first movement Travis spied was Gathod leaving the shelter he'd shared with Doug and heading toward the barns to start the morning chores. Travis rocked Cembran, watching his eyes flutter open. "Sorry, Lamb, but we need to help Gathod with the animals." Cembran smiled and kissed Travis softly before getting up and heading toward the barns. Travis followed a few minutes later.

They could hear Gathod working in the goat barn, so Travis and Cembran started with the sheep. This time of year when the weather was good, the sheep remained in the field most of the day, so there wasn't much to do. They checked that everything was all right before heading back to the goat barn to complete the morning milking. Outside, Travis stopped.

Cembran smiled, "What's on your mind?" Cembran knew him so well.

"I'd like to ask you something. I'd like to bring Arthur here to live with us." Travis didn't know the reaction he was expecting, but it certainly wasn't the one he received.

"No!" The word was vehement, his reaction instant.

"I just thought...." The words died on his lips at the look of extreme pain on Cembran's face.

"I can't do that, I just can't." The pain in Cembran's voice broke Travis's heart. Cembran turned and raced back toward the house, obviously upset. Travis didn't know what to do. He started to go after Cembran, but stopped short, deciding that maybe he needed some time. Travis figured whatever was bothering him was bigger than this.

He headed morosely back to the lake. Everyone was awake and the cleanup was well under way.

Brock noticed the look on Travis's face, "Where's Cembran?"

Travis looked worried, "I don't know. I upset him. I didn't mean too, and he took off. He probably just needs to think."

Once everything was cleared away from the Bacchanal, Travis carried things back to the house. He'd expected Cembran to join them once he'd calmed down, but Travis hadn't seen him for the past hour or so, and he was starting to get worried. He looked through the house before heading outside and down to the barns. As he stepped out of the house, Travis saw Jim and Sue coming up the path. "Travis can we…?" Jim saw Travis's face and stopped whatever he was going to ask, asking instead, "What's wrong?"

"Cembran's upset and I haven't seen him. I need to make sure he's all right." *Damn, I should have followed him instead of leaving him alone*, he thought.

"Go on, then; Jim and I will wait inside." Travis nodded as he walked briskly down toward the goat barn. Inside, it was quiet and there was no sign of Cembran. He checked out the sheep barn. Inside was the same as the other: quiet and no sign of Cembran. Damn it where was he, Travis thought, as he headed out to check the fields. Travis finally spotted him sitting behind the barn on a bale of hay, a lamb cradled in his arms like a security blanket.

Travis approached softly, "Lamb, I…."

Cembran's cheeks were streaked with tears, "I just can't, Travis." His shirt was wet and he'd been crying for a while.

"Okay, Lamb, I can accept that." Travis knelt near him, pressing their foreheads together. "There's more to this than Arthur. What's going on?"

Cembran's voice was choked and raspy, "I can't be my father. What if I turn out like him? What if…?"

Travis sat next to Cembran. "Lamb, you aren't your father and you won't act like him." He stroked Cembran's cheek, softly, "I won't do this if you don't want to. I love you more than anything." Cembran put the lamb onto the ground and threw his arms around Travis's neck. "It's okay, Lamb." Travis rocked him gently in his arms. It never ceased to amaze him that even after having lived alone all those decades, Cembran was still such a sensitive, caring, and tender soul.

"I just don't want to disappoint you." There it was, the real reason for the tears.

"Lamb, you'd have to work hard to disappoint me." Travis's lips found Cembran's on their own. He pulled Cembran to him, holding him tightly, "I love you, Lamb, more than anyone or anything." Cembran gripped him tightly, holding on like he was lost and Travis had found him again.

"Lamb," Cembran raised his head, listening. "Jim and Sue are at the house, they wanted to talk to us about something." Cembran nodded and got up. Travis kept his arms around him as they walked back to the house. "You don't have to be afraid to disagree with me or tell me how you feel. We're not going to agree on everything." Cembran nodded and leaned against Travis as they approached the door.

Jim and Sue were waiting patiently. "Has everyone left?"

Sue smiled brightly, "Yes. While you were busy, we saw them off. Everyone told us they had a wonderful time and asked us to tell you they look forward to next month." Cembran and Travis sat down.

"Travis," Jim spoke up, "We wanted to speak with you. Sue and I have been talking quite a bit over the past few weeks." Travis was wondering where this was heading. "Sue and I would like to provide a home for Arthur. In the old country, he would immediately go to live with a relative or a home would be found for him in the village. Sue and I feel strongly that we need to care for our own." A tingle went up Travis's spine; this was wonderful news.

Sue picked up where Jim left off, "We've been lonely since Brock left home and we've got a lot of years and a lot of love left to give. So we wanted to ask you if you'd take us to meet Arthur and find out how he feels."

Travis was out of his chair and hugging Sue before he could think. Then he realized what he'd done and his face colored, "I'm sorry, I got carried away."

She giggled, "You really care for this boy, don't you?" Part of her question remained unspoken.

"Yeah, I do." Travis looked at Cembran, "But Cembran and I haven't been together long enough yet to take him ourselves." He had no intention of making his lover feel uncomfortable.

"Would you take us to meet him?"

Travis grinned, "Sure, when do you want to go?"

Sue giggled again, "Today. No time like the present. That's why we stayed."

Travis was surprised and pleased. "Okay." He paused, "Did Brock tell you he doesn't know he's a satyr?"

Sue became serious, "Yes, Brock told us and we've decided we'll tell him once he's settled with us."

Travis was beaming as he looked at Cembran, who was smiling as well. "Okay, we'll leave in a few minutes. I'll call Paulette and let her know we're coming."

After speaking with Paulette, the four of them piled into Travis's car and headed to the home for children. When they arrived, she greeted them and escorted them to her office. Travis introduced Jim and Sue and explained why they were here. "Jim and Sue are interested in providing a home for Arthur."

Paulette was pleased by the offer, but she seemed a little reserved as she explained the regulations. "You need to be approved as foster parents."

Jim took out the forms he had already completed and their approval as foster parents. "My son is a lawyer; we completed the process already." Travis was surprised and pleased; they were obviously serious.

Paulette was made copies of the approval. "There are a few issues that I see. The first is that you don't live in the County."

"We asked Brock about that and he said that as long as we agree to make Arthur available to the social workers and we are willing to comply with County regulations, there shouldn't be an issue."

Paulette nodded, "That's true. My other issue is your age."

Travis spoke up at this point, "Paulette, what's the real issue?"

"I'm concerned that they may not be able to handle him. He has emotional and health problems and he's very immature for his age. He's fifteen, but emotionally he's about twelve or thirteen."

Travis was about to say something when Jim spoke up. "Sue and I have already raised a son, we can handle anything."

Travis interjected, "I've spent a lot of time with Arthur over the last month or so. He's a smart boy who needs love. Jim and Sue will give him that; they're more than capable of dealing with any emotional or health issues. Paulette, please ask yourself, is he better off here, or in a loving, caring home with people who want to be part of his life?"

"Okay, okay. Why don't you take them to meet Arthur while I finish the paperwork?" They got up and Travis led them outside. Arthur was sitting in his usual place in the yard, staring at the picture of his mother, but when he saw Travis, his face brightened and he rushed over giving Travis a big hug.

"Arthur, I have some people for you to meet." The boy looked up warily. "This is Jim and Sue Kraus." Jim extended a hand and Arthur took it without saying anything.

Sue was more forward; she scooped Arthur into her arms hugging him tightly, "You sweet boy." Arthur looked like he didn't know what to do, until he finally relaxed into the hug.

"Arthur, Jim and Sue want to give you a home."

Arthur looked up at Travis, "For how long?" His voice was small and he sounded almost fragile.

Sue was practically crying as she hugged Arthur to her again, "For as long as you want to stay, you sweet boy."

Paulette joined them smiling brightly. "I've got everything ready." She extended her hand and led Arthur away; a few minutes later she motioned for Travis to join them. "Arthur, Jim and Sue want to take you home with them. Is that okay with you?"

Arthur's gaze traveled from Paulette to Travis and back to Paulette. Then he nodded his head, "I'll get to visit you and see the lambs, right?"

Travis smiled, "Of course." He knelt down, "Jim and Sue will love you and care for you." He thought a minute, then added, "And you'll also have a cool big brother." Arthur smiled and hugged Travis tightly.

The three of them rejoined Jim and Sue. "Arthur, I'm going to take them to finish the paperwork. Would you go pack your things?" The boy nodded and headed inside. At the doorway, he turned, looked at Travis, and smiled, before going inside.

Paulette led them inside where they completed the paperwork. It took awhile to complete the forms and get everything signed. However, by mid-afternoon, they were all in Travis's car, their stomachs were full of hamburgers and French fries (Arthur's choice), and they were heading back to the farm. Arthur was in the back seat between Jim and Sue. Her arm was around him, holding him like he was a great treasure.

At the farm, Arthur was fascinated. "Can I go see the animals?"

Travis beamed, "Sure." Jim, Sue, and Arthur walked together toward the barns. As they walked, he overheard Arthur say, "When Travis came to visit, he'd bring one of the lambs or a baby goat. I like the...." His voice trailed off as they got farther away and he watched as the three of them walked down the path.

Cembran rested his head on Travis's shoulder, "Come inside." Pulling his gaze from the path, he stepped inside the house. Cembran's arms snaked around his neck, lips finding Travis's. The kiss was gentle, loving, and very sweet. "You did a wonderful thing. Travis, I'm so sorry."

Travis cut him off with another soft kiss, "Lamb, it's okay. He's better off with them and I'll be able to see him."

"I have something for you. I was saving this for your birthday, but I want you to have it now." Cembran went into the bedroom and returned a few minutes later with a beautiful wood carving. Travis took it and looked at the intricately carved figure.

His hand involuntarily covered his mouth, "Lamb, it's beautiful. It's me?" Cembran took the carving out of Travis's hand and placed it on the mantle next to the carving of his mother and brother as Travis watched through wet eyes.

Chapter Twenty-four

Travis wiped the sweat from his brow as he worked in the vegetable garden. The sun was barely up and it was already hot and sticky. That was Michigan in late July. Not that Travis was complaining; he was almost done and the heat was great for the early summer vegetables. Baskets of green beans, wax beans, peas, leaf lettuce, and spinach had already been harvested and were ready for Travis and Cembran to take to the farmers' market in town. The garden was producing more they could use and Travis figured he could turn some of their excess bounty into cash.

He smiled as he heard footsteps behind him.

"Lemmle, are you ready to go?"

Travis straightened up as he watched Cembran walk toward him, weaving between the rows of vegetables. "Travis, are you okay? You look puzzled."

"I had a strange night. My thoughts were disturbed, unsettled."

Cembran's expression darkened with concern, "Like when my father...?"

Travis shook his head, "No, not like that, but just... strange." He was confused and a little concerned that he was over-reacting. After the attacks by Cembran's father, he was sensitive to his dreams and thoughts while sleeping, and he knew something wasn't right, but he couldn't put his finger on what was wrong. "I'll be alright."

Cembran wasn't convinced, but let it go, for now. "Okay, but tell me if it continues." Cembran unconsciously bit his lip.

Travis leaned close for a kiss, getting one along with a smile. "I will, I promise." He looked around one last time, returning his attention to the task at hand. "This should be all of it. I just hope it'll all fit in the car." Travis kissed Cembran warmly before picking up the final basket of spinach and carrying it up to the house.

They showered quickly before Gathod joined them for breakfast, after which they loaded the vegetables into Travis's car.

"That is one full vehicle," Gathod smirked as he closed the trunk. "I'm glad I'm not going with you; I'd have to ride on the roof."

Travis got in as Cembran and Gathod talked briefly. "Thank you for taking care of the morning chores. We should be back this afternoon."

"No problem," Gathod grinned.

Cembran smiled as he got into the car. Travis honked goodbye as they pulled onto the road. They'd gone less than a mile when he spotted a car heading toward them. Travis recognized it; "No wonder Gathod was so happy." He slowed and rolled down the window. "Doug, going to see Gathod?"

Doug nodded slightly, "Yeah, I haven't seen him all week. Where are you headed?"

"To the farmers' market."

"Good, maybe I'll see you there later." Travis looked at him quizzically, "It's a good place to be seen, shake hands, and meet people."

"That makes sense. We'll look for you later." Travis waved as he rolled up the window and continued on toward town.

The market was a beehive of activity as Travis and Cembran located the booth that they had reserved. When he'd called, the man in charge of the market told Travis that there was one last stall available, so Travis had booked it for this week and the two following weeks so he could see how things went.

They unloaded their vegetables and spent some time setting up their stall, making sure their produce looked fresh and appetizing. As they were finishing, the people in the stall next to them came over and introduced themselves. "I'm Merle and this is my wife Jane." Travis introduced Cembran and himself. "We've been coming here for years." Their booth was filled with jars of honey and various items made of beeswax. Cembran smiled and asked about the bees, telling Jane, "My mother used to keep a beehive when I was young."

The four of them talked until the bell sounded, indicating that it was eight o'clock and the market was now open for business. Throngs of people entered the market and started moving up and down the aisles, looking to see what everyone had for sale. Travis and Cembran did a steady business for the first couple of hours, selling a lot of their beans and peas. Their spinach, however, was a huge hit. There wasn't a lot of it at the market, so it sold quickly, and within an hour of opening, they'd sold everything they had.

Merle popped his head into their booth, "How's it going?"

Travis smiled as he bagged three pounds of wax beans for a customer, "Very well." He helped the lady, thanked her, and completed the sale. "We already sold out of the spinach."

"Darn, that spinach looked good. I knew I should have gotten some earlier. Will you be here next week?" Travis nodded. "Good, put aside some for me." Merle went back to his booth when Jane signaled that she needed help.

The next hour was busy and Travis was helping a customer when he heard a gruff voice say, "Freeman, you still farming?"

Travis thanked the customer he was helping and raised his head, looking up into the eyes of Joe Palumbo. "Yes. What do you want?"

Joe leaned into the stall, "I wanted to ask you how much?"

"How much for what?" Travis figured he'd play along.

"How much do you want for the land? Name your price. One million? Two million?" Joe tried to smile, but it just looked ridiculous.

"The land is not for sale and it never will be." Travis crossed his arms in front of his chest. "And if I ever do decide to sell, I certainly wouldn't sell to a crook like you!"

Joe's face contorted into a look of absolute disgust, "Freeman, you and this…," he pointed to Cembran, "…faggot." He looked around to see who was listening, though no one appeared to be, much to his disappointment. "The thought of you two raising a kid just makes me sick."

"How did you…?"

Joe stood erect, obviously pleased that he'd scored a hit.

Thankfully, Travis heard a voice behind him, "Travis, what's going on?"

Travis turned around and smiled at Doug as he walked into the stall. "Hey, I have someone for you to meet. Doug, this is Joe Palumbo. Joe, this is Doug Green, the man who'll be replacing your brother as Sheriff." Doug laughed, Joe glared, and Merle, who'd just taken a drink of water, choked on it in the next booth.

Joe looked at Travis murderously before he took the opportunity to move on, and headed down the aisle, glaring at everyone as he walked. Between laughs Doug somehow managed a few words, "So what was that about?"

"He wanted to know how much I wanted for the land. I told him it wasn't for sale. Then you arrived and I just couldn't help throwing a little abuse his way." Travis turned to Merle and Jane in the next booth and introduced them to Doug. "Doug is running for Sheriff."

Merle expended his hand and smiled broadly, "Good to meet you." They talked for a few minutes until Doug excused himself and went into the market to meet people and shake hands.

When they were alone, Travis talked softly with Cembran, "I don't understand the comment about us raising a kid. I mean, I only talked it over with you. Something isn't quite right."

"Well, you spent a lot of time with Arthur. He probably heard a rumor." Travis nodded; maybe Cembran had a point. Whatever it was, it wasn't important now.

The rest of the morning went smoothly, and by noon, they had sold most of their vegetables and had just a few pounds of beans left, which they gave to Merle and Jane in exchange for a jar of honey. After packing their baskets in the car, Travis and Cembran said goodbye to Merle and Jane and headed back to the farm.

The drive home was pleasant and very satisfying, "Lamb, I was wondering. Next week, would you like to bring some of your cheese to market? I know we're currently producing more than we need."

Cembran thought for a minute, "Sure, if you think people will like it. We can take some next week and see how well it sells."

Arriving back at the farm, they unloaded their baskets and went inside. The house was still cool because of the large trees providing shade. Travis took Cembran's hand and led him to the bedroom, closing the door behind them. Travis stripped off his clothes, stepped into the bathroom, turned on the shower, and got in under the tepid water. Cembran joined him a few seconds later, wrapping his arms around Travis's waist.

Travis squirted some shampoo into his hand and started washing Cembran's hair and massaging his scalp. Cembran got under the spray to rinse his hair as Travis lathered soap in his hands. His soapy hands washed Cembran's body, enjoying the feel of all that smooth skin. He rinsed his lover's body and then it was his turn. Cembran washed Travis's hair and lathered every inch of his body. Travis loved the feel of those hands on his skin. There was no sex involved, at least not today, but the act of washing each other was extremely intimate and very special to both of them.

Travis rinsed off the soap and pulled Cembran to him, kissing him while he slowly rubbed Cembran's back. Stepping out of the shower, Cembran grabbed a large, fluffy towel and vigorously dried Travis's body before drying his own. He then went into the bedroom and slipped on a pair of shorts before heading into the kitchen to make a light lunch. Travis emerged from the bedroom a few minutes later.

Sitting together at the table, they talked together as they ate. "What do you have to do this afternoon, Lamb?"

"I need to check on the animals; otherwise, things are caught up for now." Travis was relieved to hear that. They'd been working furiously over the past few weeks, completing projects, making repairs, and getting the sheep sheared. "Do you have anything special we need to get done?"

Travis nodded, "I have something very special to do this afternoon." He leered suggestively at Cembran, who raised an eyebrow, wriggled a little in his chair, and smiled.

As Travis was finishing his lunch, he heard his phone ringing. Getting up from the table, he went into the bedroom to answer it. Cembran could hear Travis talking, but he paid little attention. When he'd finished his lunch, Cembran put his dishes in the sink and went into the bedroom. Travis hung up as he entered the room. Who was that, Lemmle?"

"Heinrich. He just called to tell us that the auction of some of the coins went very well. Almost all of them exceeded their estimates and a few of them went for unbelievable prices." Over the past few months, the gold coins that they'd deposited in the bank in Switzerland had been gradually sold, mostly at auction. The coins had caused quite a stir in the market and the auctions had gotten a lot of attention. So far about one-third of the coins had been sold and already they had yielded millions of dollars. "Heinrich said that the best coins haven't been sold yet. He wants to wait for just the right auction."

"That's good." Once they'd started to sell the coins, it became apparent that many of them were very rare and really valuable. Cembran and Travis had decided that only half of the coins would be sold. The remaining ones would be kept in the vault.

Even though Cembran had insisted that both their names be included on the account with the bank, Travis still thought of the money as Cembran's. "The sale of the rest of the coins that you agreed to sell should be done by the end of the year." Cembran nodded and Travis gently pressed their lips together in a sweet, loving kiss, before heading back to the table to finish his lunch.

Once he'd finished eating, Travis put the dishes in the sink, and popped his head in the bedroom, "Would you like to take a walk with me?" Travis went into the linen closet, took out an old blanket, throwing it over his shoulder, before offering his hand.

Cembran smiled brightly as he took it. "Are we going to the lake?"

"Yeah, I thought it would be cooler there."

"I need to make sure the animals have enough water first. I'll meet you there, okay?"

Travis kissed him softly, "Sure. I'll see you at the lake in a few minutes." They left the house and Travis headed down the path to the lake, while Cembran went to the sheep barn. The water containers for the sheep were full, so he checked on the goat pens. The goats needed water, so Cembran filled the containers, checked the milk storage, and headed to the lake.

Cembran emerged from the woods to a truly beautiful sight. Travis had spread the blanket in the shade, where he was lying on his stomach, his naked body glistening with a light sheen of sweat. Cembran smiled as he walked to the blanket and slipped off his shorts before kneeling next to Travis. His hands stroked Travis's hot, silky skin.

Even after years of hard work, Cembran's hands felt soft and smooth against Travis's body. "Lamb, that feels good, so good."

Cembran straddled Travis's legs, his hands massaging Travis's back with long, sensual strokes. Travis murmured his pleasure with each breath. Leaning forward, Cembran nuzzled Travis's cheek, angling for a kiss. Travis turned his head and their lips met. Slowly, Travis rolled over, pulling Cembran onto him, enjoying the solidity of his lover's body as it pressed onto him.

"I love you, Travis," Cembran whispered just before their lips met again.

The kiss built from languid and gentle to needy and passionate in a matter of seconds. A warm breeze blew across their bodies as their lips tugged and tongues explored mouths. Travis lifted his upper body, latching onto one of Cembran's nipples, swirling his tongue around the fleshy bud as Cembran moaned with pleasure. Travis switched sides and continued working those hard fleshy nubs until Cembran threw his head back in a silent cry of ecstasy. He straddled Travis's body, rubbing his ass over Travis's throbbing erection. Travis hissed as Cembran moved back and forth.

Travis cupped Cembran's cheeks in his hands, bringing his body forward. "Lean back, Lamb." Cembran obeyed until his body rested on top of Travis's as strong arms caressed his chest and stomach, while Travis's hot tongue circled his tight opening. Cembran looked up at the trees while Travis licked and sucked on his tight opening. Hands rubbed Cembran's chest, caressed his stomach, and tweaked his nipples while Travis's tongue circled, probed, and tickled his entrance.

"Relax, Lamb. I have you." Travis felt Cembran relax and he probed him with his tongue, opening him up as he thrust his tongue inside.

Cembran was moaning and whimpering loudly as he squirmed in sweet agony. "Trav, I'm gonna—" Cembran said nothing more as he came on his stomach with a small cry, while Travis continued working his opening.

Travis smiled as he rubbed Cembran's cum into the skin of his stomach. Slowly, he helped Cembran shift off his body and onto the blanket. "Love you, Lamb." Travis kissed Cembran sweetly, letting him rest.

"What about you, Lemmle?"

"Shhh." Travis stilled Cembran, "It's not important, just relax." Calmly, Travis took Cembran in his arms and held him close, letting his breathing return to normal.

Lying on the blanket, wrapped in each other's arms, was very relaxing and soon Cembran was snoring. Travis held him close, relaxing as the man he loved with his whole being, slept quietly in the shade. A short while later, Cembran's incredible blue eyes fluttered open. Travis smiled and whispered, "Hi, sleepyhead."

"Hi."

"Did you have a good nap?" Cembran nodded. "Would you like to go swimming?" Cembran nodded again and they got up from the blanket and walked into the lake.

The cool water surrounded their bodies as Travis took Cembran into his arms, pulling them together. Cembran wrapped his arms around Travis's neck and his legs around his waist. "Love me, Lemmle."

Travis's erection was throbbing as Cembran lowered himself onto Travis, taking him completely into his body. The cool water surrounded their bodies as Travis thrust slowly. Each thrust was intense. Whenever he pulled out, the cool water made his cock tingle; with each inward thrust Cembran's hot body made him throb. With each movement, Travis's desire and need increased, building into a frenzy of passion.

Cembran kissed him deeply, pulling on his lips as Travis thrust deeply into him. His cock rubbed against Travis's stomach and he moaned into his lover's mouth as he came again, between their bodies. Seconds later, Travis threw his head back as a full-body orgasm swept though him.

Cembran slipped away and unwrapped his legs from around Travis's waist. He held Travis close as their breathing returned to normal. "I love you, Lemmle; you're amazing."

"No, Lamb, you're amazing. I adore you." Travis wrapped his arms around Cembran's waist, pulling him close, and kissed him, communicating all his love with the kiss. They kissed until they started to get cold in the water, and then walked back to the blanket. They lay down, their bodies drying in the breeze. Cembran scooted next to Travis and rested his head on his shoulder. Soon their breathing synchronized and both drifted off to sleep, curled together on the blanket as the breeze bathed them in warmth.

Chapter Twenty-five

arly August was always hot and this year was no exception, which worked out well, because Brock, Steven, Jim, Sue, and Arthur were coming for a visit and Travis thought it would be a great day for swimming.

As Travis walked up the path after returning early from the farmers' market, he saw Gathod heading toward the barns. "Hey, Gathod, don't forget we're having a swimming party this afternoon. Are you and Doug joining us?" Gathod and Doug had been seeing each other for months now and they seemed good together.

Gathod returned Travis's wave, "I'd love to join you, but Doug's got a campaign stop today." Doug had been campaigning hard for weeks. All the polls showed him and the current Sheriff neck and neck.

Travis smiled, "Okay, we'll see you for lunch by the lake." Travis had invited everyone as a sort of celebration. Arthur seemed happy with Jim and Sue, and the court had just granted them temporary custody with a review to make it permanent in six months. On top of that, he and Cembran had just completed the addition to the house and tonight they'd spend their first night in their new master bedroom with its king-size bed and new bathroom. Travis was looking forward to a great day and a great night.

Last month, Travis, Gathod, and Cembran had gone to the County Fair. The three of them had had a wonderful time looking at all the animals and exhibits. At the livestock auction, Travis and Cembran purchased the grand champion goat and the grand champion ram, as well as four other sheep and six goats.

Heading down the path to the sheep barn, Travis couldn't help feeling content and happy. Everything seemed to be working out. "Yeah, I know it won't last," he told himself, "but I'm going to enjoy it." Travis looked around the farm. Sometimes he found it hard to believe that he lived here. The farm still looked as idyllic as it did when he first saw it a little over a year ago - the barns, the neatly fenced pastures, the sheep and goats grazing, and most of all, as he approached the barn, the sound of Cembran singing while he worked. Smiling to himself, Travis slipped into the barn and watched as his lover lifted bales of hay into the loft, muscles straining, his tan skin taut, glistening with sweat.

"Lamb, do you need some help?"

Cembran had just lifted the bale into the loft. He turned and smiled at Travis, "No, I'm almost done. The loft here is almost full. The one in the goat barn is full and the grain storage is near to bursting." Cembran stepped close to Travis, the scent of sweat and man making him ache.

"God, you smell good." Travis nuzzled Cembran's neck, nibbling gently on his ear. "So sexy."

Cembran smiled wickedly as he kissed Travis and turned back to his work, "We're going to need to add barn space next year. The new loft above the shed is full. I'll barely be able to get the last of the hay in this one and we'll need more as the herds continue to expand."

"Okay. We'll plan the space we need this fall and winter, and we'll build in the spring.

"Good." Cembran lifted the bale into the loft as arms wrapped around his waist. He set down the bale and turned.

Travis kissed his gorgeous, sweaty man, lingering over the kiss as his lips pulled at Cembran's. "I'm going to finish working in the garden. Those weeds are murder. I'll meet you inside in an hour." He leered at Cembran, "We'll break in the new shower." Cembran groaned a low deep growl as he went back to work. Travis watched that tight butt in those rough, worn pants before tearing his eyes away and heading to the vegetable garden. He'd tripled the size of the garden and planted a number of fruit and vegetables. He'd also planted a small orchard with apple, cherry, peach, and pear trees. It would take a few years, but they'd be a great addition to the farm.

Travis worked for an hour pulling weeds and staking plants. They'd already put up plenty of beans, carrots, and tomatoes. Cembran had made pickles that Travis was dying to taste. The melons would be ready soon, as would the sweet corn. The farm in general had done very well this year. Their wool had gotten top dollar, Travis had started taking some of Cembran's cheese to the local farmers' market along with their extra vegetables, and each week he'd sold almost everything, for very good prices, too. Today he'd left the market early because he'd sold out so quickly. Yes, life was indeed good.

When Travis saw Cembran heading up the path toward the house, he put away his tools, brushed off the worst of the dirt, and followed him into the house. Over the last four months, they'd doubled the size of the small house, adding a master bedroom, an office, and updating and enlarging the bathroom. Their old bedroom was now a guest room. They'd kept the same rustic feel in the new rooms as the rest of the house. While they'd all worked hard on the addition, Travis was particularly grateful for Gathod and Cembran's craftsmanship and skills.

The walls of their new master bedroom were paneled in stunning red oak. When the pastures were enlarged, the area they needed to clear had contained two large red oak trees. The trees were felled and the wood milled and used on the walls. The room was stunning, as was their new king-size bed that Cembran had constructed from the branches of the same oak trees. The office was paneled with yellow pine that Travis had oiled until it glistened.

He was undressing in the new bedroom when Cembran quietly joined him. He stepped out of his pants, standing naked in front of Cembran. Slowly, Travis opened Cembran's shirt, working the buttons, exposing smooth, sun-kissed skin. After slipping the shirt off Cembran's strong shoulders, he opened the front of his lover's pants, pushing them down past his hips and letting them slump to the floor. Cembran stepped out of them as Travis pulled their bodies together.

Their lips met in a deep, passionate kiss, chests pressed skin to skin, legs entwined, as Travis's hands caressed Cembran's back before cupping his hard, round butt. He murmured breathlessly, "Come with me, Lamb." Travis slowly stepped back, took Cembran's hand, and led him to their new shower. He turned on the water, and they kissed passionately as it warmed, their tongues dancing insistently. Travis got into the shower and drew Cembran to him. Their lips met again, remembering exactly where they'd left off. The water cascaded over their bodies as he carded his fingers through Cembran's thick ringlets while he pressed Cembran's back against the cool tile.

Travis inhaled sharply as Cembran broke the kiss and his full lips latched onto a nipple. Cembran's tongue circled the bud as his nimble fingers wrapped around Travis's pulsing, leaking cock. Cembran slid down the wall, kissing a path down Travis's chest and stomach before opening his mouth. His tongue licked lazy circles around the throbbing head before sliding down the shaft. He popped first one and then both of Travis smooth balls into his mouth, gently rolling them with his tongue as Travis's musky, full scent filled his nose. "Lamb, that's so good." Travis breath was coming in shallow pants as Cembran released his balls and took the large pink head into his mouth. Cembran's tongue swirled as he increased suction, and Travis's shaft was pulled into Cembran's hot, welcoming mouth.

"Ohhh!" Travis's eyes rolled as Cembran worked his cock, slowly and deftly, bringing him near the brink before pulling back. He put a hand on Cembran's chin, drawing their faces level again. As their lips met again, Travis could taste himself on Cembran's tongue, as their hard cocks rubbed together and soft skin vibrated against soft skin.

Gently, Travis spun them around so that Cembran received the spray from the shower. The hot water splashed over Cembran's back as Travis sucked and nibbled on a fleshy nipple. Cembran half moaned, half growled as Travis worked the bud into a hard protruding nub. He smiled into Cembran's chest as he felt his Lamb's knees start to quiver. Giving the nipple a reprieve, he moved his mouth to the other, working it between his lips. "Trraaav," Cembran pleaded, so Travis slowly lowered his body, kissing the smooth skin until he was nuzzling and laving his tongue across Cembran's meaty balls.

Travis knew from the way Cembran was shaking that it wouldn't take much to set him off. "I want you, Love."

"God, Lemmle, take me. I'm yours. Only yours." Cembran's voice was deep, pleading.

Turning Cembran around, Travis pressed him against the tile wall, spreading those hard globes before tonguing the tight opening. Cembran moaned constantly as Travis teased and worked it until it relaxed. Travis licked the rim while two fingers penetrated into Cembran's body. "Okay, Lamb?" In answer, Cembran thrust his body back onto Travis's fingers with a whimper. Travis curled his finger and felt Cembran shudder as he rubbed that special spot.

Travis removed the fingers and pressed the head of his cock to Cembran's entrance and held it there. "Lemmle, please, I want to feel you."

"How much?"

"This much." As Cembran uttered those words he thrust back and took Travis deep inside him in one swift movement. The air rushed from Travis's lungs as his cock was swallowed by Cembran's body. He stood still as Cembran moved forward before thrusting back again, taking him all the way to the hilt. "Fuck me, Travis!"

The water cascaded over their bodies as he thrust deep into Cembran's body. Travis pulled Cembran away from the tile and massaged his chest and stomach as he thrust deep into him again and again. Cembran threw his arms back, giving himself completely. Travis slipped his hands to his cock, stroking him with the long, slow strokes that he really liked. "So close."

"Me too."

Travis thrust deep into Cembran's body, careful not to break his hand rhythm. His lover started to quake and he cried out as he came on Travis's hand. Travis whimpered softly as he filled his lover's body with his own release. He held Cembran tight, their bodies still connected, as he slowly took the soap from the dish and lathered Cembran's chest and stomach. Their bodies separated of their own accord before Travis finished soaping Cembran's satiated body, washing his hair and running his hands over every inch of smooth, warm skin.

Once they were both clean, Travis turned off the water and wrapped Cembran in a big fluffy towel. "I love you, Lamb," Travis whispered as his lips found Cembran's.

"I love you too." Hands caressed and stroked as they dried each other before stepping into their new bedroom to get ready for the picnic by the lake.

Travis was getting things ready to carry down when Sue, Jim, and Arthur arrived. Arthur bounded through the yard, "Uncle Travis, can I go see the lambs?"

Travis had to laugh, "Sure." He smiled as he watched Arthur run down the path. Travis ushered Jim and Sue into the house. After showing them the new addition, the four of them sat in the living room.

"How is Arthur doing? He sure seems happy."

Sue smiled, "He's an incredible boy. Smart, loving, but he gets so sad sometimes. He was so excited when we told him we were coming for a visit. I don't know if he actually slept last night."

"Have you told him he's a satyr?"

Sue almost laughed, "Yes, and he seemed extremely relieved to know there was a reason why he always felt different from the other kids." She leaned forward, "He started getting his horns a few weeks ago; we've been teaching him how to mask them. He forgets sometimes, but he's learning." Sue giggled a little, "He likes one of the neighbor girls. He hasn't actually talked to her yet, but he keeps watching her as she walks through the neighborhood."

Travis couldn't help smiling. "He seems happy, and I'm glad he's adjusting. Do he and Brock get along?"

Jim smiled broadly, "Brock keeps calling him 'little brother' and Arthur seems to worship him. Every day he asks if his brother Brock is coming over. To tell you the truth, I think they're good for each other; they were both raised as only children and I think they both like having sibling."

At that moment they heard a knock on the door, "It's open." A few seconds later, Brock and Steven stepped through the door looking happy and contented, carrying dishes of food.

Cembran got up, "Brock, Steven, we're glad you could come." He took the dishes, setting them on the counter before hugging them both.

Sue got up, "What can we do to help?"

Cembran smiled, "We've got everything set at the lake, we just need to carry down the food." Everyone picked up something and headed out the door. Travis and Cembran smiled as they saw Arthur coming up the path from the barn, carrying a lamb in his arms. Cembran chuckled, "Looks like you found a friend."

"Yeah, she keeps sucking my fingers." Arthur giggled happily as the lamb reached for his hand. The lamb had been rejected by its mother, so Travis and Cembran had been bottle feeding her.

Cembran motioned to Arthur, "Come with me. I'll get her bottle, and you can take her to the lake with us and feed her."

"Cool." Arthur followed Cembran into the house to get the bottle with a look of sheer delight on his face. When they came back out, everyone headed to the lake, their hands full of food containers.

The sand was warm on his feet as Travis set out the picnic lunch. Everyone ate heartily and talked animatedly. Arthur sat on the soft sand, the lamb on his lap, nursing from the bottle. Cembran had made a wonderful summer lunch with fresh vegetables, fruit, cheese, homemade bread, and some of his wonderful beer. Sue brought some of her famous chicken salad, while Brock and Steven (actually just Steven) made a fresh fruit dessert.

After lunch, everyone changed into their bathing suits and spent the afternoon splashing and playing in the water. Brock spent part of the afternoon teaching his "little brother" some new swimming strokes. Jim and Sue waded in the water. Jim splashed Sue playfully, and soon the two of them were in a water fight that quickly escalated into an all-out war that left everyone soaked and laughing. Gathod arrived during the water fight and got drenched by Arthur before he could even change his clothes. Gathod chased Arthur around the lake and into the water, laughing and yelling the entire time.

Late in the afternoon, Cembran and Travis relaxed in the shade with Jim and Sue while Brock, Steven, and Gathod took turns letting Arthur dive from their shoulders and flipping him into the water. "Uncle

Travis, watch!" Arthur cried out as he climbed onto Brock's wide shoulders before diving into the water. Everyone applauded and Arthur beamed with pride as Brock threw Arthur over his shoulders and carried him out of the water before depositing him on the sand.

"Arthur."

"Yes, Uncle Cembran?"

"Your lamb needs feeding."

Arthur smiled as he settled on the sand, gathered the lamb onto his lap, and talked softly to the lamb while he fed her.

Travis ran back to the house, returning a few minutes later with Steven's dessert. After gorging himself, Arthur sat in the shade, lamb on his lap, stroking its soft wool as she slept. Everyone else sat in the cool shade talking. "Gathod, how is Doug's campaign going?" Travis hadn't seen Doug in weeks; he'd been so busy.

"It seems to be going okay from what he tells me. It seems that a lot of people don't like the current Sheriff, so he's trying to think positively."

"Speak of the devil." Doug emerged from the woods, joining them in the shade.

"Having a picnic?"

"Yeah," Travis got Doug a plate. "We were just talking about you, how's the campaign trail?"

"Exhausting, but I think we're making headway. I'm hopeful." The primary election was in two weeks, but since both Doug and the current Sheriff were from the same party, the primary was in fact the election for Sheriff, since no one was running from the other party.

"Well, we're all pulling for you and we'll vote early."

"We're having a rally the day before the election." Doug settled on the sand next to Gathod and started eating.

Cembran spoke up, "We'll be there." Travis smiled as he lightly nuzzled his cheek. God, he loved this man.

Arthur sat the lamb down next to Travis and grabbed Brock and Steven by the hand, practically pulling them into the water. Travis turned to Cembran, "Come on Lamb, let's join them."

Gathod and Doug went for a walk, and Jim and Sue stayed in the shade, while the rest of the boys had a jolly time splashing, dunking, and holding swimming races. They all decided that Travis was the judge, since he was the fastest anyway.

Doug and Gathod returned from their walk, concerned. "Travis," Doug motioned at him to come out of the water. "I found fresh boot-prints on the other side of the lake heading into the woods away from the farm."

"We haven't seen anyone or had any trouble." Travis wasn't too concerned, people occasionally wandered onto the property.

"I wouldn't think too much of it either, but I found this as well." Doug held up a faded, yellow safety vest, the kind used by contractors and construction personnel. "It could have been there a while and it's probably nothing, but I wanted to let you know."

"Thanks, Doug; we'll keep an eye out." Doug handed Travis the vest and he looked it over. It was faded and appeared to be dirty. It could have been there for quite some time or just a few days. Travis handed it back to Doug, "Please hang on to this. If someone's up to something, we may need it later." Doug took the vest, putting it in his pocket as he and Gathod sat in the shade with Jim and Sue, while Travis returned to the water and the swimming races.

As the afternoon faded, Sue and Jim got ready to leave. Sue called to Arthur, "Come on, it's time to go."

"But Suuueee...." Everyone stifled giggles.

Brock came to the rescue, "Mom, Steven and I are staying the night, we'll bring him home in the morning with us."

Sue looked stern, but no one was buying it. Arthur looked hopeful, his eyes pleading. "All right, but you mind your uncles and brother." Sue then looked at Travis, appalled that they'd all forgotten their manners. Travis just nodded and smiled; to him they were family, and asking permission to stay wasn't required. "Come with me, then, I brought some dry clothes for you. You'll need them for tomorrow." Arthur followed Sue to the car, smiling the whole way. He returned a few minutes later with a small bag of clothes.

Jim and Sue packed up their things, hugged Arthur, and said goodbye. "Be good, Arthur."

"I will." Arthur grinned and waved as they headed down the path to their car.

Doug and Gathod said their good-byes as well and headed down the path to Gathod's house a few minutes later. Travis could tell by the looks they were giving each other that some alone time was in order.

"Arthur, why don't you get dressed and you can help Cembran and I with the chores." Travis grinned and whispered to Brock as soon as Arthur went to change, "He'll be busy in the barns for the next hour or so. The lake is beautiful at sunset." Brock winked at Travis as he and Cembran packed up the last of the picnic items and headed back to the house.

Arthur returned a few minutes later, his clothes sticking to his body, his hair still wet. Travis just shook his head, "Would you bring the blanket up to the house with you?" Arthur threw the blanket over his shoulder and picked up the lamb, following Travis and Cembran back to the house.

Arthur put the lamb in the small pen near the house before helping put away all the picnic stuff. The three of them then went to milk the goats. Arthur had a ball milking and playing with the goats. Once they were done, Travis went back to the house to clean up while Cembran showed Arthur how he made cheese.

That evening after dinner, Brock, Steven, and Travis played games with Arthur while Cembran watched and worked on a carving. "Whatcha doing, Uncle Cembran?" Arthur had been watching him work between turns.

"I'm carving a figure like those." Cembran pointed to the mantle. He got up from his chair and showed him, "That's Gathod." His hand indicated each figure. "That one is Travis." Cembran moved his hand, "This is me, here's Jim, and that's Sue. They were done a long time ago by my brother Fartham." Cembran moved his hand to indicate the carving of Fartham, "That's him. This is my mother." Cembran paused, "And this one," indicating the block of wood he was working on, "is going to be you."

"Me?"

"Yeah. I'm doing a carving of you to go with the rest of the family." Cembran's eyes twinkled, "Probably diving off Brock's shoulders." Everyone laughed and the games continued.

"What about Brock and Steven? Are you going to carve them too?" The look on Arthur's face was incredibly earnest.

Cembran nodded, "Yes, I want to carve our entire family." He couldn't help smiling to himself as he went back to work. Arthur returned to the game and they played until bedtime.

Cembran made up a bed for Arthur in the living room. Brock and Steven said good-night and retired to the guest room. Travis brought in the lamb and it curled into a ball at the foot of Arthur's bed. After saying good-night, Travis and Cembran left Arthur to get ready for bed, and quietly retired to their new bedroom.

Their lovemaking was sensual and quiet, their passion and love transcending words. Their bodies joined and moved together in a way that seemed to join their souls, climaxing in blinding, open-mouthed orgasms that seemed to steal their breath away.

The house was quiet and Cembran was asleep as Travis got out of bed, slipped on his robe, and went to check on Arthur. He was again finding it difficult to rest. His sleep kept getting interrupted by strange feelings, like there was someone else in his mind. Travis knew his dreams weren't being attacked, but he wondered if someone else's dreams were, and he was just picking up the residual somehow. Travis reminded himself to talk about it with Cembran in the morning.

Looking into the living room, Travis smiled. Arthur was sound asleep. The lamb had shifted; its head was on the pillow, her tiny body pressed against Arthur's chest. Neither of them woke as Travis turned and went back into the bedroom, closing the door with a soft click.

Chapter Twenty-six

Steven smiled as he looked up and realized it was lunchtime. Maybe they'd have the type of lunch they'd had last week, when Brock had met Steven at his office and asked him to lunch. Steven had smiled, said yes happily, and followed Brock to his car. Brock had driven him home and once inside, had stripped him naked and fucked him hard on the living room floor.

Brock's door was open and he was swearing up a storm. Nope, not a repeat of last week. Steven was a little surprised because he'd never seen Brock act this way. Helen looked at Steven confused and wondering what was going on; this was obviously foreign behavior to her as well. Steven smiled at Helen, entered Brock's office, and closed the door. "Brock, you're scaring everyone."

The words drew his boyfriend out of his anger. "Sorry." Brock flopped into his chair. "I need to make a quick call before we go." Steven got up to leave but Brock indicated for him to stay, "It's okay, you're involved." Steven knew this must involve the farm because it was the one piece of client business that he was associated with. Brock picked up the phone.

"Travis, its Brock. I've got Steven in here with me; can I put you on speaker?"

"All right." Brock engaged the speaker phone. "Hi, Steven."

"Hi Travis."

"Brock, what's going on? Is everything okay?"

"There's a problem. The County isn't registering the land transfer and I'm not able to determine why."

"Huh?"

"I'm going to drive over there this afternoon and see what I can find out."

"Stop by afterwards and we'll talk. Is Steven coming with you?"

"Yes." Steven was shocked. He'd never participated in any actual client business before.

"Okay. We'll see you later." Brock disconnected.

"Brock, what's going on? Why do you want me to go with you?" Steven smiled as he looked at his sexy man, "Not that I'm complaining." Brock motioned for Steven to sit down.

"I could use your help this afternoon; I need an extra set of eyes, and you're already involved. Besides. I want to talk to you about something." Steven cocked his head as if to say he was listening. "I was wondering if you'd be interested in going to law school."

"Ummm." Steven was shocked, well, shocked and scared. His old insecurities surfaced quickly.

Brock saw it, "Steven, you've read every book we've written, researched cases. Hell, you know the law library better that we do and you have a good understanding of the law."

"But, what if I...."

The door was closed so Brock felt at ease taking Steven in his arms and holding him tight. "No buts, Love. You have what it takes, you're smart; you reason well. You'd make a great lawyer."

Steven pulled back, looking into his eyes, "But, I'm not like you. I don't have that killer instinct needed to win, particularly in court."

"Yes, you do. Last week when Susan was giving me a hard time, I saw you walk by my office. You looked ready to deck her. You knew I could take care of myself, but you were ready to fight for me. That's what we do, fight for others."

"Oh, I never thought about it like that, but yeah, I'd fight for you and to keep you, Brock."

"I know, Love, and I'd do that same for you." Brock kissed him gently, pressing his body against the conference table.

Steven looked around mischievously. "You know," he leaned close, whispering, "I always dreamed of...." Steven patted the top of the conference table suggestively.

Brock smiled a wicked smile before shaking his head, "You're such a pervert." Brock released his embrace and grabbed his coat, "Get your jacket, Love, we need to find out who's messing with our family."

Steven walked to his office, grabbed his coat, and let Helen know he'd be out of the office for the afternoon. He met Brock at the front door. Brock was surprised to see Steven carrying a large notebook. "I'm working on this and if there's waiting time I can make some headway."

Brock rolled his eyes, "If there's waiting time, I'll probably ravish you in the nearest closet."

Raising his eyebrows, Steven grinned, "There's that, too."

The trip North took a while longer than expected with traffic. Steven worked quietly while Brock drove.

"Steven, I've got something I want to ask you." Steven closed his notebook, looking at Brock as he pulled the car off the road and shut off the engine. "I've been thinking and I want to tell you something and ask you something." He watched Brock quietly. "I love you and I want you to share my life with me." Brock stopped and seemed at a loss for words. Steven smiled. If Brock was tongue-tied, this must be big. "This probably isn't the right place for this, but will you live with me? Share my life and my home?"

Whatever Steven had been expecting, it wasn't that. A smile lit his face as he threw his arms around Brock's neck before kissing him hard. "Is that a yes?"

"No, that was an 'oh god, yes!'" Steven jumped into the back seat, slipping his pants off. "I want you now, Brock! Right now!"

Thank goodness Brock drove a large car. He shifted into the back seat, kissing Steven, before lifting his legs and slipping two fingers into that tight, hot ass. "God, Brock, need more. Need you." Brock opened his pants and pushed them past his hips. His cock was rigid and already leaking. Brock brought his lips to Steven's as he pressed his cock to Steven's opening, pushing for entrance. "Aahhhh," Steven moaned into Brock's mouth as his cock sank fluidly into Steven's body.

Brock's lips never left Steven's as they moved together in a rhythm of love. Each thrust was met by the other again and again. Their bodies drew apart and back together again in a frantic joining filled with joy. Steven exploded into his hand as Brock filled Steven, both men crying the other's name as they came.

After kissing while they came down from the orgasmic high, they dressed before getting back in the front seat and continuing on their way. Only now, neither Brock nor Steven could wipe the grins from their faces.

About thirty minutes later, they arrived at the County courthouse still grinning like anything. Before getting out of the car, Brock turned to Steven, "I want you to pretend to be my assistant. Take notes, listen, flirt with everyone interested. We want information."

They headed into the huge imposing old County courthouse, stopping by the receptionist to ask for the Registrar of Deeds. They were pointed to the second floor. Brock went directly to the office and approached the clerk behind the desk, who asked, "Can I help you?"

She looked to be about twenty and Brock turned on the charm, "I sure hope so." Steven almost laughed as Brock flashed his brightest, "*I want something and you're putty and don't know it*," smile. "I need to transfer a plot of land, but I'm having difficulty."

She smiled back at Brock, and Steven knew she'd give Brock whatever he wanted. "Can you give me the details, handsome?" Brock handed her a copy of the current deed and she typed into her computer terminal. "There it is. Oh, it looks like the County has put a hold on the deed."

Brock flashed his eyes at her and she smiled and pulled out a map. She was obviously enjoying his attention and wanted him to stick around. She returned to the counter, "This is the plot you want to transfer. It looks like the County is interested in this land for a new park." She looked disgusted, "Like we need a park way out there."

Brock figured he'd gotten all the information he could from her, but he decided he'd try for some gossip, "Why would they do that?"

She leaned close, "The Sheriff's brother Joe has wanted that land for years. I bet they've got something going. He tried to buy the land, even paved the way for zoning approval last year, but it fell through." Brock gave her his biggest smile and left the office.

Once in the hall, Steven whispered, "That's not good, is it?"

"No, it's not. It means they're probably going to try using eminent domain to take the land from Travis and Cembran."

"You mean steal it?"

"No, they'll have to pay for it, but the land is more important to Cembran and Travis than the money."

"Oh." Steven looked sad as the impact hit him – no more farm, swimming, lambs, goats, Bacchanals, everything. "Jesus, Brock, we've got to stop them!"

Brock whispered, "We will. Come on, we've got another stop to make." He headed to the County Secretary's office on the first floor. A small, older woman behind the desk asked if she could help Brock. "Can you tell me when the next County Board meeting is and what's on the agenda?"

"Oh, sure. The next meeting is next week, August 29th." She handed Brock a set of papers. "Here's a copy of the preliminary agenda." As Brock perused the agenda he saw what he was looking for: "Discussion of Proposal to Acquire Land for New Park."

"Thank you." Brock smiled again and they headed outside, back to the car. He didn't start the car, but picked up his cell phone instead.

"Hey, Doug, or should I say, future Sheriff. It's Brock." Doug had won the primary election and he was now running unopposed in the November election, so for all practical purposes, he was the Sheriff-elect.

"Thanks, Brock, it seems a lot of people hated the old Sheriff. I won by a wide margin."

"Well, I'm pleased you won, but I expect it was your qualifications that got you the election."

"What can I do for you?" The pleasure in his voice was obvious.

"We've got a problem you might be able to help with."

"What is it?"

Brock told him what he'd been able to find out. "I think Palumbo's got a scheme going and he's got the Board hoodwinked. I mean, anyone can tell they don't need a park in the far corner of the County."

"I'll see what I can do."

"Thanks, Doug." Brock hung up and turned to Steven, "I'm sorry, Love, I've got a few more calls to make."

Steven leaned against Brock, stroking his arm, "It's okay. I like listening to you work." He pulled out his notebook, working while Brock made some more calls. Once he was finished, he started the car and headed out to the farm. "How are we going to stop them?"

Brock looked over at Steven; he'd seen him upset, but he'd never before seen him this angry. "Steven, this is what I was talking about earlier; we fight for others. We're going to develop a plan and we're going to fight! I don't know how, yet. But I know we will."

"Good. I think I have an idea, but I have some questions."

"Shoot." Brock was smiling as he drove.

"How does eminent domain work?"

"The power of eminent domain is controlled by the constitution. It allows the government to take private property for a public purpose."

"Do they have to pay for what they take?" The earnest look on his face was precious. "How is the value determined?"

Brock thought a minute, "Fair market value has be paid for the property."

"So who determines fair value?" Steven was getting into this.

"The property is appraised. Often by multiple people and a value is determined." Brock looked at Steven, "What are you getting at?"

"I'm not sure yet. I just have an idea that isn't formulated yet. Let me think about it."

Brock smiled as they arrived at the farm. "Okay. Let me know."

Travis met them at the door, extending his hand in greeting. "Come in." They stepped into the house and sat at the table. "Cembran is finishing the chores. He'll be up here soon." Brock filled Travis in on what he found at the courthouse. "What are we going to do, Brock? If they succeed in taking this land, it'll kill Cembran."

Steven was confused, "Couldn't you buy another farm?"

"It's not the same." Travis turned to Steven, "Cembran built this farm from nothing and he's lived here for 120 years or so. He's bonded to this place. If he were forced to leave, part of who he is would die."

Steven's eyes went wide, "What?"

Travis turned to Brock and then back to Steven, "Cembran looks our age, but he's actually about 310 years old and he's lived here since my great-great-grandfather owned the land."

Steven whistled, "My god. I didn't know satyrs lived that long."

"Most of us don't. It depends on a number of things. Cembran is a direct descendant of Bacchus, so his longevity is very strong. His father lived to be almost 600."

"Oh."

Travis was quiet as thoughts raced through his mind. "Cembran has become part of this land and it's part of him. If he were forced to leave, he'd wither and die."

Steven whispered softly, "How do you know?"

Travis shrugged, "I just do. I mean, when Bacchus made me a satyr, he told me to 'care for his other children' and I think he gave me the ability to recognize and know what his children need, just like I knew you were a satyr as soon as you stepped through the door. I don't know how I know, but I do. So I'll fight this with everything and every cent I have."

Brock looked perplexed, "You mean if this were my farm?"

Travis nodded, "This fight isn't just for Cembran, but for all of us, and yes, I'd fight just as hard for any of you." Travis stopped and thought, "I mean this place isn't just a farm, or just land; it's important to all of us as a community. Sort of sacred ground because it's the location of the Bacchanal and because Bacchus has been here."

Steven nodded, "I think I understand. Whenever we come here," he looked wistfully at Brock, "I feel lighter and happier, almost like I can do anything."

Travis got back to the task at hand, "Where do we go from here?"

"When I spoke to the young lady in the Registrar of Deeds office, she said she thought this could be some sort of ploy. I'm going to look into that, but I think we need to attend the County Board meeting and see if we can't stop this before it gets started. Right now it's in the talking stage."

"I agree."

"Look, I'll keep on this for you. We'll fight this all the way. Besides, I may have a surprise for them."

Cembran came in the door as they were finishing up. "Are you staying for dinner?"

"No, thank you. We've got to get back." Turning back to Travis, Brock said, "I'll call you as soon as I have anything."

Cembran looked questioningly as his lover, who put his arm around his waist. "I'll fill you in later, Lamb." Cembran nodded as they said good-bye to Brock and Steven. Once they were alone, Travis sat him down and explained what was happening.

Cembran was shaking by the time Travis finished explaining. "Can they really just take our farm?" His voice sounded helpless and already defeated.

"They can, but we're going to fight and fight hard! I have no intention of letting anyone take what's ours. No way!" Travis paused, letting himself calm down. "Brock is working on a solution and we'll have to trust him," he comforted Cembran.

Cembran turned his head to look into Travis's eyes, "There's something else, isn't there?"

Travis couldn't ever hide much from Cembran, even when he was trying to protect him. "Yes, you know I haven't been sleeping well and I've told you I keep getting these strange feelings." Cembran looked concerned and nodded. "They're becoming more intense, darker, and it's happening almost every night."

"Do you think it has anything to do with the proposed park?"

"I don't know, but I don't like it and I don't know what I can do about it." Travis sighed softly, "Let's have dinner and go to bed. It'll be all right." He hoped he sounded convincing because he was almost as scared as Cembran.

On their way home, Steven kept thinking out loud. "Brock, there seems to me to be two ways to stop this cold." Brock looked at Steven waiting for him to continue, "One, prove it's not for a public purpose."

"Right; Doug's looking into that."

"Second, make the cost of reimbursement for taking the land so high, they can't afford it."

Brock hit the brakes, "Steven, you're a genius. That's it." Brock leaned over and kissed Steven hard, "Let's get home. You deserve a reward, a big reward."

Chapter Twenty-seven

A few days after the bad news, Travis conducted the August Bacchanal. Needless to say, it was a subdued gathering. Everyone had a good time, but no one's heart was really in it and the Bacchanal broke up a little after midnight. Travis and Cembran had invited Jim, Sue, and Arthur to stay with them overnight. Brock and Steven asked to spend the night in the shelter.

The others walked back to the house together once the Bacchanal broke up. They quietly entered, seeing that Arthur was asleep in front of the dark fireplace, the lamb curled up at his feet. Sue whispered, "The only thing he talked about for days was that lamb."

Travis nodded. Thoughts of no more lambs, no more kid goats, and no more farm, and worst of all, the effect the loss of the land would have on Cembran, flew through his head. Travis looked at Cembran and he could see the same thoughts racing behind his beautiful eyes. Jim squeezed Cembran's shoulder, "Brock is working on it. It's going to be fine." Cembran nodded and smiled before saying good-night. Quietly he slipped into their bedroom, shutting the door.

"Travis, if you and Cembran need anything to fight this, money, whatever, Sue and I are here to help."

Travis choked up at the kind offer. He swallowed and smiled, grateful for their support, "Money isn't an issue, but thank you. What I need is for this to go away. Cembran is so bonded to this place. We just can't lose it." His voice trailed off.

"I know; that same bonding made it very difficult for Sue and I to leave our village. But, at least it was our choice, and that allowed us to move on. If they take the land, Cembran won't be given that choice."

Jim actually shivered. "We know Brock will find a way. He has to." The conviction in Jim's voice was somehow reassuring. Heck, Travis knew that if there was a way to end this now, Brock would find it. After saying good-night, he went into their bedroom.

Cembran was sitting up in bed, a blank look on his face. Travis cleaned up quickly and joined him in bed, their bed. Travis wrapped his arms around the man he loved with everything he had, pulling him to his body.

"I'm sorry, Trav."

"What do you have to be sorry for?" Cembran shrugged. "Lamb, we can either feel sorry for ourselves and let them defeat us, or we can fight and fight to win." Cembran shrugged again. "Lamb, its all attitude." Cembran looked at Travis furrowing his brow. "If you act defeated, you will be defeated. Look, Lamb, this could be a long battle and we need to be prepared for it." Cembran looked into Travis's eyes and the defeated look eased a little. "We're going to that meeting and we're going to give them a fight they won't soon forget." Travis kissed his love, not with passion, but with care and reassurance. "Let's go to sleep; we've got planning to do tomorrow." Cembran nodded, returning Travis's kiss before sinking onto the bed. Travis held him close, keeping him safe in his protective embrace until they finally fell asleep.

After another night of disturbed rest, Travis was awakened by a soft knocking on the bedroom door, "Uncle Travis, there's a man here."

Travis got out of bed, kissed Cembran gently, slipped on a pair of pants and opened the bedroom door. Arthur stood in his pajamas, pointing to the door. "Thank you Arthur." Travis mussed his hair before opening the door.

A man wearing jeans and a t-shirt and carrying a clipboard stepped forward. "Good morning, I'm John Stevenson. Brock Kraus called me to look at the property."

Travis was intrigued, "Okay. Do you need me to get Brock?"

"He's here now, at this hour?"

"Yes, he's here on the property. Do you need him?"

"Not really. I'll find him later. Are you Travis Freeman?"

"Oh yes, sorry." Travis extended his hand. "Yes, I'm Travis."

"Brock asked me to appraise the property. Could I ask you some questions?" He consulted his clipboard.

"All right, please come in. Would you like some coffee?"

"That'd be great, thanks." Travis put on a pot of coffee and went into the bedroom to dress.

Cembran was up. "Who's at the door?"

"An appraiser Brock asked to look at the property." Travis kissed him good morning again. "Don't worry, I'll find out what's going on." Cembran nodded as he returned Travis's kiss. When they were both dressed, Travis joined Mr. Stevenson while Cembran handed Arthur a bottle for the lamb and left to get started with chores.

Arthur was sitting on the floor feeding the lamb while Travis poured coffee and brought two cups to the dining table.

"Could you answer a few questions for me?"

Travis sat down, "Sure, if I can."

"How large is the property?" He took a sip of his coffee.

"Just over 400 acres. There are two lakes, a small stream that feeds the lakes, and a river that serves as the Northern boundary of the property. I must admit that I've never actually seen one of the lakes or the river."

"Never seen them?" He took another sip of coffee.

"No, most of the property is wild. In fact, much of it is old growth forest. My family never allowed logging on the property and it's been in the family since before statehood."

John whistled, "Can you tell me about the farm?"

"We raise sheep for wool. The wool we produce is of the highest grade and very desirable. We have a herd of goats that we milk. Most of the milk is used for cheese that Cembran makes himself."

The appraiser finished his coffee and got up from the table. "Thank you. Is it all right if I take a look around? It'll take a while."

"Sure." Travis led John outside and pointed out where things were on the property. As they were talking, Brock and Steven came up the walk. John and Brock talked for a few minutes before John headed down the path toward the lake.

"Brock, what exactly is he doing?"

"He's getting us an appraisal of the property as part of incorporating the farm. I'm also hoping it'll help us with the County, but I don't know yet."

Travis shrugged, "Oh well, come inside. I've got coffee on." They went into the house and Travis poured coffee and started breakfast. Cembran returned as Travis was putting it the table.

After a hearty breakfast and some morning conversation, Arthur took Jim and Sue to see all the animals while the young men met with the appraiser.

Mr. Stevenson consulted his clipboard, "This is an extraordinary piece of property; I've never seen anything else like it. I mean, most of the state's forests were logged, and to find a piece of land that still has the old growth intact is amazing."

"Thank you."

The appraiser turned to Brock, "I need to do some research and some figuring."

"Time is of the essence."

"I'll do my best."

"I need the information Wednesday morning. Do this and I'll make it worth your while in the long run."

John stood up and shook hands all around, "Then I'd better get started."

Once John had left, Travis and Cembran started cleaning up. "Brock, I don't understand what's happening."

"I know, Cembran. I'm trying to gather as much information as I can, fast." Brock looked around the room, his mind working. "Travis, we'll be back on Thursday morning to plan what we'll say to the Board. In the meantime, get some digital pictures of the farm and your home. They might come in handy."

"Okay."

"Steven and I need to get back to town so we can get some research done." The two of them got up to leave, "We'll see you Thursday morning." After saying good-bye, complete with hugs all around, Brock and Steven left. Travis heard them say good-bye to Jim, Sue, and Arthur on their way back to the car.

Jim and Sue took Arthur home later that afternoon, but only after he'd convinced them all to take him swimming.

Travis and Cembran spent the next three days in a whirl of activity. Regardless of the upcoming Board meeting, the farm carried on and this was a busy time of year. In addition to their regular chores, the fruit and vegetables from the garden needed to be processed and a sheep was about to give birth.

Travis asked his lover one evening, "Cembran, is this usual for this time of year?"

"No, they usually lamb in the spring." He shrugged, "Sometimes, it happens when it happens. These late births mean we need to keep a close eye on both mother and baby during the winter, though."

Travis loved the newborn, and Cembran smiled for the first time in days as he watched Travis help the sheep through a difficult birth. What really surprised Cembran was how easily he took to jobs like that. He really did seem to have a special bond with the animals in their care.

The night before the Board meeting, Travis took Cembran to the shelter by the lake. Slowly and tenderly, he undressed him, exposing his beautiful, smooth skin. Laying him on the blankets, Travis slipped off his clothes before pressing their bodies together. "I love you, Lamb. Nothing is ever going to change that."

Kisses, hot and loving, came straight from their hearts. "I love you too." Tears streaked Cembran's cheeks as they made love. He was overcome with a flood of conflicting emotions and feelings.

Travis noticed the tears, kissing them from Cembran's cheek. "Lamb, let it go for tonight, just feel." He looked Cembran in the eyes. "Concentrate on my eyes, Lamb."

Hands smooth and tender roamed over Cembran's body, but Travis's gaze didn't waver. Slowly, Travis straddled Cembran's body, lowering himself down without breaking eye contact. They moved together, their bodies becoming one, their eyes locked on one another. They climaxed together, feeling each other's orgasm ripple though their joined bodies, eyes peering into each other's souls.

Travis held Cembran close, watching the moonlight dance on the water. "Lemmle, do you know what hurts most?" Travis remained silent, hugging Cembran tighter. "We've built a family here and I feel like they're trying to take it away." Cembran thought of Doug, Gathod, Brock, Steven, Jim, Sue, and Arthur, who'd become like family to them both and who had come together because of the farm and the Bacchanal. Even Greg and Millie had become friends in just the last couple of months. He was trying to remain hopeful, but was finding it very difficult.

"Lamb, no matter what, they can't take that away from us; we won't let them."

Chapter Twenty-eight

Thursday morning, the day of the Board meeting, dawned gray and dreary. Cembran, Travis, and Gathod were all up early getting the chores done. Not that any of them could really sleep anyway; Cembran had tossed and turned for a long time. Travis had held him tight until eventually his lover did briefly fall asleep.

Travis and Gathod were working in the sheep barn, mucking out and making preparations for winter. "Gathod, how are things with you and Doug?" Travis continued to work while they talked.

Gathod grinned sheepishly, "I wanted to talk to you and Cembran about that. Doug asked me to move in with him, but he thinks he needs to live in town or closer to town when he's Sheriff." Gathod had filled his wheelbarrow and went to empty it on the muck pile. Picking up where he left off when he returned, he said, "So if I live with him, the house here will be empty. I mean, I like it, but...." Travis could tell Gathod was conflicted. "You guys took me in, gave me a home, and a family."

"Gathod, it's fine. You deserve to be happy and so does Doug. You don't owe us anything. You're family and we'll both be happy that you're happy."

Gathod looked at Travis in disbelief, "Are you sure?"

Travis dropped his tools, stepped forward and hugged him, "Of course, you goof."

"I told Doug I couldn't move until winter; there was too much to do here." Gathod was smiling and Travis could tell he was excited about the prospect of living with Doug. "He told me we'd buy a house together." Gathod looked embarrassed, "But I don't have any money."

Travis smiled, "Yes you do. We never talked about salary when you started working here, but I opened an account for you and we've been paying you for months." Gathod looked at Travis in disbelief. "I'll show you when we get back to the house." There was no way Travis wasn't going to pay Gathod for all his work.

The two men were finishing up their chores, putting away the tools, when he said, "Gathod, I'd like your opinion, your satyr opinion." The other man's eyebrows raised and he leaned on the shovel, listening. "Over the last couple of months, I've been having weird feelings and thoughts in my sleep, thoughts that aren't mine." Gathod's eyes widened. "It's not like Cembran's father's attacks and I was hoping you'd have some ideas, because these feelings – whatever you want to call them – are getting darker."

Gathod thought a minute, "I can think of a couple possibilities. You could be picking up on someone else's dreams or thoughts." His face pinched, thinking. "You spend a lot of time around other satyrs and since the attacks, you could be extra sensitive." Travis listened intently. "The other possibility," his expression darkened, "is that someone else's dreams are being attacked and you're picking up on the, for a lack of a better word, 'negative energy.'"

Travis sighed tiredly, "With Cembran's father dead, I thought this dream stuff was behind me." Frustration and helplessness were clear in his voice.

Gathod's eyes got big as saucers. "His father isn't dead, per se. From what you've told me, Bacchus took him. He's just in the realm of the gods now."

Now Travis was concerned. "You mean he's a god?" Anger tinged his voice at the thought of that cruel man.

"No." Gathod's voice remained level, "He's just with the gods. His power is very limited." Gathod changed tacks, "Don't worry about him." Gathod clasped Travis's shoulder, "The feelings during your sleep are probably nothing. Many of us get them from time to time and most of us learn to ignore them." Travis wasn't so sure, but maybe Gathod was right. Either way, he couldn't do much about it anyway.

When the morning chores were done, Travis and Cembran headed back to the house. Cembran went inside to clean up. "Lamb, I need to take a walk. I'll be back soon." Cembran nodded and went inside as Travis headed down the path toward the lake.

"Travis!" Travis turned around at the sound of someone calling him. Cembran was running down the path. "Come back to the house." He took Travis's hand and led him back.

Cembran opened the door. Their house was full of people, dozens of people. Travis saw Doug grinning from eat to ear. "What's going on?"

"I told some people working on my campaign about your farm and what was happening—"

Doug was cut off when a large man stepped forward, "We're tired of Palumbo and his brother running things. We got rid of one and we're going to get rid of the other. We'll be at the meeting tonight to show our support."

Travis and Cembran were speechless. They both stood in the doorway with their mouths hanging open – amazed by the kindness of strangers.

"We've got more people who'll be there, so we'll be able to make plenty of noise." This came from a little old lady who elbowed her way through the larger men. "We need unspoiled places like this." She seemed to be the ringleader, "Come on, folks, let's go and make calls."

Everyone filed out of the house, leaving Travis and Cembran gaping in disbelief. Travis found his voice first, "Doug, how can we thank you?"

"Don't thank me. I just mentioned the farm to Mable and she got herself riled up and started making calls. That woman can work the phones better than anyone I've ever seen."

Brock and Steven knocked on the door frame before stepping in the house as the last of the people filed out. "What's all this?"

Travis was smiling brightly for the first time in days, "The cavalry!"

Doug explained about the community support and Brock sat down at the table. "That's good, really good, and I think I've come up with a couple of other things."

Doug said good-bye and told them he'd see them at the meeting. Cembran cooked a big breakfast while Travis, Brock, and Steven started planning their strategy. Everyone ate heartily. Cembran was always a good cook, but this breakfast tasted good, really good, and like Travis, he was smiling big.

By noon they'd mapped out their strategy. Brock felt Travis should be the primary speaker and he'd be there if he needed help. "It'll carry more weight if you make the case as the owner of the property." Travis was nervous but he agreed. "This isn't a court, Travis. Here you carry more weight than I do. But I still have something that will throw them."

"Okay. Thank you for all your help, Brock, and you too, Steven."

"Yeah, thank you both for all your help; we couldn't have done this without you," Cembran added.

Brock went over some final details, then said, "We've got to get back to town, but we'll meet you at the courthouse. The meeting starts at seven-thirty and you should be up by about eight. I checked with the secretary today asking about items further down on the agenda. They think this will take fifteen minutes." Brock grinned, "They won't know what hit them."

Steven and Brock said good-bye and hugs were exchanged all around. "We'll see you tonight. Don't be nervous, you'll do fine."

As Brock and Steven turned to go, Travis was struck by a thought, "Brock, would you see if Arthur can come with you tonight?"

"Why? What are you thinking?"

"Something absolutely shameless," Travis grinned wickedly.

Brock raised his eyebrows and smirked a little, "I'll call my parents."

The rest of the afternoon Travis and Cembran kept themselves busy completing some projects and getting their chores done, but unlike most days, they did all their chores together. Usually, they worked independently but neither of them wanted to be alone with their thoughts and concerns. Doug called in the afternoon to tell them that Mable had lined up plenty of support. "They'll be at the courthouse at eight, so we're all set on this end."

That evening, they finished their chores, ate a light dinner, and got ready to go to the meeting. Steven and Brock arrived a few minutes before seven with Arthur. "Uncle Travis, what do I do?"

Travis explained his plan and Brock pronounced it "Absolutely shameless – in other words, worthy of any good lawyer."

After packing everything, they headed to the courthouse, arriving a few minutes before the start of the meeting. Travis gathered his materials and he, Brock, and Cembran headed into the meeting. Steven had agreed to stay with Arthur until he was needed.

Travis opened the door to the County Board Room as they were standing for the pledge of allegiance. The Board members were seated on a raised platform, with chairs provided for the general public. About thirty people sat in the public chairs. The initial agenda items were largely formalities and were dispensed with quickly. A number of citizen comments and questions were raised and answered.

The Board President, Keith DeArmond, announced that a new park had been proposed. "Tonight we are not giving approval for the new park, only deciding if the proposal should be pursued."

Joe Palumbo walked to the podium with his drawings and charts of the proposed park. Travis looked at the drawings in horror and he noticed that Cembran seemed to withdraw into himself. Travis saw their lake with campsites around it, their farm as a petting zoo, with hiking trails winding through the woods. Travis took Cembran's hand in his. As Joe started to speak, the door to the Board Room opened and people started filing in one at a time. Each person had a handwritten sign on a string around their neck reading, *"No Palumbo Park!"* The commissioners were listening to Joe and didn't notice them at first, but they kept coming, filling every seat and lining the walls of the Board room. Each person stood or sat so their sign was clearly visible.

As Joe was wrapping up, he brought out a board detailing the costs of the project. Included was as estimate to acquire the land. It was much less that the appraiser had quoted them, and Travis leaned to Cembran, saying "He's trying to sell them a bill of goods."

"Are there—" The Board President stopped in mid-sentence as he noticed the sea of "*No Palumbo Park*" signs in the room. "Any citizen comments?"

Travis stood up, "Yes, I wish to speak, and Joe, leave the cost estimates up there." Palumbo scowled, but did as Travis requested.

"Please state your name and address for the records."

"Travis Freeman, owner of the property in question." The Board members looked at each other. "I thought you should see the property he wants to destroy." Travis held up enlarged photographs of their home, the barns, the pastures with sheep and goats. "You are deciding whether to pursue a proposal to take our home to build a park. I also thought you should see whose home you are proposing to take." Travis motioned to Cembran, who got up and stood next to Travis. "You'll be taking our home." The back door of the room opened and Arthur entered carrying a lamb, with a kid goat following on a leash, "And you'll be taking their home." Arthur walked down the aisle and stood next to Cembran, who picked up the goat, cradling it in his arms.

A collective "Aww" went up from the audience. Travis looked at Joe Palumbo sitting in the front row. He was furious. "My family has owned this land since before statehood."

Keith, the Board President, spoke up, "Mr. Freeman, we weren't aware you were living on the property."

"I am, and the property has been farmed for decades." He skipped over the details of who had been farming it. "Now, I'd like to clear up another item."

"What is that, Mr. Freeman?"

Travis pulled out his notes. "Mr. Palumbo states in his proposal that the property can be acquired for approximately a million dollars."

"Yes, that's true."

"What did Mr. Palumbo use to arrive at that estimate?"

The Board President looked to Joe, who responded, "Rural land sells for about $2500 an acre."

Travis smirked. "I have an independent appraiser's report on the value of the property. According to their report, the land - with the lakes, stream, and river - is worth three million dollars, the farm is worth a million as an ongoing business, and the trees on the property, which happen to be old growth forest, are worth approximately six million dollars."

The Board President smiled. "Mr. Freeman, the trees?"

"Yes; there is precedent in cases like this, that you must pay for all property seized, and since this is old growth forest, which exists nowhere else in the state except in a few state and national parks, you must pay the fair market value for the trees. In addition, state law requires a twenty percent relocation allowance since this is our primary residence. Therefore, the price to acquire the land is not one but twelve million dollars. If it were for sale, which it is not."

"Mr. Freeman, we are proposing using eminent domain to acquire the land if necessary."

"I know that, but how are you going to pay for it? Your entire annual budget is less than ten million dollars and you must pay in full. I know you could float bonds, but this park will provide limited revenue and certainly not enough to repay twelve million dollars with interest." Keith looked at Joe. Travis continued, "And since this must be a public project, we will scrutinize the origin of every cent used."

"Mr. Freeman, who is 'we'?"

Brock stood up and stepped forward. "Who are you?"

"Brock Kraus, attorney for Mr. Freeman from the law firm Goode, Goode, and Kraus."

The Board President actually smiled, "Mr. Kraus, you seem to have a conflict. Your firm represents this County."

Now it was Brock's turn to smile, "Not any more. This is a copy of the registered letter that was delivered today informing you that you have been dropped as a client." Brock stepped forward and handed the letter to Keith. "Cembran Bacch," Brock indicated Cembran with his hand, "is my cousin." Brock continued, "The estimates provided by Mr. Freeman have also been validated by precedent and by independent judicial opinion."

The Board President was clearly shaken. "Thank you, Mr. Kraus; I think we've heard enough. Is there any other discussion?" The other Board members were shaking their heads and they all looked very unhappy.

Travis could see the conflict on their faces and an idea struck him. He leaned over and whispered to Cembran, "Think happy thoughts, Lamb." Travis then concentrated, thinking of the happiest times he could remember. He smiled to himself as images of him teaching Cembran to swim, Arthur feeding the lamb, and making love in the grass, flashed through his mind. Travis used those images to flood the room with happiness, carried on images of lambs, goats, and sheep. He watched as the conflict on the Board member's faces disappeared, replaced with smiles and looks of contentment.

One of the older Board members smiled broadly, "I move that we not pursue this further; the project is not viable and doesn't have public support." She smiled and indicated all the people in room.

"Do I have a second?" Keith was smiling as well.

"I second the motion."

"All in favor?"

The entire Board said "aye" and the room erupted in applause. Cembran set down the goat and Travis scooped him into his arms whispering, "Come on, Lamb, let's go home." He gathered up his notes and pictures, and they exited, weaving their way through the crowd of supporters patting them on the back and shaking their hands. Arthur followed with the lamb and kid goat, soaking up the attention like a sponge.

Outside, the night was quiet as people exited the courthouse. The audience members waved and smiled as they got into their cars. Arthur put the lamb and goat in the cages and loaded them in their vehicle. Travis hugged him tightly, thanking him for his help.

"Travis, what did you do?" Brock was smiling as he pulled him aside.

Travis smiled, "I flooded the room with happy thoughts and images, figuring happy people would be less likely to vote someone out of their home."

Brock looked very confused, "What made you think of it?"

Travis thought for a minute. As an answer, he briefly turned his eyes to the sky and Brock nodded slowly in response.

As Travis turned toward the car, he saw Joe Palumbo coming down the steps with a murderous look on his face, shaking his fists, "This isn't over, Freeman!"

"Yes, it is!"

Travis turned to see where that voice came from and he saw Doug, in his State Police uniform, and two other officers also in uniform, striding over their way. Doug was all business, "Joe Palumbo?"

"Yeah, what?"

"You're under arrest for land fraud." The two officers cuffed Joe's hands behind his back. Doug read him his rights and the two officers led him to a police car.

"Sorry I'm late; I tried to get here sooner. How did it go with the Board?" Doug asked.

Arthur practically shouted, "We won and I helped!" He was almost dancing with excitement.

Travis explained, "The Board voted not to pursue this further. It's over." His curiosity got the better of him, "What happened with Joe?" He watched as the cruiser pulled away.

"We've been investigating him for some time, but we couldn't get anything concrete on him. I can't give you details, but we were finally able to build a case and I asked if I could be the one to serve the warrant." Doug grinned with glee.

Brock interrupted the happiness, "Arthur, we need to get you home before Mom and Dad kill me for keeping you out so late."

Arthur rolled his eyes, "Okaaayyy." He hugged everyone goodbye and climbed into the back seat of his brother's car. Steven and Brock said their good-byes and headed home with smiles on their faces.

"Doug, are you still on duty?"

"No, actually I'm not, but I could use a ride home." Doug took off his hat and wiped his brow. "Mine took Palumbo to jail."

"Get in and we'll take you."

Doug looked sheepish, "I was hoping you'd take me to the farm to see Gathod."

Travis smiled, "That's what we said, Doug; we'll take you home." Doug smiled as he got in.

Arriving at the farm, Doug said good-night and headed to Gathod's. Travis smiled as he carried the lamb to the barn, placing her with her mother. "Thank you," Travis whispered as the animal curled next to her mother before going to sleep.

Travis met Cembran on his way back to the house, "All set?"

"Yes, the kid is back with his mother."

Travis took Cembran's hand as they walked back to the house, "I could use a shower."

Cembran gave Travis a sly look, "Me too." In the bedroom, Travis slipped out of his clothes while Cembran closed up the house for the night. Travis stepped into the bathroom, starting the water and Cembran opened the door and stepped into the bathroom as he was about to step into the shower.

"Lamb, you are beautiful." Travis's voice was low and gravelly. Gently, he pulled Cembran to him as he stepped into the shower. The water was barely warm, the perfect temperature for a hot day. "Stand still, Lamb."

Cembran stood facing Travis as strong hands washed his hair and massaged his scalp. After rinsing his hair, Travis soaped his hands and washed Cembran's shoulders and arms, stroking the soft skin, feeling the hard muscle beneath. Travis's soapy hands roamed down to his chest and stomach, the soft skin covering strong powerful muscles, which danced and quivered beneath his hands. "I love this," Travis moaned softly as he washed his lover's hard stomach. "Turn around, Love." His hands washed and stroked Cembran's powerful back, working his hands lower until they cupped Cembran's hard butt, fingers running along the crease.

"Trav, that's so good." Once Cembran's back was rinsed, Travis spread those gorgeous cheeks before kissing his lower back, tongue probing the crease, searching, searching. "Travis!" Cembran gasped as he found it. Travis's tongue darted around that small, tight opening, teasing, probing, laving. "Mmmm, Trav, what you do to me."

Travis's fingers reached though Cembran's legs to grasp his hard pulsing cock. Stroking gently, he asked, "What do you want, Lamb?"

Slowly, Cembran turned around, "I want you, Lemmle. My knight in shining armor. Again."

Travis captured Cembran's lips, his tongue probing as he felt Cembran lean into the embrace, giving himself over completely. "Always, Love. I'll always fight for you and for us." Kisses deep and slow shuddered through their bodies as Travis pulled them together, the water cascading over them. "Here or in the bed?"

Cembran wrapped his arms around Travis's neck, drawing him into a deep kiss. "Bed, please. I want you long, hard, and slow." His voice was deep with need. The last few days had been hard on him, very hard. Travis had been his rock through it all and he wanted to show him just how much he appreciated his strength.

Travis turned off the water and stepped out of the shower, grabbing one of the large fluffy towels, and dried Cembran's body and hair. Cembran returned the favor before dropping the towel on the floor. "Lamb, go lie on the bed, I'll be in shortly." Travis patted that incredible butt as Cembran headed into the bedroom. Travis finished up in the bathroom then joined him. Cembran was lying on in the center of the huge bed, his head on a pillow, legs spread, cock full and pulsing, the head glistening. Travis climbed onto the bed, his cock hard and swaying. "Lamb, I want you so bad."

"Take me; I belong to you, only to you."

"Then show me." Cembran's horns appeared on his forehead and Travis concentrated, his own horns becoming visible, his tail tickling his back. Travis lowered himself onto the bed, kissing Cembran hard while his hands caressed all that smooth skin. "I love that you show yourself to me and only to me."

"You, only you." Cembran could barely talk, his lips were otherwise engaged and at this stage, talking wasn't necessary. Cembran pulled his legs up, wrapping them around Travis's body, issuing an invitation that drove Travis wild with desire. After slicking himself and Cembran, Travis pushed into that hot, tight body, kissing Cembran with everything he had.

Their bodies joined; they felt as though they were truly one. They moved together, withdrawing but never separating. Travis's thrusts were long and deep, penetrating into their very souls. Words of love poured from both of them. Kisses hot enough to melt steel seared their mouths as their bodies took pleasure in each other. "Lemmle, I—" The words were cut off as Cembran's orgasm barreled through his body, wracking him with convulsions of ecstasy. Travis's own body shook and he growled as his passion flooded deep into Cembran.

Slowly as their bodies became theirs again, they separated, kissing, loving, and petting until they drifted into such sweet sleep as only love can bring.

Brock and Steven pulled away from the courthouse grinning at each other. Arthur was a bundle of excitement in the back seat. He was trying, with little success, to sit still.

"Arthur, if you calm down, we'll stop for ice cream before we get to Mom and Dad's." Arthur settled in his seat and smiled.

After stopping for their treat, Brock and Steven dropped Arthur off at Jim and Sue's before heading towards their own home. "Steven, I need to stop by the office."

"All right, do you want me wait in the car for you?" Steven yawned a little and relaxed in his seat.

"If you want, I' may be a few minutes."

"Okay." Steven put his hand on Brock's leg as they drove.

A few minutes later, they arrived at the office. Steven decided to follow Brock inside. The cleaning crew was just leaving for the night and Brock told them he'd turn off the remaining lights and set the alarm when he left. He headed to his office and Steven followed him inside. Without turning on the lights, he shut and locked the door, and pulled Steven to him before capturing his mouth.

Steven whimpered softly as Brock opened the buttons on his shirt and slipped it off his shoulders before dropping it on the floor as he maneuvered Steven to the conference table. Steven's butt bumped against the edge.

"Oh," he moaned softly as Brock lifted him onto the large table. Brock plunged his tongue into Steven's hot mouth as he opened Steven's pants. Steven lifted himself and Brock pushed his pants past Steven's hips. Steven toed off his shoes and his pants slipped off his feet, dropping with a rustle onto the floor.

Brock used his kisses to press Steven's body back onto the table. He moaned at the sight of Steven laid out on the large table. His alabaster skin stood out against the dark polished wood. "Steven, you are one handsome man."

He pulled Brock to him, letting his passion rise. He was finally able to realize that while he never saw himself as handsome, Brock really did. "Let me see you." Steven whispered.

Brock looked at him a little confused. "Show me who you really are. Make love to me as a satyr."

Brock closed his eyes and his horns became visible in his hair. Steven was panting breathlessly as he watched Brock slowly unfasten the buttons of his shirt, before taking it off and dropping it on the floor.

He moved between Steven's legs and he whimpered involuntarily as his hips started to buck. Brock always did this to him; every time he took off his shirt, Steven's body ached for him.

"You told me once that you dreamed of me taking you on my conference table." Steven nodded weakly. "I want to make that and all your dreams come true, Love."

Steven licked his lips and nodded weakly, "You made all my dreams come true a while ago, just by being you." Brock leaned forward and pulled Steven's lips to his in a scorching kiss as he pulled Steven forward until his butt rested near the edge of the table. "Take me please."

"Show me, Steven. Show me what you want."

He lifted his legs and pulled them to his chest, exposing himself completely to Brock, who bent forward, running his fingers over Steven's crease. He shuddered as Brock used his tongue to tease and probe the hot opening. He kneaded Steven's cheeks while his tongue worked the opening until Steven's head rocked back and forth on the table as he moaned his lover's name over and over again.

Brock stepped back, hands on his belt. Slowly, he toed off his shoes, opened his pants and unzipped his fly. The soft wool pants fell to the floor in a puddle. He stepped out of them, his heavy cock swinging as he came back to Steven. "Hurry, please," Steven moaned. Brock stepped to his desk and grabbed a small packet of lube from his drawer.

Steven was practically vibrating as Brock positioned himself between his upraised legs. Brock slowly sank into his hot, welcoming body. "You feel so good." Steven let his head rest against the table as Brock started to move deep in his body. He set a brisk pace, but Steven wanted more. "Please. I want everything." Brock picked up the pace as he reached to Steven's chest, lightly twisting the silver bars in Steven's nipples. He moaned and writhed on the conference table as Brock continued to pound into his body. He met Brock thrust for thrust, wanting everything his lover could give him. "That's it. Right there."

"You like that?" Brock pulled out of Steven's body and then thrust in a smooth swift movement. "Fuck, Brock, do that again!" He obliged over and over. Steven was over the moon by the time Brock buried himself in his body before leaning forward and pulling Steven's face to his. "I love you, Steven. You make me happier that I can ever remember."

Steven kissed Brock back, "And I love you." He could barely breathe as sweat rolled down his face and chest. "You fill my life in so many ways." He tightened his muscles around Brock, "You are my dream come true."

Brock wrapped his hand around Steven's cock, "I love you, Steven." He pulled fiercely, "Come for me! Show me what I do to you! Show me how much you love me!" His words sent Steven flying and he shot hard into Brock's hand, crying out as he came, his body vibrating with ecstasy.

Brock had been on the edge for a while and once Steven climaxed, he lost all control and he came deep in his lover's body, grunting something completely unintelligible. Steven went limp, splaying his body on the table as Brock collapsed onto Steven.

Steven brought Brock's lips to his, "Thank you. For the love, unconditional support, encouragement, trust, sharing my life. For everything."

Brock returned Steven's kiss, "You're welcome, Love. But you know, you're not the only one whose dreams have come true." He kissed Steven again before lifting himself off the table and helping his lover get up. After a quick cleanup, they both got dressed. "Come on, let's go home. We need to shower and get to bed."

"You're tired?" Steven was teasing; he wasn't sure he could move.

Brock winked, "I said go to bed. I didn't say anything about sleeping." Steven noticed that Brock's horns were no longer visible. He beamed at his boyfriend as they left the office, his hand slipping into Brock's as they walked to the car.

Chapter Twenty-nine

"Oh my god!" Travis sat up in bed bathed in sweat.

"Lemmle, what's wrong?" Cembran stirred next to Travis, rubbing his eyes as he turned on a small light next to the bed.

Travis turned toward Cembran, the covers pooling in his lap. "Why didn't I see it earlier?"

"See what? Travis, tell me what's wrong." Cembran was becoming concerned.

Travis tried to get his thoughts together. "Cembran, Palumbo has tried to get our land for years, first from my father then from me." Cembran nodded. "Even going to the point where I think he had you attacked and poisoned the animal feed." Cembran nodded again. "So why would he propose that the County build a park instead?" Cembran looked confused. "I mean if the land was a park, he would never get it. Why the change? I mean, he may hate me, but…."

"Does it matter, Lemmle?" Cembran's arms slipped around Travis's waist, coaxing him back onto the bed and turning out the light.

"It could. But I guess there's nothing I can do about it now." Travis kissed Cembran softly, holding him close, as he allowed his mind and body to finally drift back to sleep.

In the morning, he woke to the soft sound of Cembran's breathing. The room was lit by the first rays of dawn coming through the windows. Carefully getting out of bed, he put on his robe and went into the kitchen to start the coffee and make a light breakfast. Yesterday had been a good day. The County Board had decided not to pursue building a park on their land, and the state police had arrested Joe Palumbo, but Travis still felt that something wasn't quite right.

Travis stood in the kitchen having his first cup of coffee when a pair of arms snaked around his waist. "Morning, Lamb," Travis smiled into his cup.

"Morning," Cembran nuzzled the back of Travis's neck, his hands slipping beneath the robe to caress his stomach. "I have to start chores, but may be later we can…." Cembran smiled as his hand slid lower.

Travis twisted his head for a kiss before Cembran removed his hands. After a quick bite, Cembran headed outside. Travis went back into the bedroom to get dressed. Sitting on the edge of the bed, he made a phone call.

"Doug, it's Travis."

"Hey, Travis."

"Would it be possible for me to see Joe Palumbo?"

"Why on earth would you want to do that?"

"I have some questions that he might be able to answer."

"What kind of questions, Travis?"

"It's hard to explain on the phone."

"I'm at Gathod's. I'll stop by your place in an hour or so."

"Thanks, Doug. I'll see you when you get here and thanks again."

Travis hung up, got dressed, and went down to the barns to help Cembran with the chores. Travis filled him in on his call to Doug and what he'd asked. Cembran wasn't sure what Travis was hoping to find out. "Lamb, I think there's more behind this and I need to find out. Do you want to go with me?"

Cembran thought a minute, "No, I don't think so. I never want to see that man again." Travis nodded, understanding Cembran's feelings completely. He wasn't too thrilled at the thought of seeing Joe Palumbo again either.

Travis helped with chores and then headed back to the house to meet Doug. Walking up the path, he saw both Doug and Gathod leaving Gathod's. "Morning, guys," he called as he walked toward them.

"Morning, Travis; is Cembran milking?" Travis nodded and Gathod headed down to the barn to help while Travis and Doug went inside.

"I called ahead and arranged for you to see Joe. I have to be with you the entire time." Travis nodded. "But I still don't understand what you expect to achieve."

Travis tried to explain, but it was hard because he was operating mainly on a feeling. "Doug, Joe has been trying to buy this property for a long time, first from my father and then from me. He thinks he can develop it and make a fortune and he probably could." Doug looked confused. "If a park were built here, then he'd never be able to develop the land. So why the change?"

"Maybe he just hates you?"

Travis laughed, "I'm sure he does, but he only hates me because I'm standing in the way of what he wants. A park would add more obstacles between him and his goal. Doug, the whole park idea is completely out of character. Why?"

"You think there's more to this, then, but do you really think he's going to tell you?"

"He's not going to say anything if we don't ask."

"Okay. Let's go." Travis put the coffee cups in the sink and they headed to Doug's car. Doug drove them to the jail where Joe was being held pending his initial court appearance. He parked the car and Travis followed him into the building. Travis had to go through metal detectors, locked doors, and had to answer a number of questions. Finally, they were sitting in a small room across a table from Joe Palumbo.

"Freeman, what are you doing here? Come to gloat?"

Travis took a deep breath, wondering where to start. "No, I just had a few questions."

"I won't answer anything."

Travis had been afraid of this. Doug stepped forward and got in Joe's face. "You'll answer whatever questions he has for you. You understand?" Travis had never seen Doug look so menacing; he actually saw Palumbo flinch. Doug motioned for Travis to continue.

"You've been trying to buy my land for years, first from my father, then from me."

"So, what of it?" Joe tried to look belligerent.

"So if the County built a park, you'd never see the land."

"And?"

"So why the change of heart? Why did you propose the park to the County?"

Joe just shrugged, shook his head, and looked uncomfortable. Travis looked over at Doug, who got up and walked to the far side of the room. Travis looked back at Joe, hoping for something, anything, but Joe just sat there. So he tried again, trying to sound as friendly as he could, "What happened, Joe?" he almost whispered.

Joe just sat there, looking back at him. He was about to get up when Joe finally spoke, "I started having these...." Travis waited for Joe to continue. "I don't know what to call them, dreams, nightmares, daymares." Travis listened intently. "I started having these vivid dreams months ago, echoing my frustration with you and your refusal to sell the land." Once he started talking, Joe seemed to build momentum. "At one point I had a dream of you talking about adopting a kid. When I mentioned it at the farmer's market, the look on your face told me I'd hit a nerve, so I thought that maybe the dreams were accurate."

"What happened next?" Travis spoke softly, trying not to smile as his suspicions were confirmed and not wanting to interrupt Joe.

"I started having dreams about a park. I saw vivid images of a park on your land, hiking trails, campsites, a petting zoo, night after night, the images came unbidden to my mind. I couldn't stop them." Joe held his head in his hands. "I finally created the drawings and presented them to the Board, just to get the dreams to stop."

"Did the dreams stop?"

"I don't know. The last one was two days ago, the night before the Board meeting. I didn't have one last night." The other man looked defeated and tired.

Travis nodded sympathetically, "I think you've probably had the last one." Travis's own sleep the night before had been wonderfully peaceful. Joe looked up, "Just remember they're only dreams." He looked at Doug and indicated with a slight nod of his head that he was done.

Once they were out in the hall, Doug gave a strange look at Travis, whispering, "He sounds nuts."

Travis whispered softly, "He's not nuts. I think those dreams were the work of Cembran's father." Doug looked at him in disbelief. Travis explained briefly about his disturbed sleep and suspicions. "Trust me, it's a satyr thing." Doug nodded and they headed down the hall. Exiting the jail, they strode quickly to the car and headed back to the farm.

When they arrived, the house was empty. Travis turned to Doug, "Thank you for your help. At least we were able to confirm my suspicions. Not that there's much we can do about it, but at least we know." Doug said good-bye and headed down the path to Gathod's.

Travis headed toward the barns and found Cembran with the sheep. "Lamb," Travis smiled brightly as Cembran rushed to him, his lips already in kissing position.

After a warm kiss, Cembran asked, "Did you find out what you wanted?"

Travis became serious, "Yes, I did."

"Do you want to tell me about it?"

"I will later. Let's finish our chores." He kissed Cembran again and they went about their work.

That evening, when they were in bed, he told Cembran about his suspicions and what he'd learned from Joe.

"Travis, do you really think my father could be behind this?"

"Yes, I do."

His lover shivered against Travis's body. "What can we do?"

"Lamb, I think he's beyond us now, but I think since we're aware of him, it'll be more difficult for him in the future." Cembran nodded. "At the next Bacchanal, I'll let everyone know what I believe happened." Cembran looked at him, concern evident on his face. "Relax – the only power he has is what we give him, and if we don't think about him, he'll grow weaker." Travis saw Cembran's incredible blue eyes close and felt his body relax as he drifted off to sleep.

After Travis explained about Cembran's father, getting the unpleasant news out of the way, the September Bacchanal quickly escalated into a celebration for a number of reasons; Steven and Brock had decided to move in together, Doug's election victory, as well as the victory with the County Board. Adding to the festivities were a number of new faces, including Greg and Millie's oldest son Mark and his wife June, their younger son Phillip, and Dovino had arrived from Switzerland about a week ago.

In early September, Travis had been awakened by the telephone. "Hello," he answered groggily.

"Travis?" The voice tentative and heavily accented, "It's Dovino."

Travis immediately brightened. "Dovino, it's wonderful to hear from you, how are you?"

"I'm fine. I'm calling because I...." Dovino had come out to Travis and Cembran when they were in Switzerland last year and he'd asked if he could come to visit. "I was wondering... I mean, I'd like to come to the U.S."

"Have you talked to your father?"

"Yes, he says I need to do what will make me happy. He helped me apply for a visa and they said they'll grant it if I have a job so I was wondering if you...." His accent was particularly heavy when he was unsure of himself.

Cembran had stirred next to Travis and had been listening to Travis's half of the conversation. Travis covered the phone. "Dovino wants to come to the U.S. He's asking for a job." Cembran smiled and nodded. Travis uncovered the phone, "You have a job here on the farm if you want it." Travis heard a whoop through the phone. "When will you arrive?"

"I have a plane ticket for late next week, but I can put it off if that's a problem."

"That's fine. Give me the details and we'll pick you up at the airport." Dovino provided Travis with the flight details, then Travis put Cembran on the phone and the two of them talked for a while.

Dovino had arrived and he was currently staying in Travis and Cembran's guest room. Gathod was planning to move in with Doug in the next few weeks, and then Dovino would move into Gathod's small house.

Dovino had been a big help on the farm over the past week and he really seemed to be enjoying the Bacchanal. Travis noticed that he and Phillip seemed to be hitting it off quite well. Travis cornered him near the food tables, "Dovino, are you enjoying the Bacchanal?"

"Oh yes." His eyes were dancing and Travis figured he was smitten with Phillip. "It's different, but I think I'm going to like it here." Travis saw his eyes drift to where Phillip was talking to his father.

"That Phillip seems really nice," Travis couldn't help teasing a little.

Dovino reddened, "Yeah, he seems nice." Dovino's eyes furtively looked to where Phillip was standing.

Travis smiled, "It's all right, Dovino." Travis squeezed the younger man's shoulder, "Go have fun." Dovino blushed again and then sauntered over to where Phillip was standing. If the smile on Phillip's face was any indication, he wasn't the only one young man smitten.

Travis filled a plate and sat by the fire. Cembran joined him a few minutes later, sitting behind Travis, pressing his chest to Travis's back, while he rested his head on his shoulder. Steven and Brock joined them.

"Did Steven tell you the good news?" Brock looked ready to burst. It may have been Steven's good news, but Brock was just as happy about it as Steven.

"No; what is it?" Steven told them that he had decided to go to law school. "Where? When?"

"I'll probably start in a year and I think I want to go to Michigan State. That way I can commute from Brock's house." Brock coughed gently. "I mean our house." Steven explained that he'd sold his condo and that he was moving in with Brock in the next week or so. Both of them looked extremely happy. Brock's arms wrapped around Steven's waist and Travis could see Steven relaxing into Brock's embrace.

"Brock, before you and Steven disappear," Brock nuzzled Steven's neck gently, "I have something to tell you. As both of you know, all the land was transferred to 'Two Worlds Farm' last week with the exception of the fifteen acres on the other side of the lake."

Brock nodded, "I was wondering about that."

"I've worked with the County and created five three-acre plots - they were very helpful after the meeting – and I was wondering if the two of you would like to purchase one of those plots to use for a vacation home?" Steven looked at Brock, a huge smile on his face. "I'm going to offer a plot to Doug and Gathod as well." Both men were smiling, "I don't need an answer now, but I wanted you to think about it. I also want to put one of the plots in trust for Arthur. He'll receive it when he's twenty-five. The other two plots will remain empty for now." Travis looked at Jim and Sue, "I offered a plot to your parents, but they declined."

Brock was speechless as he looked at Steven, "I don't know what to say. We'd love it." His arms tightened around Steven's waist, pulling them closer.

Travis relaxed into Cembran's embrace, "Go have fun you two. We'll work out the details later."

Gathod and Doug were equally surprised and pleased with Travis's offer. Doug had thought they'd need to live in town, but County Sheriff regulations only required that he live somewhere in the County.

They'd agreed to think it over, but Travis felt sure they were as excited about the offer as Brock and Steven.

"Lamb, I have something special for you." Cembran leaned close, his lips nibbling on Travis's ear. "Are you ready?" Cembran nodded and stood up, extending his hand to Travis. Taking his hand, Travis led Cembran to the shelter.

There was no need for a fire, but the fireplace was filled with candles, a bucket of champagne in the corner. Travis knelt on the bedding and gently tugged Cembran to him before closing the curtain over the entrance. He opened the bottle and poured them both glasses of champagne. "Lamb, my life truly began the day I met you. I want to grow old with you surrounded by our family, the family we built together. I love you forever and always." Setting his glass on the hearth, Travis leaned forward, kissing Cembran deeply. He took Cembran's glass, setting it next to his before taking the man he loved more than anything into his arms and pressing his hard strong body into the thick soft bedding.

Cembran's hands wrapped around Travis, caressing his back as Travis slowly opened the buttons of Cembran's shirt before slipping it off his shoulders. Travis straightened up, pulling off his own shirt.

"Travis, you feel so good, smell so good." Cembran nuzzled Travis's neck inhaling deeply. Their bodies pressed together again, hands caressing as Travis opened Cembran's pants, slipping them past his hips, down his legs and off his body, before kneeling in the shelter and removing his own pants. Their bodies ached for each other as Travis lay on the bedding, pulling Cembran close.

"Lamb, I have something I want very much to give you. Will you accept it?" Travis had decided to give Cembran his Triuwe.

Cembran looked at Travis momentarily confused, then his face brightened and he realized what Travis meant, "Only if you'll accept my Triuwe as well."

"I will, Lamb, happily." Travis captured Cembran's mouth, pulling them together as their bodies pressed and rubbed against each other, soft to soft, hard to hard.

"Lemmle, I want to be with you, want you to fill me." Travis slicked his fingers, pressing them into Cembran.

"Yes, Travis, that's what I want, what I need." Travis prepared Cembran and rolled him on his back. Cembran's legs lifted for Travis. "I love you."

"I love you, too." Travis slicked himself and slowly pressed into Cembran's body until he was buried deep inside, their bodies joined together. Travis concentrated and his horns became visible. Cembran's eyes closed and his horns appeared within his tight blonde ringlets, too.

Travis was throbbing inside Cembran, but neither of them moved as he concentrated again. His chest began to glow and he could feel his mind reach out to Cembran. He felt Cembran reach back to him, and their minds and hearts linked. He could feel Cembran's emotions, his love and passion, flowing directly to him. Slowly Travis began to move. Cembran moaned softly as he retreated, and growled as Travis pressed into him. Their lips touched again and chests pressed together, joining them in a way they never thought possible, one heart, and one love.

"I can feel your love coursing through me, Trav."

"And I can feel yours, Lamb. It's a part of me; you're a part of me." Travis felt his legs and arms tingle, then his chest and back. Spots danced in front of his eyes as he erupted deep in Cembran's body, filling him with his love. Cembran climaxed with Travis, their lips pulling on one another, their eyes briefly glimpsing each other's soul.

Slowly they came down from the most intensely passionate moment of their lives. Travis cupped Cembran's head in his hands and pressed their lips together in a kiss filled with love and joy. "I love you, Lamb."

"I know; I can feel it."

"I can feel your love, too." Travis could feel Cembran's love for him deep within his heart, like a feeling of great joy and comfort welling up from within. They settled together on the bedding, Travis wiping them both with a towel before Cembran rested his head on

Travis's shoulder. He could feel a connection to Cembran that hadn't been there before. "I can feel you Lamb. You're a part of me now, the best part of me."

A tear of joy rolled down Cembran's cheek as Travis pulled them together, kissing his Cembran, his love, and now his mate. Travis could hear the music and dancing from the Bacchanal outside, but made no move to get up. He had everything he needed or wanted right here. Cembran rested next to him and supportive friends frolicked just outside. Travis reached to the hearth and handed Cembran his glass, and after a silent toast they emptied their glasses, set them aside, blew out the candles, and nestled together.

Cembran spoke dreamily, "Travis, I think you did it," his voice whispered in the darkness.

"Did what?" Travis had started to drift off to sleep.

"Do you remember how we felt that last night in the satyr village? That sense of community and acceptance?"

"Yes."

"I feel that same thing now. Here, with you and our friends, our family." Laughter from around the fire drifted into the shelter.

"Me too, Lamb. Me too."

That night, Travis dreamed. He dreamed of the time, years before, when he'd watched Cembran bathe in the lake when he was a teenager, seeing Cembran's strong, handsome body for the first time as he washed himself. After bathing, Cembran had rested in the grass, the water glistening on his body, the body Travis now knew so well.

Words formed in Travis's mind, words that weren't his own, though the voice was familiar. "I knew then that you'd make each other happy."

Andrew Grey grew up in Western Michigan with a father who loved to tell stories and a mother who loved to read them. Since then, he has lived throughout the country and traveled throughout the world. He has a Master's Degree from the University of Wisconsin - Milwaukee and works in information systems for a large corporation. He considers himself blessed with an accepting family, fantastic friends, and the world's most supportive and loving partner. Andrew currently lives in beautiful, historic Carlisle, Pennsylvania.

Printed in the United Kingdom
by Lightning Source UK Ltd.
133382UK00002B/124/P